Empty Net

TEAGAN HUNTER

Editing by Editing by C. Marie

Proofreading by Judy's Proofreading & Julia Griffis

Cover Design: Emily Wittig Designs

*To the ones who are always trying, trying, trying for people who don't give a fuck.
This is your permission to stop.*

Chapter 1

FOX

Lawson: I have an EXTREMELY important question.

Hayes: It's too early for this.

Locke: It's 8:30 at night.

Keller: Any time between 12:00 AM and 11:59 PM is too early for Lawson.

Me: So that leaves one minute of Lawson Time?

Hutch: And that's being generous.

Lawson: You know, you should all make a resolution to be nicer to me.

Lawson: Except you, Foxy. You're always nice.

Lawson: Sometimes too nice. Be meaner sometimes, will ya?

Me: Dickwad.

Keller: Damn! Coming right out of the gate hot!

Me: Shit. I'm sorry.

Keller: And now he's regressed.

Hayes: That didn't last long.

Locke: Did we really think it would?

Hutch: Foxy is too much of a good boy to be mean.

Me: Hey! I can be mean.

Me: I just don't like to. My mama would whoop my ass if she saw that text.

Me: And I'm not a good boy. Stop saying that.

Keller: I'd let your mama whoop my ass, but for totally different reasons.

Hutch: Come on. Not with the mom jokes again.

Keller: If we're forced to be in a group with Lawson, mom jokes are a necessity.

Lawson: So you're saying I can ask my VERY important question now?

Keller: No. Stop talking.

Lawson: I can't. I don't think I have an off button.

Hayes: Poor Rory.

Lawson: Poor Rory? No, more like poor Quinn. I feel terrible for her now that she's saddled with you.

Keller: Yeah, how is the hot nanny doing?

Hayes: Keller...

Locke: Careful, guys. I can hear him growling from here.

Lawson: And here we thought Hutch was the growly one.

Keller: They're both growly. At least when they want to be.

Lawson: As if you have any room to talk.

Lawson: You're the dick, Hutch is the grump, Hayes is the protective one, Locke is the old man, and Fox is the good boy.

Locke: I'm not old, dammit!

Me: Stop saying I'm a good boy. I can be bad.

Hayes: Only a good boy would say something like "I can be bad."

Keller: You forgot to say you're the obnoxious one, Lawsy.

Lawson: I'm not obnoxious. I'm lovable!

Hutch: You're obnoxious.

Lawson: And lovable!

Locke: Annoying.

Lawson: And lovable!

Hayes: Exasperating.

Lawson: And lovable!

Me: I love you, Lawsy.

Lawson: See? Told you I'm lovable!

Lawson: Now that we've established that, gather around, boys, because I have a question for you.

Lawson: What car would you give a mildly enthusiastic hand job to own?

Hayes: Is it wrong that I'm not even surprised by this question?

Hutch: At this point, I've come to expect it.

Locke: We really should be more concerned about him, but this seems perfectly in line with Lawson.

Me: I'm concerned but also intrigued to see the responses…

Keller: I have a few follow-up questions. What does "mildly enthusiastic" mean exactly? Like, do I need to smile? Do I have to make eye contact? Can I put a divider between us? And also, will the car be in immaculate condition, and does it have to be a real car? Can it be a ship?

Hutch: I'm not sure if I'm impressed by the thought you put into this or curious as to why you're so eager to offer a hand job for a car.

Keller: Or ship. We don't know yet. We're still hashing out the details.

Locke: Excellent point, Kells. Lawson?

Lawson: It can be a ship.

Keller: And?

Lawson: All other rules are agreed upon by both parties, but for the sake of this one, let's say mildly enthusiastic means you have to at least SEEM interested.

Keller: Millenium Falcon.

Hutch: Wow. That was fast, you nerd.

Keller: Call me a nerd all you want, but that thing is SWEET. Do you know how fast it can make the Kessel Run?

Hayes: You know, I really did not at all have you pegged as a Star Wars nerd, Kells.

Keller: I'm a man of surprises.

Locke: K.I.T.T.

Hayes: What's that?

Hutch: Wait…from that old '80s show? With David Hasselhoff?

Lawson: DON'T HASSEL THE HOFF!

Keller: I bet you used to watch that shit every week.

Locke: For fuck's sake… I'm not that old! I used to watch reruns. K.I.T.T. was legit.

Keller: Just admit you're old.

Locke: Never.

Me: Bumblebee.

Lawson: How is nobody picking a REAL car?

Hutch: Uh, probably because we can all afford the real car? We're not all cheap asses like you.

Lawson: I'm not cheap! I'm responsible.

Lawson: You guys aren't playing the game correctly.

Lawson: Now pick a REAL car you'd give a hand job for.

Hayes: Can we just not give other dudes hand jobs?

Lawson: BE A TEAM PLAYER, HAYES.

Hayes: I WILL NOT PARTICIPATE IN YOUR BULLSHIT SHENANIGANS, LAWSY.

I laugh, tucking my phone into my back pocket before this chat really gets out of hand. I mean, it's always a bit unhinged, but I'm in public, so I should have at least some decency, especially given that I'm ninety percent certain the older woman behind me is reading over my shoulder.

When I peek back at her, she's scowling, so I shoot her a wink. *That* gets her to smile. I chuckle to myself, turning back around as the person in front of me scoots up and begins tossing their groceries onto the belt with zero organization. It makes my eye twitch, but I mind my business as I was taught.

Halfway through the haphazard unloading, they make eye contact with me, reaching into the back of their cart. I hold my breath, waiting for that spark, that *Oh my god, I know this person!* gleam to hit their eyes. But it never does, and when they place their milk onto the belt without incident, I breathe a sigh of relief.

Usually, I don't have an issue talking with fans, but I don't like talking to them when I'm trapped in a line like this, unable to make a quick exit if they start asking questions I don't want to answer.

Like *"Why didn't you stop that goal from Pittsburgh last night?"*

Or *"How could you let two shorthanded goals be scored?"*

And *"Think maybe you need to sit out a few games? Regroup?"*

I know it's exactly what they'd ask because it's what I've been asking myself since the final buzzer sounded. My one job last night was to stop pucks, and I sucked. The rest of the team showed up, and that's the only reason we won. It certainly wasn't my goal-saving abilities.

I push the unwanted thoughts aside, trying not to dwell, especially since we walked away with two points in the end, and that's all that matters. Besides, tonight is supposed to be about fun, not hockey.

I'm sure I'm not expected to bring anything, but my

mother would hand me my ass if she knew I went to a party empty-handed. I set my basket on the belt, then unload my provisions. I'm sure the party hosts—and the rest of my team, for that matter—will endlessly make fun of me for bringing something, but it's just ingrained in me at this point. Champagne and cookies it is.

"Hey, Fox," the cashier says as I approach the payment terminal.

"Hey, Rico. How are you?"

The lanky, overgrown kid with hair down to his shoulders who smells suspiciously like pot shrugs. "Well, I'm stuck here until next year, but it's overtime, so I guess I can't complain."

I can't help but laugh at his horrible "next year" joke.

"What are you up to?" he asks as he drags one of the boxes of cookies across the scanner. "Must be something fancy with you dressed like that."

I glance down at the tux I'm wearing, then grin back up at him. "What? This old thing?"

"Yes, that old—what is it, Tom Ford?—tux you're wearing."

It's Armani, though I'm not sure that makes it any better, so I don't correct him.

"Got a thing with some teammates." I purposely keep my answer vague. Not that I think Rico would tell a soul where I'm off to—he's too cool for that—but still.

"Teammates." He shakes his head with a smile. "I love how you casually say that like you're not going to hang out with the entire Seattle Serpents team. Still wild to me that you even come through here and you don't have someone buying your groceries for you."

"I'm just a normal guy, Rico," I tell him, certainly not for the first time since I'm here at least a few times a week when I'm not on the road.

He snorts. "A normal guy who makes six point four million a year."

I don't tell him I actually make $6.6 million, which means he's right—I'm not a regular guy. I'm a professional hockey goalie being paid millions of dollars a year to play a game I love more than life itself who is off to a catered party where we'll no doubt drink thousands of dollars' worth of champagne like it's something we do every Tuesday and not even bat an eye. There's nothing normal about that at all.

He gives me my total, and I slide my black card into the reader.

"Stuck at work or not, I hope you have a good night and a happy New Year, Rico," I say as I grab my bags full of supplies I don't really need.

"Thanks, Fox. Don't party too hard, yeah?"

I'm halfway to the exit when he cups his hands around his mouth and yells, "And go Serpents!"

I hustle out of the store faster than ever, practically running to my blacked-out Denali Ultimate in hopes nobody decides to stop me. I only laugh at the absurdity of everything when I'm tucked safely inside and there have been no incidents to speak of.

My mind spins as I navigate the Seattle streets, heading toward The Sinclair, where our team's New Year's Eve party is being hosted by our captain and his girlfriend, Auden. This time last year, the hotel belonged to Auden's company, Sinclair Properties, but she sold it, having felt the luxury hotel empire was running fine without her and wanting something else out of life. Now, here we are, holding team parties there.

The Serpents got lucky with no games today and tomorrow. Otherwise, I highly doubt we'd be doing anything like this. Everyone would be holed up at their houses, ice packs on their quads and massage guns working their calves, recuperating after the game. I know that's precisely where I'd be, especially since every game lately feels like a grind.

Fuck, I should have played better last night. We had to work too damn hard for that win. For all our wins lately, actually. It's taxing for the whole team, and the worst part is that it's *my* fault. If I could just keep the puck out of the back of the net, we wouldn't have to work from behind so much. If I could push from post to post just a little faster, I could save us from going to overtime and adding those extra minutes of ice time. If I could get my glove in *just* the right position, I could keep us ahead. So many ifs, yet none of those things have happened. I need to be on my A game going into the new year because I don't know if the rest of the team can keep going like this, barely hanging on each night, thanks to all my screwups.

When Dash, our backup, is in net, it's like we're a whole different team, but I'm supposed to be the starting goalie. I'm supposed to be this team's winner, this city's champion. I'm none of those things.

I shake away my doom-and-gloom thoughts as I pull up in front of the hotel, then toss my keys to the valet—who looks *very* excited to get behind the wheel of my baby—and make my way inside to the party on the top floor.

"Why does it not surprise me that you're the first one here?" Hutch asks as I nod at the guard standing by the entrance, who lets me pass without an issue. Guess he's aware of who is on the team and who isn't.

"Or that you brought…gifts?" My captain's eyes drop to the paper bags in my arms.

"Champagne." I hike the bags higher. "And cookies."

He huffs out a laugh. "See? Such a good boy, Foxy."

That's what they call me: the good boy, the Southern gentleman. I guess I am those things, but I'm not the perfect guy they seem to think I am. For instance, I suck at my job, so there's that.

I hand off the bags to a caterer who has appeared at my side. Honestly, if you'd told me at the start of last season that our usually grumpy captain would be openly participating in a party where there's a staff and no strippers, I'd have laughed right in your face. Guess a lot changes about a man when he's fallen in love.

"Thanks," I tell them. "And feel free to take a cookie. They're white chocolate peppermint and are to die for."

They smile up at me before bustling away.

"They aren't going to try those, are they?"

Hutch gives me an incredulous look. "Uh, probably not. They're working. Do you ever stop trying to take care of other people?"

"I can't help it. It's just part of who I am." My parents raised me to always give before I take, and I've taken that to heart my entire life.

He shakes his head. "Damn Southern men and their infinite politeness."

Some people, like my favorite forward, Lucas

Lawson, say I'm too nice, and I guess those people wouldn't be entirely wrong. But it's hard not to be when it's impressed upon you from the get-go.

Part of me wonders if that's the issue with my game lately. Am I being too polite out there? Do I need to fight for my crease more? Do I need to stand my ground and ensure nobody gets in my blue paint?

I already know the answer, and it's a resounding yes.

I straighten my cufflinks. "Need any help with last-minute touches?"

Hutch gives me another look, this one saying *You just can't help it, can you?* "Son of a bitch, Fox. Go grab a drink or something before I make you do extra drills at practice tomorrow."

It's a total bluff. He can't make me do shit, but just the idea of it has me moving toward the bar anyway.

"Vodka soda, please. No ice," I request, and the bartender nods, getting to work on my drink as I rest against the bar, looking out at the space that's been decorated to perfection.

Low lighting and fairy lights make it feel like we're outside under the night sky instead of in a dark, closed-off ballroom. Several standing tables are scattered around, all draped in black linen with gold accents and a beautiful bouquet of white roses centered on each one. A photo booth is off to the side, and a deejay is set up across the room. There are not one, not two, but *four* bars, one in each corner, like whoever put this together knew what they were getting into shoving so many hockey players into one room.

"Here you are, sir," the bartender says, sliding a glass my way.

"Thank you kindly," I tell them with a nod before lifting the glass to my lips and taking a sip as my phone buzzes in my pocket.

I pull it free to find a text from my mother. I stifle a groan and, against my better judgment, open the message.

Mama: Please tell me you're not going to be alone on New Year's Eve.

Another message comes in before I can respond.

Mama: That will absolutely break my heart.

That's my mother for you, always worried about her children, no matter how old we get. It doesn't matter that I'm thirty years old and live across the country—she's still worried.

I let my thumbs fly over the screen.

> Me: Got a team thing, so definitely won't be alone.

> Mama: Oh, thank gosh. I was ready to jump on a flight to come see you.

> Me: You just saw me last week, and you'd never make it in time.

> Mama: But I could try!

> Mama: Call later?

> Me: It is tradition.

> Mama: That's my boy. Wish you were here tonight.

I know my mother would love nothing more than to always have her children under her roof. And truthfully, I wouldn't mind it since I hate being alone lately. It's one of the reasons I'm one of the first to arrive to this party. I didn't want to sit around my apartment, twiddling my thumbs for another second longer. These days, being alone leads to me watching replays, which leads to me obsessing about my game, which leads to me playing like shit. I need the distraction of tonight, something to take my mind off the way our games have gone lately, something to loosen me up so I can play better for my teammates.

I tuck my phone back into my pocket and let my eyes roam around the room. They snag on Hutch and his girlfriend, Auden, across the way, their heads together as they laugh about something. An inside joke, I'm sure.

If I had seen this display of cutesy love a few years ago, I might have made a silly comment or ribbed my teammate endlessly in the locker room. All my single teammates would have since we formed the Serpents Singles Club—or at least that's what Lawson likes to call us—which was really just a pact to remain unattached until we each got the chance to lift the Stanley Cup over our heads.

At the time, I was content with our deal, totally on board, because why not? It wasn't like I was against relationships or anything, but I wasn't looking for one either. I was good with being single and having fun. But one by one, my teammates have started falling in love, leaving our agreement by the wayside, and it's had me feeling things I never expected to feel…like *longing*.

Hutch was the first to break the promise when he met Auden before last season started. There was a lot of drama around them getting together, but everything worked out in the end. Then Lawson went and fell for Auden's twin sister, Rory. He found a puppy, stopped at Rory's veterinary clinic for help, and, in typical Lawson fashion, annoyed her until she admitted she had feelings for him too.

Our latest to fall is Hayes, who was given guardianship over his niece this past summer. With his history of causing havoc, I guess I really shouldn't be surprised he fell for his nanny, someone completely off-limits. It's entirely on brand for him. He and Quinn are happy, though, and that's really all that matters.

I'm glad they found their people. Truly, I am. But now that I see what they have, it makes all my one-night stands and short flings feel wrong. I want my own *someone*. Someone to laugh with, to debate with regarding whether you should put peanut butter on both slices of bread, someone who won't be afraid to call me on my shit whenever I need it.

I toss back the remains of my drink to stamp out the feeling of loneliness clawing at my chest, the same feeling that grows heavier and heavier by the day. I order another vodka soda, promising myself to slow down after this one. I can already feel the heat rising in my cheeks from drinking so much so fast, especially since I typically stay sober during the season and it's been a while since I've had a drink.

When I'm handed a glass this time, I take a slow sip, pacing myself. A dark-haired woman in a skintight, shimmery silver dress and sky-high black heels marches by, stopping just a few feet away. Her head is tilted low, and she presses a phone to her ear.

"No, Mother," she hisses. "Because I said *no*. Don't you know what that word means?"

A sigh.

"I don't care who he is. I am *not* going on a date with anyone you set me up with."

A pause.

"Because I'm already seeing someone! So, no, we absolutely will not be talking about this later when I calm down because I won't be calming down."

I grin at her tenacity. Good for her, sticking up for herself.

"Now, I'm getting off the phone before we both say something we regret. Goodbye, Mother."

She wrenches the phone from her ear, slamming her thumb on the screen so hard she lets out a soft yelp. She pulls her hand away and shakes it, examining her long, perfectly manicured nail.

"Dammit," she mutters, sucking her thumb into her mouth, her red-painted lips closing around it.

I shift, swallowing thickly at the gesture. There's no reason whatsoever that should have any effect on me. Still, it does, and it's just another sign of how fucking lonely I am because my mind immediately goes to *other* things I'd like to see red lips wrapped around.

I clear my throat, draining the rest of my vodka. *So much for savoring it.*

The sound draws the woman's attention, and she lifts her head, recognition all over her features. She's not the only one because I know just who it is that has my cock twitching in my pants: Lilah Maddison, Auden's best friend.

And I know for a fact she isn't seeing anyone.

Chapter 2

LILAH

Death, taxes, and my mother driving me absolutely nuts—those are the only certainties in life.

Why my mother chose New Year's Eve to get on my ass about "growing up" and "settling down," I have no clue, but here I am anyway, angrily stomping around the party I worked so hard to make perfect, all because of her.

I hang up on my mother with just a *bit* too much ferocity if my stinging thumb is any indication. On instinct, I suck the injured digit into my mouth to soothe the ache. It, of course, does nothing to alleviate the frustration flowing through me, but at least it's something.

"I won't have you embarrassing me with one of your one-night stands again."

I brought *one* one-night stand to a party with my

parents' stuffy friends years ago, and my mother has never let me live it down. Did he eat all the shrimp and steal half the silverware? Yes, but still—who even uses real silver at a dinner party anyway?

"You're reckless, Lilah. When will you grow up and settle down with someone nice and not one of those boys *you run around with?"*

This isn't the first time my mother has brought up "settling down" in the last few months. She's never once considered that I don't *want* to get married.

And why should I want to? All the marriages I've witnessed have turned to complete shit, including hers. My parents might still legally be married, but they haven't been husband and wife in ages.

I can only guess her sudden interest is because my younger sister, Sadie, is now off the market, having packed up her life and moved to Europe to live with some distant heir to a throne or something or other. I don't understand the particulars of royalty and never will, but I'm happy for her nonetheless. She met Drake while traveling for work for Sinclair Properties and fell in love. I'm glad. Now she doesn't have to be subjected to all this shit my parents are trying to pull.

I'm the sole disappointment now.

Why I won't ever be enough for my parents, I'll never know. Sure, I helped Auden build a billion-dollar empire, but I was still just a "glorified secretary" to them. I guess closing million-dollar deals and helping open and maintain luxury properties wasn't good enough. They want more, my mother in particular. She wants me to become her—hosting events that have no purpose just to impress people who are going to gossip about me behind my back.

I don't want that life, but it's the one I was born into. My family comes from old money thanks to the investment firm my grandfather passed on to my father, and things are done a certain way to uphold our family name, like getting married and popping out an appropriate number of kids to continue the line. According to my mother, that should have happened years ago, but somehow, I managed to sidestep that conversation while working for Auden. They were too busy being angry that I chose to go to college instead of staying at home and being paraded around for their friends to judge me. It took them six months before they spoke to me again when I first left for school, and it was honestly the most peaceful six months of my life.

Now that I'm "free" of Auden—their words, not mine—they're back to being on me about settling down and becoming a "proper woman," and I'm back to refusing them every step of the way. I *am* a proper woman. So what if I'm single? I'm happy that way.

Liar.

That little voice always at the back of my mind pipes up loud and clear.

Fine. I'm not exactly happy being single—I never have been. However, I don't want to be tied down, either. Just because I don't want to be alone doesn't mean I have to get married.

Someone clears their throat, and I glance up to find none other than the Seattle Serpents' starting goalie staring right at me with red cheeks and a drink in his hand, and I realize I'm still sucking on my thumb. Fox, the quintessential Southern gentleman and the definition of a good boy. The same guy who has made me blush far too many times by uttering words like *sugar* and *sweetheart* and even *ma'am*.

That last one annoys me to no end, but can I be blamed when the man looks like he does? His chestnut hair is perfectly coiffed, his jaw is lightly lined with scruff, and his brown eyes remind me of smooth milk chocolate. I let my gaze trail over the rest of him, noting how his black suit molds to his sculpted body, clinging extra tight to thighs I have no doubt could crush a watermelon with very little effort.

Fox shifts uncomfortably under my gaze, his eyes lingering on my lips, which are still closed around my thumb, and I don't miss his rough swallow or the way his stare darkens. He shuffles again when I pop it free with a loud noise, and I like it far too much.

So, I slide my pained digit back into my mouth just because I can. Fox has made *me* blush over and over. It's only fair to return the favor, right? I might have sworn off dating, but that doesn't mean I can't have fun in the meantime.

Someone calls my name from across the room, and I turn to find one of the caterers waving me over. I hold up my hand, letting them know I'll be right over. As much as I'd love to stick around and mess with Fox some more, duty calls.

He's still staring at me when I turn back around, his cheeks stained red.

"Fox," I say with a grin.

"Lilah," he responds, his voice a little more gravelly than usual, which only makes me smile more.

I toss him a wink and swear his blush deepens before I swivel on my heels. I shouldn't tease him, but it's too fun not to. He makes it so easy.

I cross the room to fix whatever has popped up now because that seems to be exactly what today has turned into—problem after problem. First, we had an issue with a few broken tables, so I rolled up my proverbial sleeves, screwdriver in hand, and got to work. It might have been the first time I held an *actual* screwdriver in my hand and not the mixed drink. Then, it was the tray of flutes being dropped and breaking all over the kitchen. It's fine. We found more.

It was a lot, but I did what I always do—I found a way to make it work.

Which is precisely what I do with our new problem—a caterer having to leave to take care of their sick child. I pivot, form a plan, and send the team back out to work. Crisis averted, I peek back into the party, the room even fuller than it was just minutes ago. The tables and centerpieces are perfectly set. The bars are stocked, and people are already waiting to grab a drink. The deejay is playing the music at a level that's fun but still allows you to have a conversation with the person across from you.

"Get out here and stop hiding!"

Auden appears before me, dragging me out from behind the door and into the party that's in full swing.

"This place looks incredible!" she says with a loud excited squeal. "I can't believe you did all this."

"*We* did all this. This is your party."

"On paper, but you did most of the work." I roll my eyes at her, and she slaps my arm. "Don't roll your eyes at me, Lilah Jane. You're just as much responsible for this as I am, even more so. Don't diminish your efforts like that."

"Not bad for a glorified secretary, huh?"

She groans. "Please tell me you didn't talk to your mother today. I thought we had a rule about not answering on holidays because we know she's going to be drinking far too much chardonnay and will probably get mouthy."

I roll my lips into a flat line, answering her without saying a word.

"I swear, that woman," Auden seethes. "I hate that she talks to you like that. If she understood half of the shit you did for me, she'd shut her trap." She winces. "Sorry, I know she's your mother, it's just…"

I shake my head. "No, I get it. She's infuriating."

"What did she want this time?"

"Oh, you know, just to remind me that I'm going to spend the rest of my life alone and bitter because I'm unmarried and haven't popped out ten kids, even though I'm barely even thirty years old."

"That's not how that works, but okay."

"*And* that she's 'found the most delightful guy' for me to bring as a date to my father's party next weekend."

"Wait—she found *you* a date? Does she not realize dating is like your favorite thing to do?"

I know Auden doesn't mean it any certain way, and this isn't the first time she's made a comment like this, but this time…I don't know. It stings a little, and I'm not sure why. Maybe it's because everyone around me is falling into serious relationships and "growing up" just like my mother says, and I'm still…well, I'm just me.

I shove the thoughts aside and nod. "Yes, she's found me a date, and I have zero intentions of finding out who that 'delightful guy' is, especially after her last attempt with Inspector Doug."

"Ugh. Those suspenders." She shudders, thinking of the guy I very begrudgingly let my mother set me up with last time. He wore suspenders, an old-fashioned detective coat, *and a monocle*…all unironically. It was terrible. "Please tell me you told her no."

"I did. I told her I'm seeing someone."

"But you're not."

I shrug. "So? I'll find someone."

"Lilah…" She lays her hand on my arm. "This is *your mother* we're talking about here. You know she's going to run with this, right?"

I wave off her worry. "Trust me, I won't let it get that far. It's just one night. No big deal."

"Okay," Auden says, but something in that one word tells me she doesn't believe me.

I appreciate her concern. I really do. But it's not like I'm planning to marry the guy. It's just one date. I'll tell my mother we broke up afterward. At least it'll keep her off my back until the next big event I have to make an appearance at.

"You know, instead of saying you're dating someone, you could just block her number…" Auden lifts her brows.

"Have you blocked your mother yet?"

She tucks her lips together, knowing full well she has no room to talk when it comes to toxic relationships with parents. Auden and her father? They're closer than close. But Auden and her mother? Well, that's a whole different story. Her relationship with her mother is just as complicated as mine, if not more so.

"All right. Fine. No more talk of mothers. Let's swing back around to how amazing this party is. Everything's good so far, right?"

"Yep. Perfect." I decide not to worry her about the latest mishap. The less she knows, the less she has to stress about, which was my goal when stepping in to help plan this.

"There you two are." Hutch, Auden's boyfriend, appears at her side with a nod in my direction. "Lilah."

"Hutch." I nod back, face straight.

But it's only moments before I break, a full smile pulling at my lips as I launch myself into his arms for a big, feet-off-the-ground kind of hug. With him and Auden dating, Hutch and I have become good friends, and I view him as the brother I never had. Not only because he treats my girl like a queen, but also because he's genuinely a good guy once you get past his gruff exterior.

"This place looks amazing." He sets me back on my expensive heels.

"Your girlfriend did all the wo—ow!" I rub the spot on my arm where Auden just pinched me. "What was that for?"

"Stop passing it off on me."

"Hutch, tell your girlfriend to stop pinching me."

"Hutch, tell my best friend you're not the boss of me and *I'm* the boss in this relationship," Auden says.

"I like to think we're fifty-fifty on that one," he answers.

Auden and I exchange a glance, then both burst out laughing.

"All right, all right. I guess I'll see myself out of this conversation. Just wanted to say how great this place looks."

He kisses Auden's cheek before taking his leave, and she sighs a little, her eyes locked on him as he walks away.

"Glad to see you're still fawning over him."

She doesn't even look bothered by my teasing. She just gives me that same dopey grin she's been giving me since they finally admitted their feelings last year.

"He's amazing, isn't he?"

I roll my eyes. "I need a drink if I'm going to have to watch all these couples moon over each other all night."

"Well, if you weren't such a curmudgeonly old lady, you too could be in a happy, healthy relationship like the rest of us," she teases.

I toss her a glare as we make our way to the bar on the opposite side of the room. We each order a glass of champagne—something light to kick off the evening—then I take in the party through a guest's eyes for the first time. I examine every inch of the room, going over all the things I would change now that people are in here. A few more tables here, taller centerpieces there. Maybe drape the lights differently.

"Stop it," Auden says.

"What?"

"I know you're picking the party apart. Knock it off. It's perfect the way it is. Besides, this is for a bunch of hockey players. I really don't think they would have cared if we had done taller centerpieces or not."

I grin. "You're doing it too."

She shrugs. "You can take the designer away from the hotel, but you can't take away the urge to design."

"Do you miss it?"

"Having such a demanding job? No, but I miss the creative aspect. I had so much fun building our house over the summer that it gave me that itch again, you know?"

I nod. "I understand that. That's how I felt planning this party."

We don't say anything, but my mind still spins with ideas, though that's nothing new because it's *been* spinning with ideas. I've spent the last year since Auden sold her company trying to figure out what I want to do next and living off the *very* generous severance package she gave me. No matter how many trips I've taken looking for inspiration, like the two months I spent in Europe getting Sadie settled there or my trip to Belize over Thanksgiving to avoid a Maddison holiday fiasco, I'm still at a loss and haven't come up with anything.

I want to do something that allows me to exercise my strengths—like planning and design—while still giving me new challenges every day so I don't grow bored. I don't know exactly what that is, but I'll figure it out. I know I will. I just have to give it time while trying to avoid my mother's latest matchmaking efforts.

"So," Auden says, taking a sip from the bubbly in her hand, "any prospects for the fake boyfriend?"

"Considering I just found out myself that I'm not single anymore, no. I haven't given it much thought beyond blurting it out to my mother."

Really, I could slap myself for doing so. What the hell was I thinking? Auden's right—there's no way my mother is going to buy it.

"Well, I know a good place to start..." She waves

her hand out at the event before us. "There are plenty of single guys here."

"You want me to date one of Hutch's teammates?"

"It's just for one night, right? And these aren't all his teammates. There are trainers and other staff here too. You could find one of them. Or a teammate's brother. I don't know." She takes another drink. "Why are you having such a hard time finding someone anyway? Don't you always have a date lined up?"

Usually, yes. I'm sort of known as a serial dater. But lately…I don't know. It's not been the same high it used to be. I used to get a kick out of all the weird dates I'd go on, used to love telling the stories, but they aren't as fun as they once were. Now, they just make me sad, and I'm unsure why.

"I'm having a dry spell," I mutter.

She gasps dramatically, so loud a few people stare. "A dry spell? *You?*"

"It's not a big deal."

It really isn't. Or at least, it didn't *feel* like a big deal until I talked to my mother. Now it's taking everything I have not to overthink her words. Am I really going to become some lonely old woman if I don't find someone to settle down with soon? I'm only thirty. That's not old. But what if one year turns to two turns to five and then ten? What then?

I don't know. All I know is that I don't *want* to settle

down. I still want fun. I still want no strings attached. Maybe even hot sex with a hot hockey player.

Ah, yes. That sounds like *exactly* what I need right now.

"Fine, I'll bite. Who's single here?"

She bounces on her heels excitedly. "Well, there's Locke."

"That's the guy with the slightly crooked nose, right?"

"To be fair, I think most of these guys have slightly crooked noses from taking pucks and sticks to the face."

I chuckle. "Fair point."

While Locke seems like a good guy, I'm not sure he's my type. He seems too responsible, too family oriented. Sure, this is just for a night, but I don't want to lead him on.

"Who else?" I ask.

"There's Keller."

"Mmm, perpetually pouty and grumpy Keller who is too good-looking for this world."

"I might be a taken woman, but even I can admit he's hot. Have you seen his eyes? It's like looking into a bottle of bourbon or something. And those tattoos? Fucking swoon."

"Right? But as hot as he is, he's a little too grumpy for me. That's more your style than mine."

"You don't know what you're missing," she says with a shrug, then continues to scan the room as more and more people pile in.

I know there are at least one or two other single guys on the team now that they've gotten divorced, but that's baggage I don't want to deal with. I want someone easy, someone chill. Someone more my speed who isn't looking for anything more than what this is.

"Oh!" Auden exclaims, champagne splashing out of her glass. "Fox!"

"Fox?"

"Yeah. He's single. He's in the club, so he has to be, right?"

Ah, right. The "club." The Serpents Singles, the group Hutch and his single teammates formed some time ago. I don't know the particulars of it, just that it includes Hutch, Lawson, Hayes, Keller, Locke, and Fox, and three of them have already fallen victim to the love bug. Why they're still part of a so-called singles club, I don't know. But it's kind of cute, all these guys using an excuse like that to be friends when all they're really looking for is companionship.

Boys are weird.

But Fox…Fox is an option I can get behind. He's definitely my type, and seeing him earlier tonight in that tux… Well, I'd like to see him out of it, too.

"You don't still have a crush on him, do you?"

I rear my head back because this is certainly news to me. "Who the hell said I had a crush on him?"

"Rory."

"Rory said what?"

The woman in question struts up to us, and I have to do a double take because seeing Rory out of her usual animal-hair-covered scrubs is always a shock, but seeing her look like *this*? Well, color me surprised.

She's wearing a floor-length black dress with just enough sparkle to it that it catches in the light. Her makeup is dark—I'm astounded she's wearing any at all—and her long, dark hair is curled loosely around her shoulders. She's a fucking knockout and looks nothing like the Rory I know and love.

"Stop looking at me like that or I swear I'm going to punch your tit."

Ah, there she is.

I step toward her to hug her, and she steps back. I laugh. "Please never change, Rory."

"Wouldn't dream of it," she says dryly, lifting her glass to her lips in that slightly annoyed, slightly amused way only she can.

I'd never tell her this—mostly because I'm pretty sure she'd roast me until the end of time with her being so anti-feelings and mushiness—but even though we clash a lot, she's one of my favorite people ever.

"You said Lilah here had a thing for Fox," Auden provides.

"Oh, right. I did say that."

"Why?" I ask.

"Because you have a thing for Fox."

"I do not!" I argue, possibly a little too loudly, several people looking our way.

Auden smiles and waves at them before turning back to us.

"I don't! I don't know why *somebody*"—I cut Rory a glare—"thinks otherwise."

"Because you were all blushy with him when those morons came to the bar and tried to convince Auden to go after Hutch."

That was a year ago! She thinks I've been crushing on him this whole time?

"First of all, you're dating one of those morons now," I point out.

"Don't remind me." She rolls her eyes, but there's no denying the smile pulling at her lips, no doubt thinking of her golden retriever boyfriend, Lawson. I don't understand how they work together considering they're complete opposites, but they do.

"Second of all, he called me *sugar* in that Southern accent. I'm fairly certain that would make any woman blush."

"Not me."

"Your boyfriend calls you Wednesday because you're Wednesday Addams incarnate. You don't count," I snap at Rory, who—predictably—looks unbothered by my words. "And I *don't* have a crush on him, so stop spreading that rumor."

"Look, all I'm saying is I wouldn't blame you if you do. He's so…polite. So…well, Fox. Has that charm that's completely irresistible, you know? It makes sense you'd be into him—anyone would."

"Again, I wouldn't."

Auden ignores her sister, turning her hazel eyes on me. "So, do you?"

"No!" I say adamantly.

It's true. I absolutely do not have a crush on Fox. Do I find him ridiculously attractive? Yes. But a crush? Not a chance.

Auden nods. "Well, if you change your mind, let me know. Maybe I can—"

"I'm so sorry to cut in, ladies." We all turn to find Hutch behind us, the new coach of the Seattle Serpents beside him with his beautiful redheaded partner. "Could I borrow you for a moment, sweetheart?"

Hutch wraps his arm around Auden's waist, tugging her close as she beams up at him, and Lawson slides in beside us, pulling Rory to him, leaving me as the odd one out. There are three beautiful couples, then me. I'm smart enough to know when I don't belong.

"I'll just..." I say to no one because nobody is paying me any attention at this point, and I don't blame them. I'd also be sidetracked if I had a tall, hot-as-hell hockey player showering me with love and affection.

I slip through the crowd that's grown exponentially, searching for a familiar face in a place where I know next to nobody. Normally, that wouldn't bother me, but tonight...tonight I could use familiar, something to distract me from my mother's words replaying in my mind.

If she came out of the gate swinging with Inspector Doug, I'm terrified to even think about the other prospects she has lined up. I need to find a date for my dad's birthday party and fast before I'm forced to confess I lied and find myself walking into the event arm in arm with a grown man in suspenders and a mustache I want to shave off.

I place my empty champagne glass on one of the trays the waitstaff is holding, immediately replacing it with a fresh one and chugging half of it to drown out my mother's voice in my head.

"You can't keep playing these games, Lilah Jane. You're embarrassing our family."

In my distracted state, I run straight into a wall.

"Whoa," the wall says, its voice warm like syrup. Big hands wrap around my waist, steadying me before I do something truly embarrassing like spilling my champagne all over their expertly pressed suit. "Easy there, sugar."

Sugar.

One word, and I know instantly who it is. This isn't a wall at all; it's a person…a very tall, well-built person if the ridges I feel beneath my hands are any indication.

Fox.

I look up into a pair of coffee-colored eyes surrounded by…freckles. He has freckles. How'd I never realize Fox has freckles? How did I never realize he smells so damn good, like soap with just a hint of mahogany? And are his eyes always this gorgeous with little flecks of amber?

"Lilah," he says with a grin that makes me feel all kinds of warm. Or maybe that's all the champagne I've had. I can't tell which.

"Fox, how are you?"

He smiles down at me. "Me? Oh, I'm fine as a frog's hair split both ways."

I laugh, wobbling a little as his grip tightens on me. "Do frogs even have hair?"

His grin slips, but only for a moment before returning even wider. "Well, no, they sure don't." He sets me right, then releases me, and I instantly miss his warmth. "Are you having a good time?"

"I am having a great time, Fox. Are you?"

"I am. It's a great party you and Auden put together."

It surprises me that he knows I helped Auden plan this party. It's not like we announced it anywhere. Auden said she was throwing a party to bring together the team before the new year, and I immediately asked how I could help. It's what we do—work together.

But I didn't know Fox knew that.

"Is that…not right?" he asks.

"No." I shake my head. "No, it's right. You're right. We worked on it together."

"I thought so. You two make a good team."

For the I-don't-even-know-how-many-eth time, Fox has me ducking my head in an attempt to hide a blush.

"Thanks," I mumble, unsure why I'm suddenly feeling shy, especially since I'm usually anything but, yet here I am, red-faced and self-conscious in front of the hockey goalie. "So"—I push my hair behind my ear—"how's sports?"

He chuckles. "Sports is good."

Our conversation makes no grammatical sense, but it makes me laugh anyway, and I could use a laugh. I could use a lot of things right now, like a romp in the sheets or another drink. A waiter approaches, and I quickly chug the rest of mine before dropping the glass on their tray and grabbing a fresh one, taking an immediate sip.

Fox's brows rise, but he doesn't comment.

"Sorry," I say anyway. "Had to talk to my mother tonight."

He nods like he completely understands, but I doubt he does. Fox strikes me as the type of guy who has parents who love him and are proud of him, not parents who always want more, more, more. I take another drink of the cool champagne, the bubbles tickling the back of my throat, my head getting all floaty, which is perfectly fine by me. The party is a hit, and after working so hard on it the last few weeks, I deserve a night to relax, a night to forget all about my mother's words.

Fox steps back, bending slightly at the waist and holding his hand out like this is some Regency romance and he's courting me. "Would you like to dance, Lilah?" he asks.

Even though there's a space that's clearly designated for dancing, nobody is out there right now. I'm sure it'll be another hour before enough alcohol has been passed around for that to happen. If we went out there now, we'd look ridiculous.

"Uh, no one else is dancing, Fox."

"So?"

"*So*, I'm not going out there and embarrassing myself in front of all these people."

"Why not? They're my teammates, not yours. Who cares what they think, sugar?"

There it is again—*sugar*. It should be such a cheesy nickname, and I'm ninety-nine percent certain I'd hate it coming from anyone else. Yet, with Fox...the only thing I hate is that it makes me blush. Again.

He lifts his brows at me in a silent, *Well?*

Maybe it's the booze running through my veins, or maybe it's just that in a room full of people, he's the only one paying me any attention right now, but I place my hand in his and let Fox lead me to the dance floor.

Chapter 3

FOX

I don't know why I asked Lilah to dance. I just know something in her eyes made me sad, and I felt she needed comfort.

Perhaps it was how her shoulders hunched inward when she mentioned her mother, or maybe it was how she guzzled down that glass of champagne, clutching it like a lifeline. I guess it could have just been that she looks gorgeous tonight, I've had too many drinks already, and I want to do something other than stand around and rehash how the season is going. She could clearly use a distraction, and so could I.

We reach the empty dance floor, and I sweep her into my arms like it's a practiced routine, settling my hand on her hip and leaving an appropriate distance between us. The deejay plays something soft and slow from the '90s as we box-step around the floor.

Lilah peeks up at me through her lashes, her blue eyes glassy from the champagne that's flowing freely. "You dance so…"

"Professionally?"

"Stiffly."

She laughs when my eyebrows rise in surprise, as no one has ever said that to me before, especially not my dance teacher from when I was eleven. Lilah inches closer until we're pressed together, her body curved against mine as we continue to move in sync.

"Much better," she says, so close now I can smell her perfume, something light and floral that I don't mind one bit. "Where'd you learn to dance?"

"If you can believe it—and you might not be able to with your criticisms—I took lessons when I was younger."

"Oh, I believe it, Southern boy. You dance like you're at a church event, not a party with a bunch of depraved hockey players in attendance."

"We aren't depraved."

She arches a dark brow at me. "I've met your teammates, remember?"

I laugh lightly. "Fair enough. Not *all* of us are depraved."

"It's okay to be depraved in some ways." She grins mischievously, her fingers playing at the collar of my suit.

I'm all too aware of what she means by her words, just like I'm all too aware of how good her body feels pressed against mine…how close my hand is to the curve of her ass, how my fingertips keep just *barely* brushing against the soft skin poking through the cutouts of her dress.

I ignore it all, instead focusing on moving us to the rhythm of the music. Another couple joins us, then another, and it's like once the gates have opened, here comes the flood as more people filter in beside us. Auden drags over a reluctant Hutch, and Hayes and Quinn pass by us, looking like two heart-eye emojis come to life. Lawson is literally on his knees, begging Rory to dance, but she's shaking her head adamantly while Keller chirps him like we're on the bench. I laugh at that, and Lilah turns her attention to them, too.

"She loves messing with him," she remarks.

"I think he might love it too."

"Probably." She shakes her head. "It's funny. I remember when Rory swore up and down there was no way she would ever fall in love. Auden too, actually. Now look at them both—completely smitten with no hope." She snorts. "Fools."

"Fools?" I ask, surprised she has such an outlook about her friends.

She turns her attention back to me. "Don't get me

wrong—I'm happy for them. Truly. I just think the whole concept of love and relationships is…well, frankly, it's bullshit."

I nod. "Ah."

She bristles, our steps faltering as she goes rigid in my grasp. "*Ah?* What's that supposed to mean?"

"It means *ah*."

"Not when you say it like that, it doesn't."

"Nothing bad. You just sound a lot like those same exact guys who swore relationships were terrible before getting into one. Now look at them—happy and in love."

"Oh. Well, yeah, I guess I do." She shrugs as we continue to sway. "Sorry. Ignore me. I'm in a bit of a mood tonight."

"Your mother?" I guess.

She nods but doesn't elaborate. Her eyes are latched on to the bowtie around my neck as she stares through me, and tightness tugs at my chest. She looks so sad, and I hate it. I hate to think the one person who is supposed to love her and treat her with respect no matter what has upset her like this, especially tonight after she's worked so hard to put together this incredible party. The night's been tainted by her mother.

"She keeps trying to set me up, and I don't want

any part of it," she confesses after several quiet moments.

"Because you don't believe in love?"

"No, because her date options suck."

I chuckle. "Makes sense. Is that why you told her you're seeing someone even though you aren't?"

"How do you know I'm not?" she challenges, tipping her chin up defiantly.

I lift a shoulder. "We talk in the locker room sometimes. I overhear things from Hutch." She looks worried by that momentarily. "All good, though. Promise."

It's true. All Hutch has said about Lilah is that he hopes she isn't going down the same road he was before he met Auden, a road of loneliness and bitterness.

"I know I shouldn't have lied to her, but she wants me to have a date for my father's birthday party next weekend, and I panicked because…let's just say the last guy she set me up with was *not* it."

She sighs, and I agree. She *shouldn't* have lied to her mother, but I can understand why she did. As much as I love my own, I wouldn't want her setting me up on dates either.

"Whatever," she mumbles. "I'll find someone."

I have no doubt she will, someone as beautiful as her, but there's still something bothering her, something else. I don't know what exactly, so I take a guess.

"Your mother is wrong."

"What?" She pulls back to look up at me. "What do you mean?"

"I don't know. I get the feeling she said something else, and I just thought you should know she's wrong."

"You don't even know what she said."

"No, but I know you." I tug her closer, my hand splayed across her lower back as I drop my lips to her ear. I want these words to just be for her. "You're kind and funny and put together this party when you have no investment in this tcam othcr than just being a really good friend to the captain's girlfriend, all while looking absolutely fucking stunning in that dress. So, she's wrong, Lilah. Whatever she said, she's wrong."

Her steps falter again, and I catch her, keeping her on pace and not missing how she doesn't respond.

Did I fuck up? Was complimenting her taking it too far? Is she completely weirded out now that I've said she looks stunning? I don't want to take it back because it's true. The way her dress is molded to her body should be illegal. And that slit on the side? The one that reveals *just* enough to make you wonder what's underneath? It's making me think things I definitely shouldn't be thinking, especially when it comes to Lilah.

But her silence is killing me, and I don't know how long passes before I blurt out, "Did I say something wrong?"

When she peeks up at me, a light laugh falls from her lips. Her eyes are no longer glassy from the booze; they're glassy from unshed tears.

"No, you didn't. You said everything right."

"Oh."

Another soft laugh as she settles further into my embrace, her head resting on my chest, her hair tickling my chin. "You're a really good guy, Fox, you know that?" she says quietly, her breath warm against me, and for the second time since I tugged her into my arms, I blush.

I've heard a lot of people say I'm a nice guy. Hell, my teammates were just teasing me about it earlier this evening, but coming from Lilah at this moment? I don't know. It's good to hear.

The song shifts from slow and romantic to a much more upbeat tune, and just as quickly as the music changes, Lilah breaks away from me, leaving my arms limp at my sides and a sudden desire to drag her back to me.

I tip my head at her. "What?"

"I…" She shakes her head. "Thanks for the dance, Fox."

Then she turns and pushes through the crowd, vanishing right before my eyes.

Wait. What?

"Lilah!" I call out, trying to reach for her, but it's useless when everyone around us is already throwing their hands up and shouting as the song instructs.

It feels like prom 2.0 in here. Everyone is suddenly on the floor, nobody aware that Lilah just pulled the fastest disappearing trick of the century, and I'm stuck standing here staring after a ghost.

Lawson jerks me back to reality, grabbing me by the shoulders and tugging me into the mix of dancers. I reluctantly follow him, still glancing out to see where Lilah fled. I can't see her anywhere now. She's gone, fading into the crowd and slipping away, the sight of her eyes brimming with tears burned into my mind as Lawson grabs my shoulders, giving me a shake.

"Come on, dude!" he yells. "Dance! New Year, New Year, New Year!"

His chanting is ridiculous, but his excitement is contagious, and I find myself shaking my head, joining in with him anyway. We dance through the song, then another and another, and soon, I have no idea what time it is, just that my mouth is dry and I might die of thirst if I don't get something to drink soon. I point to the bar, letting Lawson know I'm leaving, and he shakes his head.

"I'm good!" he yells.

I laugh. I wasn't asking, but whatever. I push through the crowd and make my way back to where my night began: the bar. The bartender remembers me, already starting on a vodka soda, and I nod my thanks. I can't help but scan the crowd, looking for a silver dress and cerulean eyes.

"Let me guess, you're looking for Lilah."

I turn to find Locke beside me, holding my drink in one hand and his own glass in the other. I was so distracted I didn't even realize the bartender set my order on the bar.

"Thanks," I say, accepting the booze. "How'd you know?"

He shrugs, taking a sip of what I assume is scotch since it's his go-to drink whenever we hang out at Top Shelf, the local hockey-themed bar we tend to frequent. "Don't know. Saw you two dancing and took a guess. I wasn't aware you were the dancing sort of friends."

"Just felt like dancing is all."

He nods but doesn't look like he believes me, and I don't believe me either.

"She looks good," he remarks.

"Hmm" is my only response. She *did* look good, but I can't stop thinking about how she peeked up at me like she was seconds away from crying when all I did was speak the truth. It has me curious as hell to know what it was her mother said to her that had her so upset.

"Who are we talking about?" Keller, easily the grumpiest person I've ever met, slides up next to us with a beer bottle in his hand, looking like he'd rather be anywhere else than here. He rests his back against the bar, looking at the dance floor with a sneer. "Look at those fucking idiots, all hopelessly in love and shit. Fools."

I laugh because it's exactly what Lilah said about them and maybe even something I could have said once upon a time, but not anymore. Now, when I look out at Hutch, Lawson, and Hayes with their girlfriends, all I see is something pure and happy, and that same pang of wanting hits me again.

I shove it down like I always do.

"Remind me why I agreed to come to this thing again?" Keller grumbles.

"Because you know it's important to your captain," Locke tells him.

Keller grunts in response, taking another swig from his beer.

"What time is it?" he asks. "I want to get out of here before midnight so I don't have to see everyone making out with one another."

I pluck my phone from my pocket to tell him and

am shocked when I see the time *and* the missed calls. It's ten o'clock—I missed calling my parents at midnight their time. *Shit.* Luckily, I know they're still awake even though it's one in the morning there.

"I'll be right back," I mutter to the guys as Locke lays into Keller about turning over a new leaf in the new year and being a better teammate like the good veteran hockey guy he is.

I slip past them and through the crowd, pushing open the doors to the balcony, shivering when the cold wind hits me. Although I've lived in Seattle for a few years, I'm still not used to the Pacific Northwest winters. This is especially true after growing up down south, where I think I saw a collective two inches of snow my entire childhood.

I settle onto a bench tucked back into a corner, as far away from the party's noise as possible, and hit the video call icon before taking another sip of my vodka soda. My mother's face fills the screen almost instantly, and I grin.

"Hey, Mama."

"Don't you *Hey, Mama* me, Arthur Francis Fox." Her eyes are narrowed. "You're late."

"I'm sorry. I got distracted."

She titters, setting the phone down, propping it against something. My father comes into the frame, a cigar unsurprisingly hanging from his lips. It's the only time of year my mother allows him to smoke it without complaint from her. Dad shuffles cards in his hands, then sends me a cheerful grin, his cheeks flushed from the spiked eggnog I know he's been drinking all night.

"My boy!" he says boisterously. "Happy New Year, kid."

"Thanks, Dad. How's the game going? You winning?"

"Oh, I'm swindling the shit out of these suckers."

His friends—Bart, Tony, and Chris, from the sounds of it—start cussing at him in unison, and all my dad does is laugh, his round belly shaking from the movement.

"You're keeping them in check, right, Mama?"

She rolls her eyes at their antics. "Someone has to."

This is their yearly tradition—poker, cigars, booze, and food with friends. I have no doubt my brother and sister are there, likely setting off fireworks as usual. It's the same thing they've been doing as long as I can remember, and a part of me wishes I were there to partake in all the fun.

"Is that my big brother I hear?"

My younger brother, Russ, pops into view, and his twin, Regan, is right behind him.

"Hey, guys," I say, grinning at them. I didn't spend nearly as much time with them when I was home as I would have liked, and fuck, I miss them.

"Artie!" Regan practically screams my nickname, tugging someone into view. "Oh my god. You can finally meet Dina!"

"Hi, Dina," I say to the blonde woman staring at my sister like she hung the moon.

"Nice to meet you," she says quietly, and I laugh.

Regan is the loudest person I've ever met—including Lawson—and it's hilarious that she's dating someone so clearly bashful.

"Where are the kids?" I ask Russ, hoping to say hi to my niece and nephew.

"Molly has them tonight." He married his high school sweetheart when he was twenty-one, then two kids later, they divorced after growing apart. Luckily for Russ and the kids, they remained good friends. "But Katie is around here somewhere," he says of his new girlfriend, who I met when I was home for Christmas.

"Okay, bye! We're going back to blowing stuff up!" Regan shouts as if being across the country means she needs to yell.

I bid my siblings goodbye as they run off to have the fun I wish I were having.

"Speaking of girlfriends..." Mama grins, and I already know what's coming next. "Anyone new in your life, sweetie?"

A pair of red-rimmed cobalt eyes pops into my mind, and for the hundredth time tonight, I wonder where Lilah has run off to. I haven't seen her since she disappeared, and I scanned the crowd far more times than I'd like to admit before I came out here. Still, she's nowhere to be found.

"Ooh, you have a look. Did you meet someone?"

I snap my attention back to my phone. "Huh? No, Mama, nothing has changed since you saw me last week."

"Just making sure you didn't go and fall in love and forget to tell me about it."

"In a week?"

She shrugs. "When you know, you know."

I'm sure my mother would think that. She was engaged to my father a month after meeting him and married him a month later. That was over thirty years ago, and they're more in love today than they were back then.

Maybe they're why I don't hate relationships as much as my teammates do. I've always had their love as a reminder that they don't always turn out shitty.

"How's the party going?" she asks. "Must be fun if you forgot to call your mother."

My mama loves me, but she takes every opportunity to guilt me. I'm pretty sure it's her motherly duty or something.

"It's fun. Just been watching Lawson make a fool of himself as usual."

"That poor Rory."

I laugh. My parents haven't met my teammates or their girlfriends, but since I tell them everything, they seem to know them and are fully invested in their shenanigans.

"Saw your game last night," my dad says, tossing cards across the table to his friends, that cigar still hanging precariously out the side of his mouth. "You played a good one, kid. That save with your paddle was incredible."

It wasn't. I wouldn't have had to make it if I hadn't given up the rebound to begin with, but my dad has never said a bad word about my game before. When I'd lose when I was younger, he'd pat me on the back anyway, and we'd go for ice cream. If I won, it was the same thing. My parents' steadfast support is the one thing I could always count on, but sometimes, I wish they'd just tell it to me straight and be honest when I play like shit.

"Thanks," I say anyway, not wanting to get into it because I have a whole list of examples of sucking lately.

It's like that when you're a player, though. Fans might see a great save or goal, while players will see all the ways they could have done better. No matter how loud someone on social media is, nobody critiques our game more than we do.

"We're looking forward to the trip you arranged for us. I can't wait to see you play in person again. It's been too long."

With me being in Seattle instead of playing in New York, where I spent most of my professional career until a horrible year sent me to the expansion team now known as the Seattle Serpents, my parents haven't seen me play in a couple of years now. So, for Christmas, I bought them plane tickets. I think my mother started shopping for rain gear about two seconds after she opened the tickets.

"But until then, we're going to watch every one of your games, kid," Dad promises.

We talk about my dad swindling his friends out of money, her shifts at the hospital and the crazy stuff her patients are doing this holiday season, and how Russ is getting in deep with Katie, leading my mother to believe that this time next year, they'll be engaged. This, of course, leads to a repeat discussion of my singlehood.

When I finally get her off the phone, I have no idea how much time has passed, just that I'm out of vodka and in dire need of another drink. I slip my phone into my pocket, resting against the building. The music thumps so loudly through the speakers that I can feel it vibrating against my back. I should probably go back in there before someone—namely Lawson—comes outside looking for me, but I can't seem to make myself move.

It's not that I'm not having a good time—I am—I just can't stop my mind from racing. From the many, many questions about my game to why Lilah looked like she was about to cry to how I'm absolutely loathing the thought of going back to an empty apartment again, it's all too much, and even this party can't distract me from that.

But maybe more vodka can.

I rise from the bench, ready to head back inside, then the doors burst open. The sound of heels clacking against the concrete perks my ears, and now I'm on edge for a whole different reason. The person moving across the balcony is the same person I've been looking for since she disappeared on me over an hour ago.

Lilah.

Her gait is a little wobbly, and I can only wonder how much she's had to drink since I last saw her. She holds her phone in her hand as she props herself up against the balcony. A loud woman shouts on the other end of the line, asking about who Lilah is seeing.

I should leave, should give her privacy, but I'm rooted in place, especially when Lilah sighs loudly, visibly upset with whoever she's talking to.

"I did not hang up on you, Mother. I *said* I was hanging up, which is vastly different from just getting off the phone. Now though—now I *want* to hang up, and I'm three seconds away from doing so."

I barely hold back my laugh at her sassiness. I don't know what's going on, but I have a distinct feeling, especially based on the irritation radiating off her, that she would be completely justified in hanging up on her mother.

"Lilah!" the older woman gasps dramatically. "Do not speak to your mother that way!"

"Well, then, maybe my mother should stop trying to marry me off to the highest bidder."

Is *that* what had her so upset earlier? Because if so, I don't blame her for crying. I'd be upset too if my parents were trying to pull off some archaic bullshit like that.

Her mother scoffs. "They're just dates, Lilah. Don't be so dramatic."

"Yes, a date with someone I've never met before who I highly doubt has any interest in me other than the fact that I'm your daughter doesn't at all sound like you're trying to pawn me off on whoever has the most money."

"Do you truly think I'm such a horrible mother that I'd do that?"

Lilah doesn't answer her, and her silence speaks volumes. The distinct sound of crying fills the air as her mother breaks into tears, but there's something about it, something that sounds rehearsed…fake.

"I'm just trying to be a good mother to you." She sniffles. "Is it so wrong that I want to see you happy?"

Again, Lilah says nothing.

"You've never once done anything your father and I have asked of you," her mother continues. "You've thrown away the education we spent so much money on. Instead, you paraded around being a glorified secretary for your *best friend*"—she says best friend like it's a curse—"instead of coming to work for your *family*, Lilah. That's how much you hate us."

Lilah groans. "I don't hate you, Mother."

"You do. You hate us, and you think I'm a bad parent when all I'm trying to do is ensure your happiness."

Honestly, it sounds like she's just trying to ensure *her* happiness, Lilah's be damned, but that's not the worst part of what I'm witnessing. No. It's Lilah's shoulders slumping down. It's how she curls into herself, how she shrinks right before my eyes. And how —and I hope I'm really seeing things—she looks like she's about to cave to her mother's whims.

"I just don't understand why you're being so stubborn right now."

"Because I already told you. I'm seeing someone."

"Since when?"

"Since… Since…" Lilah huffs. "I don't know. I haven't exactly been keeping track."

"You're lying, Lilah Jane. I know you're lying. You're not seeing anyone or else you would have mentioned him before now."

"Did you ever stop to think I didn't mention him because I didn't want to go through this whole song and dance?"

Her words might *sound* confident, but her voice is anything but. Even I can hear the shakiness in her words. She's about to blow it all.

"No, because I know you. You don't date. You just *sleep around* like some tawdry little girl instead of a woman society should respect. You're—"

"There you are!"

Lilah spins on her heels, her eyes wide as they find mine as I step out of the shadows I've been hiding in and stride toward her. I don't stop until I'm able to wrap my arm around her waist and pull her to me. She comes willingly, her breath stuttering as she crashes against me, head tipping back to peer up at me.

She looks beautiful like this in the moonlight, her hair a little wild, likely from running her hands through it, her cheeks permanently stained with red from her alcohol flush. The urge to press my lips to hers is sudden and sharp and takes me completely off guard, but I don't act on it.

Instead, I say, "Been looking for you."

"Y-You have?"

"Of course I have, sugar."

Her knees threaten to give out from under her, and it's a good thing I'm holding her up, otherwise she'd be on the ground right about now. I'd laugh if I weren't so aware of our audience.

"Lilah…" her mother says apprehensively. "Who is this?"

I turn to the camera, smiling wide. "Oh, I'm so sorry. How rude of me. It's nice to meet you, Mrs. Maddison. I'm Arthur Fox." I press a wet kiss to Lilah's cheek. "I'm her boyfriend, ma'am."

Chapter 4

LILAH

I am drunk.

That's the only sensible explanation for what I just heard. There is *no way* Fox could have said what I think he did.

I'm her boyfriend, ma'am.

"Well. I guess I stand corrected, Lilah," my mother says haughtily.

But I'm not paying her any attention. I can't seem to pull my eyes away from Fox—*Arthur* Fox—who is staring down at me with those gorgeous browns of his.

Go with it, they're saying. *Play along.*

Maybe it's the booze, or maybe it's the fact that this could save me from my mother. Maybe it's just that I want to; whatever it is, I do. I go right along with it, turning back to the camera to give my mother a *See, I told you so* look.

"Well, I suppose it's nice to meet you, Mr. Fox."
She takes a sip of her wine. "So, what do you do?"

"Me, ma'am?" Fox's drawl is more pronounced
than I've heard before. "I'm a goalie."

"A goalie?" My mother turns her nose up. "What's
a goalie?"

I roll my eyes at her snobbery. "Hockey, Mother.
Fox plays hockey."

That instantly has her much more interested in him
than before, and I have no doubt it's because my
mother is seeing dollar signs. "Professionally?"

"Yes, ma'am. I play for the Seattle Serpents."

"Well, Arthur, I had no idea you were dating my
daughter until tonight."

"You didn't?" Fox grins down at me, and it's that
same expression that had me feeling all kinds of warm
earlier. Now, I don't feel warm. I feel confused. And a
little annoyed. Yet somehow…almost relieved? And
still drunk. "Our Lilah here can be a bit shy
sometimes."

No. That's definitely annoyance winning out. I
narrow my eyes at him, and he rolls his lips together,
hiding his grin.

"Please, I don't think Lilah has ever been shy a day
in her life. Once when she was about six, she snuck
onstage at Disneyland and did a whole horribly
choreographed dance of the hokey pokey."

She laughs as if she remembers this fondly, even though we both know she scolded me for a full hour afterward *and* returned my Mickey Mouse doll to the store. It was my first and last time at Disneyland.

"That so?" Laughter shines in Fox's eyes, and I know that, unlike my mother who is pretending to think it's cute, he really does.

I shrug. "What can I say? I liked the attention."

"So, Arthur," my mother says, "how long have you and my daughter been dating?"

"Oh, well, I don't kiss and tell, ma'am." He winks at her, and I swear if she weren't already sitting, she'd fall right over. "I'll let Lilah fill you in on all those details." I drive my foot against his fancy shoes, and he grunts, but his smile never once slips from his lips. "I'm sure she's been counting the days since we first got together."

Another stomp on his foot and another pained noise from Fox.

Good. He deserves it, throwing me under the bus like this. I mean, yes, he's clearly stepping in to help me, and he's a total saint for that, but really? This is the last thing I expected to happen tonight.

"Well, Lilah?" my mother presses. "How long?"

It's funny how she looks at Fox, a man she just met, like he's the greatest thing in the world, and then how she looks at me like she's *still* disappointed in me.

"A month or so now," I answer, hoping she doesn't hear the shake of uncertainty in my voice.

"And why didn't we meet you at Christmas, young man?"

"I flew home to see my parents."

"Ah, I see. Why didn't you mention him to us?" This question she directs to me.

"Because you never let me get a word in edgewise."

"Lilah!"

Fox laughs, squeezing my hip. "She's kidding, ma'am. We didn't want to jinx anything. New relationships and all that. They take time to build, and we wanted to make sure we got it right this time."

"Aw." She sighs dreamily, and I know Auden was right. My mother has had too much chardonnay if she's falling for the show Fox is putting on. "That's just… That is *so* sweet, Arthur. Isn't he so sweet, Lilah?"

I force myself to smile. "He sure is."

"Well, I can't wait to meet you at my husband's birthday party. You will be there, correct?"

"Remind me of the date, Lilah?"

"Saturday evening," I tell him.

Fox mentally does the math, rolling team names off his lips in a whisper, and I hold my breath. Why? I don't know. I can't decide if I want him to be able to attend or not. On the one hand, it'll save me from a terrible date my mother will still set up for me because it would just be *so* embarrassing if I came alone. But on the other…well, I am still *not* dating Fox.

"Yes," he says after a few moments of silence. "Yes, I can make it."

"Oh, wonderful!" My mother claps her hands excitedly. "I'm so looking forward to meeting you."

"Likewise, ma'am. I've heard so many lovely things about you and Mr. Maddison," my new *boyfriend* says.

My mother snorts unattractively. "Oh, Mr. Fox, I highly doubt that given my daughter's displeasure toward me, but I appreciate you trying to cover for her."

Fox's hand tightens around my waist, but his smile never slips. It's the only indication I have that he doesn't care for her words, and I don't know why it brings me such comfort, but it does.

"I hate to cut this short, but would it be too much trouble if I stole Lilah away from you for a bit? I would love to have the next dance with her."

My mother clutches her chest. "Such a gentleman." She shoos us off. "Yes, yes. Go. Enjoy your evening."

"Thank you." He dips his head toward her. "You have a happy New Year, Mrs. Maddison."

She waves. "Oh, stop with that. You can call me Selene."

"Have a great night, Selene."

"You too, Arthur. And, Lilah, we'll chat later, yes?"

It's not truly a request. It's a demand. Maybe it's the booze giving me courage, but I don't dignify it with a response. I just hang up. When the screen goes black, I shrug off Fox's embrace and fling my arms into the air.

"What the hell was that, *Arthur*?" He winces, presumably at the use of his first name, and I'm glad it upsets him because again—what the hell? "How could you… Why would you…"

I can't even form a proper question right now. I'm still too stunned. Fox—the Seattle Serpents' number one goaltender—just told my mother he is my boyfriend and *volunteered* to attend a party my snooty parents are hosting. I can't believe this is happening right now. When I said earlier I'd find someone, I didn't mean someone like Fox. I meant someone who would actually survive an evening with those awful people.

He lifts a shoulder. "Seemed like you were in a pickle."

The gesture is so nonchalant. His *words* are so nonchalant, like absolutely none of this is bothering him.

"*Seemed like you were in a pickle*," I mutter, shaking my head. "You're… You…"

But again, the words don't come. How can he be so cool about this? So calm? Does he even realize what he's just done? What he's subjecting himself to? Does he know what kind of world I come from? How even though he makes millions a year, they're still going to judge him for it because he's not sitting in an office all day, bossing around minions?

He slides a hand through his hair. "I take it you're mad."

"Of course I'm mad!" I finally explode, and for a moment, I worry I'm being too loud, worry maybe someone inside will see me out here completely losing my cool and I'll embarrass Auden, but I don't care.

He can't do this.

"What were you thinking?"

Another unbothered shrug. "You needed help."

"I didn't need *your* help," I sneer, crossing my arms over my chest, the cold of the night setting in. I didn't realize how chilly it was before, too incensed by my mother's words and then warmed by Fox's touch, but now I feel the full force of the December air.

I'm not sure why I'm being so mean. Fox is nice— *too* nice of a guy sometimes, if you ask me—but this? This is taking things a bit too far.

"Really?" He raises a brow. "Because it seemed to me like your mother was winning that little battle of wills, and you were moments away from blowing your cover. She knew you were lying."

"She did not," I mutter, but deep down, I know he's right. She knew, and I *was* about to tell her the truth. I was tired of her questions, tired of hearing her words, especially because they were true.

"She did," he says, slipping his tux jacket down his arms, then closing the distance between us. I'm already warm before he even wraps it around me.

I'm pretty sure ninety-nine percent of the guys here have already discarded their coats, sporting unbuttoned dress shirts and loosened ties, but not him. *Of course* not him.

"Listen," Fox says, stepping back and putting space between us like the nice guy he is, "if you're really that upset, I won't go. You could say I had a hockey thing come up or something."

It's tempting. It really is. But I have a sneaking suspicion that would somehow be far worse than pretending to be dating for a night. And really, what's the worst that can happen? It's just one night, and at least I'll get to spend the evening with someone I know, someone I actually like instead of feeling alone in a room full of people who are undoubtedly talking about me whenever my back is turned.

I peek up at Fox through my lashes, trying very

hard not to notice the moonlight hitting his jawline, highlighting the stubble peppering it. Or the way his brown eyes seem to glimmer beneath the moonbeams. How his dress shirt is tight over his broad shoulders, tapering in at his waist with precision. Or how even though he looks reminiscent of a high school science teacher chaperoning prom with his shirt still perfectly in place, bowtie completely straight, hands tucked into his pockets, he doesn't. He looks good. *Too* good.

I swallow, then sigh.

"Fine."

His eyes widen. "Fine? Does that mean…?"

I nod. "Yes, you can be my date. I mean, it makes sense anyway, doesn't it, *boyfriend*?"

He grimaces as he lifts his hand, squeezing the back of his neck like he's suddenly embarrassed by his genius plan. I tug his jacket tighter around me, craving its warmth and relishing the scent that's entirely him, tickling at my nose while we stand there awkwardly. Me, wrapped in his jacket that's about three sizes too big and hits below my knees, and him, his hands still stuffed in his pockets and looking like he's about to tell me Pluto's a planet again or some shit.

Is this how it's going to be at my dad's party? Because if so, there is no way my mother is going to buy us dating. She might be smitten by Fox and excited that I have a date for now, but if we don't sell it, I'm never going to hear the end of it.

"So…" Fox says, rocking back on his heels. "Want to dance?"

I can't help it—I laugh. *Loudly.*

Of course Fox wants to dance. Of course Fox is completely unaffected by this. Of course he's grinning at me right now, and *of course* it's working.

I smile back. "Yeah, Fox, I'd like to dance. But first?"

"First?"

"I need a drink."

His smile grows. "I think I can manage that."

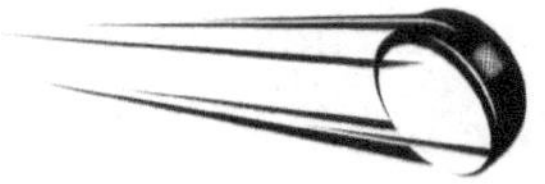

"Champagne for you, vodka soda for me."

"Thank you." I take the glass from Fox's outstretched hand, instantly bringing it to my lips. I lost my buzz from earlier with our very sobering conversation on the balcony, and now I'm on a mission to regain it, maybe even surpass it. I need it, considering I'm now "dating" a hockey player.

I gulp the drink down in record time, then hand the empty glass back to him. To my surprise, Fox says nothing. He just chugs most of his vodka and orders us another round. Fresh drinks in hand, we make our way to one of the many standing tables. I lean against it, rolling my champagne flute between my fingers, and Fox mirrors my moves. I still have his coat wrapped around me, the scent of Irish Spring and mahogany wafting about every time I move just the right way.

"So, *Arthur*," I say, enjoying the frown that momentarily pulls at his lips far too much. "How did we meet?"

"Well, *Lilah Jane*," he teases, "I think we can tell the truth on that."

"Which is?"

"You fell in love with my goalie stretches."

I laugh loudly, but it dies quickly when I realize his words might be hitting a bit too close to home. I think back to last year when Auden took me to my first Seattle Serpents game, and I couldn't take my eyes off the way Fox stretched against the ice. It was almost like he was fucking, his hips moving up and down suggestively. Of course, I knew he wasn't doing anything remotely sexual and I fully understood what was happening, but still, I let my mind wander for a moment. Probably because I was horny as hell, but whatever.

"I'm not sure that'll go over very well," I eventually say.

He grins. "Fine, then. My backup answer of 'mutual friends' will have to suffice."

"That sounds *much* more reasonable."

"And if anyone asks how long we've been dating?" he asks.

"Keep it vague. Like we did with my mother."

"Fair enough." He nods. "Your mother… She's, uh…"

"Terrible? Absolutely abhorrent? Evil personified?"

He chokes out a laugh. "Gosh, no. I just…"

"You can say those things about her, Fox. I do it all the time."

He grins again—always grinning—but this time, there's a hint of sadness to it, like he feels bad for me because that's how I view my mother. I wash his look down with a swig of booze, an inkling of that buzz from earlier already returning. Guess I didn't sober up nearly as much as I thought.

"I'm sorry your relationship with her is like that," he says, watching me closely.

I shrug. "It is what it is. Let me guess—your relationship with your parents is picture perfect?"

Even in the dim lighting, I can see his cheeks turn red, and he ducks his head like he's embarrassed by my accurate guess.

"Figures," I mutter, finishing my drink just in time

for a server to pass. I steal another glass off their tray. I'm sure I sound every ounce as bitter as my mother claimed I am, but that's because I'm not used to someone with a perfect home life. Growing up, I at least had Auden and Rory to commiserate with. None of us knew what it was like to have a family that wasn't riddled with issues.

Fox here doesn't know that struggle.

"Are they still married?" I ask, curious now.

"Thirty-five years last summer."

I whistle. "Wow. I mean, my parents are still legally married too, but it's not like they actually love each other. It's all for show. And because my father knows my mother would take him for everything in court, and he loves his money far more than he loves her."

It's the most I've ever told anyone other than Auden about my home life, and it's precisely because of the look Fox is giving me right now—pity—that I don't share that information broadly. He feels bad for me, and honestly, I feel bad for me too. But what can I do about it? It's their fault, not mine.

I take another sip of my drink, my head starting to feel that fun sort of fuzzy, and my body finally loosens up after my mother's phone call. My mother, who I definitely don't want to talk about anymore. In fact, I want to do literally anything else other than talk about her, maybe even jump out of a plane. But, since there are no aircraft around and everyone else is doing it, I guess I'll settle on relieving the tension building in my shoulders on the dance floor.

"Do you want to dance?"

Fox looks surprised for only a moment before nodding. "Yeah, let's dance."

He sets his half-empty vodka soda on the table, then thinks better of it, picking it back up and drinking the rest before setting it down and coming my way. He holds his hand out to me like he did earlier, bending at the waist like he's courting me, and this time, I'm just intoxicated enough to find it cute.

"May I have this dance, ma'am?" he asks, his drawl turned up to a ten.

I giggle. "You may."

No sooner than our fingers touch, he tugs me into his arms, spinning us both out to the dance floor. We run right into Auden and Hutch, and if they look surprised to see us together, they don't say a word.

"Lilah!" Auden throws her arms around me with a shout, and I smell the sweet alcohol on her breath as she smooshes her face against mine. "Come dance with me!"

I laugh. "We already are dancing."

"Oh. Right. Come dance with me!" she repeats.

I look at Hutch, who, based on the grin on his face,

appears to have had too many drinks himself, and he just shrugs. So we dance. And dance some more, so long that I completely lose track of the number of drinks I've had and Fox and even what time it is. I don't know anything until I hear people shouting random numbers, and even then, it takes me three of them to realize the numbers aren't random and they are counting down to midnight.

Midnight. The new year. The year I'm starting with a boyfriend. A *fake* boyfriend.

I glance around the room, searching for the man I'm supposedly dating, but he's nowhere to be found.

"Six!"

I see Auden and Hutch huddled up together.

"Five!"

Rory and Lawson with their heads bent close.

"Four!"

Hayes and his nanny-turned-girlfriend Quinn.

"Three!"

Locke is posted up at the bar, watching his teammates.

"Two!"

Keller walks out of the party altogether.

"One!"

Two arms slip around my waist, and I fall against that same brick wall from before.

No. Not a wall. It's Fox.

I spin in his arms, looking up at him as he grins down at me. That warmth I felt earlier spreads through me again, and even though I'm absolutely drunk, I know it has nothing to do with the alcohol. It's all because of those sweet brown eyes.

"Arthur," I say. Or at least I *think* I say it.

He drops his head, and for a second, I think he might kiss me. For a second, I might want him to.

Now that is *definitely* the booze talking.

But he doesn't. He bypasses my lips, his own dancing dangerously close to my skin as he makes his way to my ear, where he whispers so only I can hear, "Happy New Year, sugar."

I can't breathe. All the air is taken from my lungs and I'm unable to force any back in. I don't know how. I just know that somehow, Fox has made *sugar* the most attractive thing a man can say.

When he pulls away, he laughs at what he sees, which I assume is me looking completely dazed because, *damn, why is that so hot?*

"Come on," he says in that low drawl of his that goes right between my legs. "Let's get you home."

He pulls me through the ballroom that looks absolutely incredible, if I do say so myself. I try to pat my own back, but I can't seem to make my arm move, all my limbs suddenly growing very, very tired.

"Home?" I ask.

"Yes, home." Fox wraps his arm around me, tugging me to his side, and I'm so far gone that I allow it, snuggling into him even more as he pulls me into the elevator.

The hum of the descent is soothing, and my eyelids lower further with each passing floor. By the time we hit the lobby, I can hardly keep them open. Fox leads me outside, holding me tightly the whole way and ensuring I don't fall over. Not until we hit the sidewalk do I realize I somehow lost my heels.

"My shoes!" I try to wrench out of Fox's grasp and rush back into the hotel to grab my Louboutins, which cost way more than I'd like to admit.

"Whoa, whoa, whoa." He curls his hand around my waist, pulling me back to him. "I'll make sure someone grabs them."

"Okay, but don't let it be Lawson. I bet he'd try to wear them, and I don't want them stretched out."

He laughs, though I'm not sure what's funny. I was being serious.

"I promise I won't let Lawson wear your shoes."

I nod, hoping he keeps his word because my legs are so tired I'm not sure I can walk for another moment.

As if he knows it too, he wraps me back into his arms, holding me up again as a sleek black Uber pulls around the front.

"You're a good fake boyfriend, Arthur."

He laughs. "Thank you, Lilah Jane."

"You're welcome, *Arthur*."

Another deep rumble, the sound of a door being pulled open, and a blast of heat. It's the last thing I remember before I fall straight to sleep.

Chapter 5

FOX

I almost kissed Lilah.

It's the first thought that crosses my mind when I finally talk myself into peeling my eyes open to silence my alarm that has my phone vibrating against the table. I don't know exactly what I was thinking—and maybe I wasn't with the six or so vodka sodas I had last night—but I almost kissed my fake girlfriend.

Apparently, I have one of those now.

I also don't know why I stepped in and helped her against her mother. No, wait. I do know why I did that. Those things she was saying to her… They were terrible, and nobody—especially not Lilah—deserves to hear them from their mother. She needed help, and it cost me nothing but a night out to help her. Why wouldn't I do that?

Carefully, I pull myself up from the—*holy shit, is that*

a pink *couch?* I rub my eyes, then check again, and yep, that's a pink couch, all right. I did not have "wake up on a pink couch" on my bingo card to start the new year, but here we are.

I push myself to a sitting position on the comfortable albeit godawful ugly thing and look around. I didn't pay much attention to my surroundings last night, especially given I could barely hold myself up when I finally got Lilah wrangled into her bed, so it's like I'm seeing her apartment for the first time.

The walls are painted a pale pink that nearly matches the furniture. White bookshelves filled to the brim with what look like romance novels line one section of the room, and a huge TV is plastered against the other. There are not one, not two, but three different gallery walls, and several pairs of shoes are lined up neatly by the door. Everything has its place; even the stack of mail on the table by the door seems organized.

If I had to choose one word to describe the apartment, it would have to be *feminine,* and that's not a bad thing. Not at all. It's exactly what I expected from Lilah, the girl who, even though completely wasted, tried to run back inside because she was worried about her high heels.

Speaking of them…

I snatch my phone off the table and text Hutch to have Auden grab the discarded footwear. He instantly replies that they're already on it. Then he asks how I'm doing, and I send him back a thumbs-down emoji, which he laughs at. Hopefully, the rest of my teammates are feeling just as shitty as I am, and Coach Smith will take it easy on us during the morning skate. I scrub my hand over my face, my head pounding, likely from dehydration. I need water and maybe something greasy to eat, or there is no way I will make it through practice this morning.

I check the time: 7:12. If I move fast, I'll be able to get my truck from The Sinclair and grab a shower before heading to the barn, but I'm not sure I will be moving fast anywhere today. At 7:20, I finally drag myself off the couch and find the bathroom. After doing my business, I pad into the adjoining kitchen. It takes me four tries, but I eventually find the glasses, pulling down a mug—because that's all there seems to be—and filling it with water from the faucet.

I chug it, then refill and repeat it three more times before I'm mildly satisfied. I rinse the cup and dry it with a hand towel hanging from the stove before returning it to the cabinet where I found it. Back against the island in the kitchen, I peer to my right, letting my eyes wander down the hall to where Lilah is

—based on the snores filtering through the apartment—still fast asleep.

Shit, what was I thinking last night? I mean, yes, Lilah is a beautiful woman and I'm definitely attracted to her, but almost kissing her? That's a whole different playing field. I couldn't help myself though. She just looked so damn good standing in the middle of the dance floor, her hair wild from all the humidity and the sweat from hours of dancing. Then she called me Arthur, and I thought I might die hearing my name on her lips.

Nobody outside of my family has ever called me by my first name, not even when I was in grade school. I was playing hockey by then, so I was always just Fox. It's not that I hate my first name, it just feels foreign now. But hearing Lilah say it... It didn't feel foreign at all.

A loud *thunk* that sounds suspiciously like someone falling comes from the direction of Lilah's room, and I immediately shove off the counter, racing down the hall to make sure she's okay. I toss open the door and am greeted by the absolute last thing I expected to see today—Lilah's ass. It's completely bared save for the strip of material nestled between her cheeks. I stand there dumbfounded, utterly fucking surprised, for a long time—likely too long. Not until I hear Lilah groan do I realize I should probably do something other than stare at her.

I spring into action all at once, reaching for her, careful not to touch her anywhere that isn't covered. When I finally get her turned around, I brush the hair from her face.

"What are you… How did you…"

I suck in a breath, trying to get my racing thoughts to calm. What the hell is even happening right now? How did she end up on the floor? How did she lose her pants? What would that thin strip of material feel like between my teeth?

Stop it, Fox. Stop it right now.

I settle on "Are you okay?"

She huffs, glaring up at me with puffy eyes still coated in last night's makeup. "No."

I tuck my lips together to keep from laughing. "Why are you on the floor, Lilah?"

"Because I thought it would be a fun place to sleep."

Someone is not a morning person. Noted.

"I fell out of bed," she says with a frown as she sits up. "What else do you think happened?"

"I wasn't sure," I say honestly.

And I wasn't. I had no idea what happened. All thoughts went out of my head the second I stepped into the room and got a peek at her ass in the air. Her round, very well-sculpted ass. *Does she do Pilates?*

You know what? It doesn't matter. What matters is making sure she's okay.

"Did you bump your head? Bruise anything?"

"Only my ego," she responds, pulling at the white comforter wrapped around her. "The damn blanket got tangled around my feet."

She huffs, giving up trying to wriggle free from it, and I'm grateful. I'm not sure I could handle seeing half-naked Lilah again today.

She squints up at me. "Why are you here?"

It's a fair question, or at least it would be if she hadn't begged me to stay for twenty minutes last night. She tried pulling me into her bed, but I refused, telling her I'd sleep on the couch.

"Come on. My bed is huge. We can share it, and I'll be the little spoon." She tugs on my dress shirt in an attempt to get me to slip into her bed.

It's tempting, I won't lie. But she's drunk, and I'm not letting her make decisions like this when she's not of sound mind.

"No," I say.

"Fine." She rolls her eyes dramatically. "Then you *can be the little spoon."*

I laugh, pulling free from her grasp and laying her hands gently against her chest. "I'll stay, but I'm not sleeping with you."

"Oh my god. Did you just ask me to have sex with you, Arthur?"

I choke on my own spit. What the hell did she say?

Lilah bursts into a fit of giggles. "Oh, Foxy, you should see your face. I'm teasing. I am teasing!" She stops laughing suddenly. "But not about you staying. You're staying, right?"

I smile. "I'm staying, Lilah."

She breathes a sigh of relief. "Thank gosh. No trying to feel me up in the middle of the night, okay? Because you're cute, and I just might let you."

Then she rolled over and promptly fell asleep. Our conversation now tells me she doesn't remember a single moment, and I'm unsure if I'm glad or not. I'm curious what else she does or doesn't remember, like me nearly kissing her.

"I wanted to make sure you were okay," I tell her instead of relaying everything that happened last night.

I did want to make sure she was okay. Even if she hadn't begged me to stay, I would have anyway, even if it meant I had to sleep in the hallway outside her apartment door.

That earns me a soft, sleepy smile. Even in her state, it's cute.

"Such a gentleman." She lets out a big yawn, then falls back onto the blanket heap on the floor, tugging the blanket up around her shoulders, dangerously close to showing me that she's not wearing any pants again. "What time is it?"

"About seven thirty. I was just getting ready to leave, actually. Practice."

She wrinkles her nose. "Ew."

"Ew?"

"I can't imagine moving right now."

I chuckle. "That's fair. Are you going to stay here all day?"

"Yes."

"Can I at least get you anything?"

"Water?"

"You got it."

I push to my feet and pad back into the kitchen. I grab the same mug I used earlier and fill it with water before searching through the cabinets and her pantry for something light to eat in case she needs it. The only thing I can find is four different flavors of Goldfish, so I grab those and the mug, then head back to her bedroom.

Lilah is still on the floor, but I can tell she's still awake from her breathing. I set her provisions on her bedside table, head into her connected bathroom, and riffle through her cabinets until I find a bottle of ibuprofen. When I return to her room, she's moved, now on her back.

She cracks one eye open. "I think you might be the best fake boyfriend I've ever had, Fox."

So I guess she remembers that part of last night.

"Have you had a lot of fake boyfriends?"

She closes her eyes again. "Nope, but I can already tell you're going to be the best."

I smile, even though she can't see me.

My phone buzzes in my pocket and I pull it free to find several texts from my teammates, wondering where I am, I'm sure. I'm the perpetually early one on the team. Even though we still have fifteen minutes until practice starts, this is late for me.

"I gotta go," I tell her, backing away.

She grunts.

"I'll talk to you later?" I cross the threshold.

Another noncommittal noise.

"Bye, Lilah."

I'm just outside her bedroom when I hear her.

"Bye, Arthur."

Even though my head is killing me, I'm still dehydrated, and I'm undoubtedly walking into practice late, I still have a smile plastered to my face the whole time.

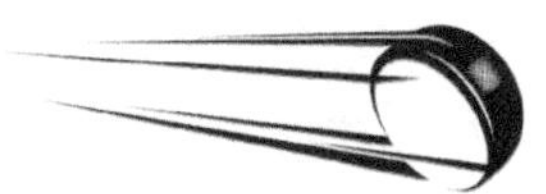

"Come on, Coach. You can't be serious."

"Oh, I'm very serious, Lawsy. Actually, I'm so serious, you get an extra lap."

He groans but wisely—something rather unusual for Lawson—doesn't say anything else.

We're all feeling the repercussions of last night. All of us except for Coach Smith, who, if I remember correctly, left around 11 PM because it was "way past bedtime." Naturally, we made fun of him for being so old after he left, but now… Now, I kind of wish I had left early, too. Maybe I wouldn't be so damn hungover right now.

But then, I also wouldn't have stayed over at Lilah's, meaning this morning's events wouldn't be burned into my mind. Even though I'm pretty sure I'm moments away from puking, I still can't get the image of a sprawled-out Lilah out of my head. It's wrong. I shouldn't be thinking of her, especially not in a moment of vulnerability like that, but still. It's right there at the forefront, no matter what I do.

"Fox!"

"Coach?"

He narrows his eyes at me. "I said, hit the net after the skate, yeah? We're doing shooting drills, and you're up first."

"Yes, sir," I say, fighting a grimace.

The thought of trying to stop pucks right now is

making me queasy. Or maybe that's just the booze trying to talk back. I don't know which.

"Go!"

Coach Smith blows his whistle, making nearly all of us jump, and we take off at a slow pace. It's funny because Lawson could easily win the fastest skate competition without breaking a sweat, but today there is no chance any of us will win anything.

"Ten bucks says Lawson pukes first," Keller says, skating beside me.

"Twenty says it's the old man," Hayes chimes in behind us.

"I'm not..." Locke swallows down the urge to vomit. "Old."

Keller laughs—or at least it sort of sounds like a laugh—and says, "You definitely can't hang, that's for sure."

"Shut up, Kells. You're barely hanging on yourself," Lawson argues.

For the first time, Keller doesn't have a comeback, probably because he knows Lawson is right. It's funny because I was drinking so much because I was dancing and having a good time, as were the other guys, but Keller? I don't know why he got so drunk, especially since he stood on the sidelines, rolling his eyes at us and shouting obscenities nearly the entire time. I'm not sure if that makes me more curious as to why he was drinking so much or sad because it was obvious he was doing it alone.

Still, it doesn't change the situation we're all in right now.

"I hate this," Dash, our other goalie, grumbles. "I'm glad it's you in net first instead of me."

"I wouldn't be so happy about that. The first few clappers will be a breeze, but they'll eventually gain energy. You're going to get the worst of it."

His mouth drops open like he's just now realizing it, too.

I laugh, then pat his shoulder. "Sorry, bud."

He hangs his head with a muttered "Fuck" as we finish our lap. Lawson keeps going as we all get set, me between the pipes and the other guys forming a poor excuse for a line. Usually, they'd be stick-handling pucks, flipping them into the air, and shooting them down the ice. Now, they're all just standing there, using their sticks like life rafts, and there's no doubt they are the only things keeping them afloat.

The first shot comes from Locke, who winces as he swings back for a slapshot, and not because he feels terrible about tossing the puck my way. He just feels bad in general. Next up is Keller, who is a little more eager to toss it my way, but it's still nowhere near his usual pace. The rest of the team take their shots, and we go through the line a few times before I swap spots with Dash, who I swear is now green, and then skate over to the bench to grab water.

"You good?" Hutch asks before squirting a stream right into his mouth. He swishes it, then spits it out onto the ice before doing it again, this time actually drinking it.

I nod. "I'll live."

"Quite a party last night."

"It really was. Didn't expect to drink so much, that's for sure."

He starts to laugh, but it turns into a grimace. "Yeah, that'll happen when Auden and Lilah get together. It's like they revert to their college days and see who can do the most shots."

Lilah.

Once again, my mind drifts back to her pert ass and the fact that I left her lying on her floor this morning. Did she ever make it back into bed? Did she take the pills I set out for her? Has she had any fluids? Something to eat? Is she even awake right now? The concern for her is at an all-time high, and I'm not sure why. Is it because she's my fake girlfriend now? Or is it just because I'm like everyone says—too nice for my own good?

"You two seemed to hit it off."

It's not a question, but it's not *not* a question either. It's almost like Hutch is fishing for something. I don't know what, but I decide not to indulge him. Something about it tells me to keep quiet, especially the whole faking-being-her-boyfriend part. Given how we're both barely functioning this morning, we haven't discussed the repercussions of our decisions last night, and I'm not sure when we will either. Maybe I should swing by her place later to check on her. And I guess maybe figure out just what all this scheme of ours entails.

"She's a nice girl."

He nods with a smile. "Yeah, she is. And talented as hell, too. Auden was so excited they were working together again, even if it was just a team party. She wouldn't stop talking about it."

Lilah was like that last night, too, though I'm not sure she even remembers. Every chance she got on the dance floor, she'd ask me what I thought about the party, if the decorations were too cheesy or if they were classy. I think I told her about fifty different times that it was the perfect combination of laid-back and classy, and I meant every one of them.

"They going to do more?"

He shrugs. "I don't know. Right now, Auden is just sort of doing whatever makes her happy in that moment, and she deserves that. They both do after how hard they worked."

He's right. They do. I wish Lilah's mother understood that instead of crapping all over her life. It might not be Lilah's name on the side of those hotels, but she helped build them just as much as Auden did. Her mother should be a lot prouder of that than she is, that's for damn sure.

I still can't believe the shit I overheard her saying last night, the way she spoke to her daughter. No—the way she *berated* her daughter. There was no pride in her voice, only criticism. And then to try to force her into dating some guy Lilah has no interest in? It's ridiculous. Yes, my mother is concerned about my dating life—or lack of one—but she would never interfere like that, especially not to try to impress her friends. Mostly because her friends don't care one lick, but still.

It's why I stepped in when I did. I'll gladly sacrifice one night if it means Lilah won't have to go on a date with someone her terrible mother sets her up with.

"Anyway, thanks for making sure she got home okay. Auden really appreciated it."

I lift a shoulder. "It was no big deal."

It really wasn't. I would have done it for anyone, even if they weren't my fake girlfriend.

"Hutch! Fox! Quit gossiping and get back to work!" Coach Smith yells, and with reluctance, we follow his orders.

The rest of practice drags by—and lasts about thirty minutes longer than usual, making me sure

Coach Smith is trying to kill us—and when I finally make it back to my truck, the only thing I want to do is grab food, go home, and sleep for the rest of the day.

Which is why I'm shocked when my truck ends up in front of Lilah's apartment building, a bag full of greasy breakfast sandwiches on the seat next to me. I stare up at the trendy-looking building with its sharp edges and mixed-material siding and try to figure out what I'm doing here.

Am I just checking on her? Am I simply being a good friend? Or am I here because I agreed to be her fake boyfriend, nearly kissed her, *and* saw her naked ass all in the last twenty-four hours? I'm unsure, and honestly, I don't care.

I snatch the food from the front seat and make my way into the building. I punch in the elevator code she slurred out to me last night, and the car takes me to the fourth floor. With a deep breath, I knock on her door and wait.

Chapter 6

LILAH

"Please stop shouting."

"I'm not shouting at all. In fact, I'm whispering because my head is absolutely killing me, and it's all your fault because you were the one who got me drunk, *Lilah*."

She says my name pointedly, and I'd laugh if my head didn't feel like it was point two seconds away from exploding. After a lot of self-encouragement, I finally pulled myself off my floor and made it to my bathroom, where I was stuck on the toilet for nearly thirty minutes because I was afraid to move again. Now, I'm lying on the couch after two cups of coffee, and I still feel like death. I can't even hold my phone up I'm so tired, so it sits on my chest as I talk to Auden.

"Nobody was force-feeding you champagne," I say.

"False. You did with that one glass."

I wince. That's true. I did do that. But I was so far gone at that point I'm pretty sure I did a lot of things sober me wouldn't have done.

Like almost let Arthur Fox kiss me.

Like beg him to stay the night and then tease him about sex.

Unfortunately, I remember both events enough to be sufficiently embarrassed, which I would have been this morning if not for the fact that I did something even *more* humiliating—showed Fox my ass. *Literally.* Thing is, I couldn't have moved even if I had tried—and trust me, I did. My body was having none of it.

I felt him staring. I felt those brown eyes of his that are far too dangerous for their own good caressing every inch of my body like he was memorizing me. For what, I don't know, but I liked it all the same.

Still, I had some sense of preservation because I managed to get my body to cooperate while he was moving around my apartment. It was strange to lie there and listen to it. I couldn't stop thinking about what he must be seeing. What did he think of my pink couch? Was it too much? Did he find it strange that I only use coffee mugs because I firmly believe everything tastes better out of a mug? Did he look at the old photos of me, Auden, Sadie, and Rory hanging on the wall? Did he wonder why I have no pictures of my parents up there? Did he look close enough to see that one of those photos is of the Spice Girls?

I don't know. I just know it was strange to have someone else in my apartment. I can only count on one hand the number of people who have been here, and I'm on the phone with one of them.

"But I'm going to forgive you," Auden says, dragging me back to the present, "because that might have been one of the best nights of my life. Can you believe I got Hutch to dance?"

"Yes. That man is obsessed with you. I'm fairly certain he'd commit murder if you asked him."

"Really?"

"Okay, you sounded *way* too excited about that."

She laughs, then groans. "I'm not sure I'm ever going to recover."

"Me either. Has drinking always felt this awful?"

"We're thirty now, so I think this is just how we live. I have no idea how Hutch went to practice this morning. I don't even remember him leaving. I think I was still drunk when he got up."

"Probably the fact that he's being paid millions."

"What's a couple million dollars?" she mutters.

I laugh—internally only because laughing out loud hurts too much—because *of course* Auden wouldn't care about a few million dollars. Her fortune from building Sinclair Properties and selling it for a huge profit far exceeds the "few million" her boyfriend makes. Even though Auden is ridiculously wealthy, she doesn't lord that over anyone. She's probably one of the most down-to-earth people I know, and it's one of my favorite things about her.

"Speaking of the Serpents, did you leave with Fox last night, or was that a figment of my very, very drunk imagination? And if so, does that mean the dry spell is officially over?"

Until now, I hadn't considered the implications of leaving the party with Fox, especially since I knew he was simply being a gentleman and had no other agenda.

"Not a hallucination, and no, the dry spell is still sadly ongoing. Fox was just doing the noble thing and ensuring I got home safely."

"So, nothing happened between you two? I know you have that crush on him."

"I do not have a crush!" It comes out much louder than I intended, and my head pounds so hard I swear I'm going to vomit.

It's worth it, though. Auden needs to know I *don't* have a crush on Fox. *I* need to know I don't have a crush on him, especially since we're pretending to date. The last thing I want is for this to turn into something it isn't. Yes, I like Fox, but I don't want him to think this is anything it isn't. I was serious when I said I don't do relationships. I don't want Fox to get invested in this, because I couldn't bear hurting him.

"Okay, jeez. No need to yell."

"Which is it—was I yelling earlier or just now?"

"Both." I roll my eyes. "I mean, you said *sadly* the dry spell is ongoing, implying that you wanted it to be broken."

"Not with Fox," I insist. "Because I don't have a crush on him."

"I believe you."

But I don't tell her the other part. I don't tell her I'm apparently dating this man I don't have a crush on. I don't know why I keep quiet about it. Maybe because it's not that big of a deal, and it's just for one night. Or maybe because I'm scared she'll tell me I'm making a huge mistake, and the last thing I want is for her to be disappointed in me.

Whatever it is, I keep it to myself.

"Well, boo."

"Boo?" I ask.

"Yeah. I don't know. I just thought… I thought you and Fox would make a cute couple, you know? He's so nice and reserved and such a Southern gentleman, and you're…"

"A complete mess?"

She laughs. "Not at all. You're just *you*, you know? You're loud and free, and you're Lilah."

I nod because I know what she means. Fox and I make zero sense together, and I fear my mother will realize it the second we walk into the party. She's never going to believe we're actually dating.

"Thank you?"

"It's a good thing. I promise."

"Well, I—"

A knock interrupts me, and I stare at the door, confused. *Who the hell could this be?* I didn't order anything, and the only other people I know who know where I live are currently busy.

"Was that you or me?" Auden asks, just as surprised.

"Me." I slowly pull myself from the couch, trying not to upset my stomach more than it already is. Maybe chugging two cups of coffee with nothing else in my system wasn't the best idea.

"Who is it?" Auden asks as I switch her off speakerphone and bring the phone to my ear.

"I don't know. But if you hear me scream, call 911 and tell them I give incredible blow jobs."

"What do your fellatio skills have to do with anything?"

Whoever it is knocks lightly again as I finally get to my feet. They're patient; I'll give them that. I just wish they would go away because I am *not* buying what they're selling.

Still, I'm curious.

"They'll get here faster because of the promise of great head."

Auden laughs as I inch closer to the door, the room spinning with each step. I push up on the balls of my feet when I get close enough to see through the peephole. It's not someone trying to sell something, nor is it a lost delivery person.

No. It's the very last person I expected to see again today.

"Fox."

"What about him?"

"It's Fox," I hiss. "He's at my door."

Auden gasps. "Shut up."

"I'm so serious."

"What is he doing there?"

"I don't know."

"Answer the door! Maybe he's there to help you with your dry spell. Maybe he's—"

"Oh my god, I hate you. Call you later. Love you. Bye."

I don't wait for her to say anything else before hanging up. Mostly because I absolutely *need* to know *why* Fox is standing at my front door. With a steadying breath, I pull it open. And, in typical Fox fashion, he's smiling. *Smiling!* Like he's not hungover and doesn't feel like he's been run over with a tractor-trailer, then left for dead on the side of the road.

I groan. "Stop it."

"Stop what?" His grin stretches wider.

"Stop smiling at me like that."

"Like what?"

I roll my eyes, then push away from the door, leaving it open behind me. Fox takes that as his cue and steps into my apartment, following behind me as I slowly make my way to the coffeepot for my third cup this morning. I grab the mug I used for the other two, refill it from the dwindling supply in the carafe, and grab my favorite creamer from the fridge. I pour in a healthy amount before taking a sip.

I instantly gag, spitting it right back into the mug.

"What the hell was that?"

Fox laughs. "Orange juice."

"What?" I look at the counter and, yep, sitting right there is a jug of orange juice instead of my beloved butter pecan creamer. "Why didn't you stop me?"

"I don't know your coffee order and just figured…"

He trails off, rounding the kitchen island to me. He takes the mug from my hands, steers me to a stool, and gently pushes me down.

"Stay," he instructs.

My lips twitch with a grin as I watch him move around my kitchen, looking entirely at ease. He dumps the horrific orange-juice-and-coffee combination, then refills the mug with fresh joe before grabbing the correct orange bottle from the fridge and splashing some in. He peeks at me over his shoulder, a dark brow lifted in a silent question.

"A little more," I request.

He pours what looks like the perfect amount before recapping the creamer and setting it back in the fridge in the exact spot he got it from, and I wonder if that's because he's noticed that I tend to like things in a particular spot or if that's just who he is too.

He brings my coffee to me, then settles back against the counter, watching me as I bring it to my lips and take a drink. As I suspected, it's perfect. The creamer-to-coffee ratio is just the way I like it. I take another few sips, then smack my lips.

"So," I say to the man who stands there with his arms across his chest, watching me like he's afraid I might fall over at any moment. "What brings you by?"

He nods to the counter, and that's when I realize there's a bag sitting there. It's grease-stained and absolutely calling my name.

I peek back at him, brow raised. "For me?"

"Yep."

I practically dive for the bag, and he laughs over the crinkling of brown paper. I open it to find what looks like a sandwich and a big box of hash browns, and my gosh, does it smell so good. I immediately reach for a fried potato round, tossing it into my mouth and sighing when the fried-food flavor settles over my tongue.

"You're the best."

He grins—not that he's ever stopped—and pushes off the counter, stalking toward me. "That's the second time you've said that today. Keep it up, and I might just get a complex."

I'd blush if I felt an ounce of mortification over it, but I don't. I'm too happy right now because he brought me food.

Fox reaches for the bag and pulls out two sandwiches and another thing of hash browns. He passes me a set and keeps the other for himself, setting napkins out in front of each of us. I immediately take a bite of the sandwich while he moves back to the coffeepot. He grabs a mug from the cabinet, pulls the orange juice from the fridge, and pours himself a generous glass before clinking it against my cup.

"Cheers," he says before taking a sip.

I groan. "No. No cheers. I can't do any more cheers."

He laughs. "Too much cheersing last night, huh?"

"Way too much." I pop another hash brown into my mouth. "Remind me never to drink like that again."

"Never drink like that again." He winks at me before taking a huge bite of his bacon, egg, and cheese breakfast croissant, grease coating his fingers. When he sucks a digit into his mouth, I have to look away.

There's no reason at all that should be attractive, yet I still find myself rubbing my thighs together. *It has to be my dry spell. That's all.*

I push away all naughty thoughts and stuff another tot into my mouth.

"You know, I always thought potatoes were such an interesting food."

He lifts a curious brow across from me, his mouth full as he takes another bite, his sandwich nearly gone in just two and mine still sitting practically untouched.

He chews and swallows. "Interesting how?"

"Well, we eat them for breakfast, lunch, and dinner, you know? It's still a potato. We just call it something different. Like these little things." I hold up the round, pressed, deep-fried potato. "This is a hash brown, hash round, tater tot, *and* breakfast potato all in one. It just depends on who you're asking."

He nods. "That's an excellent point. And it's why they're my favorite food group."

He tosses one into his mouth, then grins—*again*. I want to hate that he smiles so much because who seriously does that? But I can't. It's...cute. *He's* cute.

I ignore that thought of mine.

"Not that I'm not completely grateful for it, but you just decided to bring me breakfast because…"

Red fills his cheeks and even stains the tips of his ears. He squeezes the back of his neck. "I, uh, I figured I'd better check on you after how I left you this morning. You were really out of it. Just wanted to make sure you were okay."

"Okay as in I didn't pull an Elvis and die on the toilet?"

A loud laugh bursts out of him, and I flinch at the sudden noise, grabbing my head as the throb moves right through me again. The room spins once more, and yet again, I regret my choice to drink so much last night.

"Shit. Sorry," Fox says.

"It's okay. It's not like I didn't know what I was doing drinking that much."

"If it makes you feel any better at all, Lawson was the first to vomit at practice today."

I smile. "You know what? That *does* make me feel better."

"Keller did, too." He laughs lightly. "So, how are you really feeling after last night?"

"Well, my stomach is killing me, and as delicious as this breakfast is, there's a really good chance it's going to wind up in my toilet later."

"That's…unfortunate. But I meant the whole your-mother-thinking-we're-dating thing."

"Oh. That."

He chuckles. "Yeah, that. How, uh, how are you feeling about it this morning? Want to renege on it?"

Yes!

It's the first thing to pop into my head, and I realize how true it is. I absolutely do want to take it all back. But…I can't seem to find it in me to say so. The pros of this agreement far outweigh the negatives. Especially since I woke up to no less than four texts from my mother this morning about my new boyfriend. She's clearly already invested in this. We have to see it through now.

"I'm good with it. Are you still okay with it? Want to back out after seeing my ass this morning?"

If I thought his cheeks got red before, it's nothing compared to now, and I experience entirely too much satisfaction while observing it as I sip my coffee calmly, watching him squirm under my gaze.

"I, uh, I'm sorry. I shouldn't have looked."

Even though I should expect it, it's somehow the last thing I thought he'd say.

"Kind of hard not to at that point, yeah?"

He clears his throat, moving from one foot to the other. "Still. If my mama knew…" He shakes his head. "It wasn't very gentlemanly of me."

I shrug. "It's fine. I'm sure your mama would have understood."

He smiles warmly. "Honestly, yeah. She probably would have laughed."

"Do you have a good relationship with her?"

"I do. She's the best. I know it's not 'cool' for a guy to love his mother—the guys tease me for it all the time, even though some of them are total mama's boys themselves—but I love mine. She's too amazing for me not to, you know?"

I don't know, actually. My relationship with my mother is rocky at best. But I'm glad it's not like that for Fox. I think it would break my heart if that were the case. He's too good of a person to have shitty parents like mine.

"That's actually who I was talking to last night before you came out on the balcony. I was calling my family. Tradition and all."

"That's really sweet, Fox."

He shrugs like it's no big deal, but to me, it is a big deal. I would kill for a relationship like that with my parents. I wish the two people who should love me unconditionally actually did, wish they didn't put all the expectations on me that they do. I wish I were enough for them.

I take another drink of my coffee to swallow down that realization, then stuff another fried piece of potato in my mouth while Fox finishes his sandwich. I still can't believe he brought me food and came over to check on me. It's further proof that we don't belong together. He thought about taking care of me today while all I thought about was my missing Louboutins and which app I'll use to order dinner.

"Anyway," Fox says, pushing off the counter, wadding up his wrapper, and tossing it into the paper sack. "I just wanted to stop over and make sure you were good and didn't need me to take you to the hospital for one of those IV things to rejuvenate you."

That honestly doesn't sound like a bad idea. I could probably use that right now.

I wrap up my sandwich, saving it for later, and hop off the stool. "Thank you. You really didn't need to come over, but I appreciate it."

Another shrug, like *this* isn't a big deal either, when again, it is. I have a feeling he does that a lot—big things that don't feel big to him. He's just that kind of guy.

I decide I like that about him. I like that he's good, that he's nice. I've never dated a nice boy, let alone fake dated a *really* nice one.

We clean up from our impromptu breakfast, and Fox even rinses his cup in the sink before placing it upside down in my dishwasher. He goes as far as to top off my coffee with the rest of the brew in the carafe *and* adds just enough creamer to it again. It's weird how comfortable it all seems, like we've done this every morning for years.

When I walk him to my door, he stops, and I nearly crash into him.

"Sorry," he mutters, his hands coming out to steady me, and I swear my skin feels like it's on fire under his touch.

I'm sure it's just because I'm cold from being dehydrated.

"I hope you're not mad at me for imposing on your call with your mom last night. I've had some time to reflect this morning since the vodka is out of my system and I realize it was really rude of me to throw myself into your conversation under the guise of helping you. If you don't want me to attend the party next weekend, I won't. I'll bow out and call your parents myself to tell them I'm to blame for you being dateless."

I can't help it—I smile up at him.

"What?" he asks after several moments of me just standing there staring at him like a total creep.

"Nothing." I brush my hair—which I'm sure is a complete mess—out of my face. "You're right. It *was* rude, Fox. But it was incredibly sweet, and I'm good with this arrangement. In fact, I think I'd actually really like to go to the party with you."

Both of his brows rise high. "You would?"

"Yeah." I hold up my hand and begin ticking off the reasons on my fingers. "You're a total gentleman, you're a really good dancer, you look really hot in a tux, you keep me supplied with alcohol, you bring me breakfast the morning after, *and* you didn't even make a pervy comment when I showed you my ass. You're the total package."

Once again, his cheeks pinken, and I mentally high-five myself. I swear I could make a game out of getting him to blush.

"That's, uh, that's nice, Lilah. Could we circle back to the part where you said I was hot in a tux?"

I roll my eyes, then pull open my front door. "Go home, Fox. I'll see you next weekend."

"Yes, ma'am," he says, tipping an invisible hat at me.

Not that I'd ever tell him this, but the room gets spinny again, and this time, it has nothing to do with my hangover.

Chapter 7

SERPENTS SINGLES GROUP CHAT

Lawson: Can we please talk about how I am STILL hungover from New Year's?

Lawson: And how even though I'm still hungover, I AM A GOD WHO SCORED NOT ONE, NOT TWO, BUT THREE MOTHERFUCKING GOALS.

Lawson: BOW TO ME, YOU PEASANTS!

Keller: Wow. A hat trick. That's like SO amazing, Lawsy.

Lawson: I know you typed that with the utmost sarcasm, but I also know deep down, you sincerely meant that.

Keller: I absolutely did not.

Lawson: Liar.

Hayes: I would just like to point out that you got a hatty against the goalie with the worst save percentage in the league. Just sayin'.

Lawson: Fox, weigh in here. Does it still count?

Fox: Of course it counts.

Fox: And it doesn't make it any less hard. You should be proud of yourself, Lawsy.

Lawson: Aww. Thanks, Foxy. I love you.

Fox: I love you too.

Keller: Fuck me. Please do not start with all that sappy shit again. I can't stomach it.

Lawson: You're just mad because nobody is saying they love you, Kells.

Keller: Again, liar.

Locke: I don't know. I think Lawson might be right.

Lawson: I'd offer to high-five you for that, Locke, but I don't want to hurt your brittle old bones.

Locke: Never mind, Keller. Continue being mean to Lawson. I'm fine with it.

Lawson: Aw, man.

Hayes: Your own fault for screwing that one up.

Lawson: I was only teasing!

Lawson: Locke, come back and love me!

Locke: I'll pass.

Lawson: Foxy?

Fox: I still love you, man.

Hutch: That was sweet. Now, can everyone please shut up? You're blowing up my phone, and I'm actually trying to get shit done on our day off.

Lawson: Liar. I bet you're sexting with Auden.

Hutch: We don't sext.

Hutch: We video call.

Hutch: And you're just jealous because Rory only talks to you when no one else is around.

Lawson: FALSE! Did you see us at the New Year's Eve party? She danced with me in front of everyone!

Hayes: Uh, was that actually dancing? Or did you just awkwardly grind on her while she stood there?

Lawson: It was totally dancing.

Hutch: Sure thing, Lawsy.

Locke: Keep telling yourself that, bud.

Keller: It was quite possibly the most disturbing thing I've ever witnessed.

Fox: Aw, man. I missed it.

Locke: That's because you were busy with Lilah.

Hayes: Wait. Auden's best friend Lilah?

Keller: Yep. They were all over each other.

Fox: We were not.

Fox: We were just dancing.

Fox: At an appropriate distance apart.

Keller: Her ass on your crotch was not an "appropriate distance."

Hutch: Yeah, it was a bit much at times. Lilah's like a sister to me now. But one I like.

Locke: Wow. What a dig to your actual sister.

Hutch: STEPSISTER.

Hutch: And she's evil, remember?

Locke: Isn't she going through a divorce still?

Hutch: She is. Been going through it longer than she was actually married.

Locke: Have you thought about being nicer to her, then?

Hutch: No because she's still evil. Trust me. And be thankful you've never met her.

Lawson: Can we please go back to the conversation at hand?

Hayes: Which was?

Lawson: Fox and Lilah getting freaky on the dance floor.

Keller: The only freaky thing was your dance moves.

Lawson: Excuse me. I am a GREAT dancer.

Keller: Who said? Your mom?

Keller: Speaking of her... How's she doing, Lawsy? Missing me?

Lawson: Keller, I swear...

Keller: What? What are you going to do about it?

Lawson: Punch you.

Keller: HAHAHAHAHAHA

Keller: Make my day and try. Please. I am begging you.

Fox: Come on, guys. Let's play nice.

Hayes: I feel like this IS them playing nice.

Locke: Sadly, you might be right, Hayesy.

Fox: They love each other. They just won't admit it.

Hutch: Not true. Lawson will admit it freely. It's Keller holding back.

Keller: Because I don't love him!

Fox: You do too. Stop being mean and tell him you do.

Lawson: Yeah, Kells. Tell me you love me.

Keller: Swear I'm blocking all of you.

Lawson: You'd never.

Hayes: Not happening. You'd miss us too much.

Keller: Ugh. Don't start that shit too, Hayesy. You're starting to sound like Lawson.

Hayes: Rude.

Lawson: What a beautiful compliment, Kells.

Hutch: I'm with Hayes on that one.

Lawson: GASP! You could be my brother-in-law one day, Hutchy, and you're choosing Hayes over me?

Hutch: Yeah, and I have zero issues with doing so.

Lawson: Why is everyone so mean to me?

Lawson: And why is nobody talking about how Fox and Lilah were GETTING FREAKY ON THE DANCE FLOOR? THEY WERE BUMPING AND GRINDING!

Hayes: Because we don't care.

Hayes: And don't say bumping and grinding. It's weird.

Hutch: I kind of care.

Hutch: But also I don't because we're all grown-ass adults and can do what we want.

Lawson: Well, I'm just saying. There's something going on there. I can tell.

Fox: Why are you talking about me like I'm not in this group chat too?

Lawson: Because I talk about EVERYONE like they aren't in this group chat.

Locke: That's fair. He does do that.

Hayes: It's annoying, but we just expect it at this point.

Keller: I vote we kick him out.

Hayes: Motion seconded.

Locke: Thirded.

Lawson: Wait...

Hutch: I am 1000% on board with that, especially if it means you assholes shut up.

Lawson: OMG, YOU ARE A TERRIBLE POTENTIAL FUTURE BROTHER-IN-LAW!

Lawson: I WILL REMEMBER THIS, REED HUTCHINSON!

Hutch: I'm fine with that.

Keller: Foxy?

Fox: I think he should stay.

Keller: LOL, just kidding. It's 4–1. He's gone.

Keller: Bye bye, Lawsy!

Lawson: NO! No, no, no!

Lawson: I'm not going anywhere.

Lawson: You aren't kicking me out. It's not happening. RIGHT?

Lawson: Guys?

Lawson: GUYS???

Lawson: SOMEONE COME BACK AND LOVE ME!

Fox: I still love you, Lawsy.

Lawson: This is why you're my favorite, Fox.

Lawson: I take back all I said about you getting freaky with Lilah on the dance floor. You do you, baby. You do you.

Fox: Uh, thanks, I guess?

Lawson: Any time, bestie. <3

Keller: Fucking hell. I really hate this group chat sometimes.

Lawson: LOVE YOU, KELLER!

Keller: Once again, I am begging you, DELETE ME.

Chapter 8

FOX

"Sorry!" I yell as I race up the first portion of what looks to be a never-ending staircase to where she's waiting for me. "I know I'm late. We had a promo thing that lasted forever, and then there was traffic because this is Seattle, and that's just the way of life here, and I'm just so…sorry."

The last word slips off my lips in a whisper as I get a look at my date for the evening. Lilah looked gorgeous at the New Year's Eve party, but tonight? In a floor-length midnight-purple dress that hugs every inch of her curves? Well, I probably shouldn't have worn such tight pants, that's for sure.

My cock grows hard against my slacks, and I hope like hell my lateness is enough to distract Lilah from the fact that I have a boner right now. I try to think about any and everything else, something to distract me, but it's no use. Instead, I pretend what's happening in my pants isn't happening as I close the gap between us.

"You look… Well, breathtaking is a word that comes to mind."

In a rare moment of vulnerability, Lilah blushes, and I take entirely too much pleasure in that.

She brushes a hand over her hair, which looks flawless. "I bet you a hundred bucks my mother will have something to complain about when we walk in there."

I hate that she's likely right.

"And I will gladly tell her she's wrong."

Her blue eyes flash toward me, and I'm rewarded with another blush.

"Come on," she says, wrapping her hand around my arm. "We'd better get in there before she sends the army out looking for me."

"I don't think that's possible."

"You'd be surprised by the connections she has."

She says it so casually I might actually believe her, and for the first time, I'm nervous about meeting her mother.

"Remind me again everything you've told her?" I say as we climb the rest of the impossibly tall set of stairs.

Lilah texted me a few times while we were on the

road for two games earlier this week, letting me know her mother had called her at least thrice daily to discuss our relationship. Apparently, she's taken it upon herself to make up whatever she wants. Last I heard, our first date included a ride on a donkey down Queen Anne Hill. No idea where we got the donkeys or gumption to do this, but it made me laugh nonetheless.

"Well, we met through mutual friends. You made the first move after crushing on me for months, and you fell completely head over heels for me because my rack looked incredible on our first date."

"On our donkey ride?"

"The one and only."

"And your mother believes all this?"

She laughs loudly. "Absolutely not. But she doesn't have a choice, does she? We're dating."

"And your father? What does he think?"

She pats my arm as we reach the top of the stairs. "Oh, Arthur. You have so much to learn. My dad couldn't care less."

There she goes again, calling me by my first name. I don't think I've ever liked someone saying it so much. But as much as I enjoy it, her words still make me sad. I wish her parents weren't so horrible to her and were more involved in her life outside of what they want for her. She deserves that.

I stop walking, and she comes to a halt along with

me. Even in her heels, she's much shorter than my six-foot-five frame, tilting her head back to look up at me.

"Yes?" she asks, her long, dark lashes perfectly framing her gorgeous blue eyes.

"I…" I roll my tongue over my bottom lip, and she tracks the movement before dragging her stare back to mine. "I just want you to know if these people treat you like shit in front of me, there's a good chance I'm not going to be able to hold my tongue. I can't be responsible for what comes out of my mouth."

Lilah blinks once, slowly. Then again.

And finally, the corner of her glossy pink lips kicks up.

"Good," she says.

"Good?" I echo.

She lifts a delicate shoulder. "Honestly, it kind of turns me on when you say things like that."

I choke. Fall right into a coughing fit so bad Lilah beats on my back, trying to get me to breathe properly.

"You okay?" she asks when I've finally calmed down.

"You can't say things like that, Lilah."

"Why not?"

"Because it makes me like you."

"You should like me, *boyfriend*." She winks at me, then loops her arm back through mine. "Come on. Let's get this shitshow over with."

We walk into the hotel—which doesn't look half as good as The Sinclair if I'm being honest—and follow the signs to the ballroom.

"You grew up with Auden, right?" I ask Lilah.

"I did. We've been best friends since we were ten."

"So your parents should know her." She nods, even though it's not a question. "How come this party isn't being held at The Sinclair?"

Lilah snorts, the noise so loud it echoes off the high ceilings. "My parents aren't the biggest fans of Auden."

"What? Why? Auden's awesome."

"She *is* awesome, possibly the greatest person I know, and I love her like a sister. But I grew up with a lot more money than Auden did."

"Her father was an NHL player, right?"

"Yes, but it was never enough for them. They considered them to be rich but on the lower end of rich. Which I find extremely funny now considering Auden's net worth is more than my father could ever imagine." Lilah grins like she's immensely pleased by this, and I can't say I blame her. It makes me even more proud of Auden than I already am. "Another reason they were so upset I continued working with her."

I still don't understand how they can be so unimpressed by what Lilah has done for Auden's company, don't get why they talk about her job like all she did was staple papers together all day—not that there's anything wrong with that—never mind keep Auden's business going for her. I'm now even less excited to meet these people, and the bar was already incredibly low.

"Why are you attending this party again?"

She trips like my words have caught her off guard, and I catch her effortlessly.

"Thanks," she mutters as we approach the two doors between us and this party I have a feeling Lilah doesn't want to be part of. "I don't know. I'm…I'm being a dutiful daughter, I guess. Have you ever felt like that before? Like you're doing something you don't want to do just to be a good child to your parents?"

"Why do you think I'm such an incredible dancer? I didn't want those lessons, but my mother insisted."

She laughs. "Yes, that's exactly the same thing, Fox."

It's not, and we both know it, but maybe humor is the only way she can get through this. When we're just a few feet from the doors, Lilah stops, her arm falling away from mine as she stares down the door. She takes a deep breath, then another, like she's readying herself for battle, and for her, she really might be.

"I'm right here," I tell her softly, reaching my pinky finger out and tracing it against hers.

She glances down at where our digits touch, a small smile on her lips.

"My hero," she mutters, and even though she's going for sarcasm, there's a hint of sincerity to her words, and it has my chest feeling tight in a way I'm not expecting.

I've known Lilah at arm's length for the last year and always thought she was fun, a total good time. But seeing this other side of her lately? It's making me question everything I've known about her, and it makes me like her even more.

She slips her hand into mine, then squeezes it tight. "Here goes nothing."

The staff pulls open the doors in sync as if they've practiced it, and we're instantly hit with the sound of classical music. I can't help but laugh—nearly every person is dressed in a muted color and over the age of sixty, at least. This is such a far cry from how we spent last weekend.

"What's so funny?" Lilah asks, looking up at me.

"It's just…" I shake my head. "Well, last week, we were dancing to nineties and early 2000s music, and now it's Vivaldi. Based on the color scheme here, I'm pretty sure this is secretly a funeral."

"Why do you think I had so much fun last weekend? I knew this one would suck. I—oh, champagne!" She snatches a glass from the tray a server holds and immediately tosses it back like a shot. When she notices me staring, she lifts a single brow. "What? I'm just pre-gaming."

I shake my head but can't help but grin as we push through the party, searching for Lilah's parents, I assume. Several people smile at us, some even whispering behind their hands as we pass, something I've only seen happen in movies, but we don't let that stop us.

We don't stop until we come face to face with the woman I saw on the phone, and I'm instantly blown away by how much Lilah looks like her mother in proper lighting. Selene's hair is pulled back in a sleek bun, her eyes the same shade of blue as her daughter's, and even the way she holds her nose just slightly upturned is the same way Lilah carries herself. It's eerie.

"Lilah!" her mother exclaims, throwing her arms wide and pulling her daughter into a tight hug.

To most people, it looks like a sweet embrace, but to me? Well, I can see the rigid set of Lilah's shoulders, can see how stiff she is against her mother's touch. I can *feel* the tension radiating from her, and that's after a glass of champagne.

Her mother grabs her cheeks, smiling at her like she's the greatest accomplishment in her life, but I still see the way the woman subtly fixes Lilah's makeup under her left eye, how tight her grip is, how her blue gaze hardens, and how forced her smile becomes with each passing second. I've never seen someone so subtly cut someone down before.

"I am *so* happy you could join us," Selene says as she releases her daughter.

Translation: You're late.

"I wouldn't miss it," Lilah tells her. She steps back, immediately twining our fingers together once more. Something about it feels desperate, like she's not seeking me out for show but for support.

I'll gladly provide it. I squeeze her hand three times, silently repeating my words from earlier, hoping she catches it.

I'm right here.

She squeezes mine back twice.

Thank you.

Or at least that's what I take it as.

"Where's Dad?" Lilah asks.

Her mother waves her hand. "Your father is around here somewhere." Her eyes swing my way, and I hold her sharp stare, refusing to back down. "Aren't you going to introduce me to your *boyfriend*, dear?"

Another squeeze from Lilah.

"Mother," she says, dropping my hand, "this is Arthur Fox. Fox, this is my mother, Selene Maddison."

"Fox?" Selene asks. "You go by your last name?" Her nose turns up at this.

"Hockey thing," Lilah explains.

I take Selene's hand in mine, pressing a kiss to the back of it. I hold eye contact with her the entire time, just as I was taught.

"It's so lovely to finally meet you, Mrs. Maddison, and may I say, you look even more gorgeous in person."

Just like that, the ice is broken, and her mother's nose comes back down, her shoulders relaxing. She grins, and it's a far different smile than she gave her daughter. It's warm. Genuine. *Loving.*

"I thought we talked about this. You can call me Selene."

"Sorry, ma'am."

Selene laughs, tittering. "Oh, my. I like you, Arthur." She rejects using my preferred name, and I like it far less than when Lilah says it. "Come. I'd love for you to meet my husband."

Selene all but pushes her daughter out of the way, twisting her arm around mine and pulling me through the party.

"Sure. I'll just follow along," Lilah says quietly behind us, and I barely contain my laugh.

Selene leads us to Lilah's father, who is gathered

with a group of men with potbellies, barely there hair on their heads, and beady eyes. Somehow, they all look different and completely the same at once.

"Deacon, my love," Selene calls just as the group falls into fits of boisterous laughter.

Her face contorts into frustration before snapping back into an amiable smile, as if she's remembered she's in public. Her inside feelings show on the outside, interrupting her façade of perfection.

"Deacon!" she says, more sharply this time, her smile still creepily in place, hand still hanging on to my arm. Her grip is growing tighter by the second, thanks to escalating irritation.

A man—who I assume is Deacon based on his reaction—snaps his attention to Selene and breaks into a smile.

"My beautiful wife!" he bellows, and if I had to guess from the ruddiness of his cheeks, Deacon here has had quite a few drinks. His eyes drift to me, and there's not a shadow of displeasure in them. I'm unsure if I should be unarmed by that or not. "Who is this?"

"This, my love, is Arthur Fox. Lilah's *boyfriend*."

It's the second time she's said it like that, and I can't tell if it's because she thinks lowly of me or of the term boyfriend, like it's not good enough. That would track, considering everything Lilah has told me about her parents.

"Ah. Right. The *boyfriend*." He says it in the same way his wife does, and it has me grinding my molars together, especially when he looks at his friends and rolls his eyes.

What is wrong with these people?

He steps toward me, hand outstretched. "Nice to meet you, boy. What do you do for a living?"

It's the same thing his wife asked me on New Year's Eve. Is that all these people care about? What someone does for a living?

"Now, Deacon, I told you that," Selene says as I grip her husband's hand in mine. "He's a professional hockey player, remember?"

"How could I forget that?" His grasp is limp, as if he never learned how to shake hands properly. "How's the season going?"

I release his hand, trying not to react to my least favorite question. I don't want to talk about hockey. I just want to be here to support Lilah.

"Okay so far, sir," I say anyway.

"You lost your last game," one of his friends chimes in, reminding me of my awful performance where I let in three goals through the first period. We ended up coming back to tie it up but lost in overtime. We still got a point, but it always hurts to leave one on the table.

I hold back my grimace. "You're right. We did. But we're still third in our division."

Yet, even as I say it, I know it's not good enough because we're not first. A part of me gets it because I want that number one spot, too, and nobody beats me up over that fact more than I do. But we're in a good position right now. We're a playoff team, and we're enough points ahead of the other teams in our division that it's not something we need to worry about right now. I need to keep reminding myself of that.

"Fox, I'm thirsty. What do you say we go grab a drink?" Lilah pushes her way between me and her mother.

Selene huffs. "Really, Lilah? Is it always about drinking with you?"

"Well, when it comes to—"

"Yes." I interrupt because I have the distinct feeling what she was about to say would cause quite a stir. "I could use a water myself. Excuse us."

I pull Lilah away before anyone else can say anything, the girl on my arm clenching her teeth together included. She seethes the entire way to the bar, where she promptly orders two shots of vodka.

The bartender wisely only hesitates for a moment

before realizing she's being serious, then pours the shots. I'm sure nobody else here is doing shots, but I'm also sure nobody else here needs them as badly as Lilah does. She downs them back-to-back, then asks for a glass of champagne, which she drinks half of.

I don't say a word, silently accepting the champagne the bartender offers me but not taking a sip. I've officially sworn off drinking during the season after last weekend. Several minutes pass before I dare to speak, and when I open my mouth to do so, Lilah finally explodes.

"Can you *believe* them?!"

Based on what she's told me about her parents, yes, I can. But I don't dare say that out loud. Lilah needs this moment, so I let her have it, silently standing by as she rants.

"God, my mother is just… Ugh. And then my father's friends are so… And then he said… And he just… They are so…"

None of those were complete sentences, but they didn't need to be. I get it all the same. She wasn't exaggerating—her parents truly are awful. While I want nothing more than to put these people in their place, the only way we're going to do that is by having a good time tonight despite how many times they try to knock us down. We can't let them win.

She takes another drink from her champagne, this

time much smaller than before, and then looks up at me. "I'm so sorry, Fox."

Lilah is the absolute last person I need an apology from.

"What the hell do you have to be sorry about?" I ask.

She points toward where her parents are buried deep within the crowd to which neither of us belongs. It has nothing to do with how we're dressed. No. It's everything else about us that doesn't fit in here. These people aren't nice. There's a distinct coldness to the air, a fakeness that permeates the space. But I'm not letting that scare me away.

"It's fine," I say, even though we both know it isn't. "I can handle them."

"But they were so awful about your game. Which you play very well, by the way."

"Do you watch?"

"Huh?" she asks over the lip of her glass, which is halfway to her mouth.

"My games. Do you watch them?"

She shrugs, sipping her drink, then tucking a strand of hair behind her ear. "I mean, I watch Hutch play with Auden, if that's what you're asking."

"But do you watch me?"

Why the distinction is important, I'm not sure, but it is. I want to hear that Lilah watches me.

She swallows. "Yes, Fox, I watch you."

"Good."

"Good?"

"Yeah." I nod. "And stop apologizing for these assholes. It's not your fault they're like that."

"No, but it's my fault you're here. You're doing me a favor. That favor didn't include being treated like shit."

"You warned me, Lilah. Several times in different ways. I knew what I was walking into." I didn't think it would be this bad, but still. "So, stop. It's fine. It's just one night, right?"

She nods. "Right."

"Then we got this."

She blows out a breath. "Okay. I just…" Another exhale. "Thank you, Fox."

"Of course," I say, meaning it. *Of course* I'd help her like this. I like Lilah. I wouldn't leave her to deal with these people on her own. "Now, I'm going to use the restroom, and then we're going to dance, drink some more, and have the absolute time of our lives. Deal?"

She offers me a small smile. "You had me at drinking."

I laugh, shaking my head at her before pushing off the bar and through the crowd, searching for the restroom. A few people stop me on my way, asking me who I am and who I'm here with. Some even recognize and congratulate me on getting a point in the last game, which definitely feels like a backhanded compliment.

I'm almost out of the crowd when a deep voice that sounds familiar has me stopping in my tracks.

"We aren't letting that continue, right?" Deacon asks, every word dripping with disgust.

I step a little closer, staying just out of their periphery as I do something my mother warned me against so many times over the years—I eavesdrop.

"Of course we aren't, my love," Selene says. "This *hockey player* is just a phase." They have no clue I'm even standing here, no idea I can hear them clearly. "She's upset with me because I set her up with Doug Peterson."

Deacon groans. "Of course she is. Doug is a loser."

"He's CEO of Peterson Projects!"

"Only in name. His father is still the one pulling the strings because Doug can't close a deal to save his life."

"Fine. Then *you* be the one to find someone who wants to date that *train wreck*," her mother hisses.

Train wreck? Is that what they think of their daughter?

"I will, and I'll damn sure do better than Doug Peterson or some hockey player in *third* place. Can't even find someone who isn't a loser on the ice." He huffs. "I'll find someone good enough for her, someone who would benefit this family, too, whose name will make a good addition. I'll get her back on track. Don't worry, love."

I'm not mad they're insulting me. Not at all.

No. I'm mad that even though Lilah has told them over and over to butt out of her love life, even though she's showing them she's in a relationship—albeit a fake one—they are *still* trying to interfere. Fuck them, and fuck that.

I turn on my heel, returning to where I left Lilah at the bar.

"That was fast," she says when I reappear. "Or did you need help finding it? Or help in general? While I like you, I don't know if our relationship is that deep. I—"

"Do you trust me?"

She blinks at my interruption. "I…" Her brows draw tightly together. "Yes, I trust you, Fox. What's going on?"

"Come with me."

I grab her elbow, tugging her back through the crowd to where I last saw her parents scheming, but they aren't there.

"Where are you taking me?" she asks as I redirect us, keeping my eyes peeled for her parents.

"Where did your mom and dad go?"

"What? I don't know. I wasn't keeping track of them. I was working very hard to pretend they weren't even here, which I suppose is a little ridiculous since this is their party, but can I really be blamed?"

"This way," I tell her, dragging her to the right.

There, through the crowd of pretentious assholes, are her parents. All their friends have gathered around them—good; I'm glad they'll be here to witness it. Then they won't be able to deny it later.

I stop when I'm at the edge of the little circle they've formed and clear my throat. All eyes snap my way.

"Oh, Arthur! There you are. We were just talking about you."

I'm sure you fucking were.

"Lilah and I have an announcement to make."

"We do?" the woman at my side asks, her eyes wide as she stares up at me. "Fox, what are you…"

I wrap my arm around her, grinning down at her. "Now, sugar, don't be shy. I know we talked about waiting, but I couldn't any longer."

"Couldn't wait…" she mumbles, her eyes falling to slits.

Trust me, mine say back to her.

She briefly worries her bottom lip between her teeth before giving me the subtlest nod.

"Nope." I turn to her parents. "Mr. and Mrs. Maddison, I know this might come as a surprise. It might be a little sudden, but I love your daughter. I love how smart she is, her work ethic, and how strong she is. My mama always told me if I love something so much I can't live without it, I should make sure I never let it go. So, that's what I'm going to do. I've asked Lilah for her hand in marriage, and she's accepted."

Her mother's knuckles turn white against her wineglass. She grips it so tightly I fear it's seconds away from breaking.

"Lilah…" she says tightly. "Is this…is this true?"

I squeeze Lilah's hip, hoping she understands what I'm doing.

"It's true, Mother," she says, laying her hand on my chest. "It happened on New Year's Eve, under the stars. Isn't that so romantic?"

"That is…" Selene glances around at the people looking at her expectantly. When she realizes she's being watched so closely, she breaks into a smile that *almost* looks genuine. "That is *so* romantic. I'm so happy for you two!"

Then she's throwing her arms around my neck and tugging me down, and I let her because we're winning. Lilah and I are triumphing in this battle of wills right now, and I love watching Selene and Deacon's plans crumble right before their eyes.

She moves on to her daughter, hugging her tightly, and then Deacon steps up. He clasps his hand in mine.

Weak shake.

"I'd have liked to know about this beforehand," he says quietly.

Weak shake.

"I understand, sir, and I'm sorry about that, but I'm not sorry for loving your daughter."

Even *he* can't help but smile at that.

They step back, and Deacon throws his hands up in the air.

"I just got the best birthday present ever—my little girl is getting married!" he yells.

"Finally!" Selene tacks on, unable to stop herself from throwing one last dig at her daughter.

"Kiss her!" someone hollers.

"Yeah, give her a kiss!" another stranger adds.

It's so weird that these people I just met are so invested, but I get the feeling they aren't going to let up anytime soon, especially when I see the look on her parents' faces, each waiting for the same thing as if they refuse to believe it until they see it.

Shit. I *have* to kiss her. I don't have a choice.

I turn to Lilah to ask her if it's okay, but it's pointless. It's pointless because the second I turn to her, she winds her hand into my hair, pulls me down, and presses her lips against mine.

I'm kissing Lilah.

Or Lilah is kissing me.

I don't know, and I don't care. All I know is she tastes like vodka and champagne and far, far, far too fucking good for it to be legal. Her lips are soft and sweet, working slowly against mine as her fingertips scrape against my head. I'm not sure which one feels better or if it's just the combination of the two. Either way, I don't want it to stop, especially with how good her body feels pressed so close.

But sadly, just as quickly as it begins, it's over. She releases me, pulling away with a saccharine grin aimed at her parents, the kind of expression that says, *There. Are you happy now?*

Right. This is fake. This is one hundred percent all for show.

I clear my throat, ignoring my shaking hand as I drag it through my hair to straighten it. I don't know what the hell that was, but I do know that even though I shouldn't, I want to do it again.

I look over at Lilah, who is talking with one of her parents' friends, and she appears completely unfazed by our little show. Did she not just feel what I felt? Did the earth not tilt just a little? Was she not affected by that kiss at all?

I don't have time to worry about it. I'm too busy being peppered with question after question and congratulations after congratulations. It's a shitshow, and we're asked when we're getting married about eight different times before Lilah announces she'd like to talk to her *fiancé* in private.

I don't miss how pointedly she says it as she drags me through the party. She doesn't stop until we're both tucked into a small bathroom—which I definitely wouldn't have found on my own—the door shut behind us.

One. Two. Three.

That's how many seconds it takes before she whirls on me and all hell breaks loose.

"What the hell was that?!"

Given she just kissed the daylights out of me and then acted like it didn't happen, I could ask her the same thing, but I guess telling her parents we're engaged is the more pressing issue right now.

"Okay, look," I start, holding my palms up, "I know that was a little out of left field, but—"

"A little?!" She throws her hands into the air. "That was more than a little. That was completely… completely… *What the hell?*" she repeats.

"I had a good reason."

She crosses her arms over her chest. "Oh, it had better be *really* good. In case you just blacked out back there, you told my parents we were engaged. *Engaged,* Fox."

"I know, and that was intentional, but in my defense, I did tell you I couldn't be held responsible for what comes out of my mouth if I heard them tearing you down, and I did. I was on my way to the bathroom, and I overheard your parents discussing us. Discussing *you*, really. They…" I grit my teeth, trying to keep my cool just thinking of those awful people. "They aren't just upset that you're dating a hockey player, okay? They're pissed you're not following their orders. They want you to date someone with more… status. Someone who will help pad their pockets in the end. They want to break us up as soon as possible to get you 'back on track,' whatever that means. So that means this?" I wag my finger between us. "This ruse isn't working. It's not enough that we're dating. They needed more."

"Of course they did. They always do." She shakes her head. "As sweet as that was of you, Fox, it's also absolutely insane. I can't ask you to do this."

"Maybe, but you're not asking me to do this. I'm volunteering."

She narrows her eyes. "You know what I mean. This is too much. Pretending to be my boyfriend for an evening is one thing, but pretending to be engaged? That's a whole different level."

"Does it mean your family is off your back and you're safe from them?"

"Well, yes, but—"

"Then it's not too much." I shrug.

She twists her lips, nodding. "Fine. Say it's not too much. Then what? How far are we supposed to take this? A month?" She lifts a pointed brow. "Two months? Six? Are we supposed to actually get married? This is too much of a slippery slope. I'm not letting you do this. I'm telling them the truth."

She turns, ready to march out there and confess, but I grab her arm before she can get far.

"Lilah, wait."

She looks down at where my hand is curled around her arm, and I release her, showing her my palms.

"Just wait a second, okay?" I drag a hand through my hair, stalling because I don't know what to say.

She's right. Being her stand-in boyfriend is one thing. Marriage is another. But I just fucking loathe the idea of her parents trying to marry her off, pressuring her to find someone, forcing her into these dates. Sure, she could say no, but they're her parents. She won't.

"Look, I don't have all the answers right now, all right? But I *do* know this is saving you from a lot of torment in the meantime, and, to me, that's worth it. We can figure everything else out later. I mean, the worst that happens is we spend time together and keep you from being married off to some creep."

"No, the worst that happens is this gets taken entirely too far, and we end up married."

I wince at the harshness in her words. "Is the idea of marrying me really that awful?"

"No. Getting married in general is really that awful."

Right. I almost forgot Lilah would make a perfect addition to the Serpents Singles Club.

"Then I'll let you dump me horribly and publicly before it comes to that. Deal?"

"That doesn't sound terrible." Her lips—the ones I now know taste so good—twitch with a grin. "Getting my parents off my back doesn't sound bad, either. They've been extra awful lately and I have enough on my plate, trying to figure out what I want to do with my life."

It delights me that she's coming around, and I'm not sure what to make of that. Maybe it's because this would keep me from feeling lonely. Or maybe it's because I hope it'll distract me just enough that I loosen up on the ice and stop pucks a little better. Or possibly it's because of our kiss.

I don't know. All I know is I want to do this for Lilah. Sure, it's stupid and risky, but so what? We'll have some fun, screw with her parents a bit. It's not hurting anyone, so why not?

"Fine," she says after several quiet moments. "Fine. Let's do this, then."

"All right. Just no falling in love with me, yeah?"

She rolls her eyes. "Not happening."

"We'll see about that, *fiancée*."

I wink at her, and she blushes. It's my first sign we might have bitten off more than we can chew.

Chapter 9

Another drink and four dances later, I'm feeling better about my decision to attend this party, and I'm certain it has everything to do with the man doing the chicken dance across from me—my new *fiancé*.

I have zero idea why Fox is doing the chicken dance when the chicken dance song is not playing, but it makes me laugh, and I could use a laugh right now. It's safe to say this evening is turning out nothing like I thought it would.

I'm engaged. To Arthur Fox. A man I *kissed*.

I kissed him, and I have no clue why. Maybe it's because everyone was staring at us so expectantly. Or maybe it's because *I* wanted to throw *him* off-kilter like he did me by announcing to my parents we're engaged. While I'm still reeling from this development,

I can't help but admire why Fox did what he did—he was trying to protect me. If that's not the sweetest thing ever, I don't know what is. How could I possibly be mad at him knowing that? How could I be upset when all he's trying to do is help?

Are we idiots for doing this? Yes. But am I okay with that? Also yes, especially knowing my parents are *still* trying to interfere with my life, even after I've told them I'm in a committed relationship. It doesn't matter that it's not real. My word should be enough for them, yet it's not.

"You're ridiculous," I tell him. "People are staring."

"Yeah, but it got you to laugh, so I don't care."

That same warmth I felt on New Year's Eve slides over me, and I try hard to ignore the implications of that, mainly because it means it wasn't just the alcohol making me feel warm and fuzzy.

It was Fox.

That realization smacks me right in the face, nearly knocking me over, and my movements slow.

"You good?" Fox asks, still enthusiastically "clucking" his way through the song.

I hate that I like it. I hate that he's being so embarrassing and all I can do is laugh and join in with him. I hate that he stepped in to help me again. I hate that he cares enough to do it. I hate that he's just a really good guy, and my parents are terrible people who will probably squash that right out of him. And even more, I hate that I'm willing to let it happen to protect myself.

"Bathroom."

It's all I manage before I disappear through the crowd, needing an escape from…well, just about everything. From my guilt that I'm basically walking an innocent man to the gallows. From my parents' voices that are constantly inside my head. From the fact that this went from one innocent date to an *engagement*, and I'm just allowing it. Add in the fact that Fox—sweet, handsome Fox—is just dancing away without a care in the world right now, and I can't handle it. I need to breathe.

I regret the choice instantly. I'm stopped every few feet to accept congratulations on my "engagement" and to be inundated with questions about dates and even plans for babies. It's all too much, and if I don't get free soon, I might explode. When I finally push through the crowd, I draw in a deep, steadying breath, trying to get my heart to stop racing, but I can't. All I can hear is my mother's voice in my head.

"You're reckless, Lilah."

She's right. I am reckless. *This*—our ruse—is reckless.

"Where's your ring?"

I jump, whirling around to find my mother standing alone in a dark alcove like some evil character in a movie, waiting to make their move on their latest victim. I was so lost in thought I didn't even see her there.

"Mother!" I grab at my chest, my heart racing like I've just jumped out of a plane or something equally firmly on my Never Doing That list. "What are you doing?"

"Where's your ring?" she repeats, her eyes dropping to my very bare left hand.

For someone recently engaged and so in love they couldn't wait to brag on it any longer, I should probably be sporting something to show that, but I'm not, because this is fake. She doesn't know that, though.

"It's, uh…" *Shit, shit, shit. Think, Lilah.* "We haven't picked it out yet," I rush out, and I know right away it's the wrong thing to say.

One of her overly plucked brows rises. "You're telling me this man proposed with no plans? Not even a ring?"

"It was very spur of the moment."

"Yes, that much is obvious. He didn't even ask your father for permission." She hums, and who knew a hum could sound so disapproving? "That's fine. You'll take your grandmother's ring."

"What?" It bursts out of me in a panic. I clear my throat, taking a deep breath. "I just mean… Are you sure?"

My mother tips her nose high. "Of course I'm sure, Lilah. That ring was always intended for you. You should wear it."

"You're not saving it for Sadie?"

She sighs like she's annoyed with this conversation. "It goes to the oldest daughter. You know that."

Shit. I forgot about that little detail.

I swallow. "Then I'll wear it."

"Great."

"Great," I echo, but it doesn't *feel* great.

I don't want to wear that ring. Not only is it hideous and not my style, it doesn't belong on my finger. I'm not engaged. Guilt about our lie creeps in, but I ignore it, cramming it down to deal with later.

"Your father and I are going out of the country for a vacation tomorrow"—*that's news to me*—"but let's have lunch when we return. I'd love to get to know your new…*friend* better."

The last thing I want to do is have lunch with my mother and Fox, but even so, I nod. "Okay."

"Great. I'll have Debra reach out and coordinate things next week. Sound good?"

I want to say: *Having lunch with you is the last thing I want to do.* Or: *The thought of sitting in a restaurant with you, pretending to be a loving mother-daughter duo, sounds like literal torture.* Or even: *Do you even really want to have lunch when you're having your assistant reach out to coordinate instead of doing it yourself?*

But I keep those private thoughts just that.

Instead, I nod. "Okay."

A grin that could rival any supervillain spreads across her lips as she clasps her hands together. "Perfect. I will see you then."

She spins on her heel and walks away without another word. No goodbye. No small talk about her and my father leaving. Nothing. She just goes, leaving me to stare after her, trying to figure out what Fox and I have gotten ourselves into, and how exactly I will tell my fake fiancé we're having lunch with the devil herself.

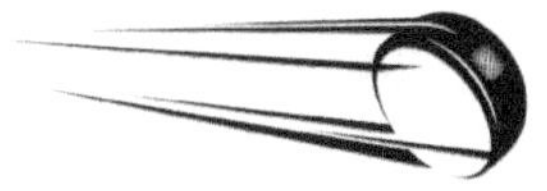

"Can I ask you something?"

"We're engaged now, Lilah." Fox tosses me a wink as we wait for the valet to pull his car around after finally escaping the party. We stayed far too long if you ask me, and I'm glad to be out of there. "You can ask me anything."

My lips twitch. He's so casual about it, making me even more curious.

"Why are you in the Serpents Singles Club? I mean, none of those other guys would have stepped in to help me like you did if that meant pretending to be in a relationship."

"I like to think they would have. They talk a big game about hating love and all that stuff, but I don't think they really do."

"Do you?"

"Not at all."

"Then why'd you join the club?"

He shrugs. "Because it was something to do."

"Come on." I bump my shoulder against him. "It has to be more than that."

"It's really not. I believe in love. After seeing my parents married and still in love after so long, I kind of have to, right? I just… I don't know. It was an easy excuse to focus on my game and nothing else."

"And now?"

"Now…" He exhales heavily. "I think I actually need to focus *less* on my game."

"How does that work out?"

He runs a hand through his hair. "A lot of being a goalie is a mental game. Yes, I have to be good enough to make saves consistently, but it's possible to be *too* into the game. Sometimes, you just have to go out there and have fun, you know. Be loose."

"And that's what you're struggling with? Being loose?"

He nods. "Yeah, I think so. At least, I hope that's what it is and that I'm not just washed up."

He chuckles, trying to play it off as a joke, but there's a hint of honesty behind his words. He actually thinks he's playing badly, and that couldn't be further from the truth. But he has to be the one to believe it, not me.

"Well, what do you usually do to relax?"

His back snaps straight, and he looks at everything but me. It takes all of three seconds to realize why.

"Let me guess—sex?" His cheeks turn a deep red, and I know I'm right. "Then have some."

He coughs out a laugh. "Are you offering, *fiancée*?"

Images of Fox and me sweaty and out of breath beneath my pink sheets filter through my mind, and my nipples pebble beneath my silky dress. It has nothing to do with how cold it is out here. I'm perfectly warm under Fox's jacket because of course he gave it to me again.

I clear my throat. "Speaking of that…" His brows shoot up. "Get your mind out of the gutter. I meant speaking of us being 'engaged.'"

"You don't have to use air quotes, Lilah. We both know this is fake."

"Still, it feels weird to say, doesn't it?"

"A little."

A lot, but I don't correct him. "Anyway, my mother cornered me and asked about my ring. Or I guess lack of ring would be more accurate."

"Oh." He slips his thumb over his bottom lip, and I track the movement, remembering how good his lips felt against mine just two hours ago. "I hadn't thought about that."

"No, I suppose you didn't have time to before throwing me under the bus."

He grins sheepishly, and it'd annoy me if I didn't appreciate it so much. Truthfully, I could have stopped him right there. I could have ended the whole charade with one little word. But I didn't. I went along with it. I'm to blame for this as much as he is.

"Well, I guess we could go shopping for one."

I laugh. "You are *not* buying me a ring, Fox. You've already done too much. Besides, I'm to wear my grandmother's ring."

"Your grandmother's ring? And I thought it was supposed to be my family who should be the traditional ones, being Southern and all."

"Um, did you forget my mother is trying to marry me off to the highest bidder?"

"Too bad for her. I don't share."

He's teasing, but it doesn't make my heart stutter any less, which instantly reminds me of the kiss from earlier because that's exactly what happened then, too. I ignore it now, just like I did then.

"Anyway, she wants to bring the ring to me when she and my father return from vacation."

"Okay," he agrees with a shrug.

"At lunch."

"All right."

"Like a *public* lunch, Fox."

He chuckles. "I understood that, and that's fine."

"You're good with this being public?"

"I really don't think anyone is going to make a big deal out of us going to lunch together, do you?"

"Well, no. I guess not. I just…"

My words are cut off as the valet arrives with his truck. After signing a few things for him, Fox generously tips the guy. Then, he opens my door, rounds the vehicle, and slips in next to me.

"How are you so okay with all of this?" I ask him once we're tucked into the car, him looking far too good as he shifts into drive, one hand on the wheel and one on the shifter.

"I don't know. I guess it all just doesn't seem like that big of a deal to me. A party here, a lunch there.

It's whatever. I'm still getting to spend time with you, so it's nothing."

I like how he says that. *I'm still getting to spend time with you.* Like *that's* what he's getting out of all of this. It's sweet.

"When does she want to do lunch?"

"I'm not sure. She said she'll have her assistant reach out to set a time and day."

"She has an *assistant*?"

I nod. "Two, actually. Don't ask me why. A demanding social schedule, I assume."

He lets out a low whistle. "Rich people are wild."

I crack out a laugh. "Tell me about it."

We ride in a comfortable silence for several minutes, my mind racing with so many thoughts. This night didn't turn out how I expected, but given the easygoing nature of the guy next to me, I might actually be okay with that.

The planner in me is dying inside about how up in the air this whole situation is, but for once, I kind of like the thrill of being surprised. And even more, I like the thrill of surprising my parents at every turn. The look on their faces earlier when they found out I was engaged…it felt like sweet, sweet revenge for every silly stunt they've pulled over the years. I still feel terrible that Fox is stuck in the middle of all this, but if he's okay with their crazy, then I guess it's okay.

At least I hope it is.

"I think we should go on a date," Fox announces, so suddenly I choke.

Like full-on have a coughing fit right there in the confines of his fancy car. I might die. Or maybe I'm being dramatic. I don't know. All I know is Fox just asked me on a date.

"A date?"

"Yes, a date. We're definitely doing this all backward, but I think we should go on a date. Get to know each other."

"A date sounds like…well, dating, which is what I was trying to avoid with my parents."

"True, but this is a date with me. That's different, right?"

It is different, and that might be the problem.

"And besides," he continues, "we're supposed to be convincing your parents we're together—we don't want to be tripping over each other at lunch with your mother."

Dammit. He's right again, though some of me wishes he wasn't. The more time I'm spending with him, the more I'm *enjoying* spending time with him, and I don't know if that's a good idea, especially if we're trying to keep this ordeal we've gotten ourselves into in check.

"Rules!"

"Excuse me?"

"Rules," I repeat. "We should set some ground rules. I mean, I think dating is okay, but maybe we should set some rules before we go."

He nods. "That's not a bad idea. Got any locked and loaded?"

"We probably shouldn't see other people."

He huffs out a laugh. "That's not a problem for me. I haven't been on a date in… Shit. Years, probably."

"*Years?*" I wince at how incredulous I sound, even to my own ears. "Sorry. Not trying to judge, but…"

"But you are?" He laughs lightly. "Yeah, it's been years." He lifts his shoulders again as he navigates the streets of Seattle, heading toward my apartment. It makes me sad our night is ending. Even with all the madness of today, I've had fun with him, and I'm not sure I want to let that go. "Hockey takes up a lot of my time, and the last time I tried to date, it didn't turn out so well."

I'm practically bouncing in the passenger seat of his very fancy car, wanting desperately to ask what happened, but I don't. Instead, I roll my lips together and keep my curiosity to myself.

As if he knows, he laughs. "You can ask, Lilah."

"What happened?" It's out of my mouth before he's even finished his sentence.

Another laugh. "I don't know, honestly. We were fairly serious, then one day, she just started listing off all the things she hated about me, like eating the same meals before games, my need to take a pregame nap, how she didn't want to follow me across the country for hockey, and the next, she was packing her stuff, and that was that. We were done."

"You lived together?"

"Sort of. It wasn't official or anything, but she had a lot of stuff at my place, that's for sure. The bonus was getting my closet space back."

He might joke around, but there's no mistaking the hurt in his voice. It's obvious the breakup came out of nowhere for him, and I can't imagine it felt good for someone to just list out all the things they don't like about you, especially since they have so much to do with a huge part of his life.

"I'm sorry, Fox."

He glances over at me, his brows raised in surprise. "What for?"

"She obviously meant something to you, and she hurt you."

He opens his mouth to say something, then thinks better of it, shaking his head. "It is what it is. Besides, it worked out for the better. Because of our breakup, I got to join the Serpents Singles Club."

Of course he spins it around to something positive. That's just the kind of guy he is.

"Anyway." He clears his throat, shifting in his seat as he makes a left. "You don't have to worry about me seeing other people. I promise you'll be the only person I'm fake engaged to."

Another joke. Another grin I like far too much.

"Sounds fair. Any other rules we should instate?"

He thinks for a moment before saying, "Kissing?"

All the air is sucked out of the car. Or at least that's what it feels like because I suddenly can't breathe. All I can think of is our kiss a few hours ago. Fox's lips against mine. The way his body pressed against me. How good my hands felt in his hair. How natural it was, like we'd kissed so many times before.

How it made my entire body tingle, and I felt it right down to my toes.

How I *still* feel it.

And how I wish I didn't.

"Stop!" I yell, and Fox slams on the brakes.

The car skids to a stop, and he looks over at me in shock.

"Holy shit. I… Are you okay?"

"Yeah, I… Sorry." I attempt to swallow around the knot that's formed in my throat. "It's just…you won't be able to find parking anywhere near my apartment. Here is fine."

Fox's brows draw together, but he doesn't say anything. Instead, he parallel parks like a professional and throws the car into park. We sit in silence for several moments, the only thing to be heard is my harsh breaths as I try to regain control of my breathing.

And he lets me. Fox lets me have that moment.

I'm not sure how long it lasts before he quietly gets out of the truck, crosses around the front, and pulls open my door for me. I accept the hand he holds my way and let him lift me from his truck, making sure my dress doesn't drag against the ground.

Fox's hand finds the small of my back as he leads me down the sidewalk to my apartment. He lets me keep quiet the whole way, offering nothing but his soft touch and reassurance that he's there. Why does he have to be so nice? Why does he have to be *such* a gentleman? Why can't he be more like all the other tools I've dated?

We walk into my building, and Fox follows me to the elevator because *of course* he's walking me all the way to my door, even though there's no way I'll get lost between here and there. The ride is quick, and we're standing in front of 4D before I even realize it.

"Well, this is me." I hitch my thumb toward the door.

He laughs. "See you tomorrow?"

I tip my head to the side. "Tomorrow?"

"I have a game. Hutch mentioned you and Auden are coming. Is that not right?"

Shit. With everything that happened tonight, I completely forgot.

"I'll be there."

His brows rise. "Really?" He grins, shoving his hands into his pockets and rocking back on his heels like he's trying to contain his excitement. "Good. That's good."

I laugh. "Yeah, that's good."

I turn to unlock my apartment, then push open the door.

"Lilah?" Fox says as I step over the threshold.

"Hmm?" I ask, turning toward him.

"You can kiss me."

For the second time tonight, his words steal my breath away.

"I…"

He shrugs, like what he's said is no big deal. "If you want, I mean. You can kiss me if you want to."

Then he steps forward, pressing his lips to my cheek, his five o'clock shadow scraping against me in the most delightful way.

"Good night, sugar," he says softly, then he dips his head before turning back toward the elevator.

I don't say anything. Where would I even start? No.

I just stare after him with wide eyes, my jaw dropped in surprise.

Fox steps into the car, facing me, and just as the doors close, he winks. It's the last thing I see before he disappears, and I'm left with the realization that Rory was right—I absolutely do have a crush on Fox, who is now my fake fiancé.

And I have no clue what to do about it.

Chapter 10

"No, no, no," I chant as the Edmonton player barrels down on me.

He's the leading goal scorer in the league and the absolute last person I want with the breakaway, but that's exactly what's happening right now. I get my glove up, ready and hoping—*praying*—he misses this shot. I track the puck, trying to predict where he will let it fly off his stick. Then he drags it back and shoots.

It zings right over my glove and into the back of the net.

"Fuck!" I shout as he zooms by, his teammates coming up to crowd around him and congratulate him on tying the game with less than ten minutes to go.

"Sorry, bud," Hutch says, skating up and tapping me on the pads. "That was my fuckup."

"Should've had my glove in the right place."

"No, I should have kept it in the zone and pushed harder to beat him to the puck. You're off the hook, man."

He gives me another tap before skating away, and I shake off his words. Hutch is wrong. I should have been able to save that. Yes, I was just facing down someone who is lighting up every goalie in the league, but still. That was an easy one. I knew where the puck was the whole time. The shot was simple, lackadaisical even. I still managed to miss it.

It was my fault again, and I know why—I'm distracted. I can't stop thinking about Lilah and her sweet lips and the way her body felt pressed against mine. I can't stop thinking about the look she gave me when I told her she could kiss me if she wanted, the want that sparked in her gaze. Considering how much I enjoyed it the first time, it would be monumentally stupid to kiss her again. Yet, I want to.

Bad.

I'd be lying if I said I wasn't hoping to see her during warmups, but neither she nor Auden were where Hutch expected them to be. It took everything I had not to ask about her. I was relieved when I overheard his conversation with Lawson about how the girls got distracted by nachos, and all was good.

It wasn't enough, though. I still have her stuck in my head and need to get her out. We have a game to win. I shake off all thoughts of Lilah and the bad goal, reining my focus back in on what I need to do to get us this other point. I breathe in, then out.

In. Out. One, two, three.

In. Out. One, two, three.

My head begins to clear, and the noise of the crowd dims as the ref drops the puck again. We win it back, passing it back and forth until we find an open path and rush into the Edmonton zone. The boys toss the puck in deep, Lawson hurrying after it, taking the hit to make the play. He whips it behind the net to the waiting open man. Thomas dekes the opposing player, then drives the puck to the net, tossing it lightly on goal. Their netminder flashes out his pad, kicking it away and almost right onto the waiting stick of Hayes, who, on one knee, launches it toward the net.

The goalie makes an incredible glove save—the exact one I should have just made to stop them from scoring—and the crowd collectively groans in frustration as we miss the chance to gain the lead again.

We reset, and this time, Edmonton wins the puck and tries to rush into our zone with it, but we don't let them, even stripping them of it when they get caught sleeping, giving us a two-on-one breakaway. Hayes and Lawson whip the puck back and forth and back again, dragging the goalie out of his crease just enough to bite on Hayes's fake shot before he zips it right to the tape on Lawson's stick and tosses it into the yawning cage.

One flick of the wrist later, we have our lead back.

"Yes, baby, yes!" I yell as I skate up to the end of the bench as Lawson, Hayes, Thomas, and our two defensemen skate by, bumping fists with the team.

"You see that, Foxy?" Lawson asks, grinning proudly.

"Oh, I saw. Fucking rights, boys!" I shout to the guys as they skate by and high-five my gloved hand.

I peek at the clock. There's still a lot of time left to play. If we're going to come out with this win, we have to play our best hockey of the game right now.

"Come on," I say to myself as I skate back into my crease. "You can do this."

The ref drops the puck, and it's a mad scramble, but Edmonton wins it and immediately gets to work, throwing the puck in deep and slamming our players into the boards with much more force than they've used all game. They're pissed now. They're going to be throwing everything at the net, trying to tie the game again.

With just five minutes to go, they attempt to go five-hole, and I get my pads down just in time to block it, covering the puck with my glove to get a whistle. We go for another face-off, and once again, they win. They shoot it toward us, and I cover the puck, earning us a whistle. Another reset and they do the same thing again, this time pulling the goalie once they gain possession, then driving toward the net.

"Fuck!" Keller calls, the puck zinging off his leg. He goes down in a heap but keeps in the play, swinging his stick back and forth to block a pass. It's fucking ballsy, and I love the guy for it, especially when he gets back to his feet and intercepts another shot, launching the puck down the ice for an icing call.

We can't change, which sucks because we've been hemmed in our zone for far too long, but it's worth it for the break.

"Holy shit," Keller grumbles, his hands on his knees as he works to catch his breath and stretch out the pain in his leg.

I skate over and tap him with my stick. "Thanks, Kells."

He gives me a twisted grin. "Any time."

I think he could mean it. Keller lives for the game's physicality, happy to play the enforcer role.

Edmonton wins another face-off, and we're back to battling. We *finally* catch a break on a bad bounce, the puck going out of the zone but not far enough for icing, and we get a much-needed line change, but it's risky. Edmonton is fast. Suddenly, they're barreling into our zone with a speed we don't have, and we just don't have the ability to keep up as they fire the puck right at me. Their first attempt pings right off the crossbar, and the crowd's cheers echo through the building. If we come out of this with two regulation points, I might have to kiss that damn bar later.

They pick up the rebound and try again—I stop it with my blocker. Another free rebound and another rush from their forwards. It's a mad scramble in front of the net, and I'm barely able to track the puck, so many sticks and skates in my way. I'm down. I have the puck just under the edge of my glove, but it's not completely covered, and Edmonton knows it too, poking at me, trying to get it past me.

And it fucking works.

The buzzer sounds, indicating a good goal, and I sit on my ass, hanging my head as the opposing team rallies together, cheering because they've tied up the game with just under a minute to go. The crowd is stunned silent, and someone pats my head. I don't know who, and I don't care. It does nothing to make me feel better about failing my team again. We're going to overtime. There's no doubt about it. Another point we're giving away, and it's all on me.

The boys win the next draw and drag the puck back into our zone, both teams content with where we're headed, and when the final buzzer sounds, signaling the end of the regulation, I don't bolt toward the bench. I rest there, elbows on my pads, trying to reconcile how I once again let my team down.

"Shake it off," Locke says, skating up to me. "We got this, Foxy."

I nod, tapping the posts before grabbing my water bottle and pushing off. I peel off my mask and skate to the bench as the guys gather for a quick session with Coach while the ice crew cleans off the snow.

"We're winning this," he says sternly. Coach Smith is a controlled man. He commands our attention without being flashy and isn't one of those coaches who gets riled up easily. But I can tell in his voice that he's unhappy about our play. I don't blame him. I'm not happy about it either. "We're not letting them come into our barn and leave with two points. Lawsy, you're on the face-off."

"Got it," Lawson responds, laser focused, which doesn't happen often with him. He's as determined to win this as I am.

"Get the puck and get it up the ice as fast as you can. Fire everything. Don't wait for the pretty goal. We aren't looking to make the highlight reels tonight. We just want that point, you got it?"

"Yes, Coach," the team says as one.

Coach Smith nods. "All right. Let's go finish this thing."

His eyes collide with mine as I squirt some water into my mouth, and we have a silent conversation.

It wasn't your fault, he says. *Get back in there and do your job.*

I dip my head at him and skate away from the bench, taking my time getting to the net. I don't know how it happens, maybe intuition or just pure fucking magic, but when I lift my head, I see the prettiest pair of blue eyes I've ever seen.

Lilah.

She sends me a wave, a soft grin on her just-as-soft lips. I instantly smile back, and I try not to read too much into that as I skate into my crease, never once taking my eyes off her. The fans are going crazy around her, pounding on the glass and gearing up for the thrill of bonus hockey. But they aren't my focus right now.

She is.

I squeeze my water bottle. Normally, I'd track the streams and droplets that fly into the air, a trick I learned to help me focus, but I don't bother this time. I'm feeling more dialed in than I have all game. And I think it has to do with the dark-haired beauty who can't take her eyes off me.

The music swells in the arena, and the in-house announcer comes over the PA system to rile the fans up for overtime. Just as they start their spiel, someone grabs Lilah's arm, and I notice for the first time that Auden is next to her, Rory on the other side.

Auden leans over and whispers something into Lilah's ear, dipping her head toward me. She rears back from her friend, her face annoyed, and she rolls her eyes, then slides them back over to me, a smile playing at her lips. I don't know what's happening—and I'm not sure I want to—but I do know all the nerves I was feeling earlier are gone, and it definitely has something to do with her.

You got this, she mouths.

I grin, grabbing the top of my mask, ready to pull it down and earn us that extra point. She holds up her finger, then spins around, and that's when I see it—my name and number right across her back.

Fox

35

I don't know why I love it so much. I don't know why it makes my heart race. But I do know one thing, and that is that Lilah is right—I do have this.

I pull my mask over my face and get set for the face-off.

I'm winning this hockey game…and I'm doing it for the girl in the stands.

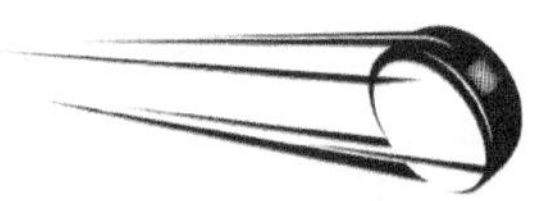

"Hell of a win, boys!" Lawson claps me on the back, his usual happy-go-lucky grin back in place as he lifts his glass into the air. "To Foxy!"

"To Foxy!" my teammates say, a mix of beers and water being thrust into the air.

We don't celebrate every win at Top Shelf, our favorite local haunt, but when it's our first home game of the new year and we take home the W, we're definitely going out afterward.

"Another round, fellas?" asks Chaz, the guy who has spent far too much time slinging drinks our way.

A few of the guys say yes, and a few say no. I'm in the no category, even though I'm drinking water. My stomach still revolts at the idea of anything involving alcohol.

"I'll take another," a smooth voice says from beside me.

I grin, turning my head to find Lilah next to me. Lilah, who is *still* wearing my jersey. It did something for me during the game, and it's doing something to me now, that's for damn sure. I try to ignore it and the warm feeling coursing through me, but it's hard to overlook.

"Hi." She grins up at me.

"Hi yourself, *fiancée*," I say back.

Her nostrils flare, eyes widening as they dart around to ensure nobody heard that.

They didn't. They're too lost in their own worlds to pay us attention. Auden and Hutch are cozied up together. Rory's staring at Lawson with stars in her eyes as he regales her with some—I'm sure absurd—story. Hayes and Quinn are wrapped up in a conversation, and the rest of the guys are sitting around shooting the shit. Nobody cares what we're doing.

Still, Lilah grabs my arm, tugging me closer, and I go willingly because I can't resist.

"So, did you have fun tonight?" I ask her.

She nods. "I did. I always have fun at games. The food is the best."

"Yeah, I heard that's why you missed warmups."

I don't realize the implication behind my words until a catlike smile stretches across her lips. "Why, Arthur, were you looking for me?"

I drag a hand over the scruff on my face that needs shaving. "I, uh, wasn't *not* looking for you."

Somehow, her wide grin grows even more, her cerulean eyes sparkling as Chaz slides a fresh drink her way.

"Thank you," she says to him, bringing the straw to her lips instantly. I do my absolute best not to pay attention to the way her tongue peeks out, sliding around the plastic. Yeah, definitely *not* noticing that at all.

I clear my throat, looking away and ignoring the tightening in my jeans.

"Don't worry. It's just a Shirley Temple. No booze. I think I need to lay off it for a while."

I look back over at her. "I wasn't worried. You're an adult, Lilah. You get to decide when you've had enough."

That earns me another smile, and I don't know what I'm saying to get so many of them, but I'm not mad about it, especially since every time she flashes me one, that cobweb of loneliness that's built up inside my chest loosens.

"So, were the nachos worth missing my goalie stretches that had you falling in love with me?"

She slides her eyes my way at my reference to our conversation on New Year's Eve. "Honestly? Yes. You look good and all doing your stretches out there, but those overpriced nachos are my favorite thing in the world."

"Bet I could make you much better ones. In fact, I'm thinking that's what we do for our date."

Her eyes spark. "You want to cook for me?"

"I'm not sure making nachos really counts as cooking, but yeah, I want to cook for you."

She looks surprised by this. "I've never had a date cook for me before."

I'm not sure if that makes me happy or sad, but it's

definitely telling about the kind of men she usually dates.

"Then it's settled. You come over, I'll make nachos, and we can tell each other all our dirty secrets."

She quirks a brow, rolling her straw between her fingers. "How dirty are we talking?"

"And you said *my* mind was in the gutter." I shake my head with a grin. "Whatever we need to know to convince your mother of our undying love."

Her shoulders deflate, and I know instantly it's because I brought up her mother.

"Shit. She hasn't been bothering you more, has she?"

She waves a hand. "It's nothing I can't handle. Just a barrage of texts today, playing twenty questions about our relationship—which reminds me, our second date was to the soup kitchen. You're a very charitable man, Arthur Fox."

"I *am* a charitable man. I volunteer there at least once a month."

"Stop it. You do not."

Her eyes widen when she realizes I'm not joking.

"Seriously?" she asks, her surprise evident.

I shrug, feeling a bit shy suddenly. "Yeah. I feel like it's the least I can do to give back."

"Are you a Disney prince?"

I laugh. "What?"

"No, seriously," she says, still staring up at me like I'm some sort of god. "Are you a Disney prince? Because that's total fictional man material right there."

"I can assure you I'm not a prince."

"Well, if I ever meet your parents, remind me to praise them for raising such an incredible human because you are unlike any man I've ever met, Fox. If only my other boyfriends were half as good as you, I wouldn't need a fake fiancé. I'd be married already."

An odd surge of jealousy hits me out of nowhere at the thought of her married to someone else. It's not like I have any claim over her, but something about hearing her say that *makes* me want to have a claim, and that's just never happened to me before.

I brush it away, grinning down at her.

"My mother would be pleased to hear that, I'm sure. She always loves being praised for her parenting skills."

"What's it like to have normal parents?"

It's sad that Lilah even has to ask a question like that. It's sad for *anyone* to ask a question like that. I know I'm lucky to have the kind of parents I do—people who love me unconditionally—but I forget sometimes just how fortunate I truly am.

She shakes her head. "Anyway, enough of the sad stuff. *I'm* going to use the restroom, then get out of here. I've had too many nights past my bedtime lately, and it's catching up to me." As if on cue, she yawns and points at the action. "See? I need sleep."

"Let me drive you home."

"It's fine. I'll order an Uber."

"That wasn't really a question, Lilah."

Once again, her eyes spark with something I can't quite place, and she nods. "Okay."

"Good."

She points toward the bathrooms. "Be right back."

I watch her walk away, which means I see when she dares a peek at me over her shoulder. I grin, loving how she quickly looks away, walking faster. I'm not sure if it's in an effort to rush away from me or due to the desire to get back quickly. Either way, it makes me laugh.

"What's so funny?" Locke asks, his heavy hand landing on my shoulder.

I look back over to where Lilah disappeared, then shake my head. "It's nothing. Nice pass to Ritchie out there earlier."

He shrugs like it's no big deal, but we both know that goal wouldn't have happened without Locke's perfectly placed pass up the ice that gave us the breakaway. His passing skills are the biggest reason the Serpents brought the veteran player to Seattle.

"Wasn't as cool as that kick save you made."

"Oh, you mean that lucky-as-fuck one? I had no clue where the puck was."

"Did anyone?"

No, probably not, but as the goalie, I shouldn't have lost sight of it like that. We all know that was a desperation move, and we got lucky with it.

"Stop beating yourself up," he tells me like he can read my mind. "We got the points. That's all that matters, yeah?"

"Yeah, but look how hard you guys had to work for it because of me. Have you seen my save percentage this year? The only reason we're where we are is because we're outscoring the opponent. It's definitely not because of me."

"It's a team effort, and you know it. So stop it." He points a severe finger at me. "I'm being so fucking for real right now. Lighten up, Foxy. Get loose. Stop putting so much pressure on yourself."

He's right. I know he is. But it's hard sometimes, especially when I *know* I could be doing better. The best I played all night was during overtime, and—

Holy shit.

It hits me: the best I played all night was during overtime *after* I saw Lilah in the stands. Is she the reason I played so well? I don't know. All I know is that maybe that's why I was on the balcony the night she needed help. Maybe I was out there for a reason, to help her so she could help distract me from my game a bit, get me out of my head.

"Yeah," I say. "Yeah, maybe you're right."

"I think I know a good place to start too." He flicks his chin, and I look over my shoulder to where he's gestured.

There's Lilah, coming out of the dim hallway, tossing her long, dark hair behind her shoulder and looking like she's walking a runway instead of through a dingy sports bar. Fuck, she looks good tonight, and I don't just mean because she's wearing my number on her back. While that's been extremely hard to ignore, it's more than that. She's just gorgeous, effortlessly so.

But as badly as I want to, I can't go there. We're already playing a dangerous game, pretending to be engaged. We shouldn't push this further than we already have.

"Nah," I say, turning back to Locke. "There's nothing there, man."

"Right. Sure. Whatever you say, Foxy," he says disbelievingly as Lilah approaches.

"Ready to go?" she asks, pulling her jacket off the back of her chair and shrugging it over her shoulders. "Hey, Locke." She smiles at my teammate, and I hate that I hate it so much.

I pretend it doesn't bother me, placing my hand on

her lower back and waving her forward. "After you, ma'am."

She lets out a loud laugh, shaking her head. "Always the gentleman, Fox."

She rushes off to hug Auden goodbye, and Locke leans in close.

"Always the gentleman, even when you don't want to be," he says, low enough so only I can hear him.

I shoot him a warning glare over my shoulder, which causes him to laugh, and then I meet Lilah by the door.

"You looked a little upset back there. Everything okay with Locke?" she asks as we step out into the cold January night.

"Hmm? Oh, yeah. We're fine," I say, brushing off her worry. "He was just being an ass."

He was being an ass, but he was also right. I *am* being a gentleman, but for the first time in my life, I don't want to be, especially when it comes to Lilah.

Chapter 11

LILAH

"Holy shit."

Fox stares down at me with his mouth agape. Those beautiful brown eyes that I seem to be getting lost in more and more often are wide with appreciation as they drag over me.

"You look incredible," he says quietly, still unable to take his gaze off me.

It's been a week since I last saw him, which means I've had time to let my nerves build about this date of ours. It seems so silly because we truly are doing things backward, getting engaged and then dating, but it didn't stop me from panicking about tonight. I changed my outfit no less than five times and even left my apartment just to get down to the lobby of my building and race back upstairs to change again.

I can't recall the last time I was nervous like that.

Maybe in college, when I went on a date with the star quarterback, only for him to never call me again? I don't know. All I know is until Fox opened the door, I had a giant hole in my stomach.

But now, with the way he's looking at me… Well, all I feel is beautiful, even if I am wearing something simple. I finally settled on a maroon long-sleeved top that hugs me in all the right places and dark wash jeans that look stitched for me and me alone. I paired the outfit with heels and went light on my makeup—something that says, *This is a date, and I tried hard but not too hard.*

Looks like Fox went the same route with jeans and a simple gray button-up shirt that's undone just enough to show a tuft of dark hair peeking out the top, the sleeves rolled up to his elbows. And no socks. I have no idea why I find that part so ridiculously attractive, but I do. His hair is still wet like he just got out of the shower, and he runs a hand through it, another thing I find entirely too alluring.

"Come on in," he says, stepping aside to let me pass, fresh Irish Spring hitting me as I do.

When I step into Fox's apartment for the first time, it's nothing like I expected. With soft gray walls, dark furniture, and low lighting, it's cozy yet modern and perfectly suits him.

"It's not much." He closes the door behind us, his

warmth seeping into me as he stands at my back, pulling my coat from my arms and hanging it next to the door, right beside his. "But I don't spend much time here during the season and even less in the summer since I often go back home or travel abroad, so it is what it is."

"It's cute," I tell him, glancing around, wanting a closer look at everything. "I'm sure making something yours is hard when you spend so much time traveling and never knowing if you'll be traded or not."

"It definitely makes settling in difficult, that's for sure. Come on."

Fox motions for me to follow him, leading me right into an open-concept kitchen with a large island in the center, matching appliances, and an oversized fridge tucked into the wall. There's a breakfast bar and a table for two near a giant wall of windows that is already set.

He rounds the island in the middle of the room, settling in front of the stove as he stirs this and that, adding a few sprinkles of seasoning. Whatever he's making smells incredible, and my stomach rumbles loudly at the scent.

Fox doesn't miss it, laughing at the sound. "Dinner will be ready in just a few," he promises. "Would you like something to drink while we wait?"

"Sure."

He moves to the fridge, pulling out a pitcher of something light green. "I made some sparkling jalapeño lime lemonade, if you're interested."

"You *made* it?"

He shrugs. "It's not too hard, and I enjoy being in the kitchen."

Every other guy I've ever dated has dropped fortunes on fancy meals that leave me hungry, so *of course* Fox is nothing like that.

When he first suggested we go on a date, I thought it might be a terrible idea. We're already walking a thin line, so throwing dating into the mix? It's not exactly ideal. But now that I'm here in his apartment and he's cooking dinner for me and grinning at me like that... well, there's nowhere I'd rather be.

"I'd love to try it."

"If you hate it, it's okay." He reaches into the cabinet and pulls out some cups while I'm busy watching how his back muscles stretch against his shirt. "But if you love it, I might just do a jig."

"A jig? Even if I hate it, I'll say I like it just to see that."

He shakes his head as he turns toward me, holding our drinks. "Gotta be honest."

But I'm not paying any attention to his words. How could I when I see what he's holding toward me?

A mug. He noticed.

"What?" he asks when I don't take it immediately. "Having second thoughts?"

"I…" But no words come out. They can't. They're stuck behind the lump that's firmly wedged in my throat.

I have no idea why I'm getting so emotional over something as silly as a mug that reads *World's Best Goalie*, but here I am.

You can kiss me if you want to.

That's what Fox told me when standing outside my door, and though there have been several moments when I've wanted to since then, none of them have been as persistent as this one. I want to kiss him so badly right now that it physically hurts. He noticed. Fox noticed, and it's the sweetest, simplest thing in the world.

"Lilah?" he asks softly.

I give myself a shake, finally accepting the lemonade.

"Sorry," I say, curling my hands around the mug. "I just…" I blow out a breath, then finally look up at him, his brows still pinched together in concern. "You gave me a mug."

He lifts a shoulder. "I noticed you like mugs."

"Yeah, but *nobody* ever notices. Not even Auden. All she does is complain that I don't have any other glasses."

He shrugs again like it's no big deal, but it feels like a big deal. Fox is just my fake fiancé. He's just doing me a favor. He's not supposed to be wooing me, which is definitely what's happening right now, intentional or not. "Maybe it's because I'm a hockey player, and we're sort of known for our quirks, so I didn't even think twice about it."

"Everyone thinks twice about it."

"Then maybe I just didn't care." And fuck me if those words don't hit me right in the chest.

Should I really be surprised, though? Fox has taken all this wackiness, like our engagement and my parents and my pink couch, with a grin on his face. Why would this affect him?

He waits for me to challenge him again, but I have nothing. So he lifts his mug and says, "¡Salud!"

¡Salud! because he remembers we're still not cheersing.

With a grin, I lift my mug to my lips and take a sip of his *homemade* lemonade, and it was well worth the wait. A perfect blend of sweetness and spice explodes over my tongue, and it's officially the best lemonade I've ever had.

"Well?" he asks when I don't say anything.

"I hope you're ready to dance because this is damn good, Fox."

He sets his mug aside, then puts one hand behind

his head, holding his other arm out straight ahead of him, and proceeds to do the sprinkler like he's some dad who finally made it up on the Jumbotron at one of his games. I laugh, shaking my head at his antics, especially with how proud he looks.

"You're ridiculous," I tell him, but I still can't stop smiling, and neither can he. That seems to be a recurring theme when it comes to Fox. It's something I could get far too used to if I'm not careful.

"Would a ridiculous man agree to be your fake fiancé for an undisclosed amount of time, then ask you on a date to get to know you better?" He winks at me.

I roll my eyes. "That sounds exactly like what a ridiculous man would do. Speaking of that…"

"Uh-oh."

"No uh-oh. Or maybe uh-oh. My mother called and has finally found time in her schedule. She wants to have lunch on Tuesday to give me my grandmother's hideous ring."

"I have a game on Tuesday."

"That's what I told her, but she's insisting it be Tuesday. I guess her schedule is just *so full* she can't possibly do it any other day."

He shrugs. "Then I'll make it happen."

"Fox…"

He holds his hand up. "It's no big deal. I'll make it happen."

"You know, you're being way too nice about this whole thing. It makes me think you might have some ulterior motive."

"No motive. I just…" He sighs, scratching at the dusting of hair lining his face. "I don't know. In some way, you're doing me a favor allowing me to do this."

I tip my head to the side. "How so?"

"Well, it gives me something to do, for one. Helps me take my mind off the game, which is nice. And I don't know…" He blows out a long, slow breath, then rushes out, "It'snicetohavesomeone."

Somehow, I'm able to decipher it, probably because I get it. It *is* nice to have someone, no matter the circumstances. Love and relationships may not be for me, but that doesn't mean I don't like to have someone to spend my time with. Actually, I could say that's exactly why I've spent so much of my time dating around. I *like* being with someone else and hate being alone.

So, he's right. It *is* nice to have someone, even if it is fake.

"But how long are we going to keep this up?"

"As long as you need."

"Fox, I—"

"No," he says, pushing off the counter. "Nope. We're not going over this again. You're not going to say I can't do this. I'm doing it, and it is what it is. Deal?"

He's so serious, his tone sharp. He means it. He wants to do this for me.

Maybe I should just let him and accept his help. I've tried doing this my way, and it's done nothing to get my parents off my back. Hell, before we announced our engagement, they were pushing even harder than before. Maybe I should let someone else take the reins on this thing.

"Fine," I relent. "But if at any time it gets to be too much, just yell 'Brussels sprouts.'"

"Brussels sprouts?"

"Yeah, Brussels sprouts. It'll be our safe word because nobody really likes Brussels sprouts, and they should make everyone pause."

"I like Brussels sprouts," he says.

"Fox…"

He laughs. "Fine. Brussels sprouts it is." He shakes his head with a grin. "Now, how about a tour while dinner finishes doing its thing?" he asks, pointing his thumb toward the food still sizzling on the stovetop.

"A tour sounds nice."

Fox sweeps his hands out wide. "Well, this is the kitchen."

"Wait. So you mean the room with the stove, oven, and refrigerator *isn't* your bathroom?" I side-eye him. "I am *so* glad I have you here to direct me."

Fox rubs a hand over the scruff that's lining his

face, and I track the movement, trying very hard to ignore the way my brain is screaming at me, saying, *I bet that'd feel good between my thighs.*

He kicks his lips up in a half grin. "Can you tell I've never hosted anyone before?"

I raise my brows. "Never?"

"Some of the guys have been here, but they're idiots. I don't have to impress them by showing them my apartment."

"You're trying to impress me?"

His cheeks redden, and he clears his throat. "Want to see more?"

I nod and let him lead the way from the kitchen into the living room, our mugs of heavenly lemonade in hand. To my surprise, a few paintings hang on the walls, something I don't think I've seen in a guy's place in…well, ever. The guys I've dated all have movie posters up or scantily clad women, nothing like the modern designs he has.

"Wow. I love these," I say, stepping up to one featuring multiple shades of blue.

"I can't take the credit for it. My family may call me Artie, but it's my sister who is the artistic one. She did these. Incredible, right?"

"I have questions. First, your family calls you *Artie?*"

"Unfortunately."

I can't help laughing at the pained expression on his face.

"It's cute."

"It's terrible, and you know it."

"No, seriously. I like it…*Artie*."

"Watch it," he says, eyes narrowed over the rim of his mug as he brings it to his lips, and it's kind of…hot.

He's not truly mad, but something about the idea of seeing a grumpy Fox excites me. I don't think I've seen him like that before.

He takes a drink and smacks his lips. "What was the second?"

"Huh?" I ask, already having lost track of what we were talking about, distracted by his adorable family nickname and scowl.

"You said you have questions. What was the second one?"

"Oh! How come you never told me you have a sister?"

He shrugs. "I don't know. It never came up."

"That's definitely something your fake fiancée should know. Anything else you're hiding from me, *Artie?*"

Another glare, and I delight in it far too much. "Nope. I think that's about it. Just two younger siblings, one sister and one brother."

"Hmm" is all I say, then I point to the photos lining

the bookshelf tucked away in the back of the room. There are very few books for such a large shelf.

"Are these them?"

"That'd be them." His grin is back in full force, and he walks me to the photos. "They're twins, so I was the outlier for my parents. That's Russ with his kids, and yes, they're twins too." He points to a man squatting down next to two nearly identical children. "And this is Regan with her dog Cricket. He's like seventeen or something and still going strong. It's wild." He points to the next photo, a young couple in what looks to be a courthouse, both wearing casual clothes but clearly getting married. "And those are my parents, Bonnie and Roy." He goes to the next picture. "This is all of us at Christmas this year."

I study each picture, especially Fox in his Christmas pajamas that match the rest of his family's attire.

"Your whole family is beautiful," I tell him, unable to take my eyes off them.

They all look so happy, like an actual loving family. I can't remember the last time mine took a photo together that wasn't for a paper.

"Are you kidding? My brother is ugly as hell. And my sister's index toe is freakishly long."

I laugh because he sounds exactly like a big brother should sound. I'd say the same thing about Sadie, too, and I wonder briefly what she would think of my deal with Fox. She'd probably laugh, then air high-five me from thousands of miles away for messing with our parents.

I drag my finger over the spines of the few books he has decorating his shelves. "You read?"

He sighs. "I try."

I tip my head at the obvious frustration in his voice. "Try?"

"I, uh, I don't read very quickly." A shrug. "Just always how it's been for me. It takes me a long time to concentrate and absorb what's on the page. It can sometimes take me a month to finish a book most people can finish in a day, so school was really hard regarding reading assignments. Now, as an adult, I tend to do audiobooks more than paperbacks. It's easier."

His confession tugs at my heart. Not because I pity him—nothing he said deserves my pity—but because it's clear this is something about himself that bothers him. I love that he doesn't give up despite his struggle and keeps trying. He doesn't let it deter him. He just finds a way to adapt. It's admirable.

"Want to see my bedroom?" he blurts out.

I pause. He pauses.

Silence. Complete and utter silence, which is really unhelpful considering all the images currently filtering through my mind, like how *we'd* look there, his sheets nothing but a tangle around us. I wish I could say it's my first time having those thoughts, but that'd be a lie. I've thought about it far too often over the last few days, especially since his game.

I'm unsure if Fox realizes the arena broadcasts the warmups on the screens throughout the concourse. He probably wouldn't have made a joke about me missing his goalie stretches the other night if he did, since I didn't actually miss them. I saw them, and I watched every last second. In fact, I was so engrossed I didn't even notice that the concession stand worker put fire sauce on my nachos instead of mild, which definitely had me sweating the whole night.

It was worth it, though, to see his moves. I know those stretches help them, but damn if they don't look wildly sexual, especially when you know just how good of a kisser one of the guys doing them is. I was hot and bothered long before I tried the fire sauce, and I'm hot and bothered right now, and it has nothing to do with the mug of jalapeño lime lemonade in my hand.

I squeeze my thighs together as subtly as I can, trying to chase away the ache between them that's been steadily growing. Fox laughs, breaking the tension, then runs his hand over his jawline again, a nervous tic I find all too endearing.

"That came out way more sexual than I intended," he says, the tips of his ears red.

I laugh, too, pretending I am *not* thinking about everything I'd like to do with him in said bedroom.

Nope. Not thinking of that at all.

"Come on." He brushes by me, careful to avoid touching me, then leads me down the short hallway with three doors.

He points out the bathroom first, then his bedroom at the end. When he pushes the door open, I'm hit with that same warm-mahogany-and-Irish Spring scent I've come to associate with him. I don't know what cologne he uses, but it's officially become my favorite.

A crisp black blanket covers his neatly made bed, and I wonder if he made it because he knew I was coming over or if he's simply that neat. Given the state of the rest of his apartment, I'm betting on the latter. I tear my eyes away from it as quickly as I look at it, trying not to focus on it too much, fearing those images might pop right back to the forefront of my mind, and I focus on the rest of the room: clean and organized, which is exactly what I expected.

When we backtrack down the hall, he passes by the remaining door in the hall on the way out, and I stop.

I point to it. "Will this take me to Narnia, where I'll find a lion and witch?"

He chuckles. "Uh, no. That's just m-my...office. Nothing really to s-see in there."

My eyes fall to slits at the shakiness in his voice. "Fox, you just showed me your bedroom where all we did was stand in the doorway without a fun sexual innuendo or you trying to take advantage of me. Now you want to pass by your 'office' because there's nothing to see in there? Not a chance."

I grab the handle, pushing the door open, and he lunges at me.

"No! Wait! I—"

But his protests are futile. I've already opened the door and found that Fox—the sweet, Southern gentleman I'm pretty sure would never hurt a fly—lied to me.

"Now, *this* is a secret," I say, stepping into the room that isn't an office. No. It's more like a shrine mixed with an office. Or, from the looks of his setup, a gaming room. "What is all this? Are you worried I'll think you're a nerd for gaming?"

"You know that's a gaming computer?"

"I'm full of secrets, Artie." I shoot him a wink, which makes his blush deepen even more.

"Look," he says, following me into the room, "I know this probably looks really weird, but I swear there's a good reason for it all."

I quirk a brow at him. "Really? Because I'd love to hear it."

"Well…"

He picks up one of the hundreds of glass and ceramic turtles on the shelves, which take up an entire wall of his "office." He holds it out to me, and I take it. I study the little figurine carefully, loving the details of the green and brown. It looks almost lifelike, like it might tuck its head back into its shell at any moment.

"Do you remember those videos they showed us in school about how horrible plastic is for the ocean? The ones of the poor sea turtles with straws stuck up their noses or those six-pack rings that hold soda cans together? And we were supposed to 'Save the Turtles' by recycling and cutting those up?"

"I remember." I set the small turtle down and pick up another figurine, admiring the details of it. "They were traumatizing. It's why I only use paper straws even though they totally suck and disintegrate within five minutes." It hits me, and I gasp. "Please tell me little baby Fox took that to heart and decided to save all the turtles?"

He nods. "He did. *I* did. I, uh, rescued many, many turtles over the years until my parents said enough and I had to pick hockey or the turtles. I picked hockey, of course, but I continued rescuing the turtles in other ways by collecting these little guys." He grabs another figurine from the shelf, holding it so gingerly, and I smile at how extra tiny it looks in his giant hands. "Then my parents got in on it, and eventually my siblings, too. It took on a life of its own, so now I have this."

He sets the turtle back on the shelf, then takes the one I've been holding and puts it back in its place, his touch light and loving. It's so sweet and gentle, and I think this might be my favorite moment with Fox so far. He's always been a little soft, but seeing this side of him, knowing he's kept all these figurines to "save the turtles" in his own way… I don't know. It makes me like him more than I already did, and I already liked him a lot.

You can kiss me if you want to.

And for the second time tonight, I want to. I want to press my lips right to his and kiss this wonderful man. He's so good and so pure and so much more than I thought he was. I'll admit I had some preconceived notions regarding hockey players being meatheads. I knew I was wrong about that when Hutch proved otherwise a long time ago, but now that I'm spending time with Fox, I can see how wrong I really was.

And that might be more dangerous than me wanting to kiss him again.

"What?" he asks when he looks over at me, and I know it's because I'm beaming at him like a total fool.

"You, Arthur Fox, are somehow nothing and everything like I thought you would be."

"Is that a bad thing?"

"No." I shake my head. "It's a good thing. A very, very good thing."

He grins, and I swear I feel its warmth down to my toes.

"Come on," he says, holding his hand out to me. I slip mine into his, curling our fingers together like it's second nature. "Let's go have some nachos."

Chapter 12

FOX

"So?"

Lilah holds up a messy cheese-and-sour-cream-covered finger, chews, and swallows. But she doesn't answer me then. No. First, she takes a sip of her sparkling jalapeño lime lemonade, letting out an exaggerated *Ahhh* before setting it back down and dabbing at her lips with a napkin.

I get the feeling she's enjoying the fact that I'm sitting on the edge of my chair, awaiting her reaction far too eagerly.

Finally, she sets her napkin down and looks me in the eyes. "I think we should get married."

I laugh. "Apparently, we're already getting married, sugar."

"Oh, right." She pokes her tongue into her cheek, contemplating. "Let's have sex, then."

Fun fact: jalapeño lime lemonade does, in fact, burn when it comes out of your nose.

Lilah beats on my back as I choke thanks to her *very* sudden suggestion we have sex. That suggestion has my pants tightening, and that's even while I struggle to breathe. I'm not sure if that's a new kink being unlocked or what, but it's certainly a recent development when I'm trying not to die.

"Sorry," she says, though she doesn't sound sorry at all; she's barely able to get the word out amidst her laughter.

I cough, reaching shakily for the glass of water she hands me. I'm thankful I had the foresight to grab it just in case dinner was too spicy for her. After chugging half of it, I take my first real breath in what feels like hours instead of seconds and sigh.

"I was…not…expecting…that," I manage through labored gulps of air.

She giggles, and it's so cute I almost forget she just nearly killed me. "It's the only thing I could think of to repay you because these nachos might be the best nachos of my life."

"Sex for good nachos. Got it." I take another long pull of water, then set it down. "I'm not sure that's an equal payment, but if you insist…"

I reach for the button on my jeans, pretending to

undo it, and she yelps, rushing to stop me. I fight back laughter the whole time.

"Stop, stop! I was kidding!"

I level her with a faux glare. "Come on, Lilah. Don't be a tease."

"But teasing's my favorite," she says, winking at me, and I think she might be serious. I think Lilah likes to tease. *A lot.* And I like it far more than I probably should.

We're close. So close I can smell her perfume—that same light floral scent from New Year's Eve I have burned in my memory—and feel the warmth radiating off her. Her lips part just slightly, her breaths uneven as her gaze flicks between my eyes and my mouth.

You can kiss me if you want to.

I remember my words from the other night, and I wonder if she remembers them, too. If she were to kiss me right now, I'd let her. I shouldn't. *We* shouldn't. But I'm not sure I'd be able to stop myself.

Her eyes drop lower to where her hands are *still* on mine, dangerously close to my cock that's pressing against my zipper, and I'm sure she can *definitely* see I am not mad about our proximity.

Fuck. How pathetic am I that I'm getting a boner because I'm sitting close to a beautiful woman? It's like I'm sixteen all over again.

I clear my throat, and she rips her hands away,

scooting as far from me as possible, ducking her head. The tension in the room is palpable, our silence deafening. It's easily the most awkward things have been between us, and I've seen her naked ass.

Shit. Why'd I have to go and think about that? Picturing her perfectly pert ass does nothing to help the *growing* situation in my pants.

Think about something else, Fox. Anything else. Think of your save percentage this year. Think about how you let in that soft goal last night.

That's enough to help calm my cock a little as we turn back to our meals. We eat silently for a long time, both plates nearly empty when Lilah asks how practice went this morning.

I reach up and massage my neck, which tightens with tension at the mention of hockey. "It was fine."

"Just fine?" she asks, popping a meat-and-cheese-loaded tortilla chip into her mouth, a little moan escaping her.

I do my best to ignore it.

"Yeah, just wasn't entirely up to par. I've, uh, been a bit off my game lately, even in practice."

"Aren't you guys like third in your division?"

"Fourth." We slipped a spot, and it was all thanks to my shit goaltending, which meant we gave up a two-goal lead with less than five minutes to go. Keller sold himself out to try to save us, but it wasn't enough.

"Then what's the big deal? I mean, I know I'm new to the game and all, but isn't that good?"

"It's not bad, but we could be in a better position, especially with the playoffs coming up so soon. Need to pad points now while we can because other teams will be pushing."

"There's still a lot of hockey left to play."

I grin. "You sure you're new to the game? That sounds like a seasoned approach right there."

She shrugs. "I might have picked it up watching a game or two this week."

She's been watching my games? So much for my cock calming down. The idea of Lilah sitting in her apartment, curled up on her pink couch, watching my games, excites me far too much.

"Have you been keeping tabs on me, sugar?" I tease.

She startles at the nickname, dropping her perfectly good chip right back onto her plate, and I grin, really liking that it affects her.

She recovers quickly, pushing her shoulders back. "So, what are you going to do to fix it?"

I like that she doesn't try to talk me up and tell me I'm doing fine and to get over it. She sees it's a struggle for me and me alone, sees that no amount of kind words will make me play better.

"I don't know, honestly."

And I truly don't. I know how I usually try to loosen up, but sex isn't exactly on the table right now, not with me "dating" Lilah. We don't need to complicate this thing between us any more by throwing sex into the mix.

"Let's have sex, then," she announces again.

Even though my pants tighten even more, I laugh off her words. "Nice try, Lilah. You're not getting me with that a second time."

I rise from my chair, take my empty plate, and reach for hers. She nods, and I grab her plate, carrying them to the counter. After tossing our scraps into the trash, I dump the dishes into the sink to deal with later and turn to clean up the kitchen. I'm acutely aware of Lilah behind me. I can feel her staring as I grab a glass dish from the cabinet above me for the leftover chicken.

There's none of that light and fun air from earlier, no laughter. No amusement at all. It's static. Stilted. Lilah's chair scrapes against the floor, and I try not to react to the noise, try to focus on nothing but the task at hand, but it's pointless. All I can do is count her steps as she gets closer and closer.

Eight.

Nine.

Ten.

She's behind me now, her heat pressing at my back,

and I act like she's not. I don't trust myself right now; I might do something really stupid like turn around and kiss her.

"Fox," she says, my name a mere whisper. "I wasn't joking."

I swallow. Hard.

Because I knew she wasn't. Deep down, I knew she wasn't teasing at all. She meant every word, and as much as I didn't want to like each one, I did. *Do.* I really fucking do.

"Fox," she says again, tugging at my arm, and I let her turn me until I'm facing her.

God, she's beautiful. Her blue eyes pop against the dark red of her shirt. Her hair hangs loosely around her shoulders, and I've been fighting the urge to wrap it around my fingers all night, wanting to see if it's as silky as it looks. I want to kiss off every bit of the pale pink lipstick on those lips I've dreamed about since our kiss.

"I want to help you."

"Help me?" The words come out strangled like someone is holding my throat and restricting my air supply. Weird because that's how I feel right now as she stares up at me and tells me she wants to help me by having sex with me.

"Yeah. Help you. You say you need to relax, right?

Well, this—*I*—could help you. You're helping me, so it's only fair, right?"

I shake my head. "No, Lilah, that's not fair. I'm not helping you so you'll sleep with me. I'm helping you because I want to."

"I know that. And I'm not really saying I want to sleep with you because I want to help you with your game. It's called a façade."

"Façade?"

"Yeah, a front. A smokescreen. Pretense." She chuckles, stepping closer. "I can pull a bunch of other words out of my Scrabble-loving head, but none of them will work better than this. Fox, I want to sleep with you because I want to sleep with you." Another step. "Because I haven't been able to stop thinking about our kiss and how I want to kiss you again. Because your damn goalie stretches got to me. Because you served me *homemade* sparkling jalapeño lime lemonade in a mug. Because you save turtles." Another step as she pushes up on her tiptoes, her breath ghosting against my lips. "Because I *like* you, Arthur Fox."

I swallow thickly, blood thrumming in my ears.

Because I like you, Arthur Fox.

Arthur.

I drag my tongue against my lips, just barely missing hers.

"You…like me?"

She nods, her stare on my mouth. "I do."

Another rough gulp. I have no idea what to do with that confession.

I like Lilah, too. A lot. I didn't think going to a stuffy birthday party or seeing her in my jersey or hanging out with her at Top Shelf or making nachos for her would make me feel that way, but here we are.

"Do you remember when you said I could kiss you if I want to?"

I nod. "I remember."

"Well, I want to, Fox. I really, really want to."

I want to say something cool like, *What are you waiting for?* But I don't have it in me.

All I can manage is, "Lilah."

It's the last thing I say before she presses her lips to mine, and my whole fucking world flips upside down. My hands fall to her hips on instinct, and I pull her to me, dragging her up until her toes are barely touching the floor as she kisses me with fervor. Her hands crash into my hair, tugging me in and hanging on just as tightly as I am like she's afraid this is all going to disappear soon.

And it should disappear. We shouldn't be doing this. This is a very, very bad idea that feels so, so good.

Stop this, Fox. Stop it now before it's too late.

But I don't listen to myself. I can't. She feels too fucking good. Too right. Too much like…*mine*.

That brings me right back to reality because she's not mine. What we're feeling is because of the situation we got ourselves into. That's it.

"Wait, wait, wait," I whisper, pulling away even though every part of me says not to because this feels better than anything I've ever experienced in my life, and I want more of it so damn badly that my hands are shaking.

Still, this is a big deal right now. It was all supposed to be fake, just a favor, and her lips on mine don't feel fake at all. What she's suggesting isn't fake. It's all too real and feels all too good, like something I could get dangerously addicted to if I let myself. And while I really want to let myself, I know I shouldn't.

"We shouldn't."

She juts her bottom lip out in a pout, and I hate that I want to lean forward and sink my teeth into it. "Why not?"

"You know why not, sugar."

"But I don't," she says, pressing closer to me again, and I groan. She's warm and soft and feels like absolutely everything I want right now. "I don't understand why not. We know what this is, Fox. We know there are no other expectations. Why not have some fun?" She dances her fingers over my chest like she can't help but touch me right now. "Because isn't that what this whole thing is supposed to be about? Having fun?"

"Having fun messing with your parents. Not having fun like this."

She drags her fingers down my chest, tracing over my abs, not stopping until she's brushing the edge of my jeans. "It can be both."

She tugs my shirt, her soft touch tickling my bare skin, and I might have had too much spice tonight. I must have. It's the only explanation for why I'm sweating so much from such a small touch.

"Lilah…" I say. No, I *beg*. "It's a bad idea."

"I don't think it is. I think you *want* it to be a bad idea because if it's not, you might have to admit you're not always a gentleman, admit you want this and you want to do dirty, dirty things to me…use me. You want to fuck me and release all this tension you've been holding on to so you can play better hockey." She tugs on my jeans, dragging me closer, her lips mere centimeters from mine. "And honestly, Fox, I want you to."

She's right. I do want to do dirty, dirty things to her. I want to bend her over this countertop and pull those jeans that make her ass look so damn good right down her legs. I want to push myself between her thighs and taste her until she's screaming my name.

Then I want to slam into her, fuck her until her legs are nothing but jelly and I'm all she feels tomorrow when I'm between the pipes, winning us a game. Because I *do* think this will help with my game. Tremendously, actually.

So, yes, I want this, but it doesn't change the fact that I shouldn't.

"Please, Arthur. Let me help you. Let me do this for you."

I don't know what does me in, don't know if it's the way she says my name or her pleading, but I don't care. Not when she's staring up at me with hooded eyes, her hands still toying dangerously close to the button on my jeans. And especially not when I don't want to resist her anymore.

"Oh, what the hell?" I mutter. "Fuck it."

Then I grab her, sliding my hands into her hair that's just as silky as I hoped, and drag those soft, plump lips of hers right back to mine, kissing the hell out of her. She gasps into my mouth, then again when I swing her into my arms and spin us both around, dropping her onto the counter and pressing between her knees. I drag her to the edge of the stone, fitting myself against her, wanting her to feel just what she's been doing to me.

If the soft moan that leaves her is any indication, she definitely feels it.

"This is a bad idea," I tell her, trailing my lips from hers and down her chin, sucking at her neck.

"Maybe, but it feels good, doesn't it?"

"Mmm," I hum, sinking my teeth into her soft flesh.

"It's just fun," she says, and I'm not sure if she's telling me or reminding herself, but I don't really care.

I grab the hem of her shirt, tugging it over her head and tossing it aside as I admire the lacy black bra that does nothing to hide her hard nipples.

"Just in case I forget to tell you later, you look stunning, Lilah."

Her breaths stutter with surprise, but I pay no attention, already placing my lips right back on her, kissing her softly just over where her heart beats wildly. Her fingers slip into my hair once more, holding me to her as her head lolls back. A soft sigh leaves her lips like there's nowhere else she'd rather be.

There's nowhere else I'd rather be, either—except maybe between her legs with my tongue teasing her until she's begging for mercy.

"Arthur…" she breathes out.

"What do you need, Lilah?" I ask, still pressing kisses to her chest. "Tell me what you need. Tell me what you want from me."

"Everything." She huffs out a laugh. "I want everything. I want…"

But she says nothing else, and I get the feeling she definitely wants something but is too afraid to ask for it, and Lilah is never afraid. I don't want her to be. I want her to be herself. I want her to get everything from this she's looking for.

"Then take it from me, Lilah. Take what you want."

She tugs at my hair, pulling me away from her, then jumps off the counter, her body sliding against mine in all the right places.

"Take it," I tell her again, and it's like something snaps inside her.

She rolls her shoulders back and pushes on my chest. I stumble backward with the movement, already loving this side of her that fits her so well. Lilah has always been a force to be reckoned with. It makes sense to me she's the same in the bedroom.

"Go to the couch and sit."

I don't dare question her. I do as I'm told, brushing past her and practically running to the living room. I sit on the dark gray leather couch as instructed, watching as she saunters into the room, looking like every bit of a wet dream. She continues until her knees touch mine, staring down at me with heavy-lidded eyes.

She reaches forward, softly running her hand through my hair. Suddenly, her grip turns just rough enough to hurt but still be enjoyable as she swings her legs over me and climbs into my lap. She scoots until we're fitted together perfectly, my aching cock pressing against her warm center, and I set my hands on her waist but do nothing else, letting her set the pace here.

She places her thumb against my lips, tracing them lightly like she's trying to memorize them. Needing to taste her, I slide my tongue out, brushing against her fingertip, and her eyes narrow like I'm in trouble.

For the first time, I think I like being in trouble.

"Do you need something to suck on?" she asks, and I nod. "Then pull my tits out and put your mouth to good use, Arthur."

I don't think I've ever moved faster in my entire life, and that includes the time I made a stick save against one of the best players of all time when New York took a penalty shot in game five of a conference showdown. I yank down the cups of her bra, revealing the tits I've been longing to see, and waste no time leaning forward, pulling a rosy nipple into my mouth and closing my teeth around it before chasing away the sting with my tongue.

Lilah moans, rocking her hips lightly against my cock that's begging for any relief at this point. It's not enough, but damn, does it feel good. I tease her, moving between sucking softly and nipping at her until she's wiggling against me, searching for me.

"Take it," I remind her, and once again, there's a spark in her blue eyes. "I'm only going to do what you tell me to do."

"I want to touch you."

"Then touch me, sugar."

She drags her hands over my chest like she did in the kitchen, then down until she's pulling at the hem. I sit forward, letting her tug the material off me just as I did her earlier. I settle back against the couch as she runs her fingertips over me once more.

"You're beautiful," she murmurs, not taking her eyes off me, and I like the appreciation in them probably far more than I should. I'm not stupid; I know I look good. I spend a lot of time training for hockey. Still, it feels good to be stared at like I'm the last donut sitting in a pastry display.

"I don't think anyone has said that about me before."

She lifts a shoulder, then snaps open the button on my jeans. "It's true."

"Th-Thank you," I stutter out as she drags the zipper down.

There are no pretenses as she slips her hand right into my boxer briefs and takes my heavy cock in her hand. I don't know which of us sighs the loudest, but her touch is enough to have me breaking the rules, and I reach forward to kiss her again. I can't help it, and I don't think she minds anyway, her tongue sliding against mine instantly as she touches me in slow, nearly painful strokes. Once again, it's not enough, but it'll have to do with the confines of my jeans keeping us from more.

"Off," she murmurs against my lips.

"Hmm?"

"Take your pants off," she instructs like she knows exactly what I'm thinking.

She slips off my lap, pulling my jeans down along with her as she falls to the floor at my feet. It's so fucking hot seeing her like this, her hair loose around her shoulders, lips puffy from my own as she stares up at me with pure fucking want.

"Do you want me to suck your cock, Fox?"

I sink my teeth into my bottom lip to keep from groaning and nod.

She grins. "I thought you might."

She leans forward, kissing the inside of my thigh, and I let out a shaky breath.

"I'm going to." Another kiss, higher this time. "I'm going to suck you until you're spilling down my throat, Arthur." Another kiss and her lips are so goddamn close to my cock I could cry. "I'm going to swallow your load and love every damn second of it."

It's what I want too. So fucking badly. I can't remember the last time I wanted anything more, actually. She kisses me again, her nose nudging against the one part of me where I really want her touch, and I barely hold back my sigh.

"Is that what you want too, Arthur? Do you want to fill me with your cum? Do you want to see it dribble down my chin? Do you want to taste yourself on my lips?"

I nod fervently, and she laughs lightly.

"Good. That's what I want, too." She hooks her hands into my boxer briefs, her eyes locked on to mine. "And that's exactly what I'm going to get."

With no other warning, she pulls me free and her mouth is on me. I'm dying. I have to be. There's no other reason for the blinding white light behind my eyes. I've finally kicked the bucket, and it has everything to do with the lips currently wrapped around me.

"Holy fuck, holy fuck, holy fucking shit," I say as she expertly moves her lips over me.

She giggles, and I feel it everywhere. I slip my hand into her hair, holding it back for her when it falls into her face, and she pulls off me.

Lilah levels me with a severe look. "Don't you dare try to take charge. You do, and I'll stop. Understood?"

I gulp, nodding.

She smiles, her lips ghosting against the head of my cock. "Good boy."

Good boy.

I've been called a "good boy" a lot in my life, but I've never loved it as much as I do now.

Lilah sucks me right to the back of her throat, her mouth the perfect pressure as she works me over, and I let her. I don't try to take control or pump from beneath. I let her do whatever she wants just like the good boy she says I am. She trails her nails lightly over the inside of my thigh, cupping my balls and rolling them gently in her palm, and I groan because god, how does she know? How does she fucking know it's just what I need?

Lilah nudges my legs wider, and I let her, slipping lower on my leather couch as she slides her finger lower, right to that spot behind my balls that are tighter than I've ever felt before. She presses against me, and I was wrong before. *Now* I'm dead because *holy shit* that feels so good.

"Fuck," I say, though it comes out more of a groan, and she laughs again. I love it and hate it all at once. "You're killing me."

She doesn't seem to care. She just keeps sucking on me and pressing on that spot. My orgasm builds and builds, the base of my spine tingling with anticipation. Then with one more press—this time right to my tight ring that nobody has ever touched before—I do exactly what she wants, and I spill right down her throat with no warning.

Lilah's as caught off guard as I am, but she doesn't let that stop her. She swallows back my cum, trying to catch it all, but it's a fruitless effort. There's too much of it, and it slips down her chin. I can't help myself—I grab her by her hair and pull her back to my lap, kissing her and tasting myself on her lips just like she asked for.

"That was incredible," I say against her mouth as we both try to catch our breath.

"And just think, I'm not even done with you."

I don't know how, but the promise has my cock twitching against my thigh. I've never been ready to go again so quickly before. Of course it would be different with Lilah.

"What do you want next?" I ask, my voice muffled as I nuzzle my nose against her neck, needing to touch her in any way I can right now.

"I was thinking you could take me to your bedroom and fuck me until I can't walk straight."

I growl in appreciation, and she laughs.

"I take it you like the sound of that."

I nod. "Very much so."

"Then what are you waiting for? Fuck me already, Arthur Fox."

I've pushed onto my feet before she can finish her

sentence, hauling her right up along with me as I kick off my underwear the rest of the way and march us back down the hall to my bedroom while she chuckles the whole way.

"In a hurry?" she asks.

"Sure am."

Another giggle quickly turns to a gasp when I drop her to my bed and crawl over her. She's not laughing anymore, not when I kiss her hard and fast or when I drop my hands to the top of her jeans, and definitely not when I unsnap them and drag her zipper down, the sound loud in the otherwise quiet room. This is as real as it gets now, and we're just moments from not being able to turn back.

And dammit, I don't want to. I don't want to walk away from her. Not now, not even when I still think this is a terrible idea. I want this too damn badly. I want *her* too damn badly.

"Stop," she says, mouth ghosting over mine. "Stop overthinking this. It's just fun, right?"

"Just fun," I echo as I slip my hand inside her jeans, getting my first feel of her.

She's wet. So fucking wet I can *hear* it, and it's the sweetest sound in the world, even better than a packed arena chanting my name.

"You feel so good," I tell her. "Want to taste you."

"Please," she begs.

It's all she has to say. I drop to my knees and pull her jeans and panties from her body, fitting myself between her spread thighs and dragging my tongue over her with no words spoken between us. Her back curves off the bed with a loud sigh, like *this* is what she's always wanted.

I think it may be what I've always wanted, too.

Her hands find their way into my hair again, and I let her control me, tell me what she wants. I like giving up control to Lilah; I like having her be in charge. Just like I like the sounds she's making, how her legs shake around me, how her tugs on my hair are getting rougher and rougher as her breaths grow more and more ragged.

"I'm so close," she says through harsh breaths.

"What do you need?" I ask her.

"You. Just you."

So that's what I give her. I slip my tongue over her dripping wet cunt and suck her clit into my mouth. I curl my fingers inside her, applying pressure to a spot I have a feeling she'll love. She rewards me with more pants. More tugs. More needy whimpers that are like music to my ears.

"Arthur, Arthur, Arthur," she chants, and I grin around her, adding *just* a bit more until there are no words, just sounds as she falls apart around me.

I've barely caught my breath before she's pulling

me up and pressing her mouth to mine. She rolls me onto my back and crawls on top of me, my cock nestled right against where I just was between her legs, and she grinds against me, already desperate for more. I'm desperate, too.

"Condoms?" she asks.

"Uh…" I rack my brain, trying to figure out where I stashed them. It's been so long since I've done this, I don't even know if I have any.

"It's okay. I have some in my purse."

She slips off me and hurries out of the room, and I let her, lying back and trying to catch my breath. What is even happening right now? I'm about to have sex with Lilah Maddison, my fake fiancée. We're crossing a line, and I don't have it in me to care.

Lilah comes bounding back into the room in record time, ripping open the condom with her teeth and sliding it over me before resuming her spot on my lap.

I like her there. She fits. *We* fit.

She kisses me softly, her hips sliding against mine, teasing me until I can barely take it anymore.

"Take it," I remind her.

And she does. She sinks right down onto my waiting cock, and we both sigh with relief as I slip inside her for the first time.

"Oh, *fuck*," she mutters, taking me inch by inch, slow and torturous.

"I agree."

"You feel so…" She takes another inch. "You're so big, Arthur. I can't take it all."

"You can," I tell her, reaching up to pluck at her nipples. "You can take it, sugar."

She shakes her head but slips down the last little bit until she's fully seated on my lap, not even a half inch of space between us.

"There you go," I tell her, bringing her down to capture her lips with mine. "You did so good."

"I did." She nods as she moves her hips slowly and methodically, trying to adjust to me.

When she feels more comfortable—or maybe even uncomfortable with the need for more—she pushes up, sitting back, the angle changing so much that she feels even tighter, and I have to work harder to breathe. Lilah tosses her head back, closing her eyes as she finds a rhythm, and I watch in awe as she rides me, bringing me closer and closer to another orgasm.

She's fucking gorgeous like this, her cheeks stained red with exertion, sweat dotting her forehead. She's still wearing her bra, her tits still spilling from the cups, like she wanted this so badly she couldn't even bother fully undressing, and I'm perfectly okay with that. Her movements grow hastier, more frantic like she's chasing something just out of reach, all while I do everything I can to hold back and not come too soon.

"Lilah…" Her eyes flutter open, and she looks down at me with those damn blue eyes of hers that I can't seem to look away from. "Take what you need," I remind her.

"I need you to fuck me, Arthur. *Hard.*"

She doesn't have to tell me twice. I flip us until she's beneath me, and I slam back into her so hard she lets out a pleased cry. I don't stop. I fuck into her as requested. Almost punishingly, and I don't know why. Maybe for making me keep my hands to myself. Maybe for teasing me earlier in the kitchen. Or maybe because I'm just mad at myself for giving in to her so damn easily and possibly ruining everything. Whatever it is, I don't stop, and she doesn't ask me to.

No, she asks for more. *Begs* for it even. And I give it to her until she's calling my name and squeezing my cock as she comes. I follow right after her, unable to hold back anymore, then collapse on top of her, my head on her chest. I lie there listening to her heart race as Lilah holds me in her arms, her nails tracing lightly across my back as she kisses the top of my head.

"Now, *that* was a very good boy," she says, and I laugh.

But she's right. I am a good boy. *Her* good boy.

And as much as I shouldn't, I can't fucking wait to be that for her again.

Chapter 13

I don't want to do this. I don't want to do this at all. I want to be anywhere else but here right now.

No. That's not true. Not *anywhere*. I know exactly where I'd rather be right now: back in Fox's bed, snuggled up next to him after the best orgasms of my life.

That's where I wish I were instead of at an entirely too fancy restaurant I don't want to be at for a lunch date with the Wicked Witch of the West. But here I am anyway, in a dress my mother brought to my apartment after she showed up unannounced to "ensure my attendance," as if I was going to bail or something. I sit with my hands in my lap as she lays into the poor server because they dared to offer her red instead of white wine. I don't understand why she's bitching—we both know she's going to drink a bottle of both.

I check my phone while she's distracted, hoping for a message from Fox, but there's nothing. He's late, and I hate that he's late. Not because I care—I get it, his schedule is a bit insane—but because it means I have to endure all this with my mother alone with no buffer. And because I would have liked to see him, even if only for a moment before coming in here.

We haven't had much chance to talk since our date at his house, which ended in a marathon of sex that I can *still* feel even days later. I was one hundred percent teasing him the first time I suggested sex. The second? I meant it, though I didn't even realize I did when I first said it. He just looked so upset about his game, and I remembered him saying it's how he usually relaxes, and I don't know…I wanted to be that for him. I wanted to help him.

Oh, who am I kidding? I just wanted him.

I don't know when exactly that happened, but all the little things suddenly added up. Him taking me home on New Year's, bringing me ibuprofen and a greasy breakfast the morning after, standing up for me at the party, making me nachos because he knew I loved them… So many little things turned into one big thing, and I gave in to everything I was feeling. He told me to take what I wanted, so I did.

Nobody has ever let me be in charge like that before. It's like Fox knew that was what I wanted, what I *needed*. And he didn't judge me. He just let me be me. I wish he were here so I could thank him for that.

"Your *fiancé* is late," my mother says as if I don't know that the whole reason we're having this lunch isn't present.

"His hockey schedule keeps him very busy. When you decided to set this lunch for today, I warned you that he might run late due to it."

My mother called the morning after Fox and I slept together and demanded we be here for lunch. It didn't matter to her that Fox had practice before his game tonight. It was what she wanted, and because Fox is who he is, he accommodated her, even when I tried to shut her down.

"Right. *Hockey.* Such a violent game." She says it with such disgust. Maybe if she knew how hard he worked or all the sacrifices he's made for it, she'd appreciate it more, but knowing her, she wouldn't. So I don't bother with trying to explain it to her. "And what have you decided to do with your life, dear? Are you going to be a hockey wife? Isn't that what Auden gave up her company to do?"

I bite my tongue—literally—because we both know Auden has done so much more with her life than my mother is giving her credit for and shrug. "I'm not sure.

I'm still trying to figure things out since she sold Sinclair Properties."

"That was a terrible deal she took. She could have made so much more money had she held out for a bit longer and didn't take the first thing she was offered."

"It wasn't about the money, Mother. She already had enough when she decided to sell. It was about finally putting down roots."

"Right. Because that father of hers moved her around so often. What kind of man raises a child like that?"

A damn good one is what I want to say, but I don't get the chance. Fox comes barreling into the restaurant, drawing several heads his way, mine included.

He looks good. I've seen him in a suit a few times now, and they always look perfectly tailored to him, but I like something about this simple side of him even more. His slacks are pressed neatly, and he wears a soft blue sweater, a collared shirt underneath. He looks preppy, like a frat boy playing dress-up, and normally, I wouldn't be attracted to it at all, but I am. I am so beyond attracted to it that I can't look away. Those brown eyes of his that I looked right into as he fucked me so hard my legs shook for ten straight minutes after find mine, and he smiles.

My mother follows my line of sight, looking pleasantly surprised.

"Well, he cleans up nicely. I'll give him that," she says as if he wasn't wearing a suit the last time she saw him. Further proof that nothing will ever truly please her.

She stands when he approaches the table, but he doesn't stop to greet her. No, he passes right by her and sweeps me into his arms, pressing his lips to mine in a chaste yet searing kiss. I'm not proud to admit that I'm out of breath when he pulls away.

"Hi," he says simply, that all-too-familiar smile pulling at his lips.

"Hi yourself," I say back, my own grin that I can't seem to get rid of when it comes to him firmly on my face.

He sets me back on my feet and finally turns to my mother. "Selene," he says, just a hint of that Southern drawl of his coming out as he takes her hand and kisses the back of her knuckles. "It's wonderful to see you again."

She looks momentarily affronted but soon melts under his grin. "Arthur, I'm so glad you could make it."

"I apologize for being late." He holds the back of her chair as she settles back into it, then slides it forward. "Practice ran a bit longer than expected."

"Oh, that's quite all right," my mother says as if she wasn't just complaining about his profession minutes ago.

Fox strides back to me, pulling my chair out just like he did my mother's. Only when he slides my chair toward the table, his hand brushes against the back of my neck, a reminder of the way he held me to him as he spilled down my throat the last time I saw him.

I waited for the morning after our night of sex to turn awkward, but it never did. If anything, it helped make things easier between us. We weren't pretending not to be attracted to one another anymore.

Fox settles into the chair beside me, his thigh pressing against mine—*did someone turn up the heat in here?*—and I swear he scoots his chair even closer.

"I've already ordered some starters and a bottle of wine," my mother announces.

"Unfortunately, I'll have to stick with water for this lunch. I have a game to play tonight."

My mother hums disapprovingly, lifting her half-empty glass of sauvignon blanc to her lips. "Well, more for me, then. Lilah, you should probably cut back, yeah? You were such a chunky little girl. I know you swell up easily. You don't want to be puffy for the wedding."

Embarrassment floods me. Is she seriously doing this right now? In front of Fox? Ugh. I can't imagine what he thinks of all this. Does he think I'm weak, letting her talk to me like that? Or worse, does he agree with her?

Fox's hand finds the back of my neck again, massaging it, requesting my attention, and I turn to him. There's no judgment in his eyes, but there is something else, something I can't entirely place my finger on. It feels familiar but out of reach.

"Just in case I forget to tell you later, you look stunning, Lilah."

I'm taken right back to the last time he said those words to me when I was sitting on his countertop in nothing but my bra.

"Thank you," I tell him, pretending my cheeks aren't on fire right now.

I peek over at my mother. She watches us with hard eyes, and I can't tell if she's pissed that I didn't take her bait like she hoped or if she's looking for a crack in our façade. Truthfully, I don't think she will find one because even I'm struggling to.

She reaches into the oversized purse hanging off the back of her chair. "I've brought along your grandmother's ring. It's about time I was able to give this to you. I thought you might never settle down."

I ignore her jab as she reveals a giant brown box. As a child, I was told countless times not to touch it. She flips the lid open, and there sits the ring I'm supposed to wear. It's just as gaudy as I remember it being. I reach for it and barely manage to pull my finger away before my mother snaps it closed.

"I'd like Arthur to give it to you."

"Oh, sure," Fox says. "I can do that."

"*Properly*," my mother says, brow arched.

Properly? Does she mean… *Oh god.*

"What? Mother, no. That's—"

"It only seems right, Lilah Jane, since he proposed the first time with no ring. Don't you want a lovely story for your children one day? Or would you rather tell them about how their father proposed without a plan or a ring?"

None of those things. I don't want to tell my future children any of that because I don't even know if I *want* children. But saying that would open a whole new can of worms I'm not interested in discussing right now.

"Your mother is right, Lilah."

I swing my head toward Fox. "She is?"

He nods, leaning close to me. "You deserve a proper proposal. Let me give you one."

I want to scream, tell him this isn't a proper proposal because it's not real, but that would ruin everything. So, I nod.

Fox pushes his chair back and takes the box from my mother's hand. She looks smug as if this is the smoking gun that will blow our whole con to bits. But I guess she's not betting on how good of a man Fox is.

He holds the garish box in his hands, running his

fingers over it before taking a deep breath and dropping to his knee before me. I look around the fancy restaurant. Everyone stares at us, captivated by what's happening, having no clue we're playing the ultimate game of charades.

I pull my chair out to face him, trying to tell him with my eyes, *You don't have to do this.*

All the while, his say, *Let me do this for you.*

"Fox, I—"

"Lilah Jane Maddison," he announces loudly, his voice booming above mine, silencing my protests. "I fell in love with you on our first date."

I roll my lips together, trying to hide my smile because I know as well as he does our first date was just days ago.

"You were radiant, sitting atop that donkey eating a footlong corn dog you had dipped in chowder," he says, his eyes dancing with laughter, that smile I've come to love so much teasing the edge of his lips. "I knew then that our love was the kind you hear about in fairy tales."

I don't dare peek at my mother because I know I'll lose it.

"I wasn't looking for forever, but that's exactly what I found in you. You…" His eyes soften, the humor in them dying out, and it's so sudden that my throat tightens as I stare down at him. "You brought something into my life I didn't know I was missing."

Something in his voice begins to change, quiets, and the rest of the room fades away. It's just us now: Fox on one knee, holding my hand and peering into my eyes, which are beginning to sting.

"You're brilliant and kind and beautiful. And your wit might be my favorite thing about you. You make me laugh and smile. And you make me really, really damn happy. It would be an absolute honor to be your husband. So, what do you say, Lilah? Will you marry me?"

My throat burns, and it's hard to find air. I don't know what I expected from this, but it certainly wasn't that. It wasn't just Fox calling me brilliant or beautiful. No. It was more. It was the rawness in his voice when he said I was what he was missing because it sounded so real. Like he truly *was* missing something.

It reminds me of his confession that it's nice to have someone. Is Fox lonelier than I thought? Does this mean more to him than he's letting on?

"Well, Lilah?" my mother asks, pulling my attention, and I look over to find even *she* has tears in her eyes. "Answer the man!"

I turn back to Fox, who is staring up at me expectantly, waiting as patiently as ever.

"Yes, Fox," I say quietly, praying he doesn't hear the shakiness in my voice. "Yes, I'll marry you."

He blows out a relieved breath, perfectly playing the part of a worried boyfriend.

"She said yes!" he exclaims, and the rest of the restaurant cheers.

Fox opens the box, revealing the hideous ring he can't help but widen his eyes at. He gingerly tugs it from the silk-lined holder and slips it over my finger while I try not to wince at the sight of it. Once upon a time, when I was a very little girl and had much different thoughts about love and marriage, I dreamed of a ring. This thing? It's nothing like what I wanted. A hundred tiny diamonds surround a squared, four-carat diamond in the center. Inside the band are four smaller stones, two on each side, resembling rubies.

If this were an alternate reality in which I actually wanted a ring on my finger, it would be something simple and nothing as extravagant as this. But this isn't an alternate reality. *This* is my reality, my future, if I don't find the courage to stand up to my parents.

"That was lovely, Arthur," my mother says as he presses his lips to my cheek, then resumes his spot next to me. "What do you think of the ring? Gorgeous, isn't it?"

He smiles at her, and if I didn't know him better—

which I definitely do—I'd believe it was genuine. "It's lovely, Selene."

She lifts her glass, grinning at him over the rim, seemingly pleased with his answer. "Now that that's out of the way, we should discuss your engagement party."

"Our *what*?!"

My outburst has many people looking our way.

"Keep your voice down, dear," my mother says, her eyes narrowing. "I don't know why you're so surprised. We hosted one for your sister. We'll do the same for you."

Ah, yes. Sadie's engagement party. How could I forget? I got caught making out with one of her fiancé's friends in the bathroom. If I think about it, it was the catalyst that set my parents off on this *You need to settle down* mission they've been on.

"Perhaps you'll keep your clothes on at this one," she says, taking another pull from her glass and emptying it in record time.

I glance over at Fox, whose brows are raised. I shrug, and he grins, giving me a subtle headshake, but there's no judgment in his eyes. I mentally add that to the list of things I like about him. He doesn't hold my past against me, which I certainly can't say for my mother.

A server appears, refilling my mother's glass as she

asks, "What do we think about the spring? That's a lovely time to host a party."

"Mother, I—"

"I think the spring is nice," Fox agrees with her.

"Wonderful. We'll plan the party for then. I'll get my assistant on it, and we can get the invitations out ASAP. Hopefully, people will RSVP, even with such short notice." She gives us a pointed look. "Now, would you like white or off-white linen?"

That's how we spend the rest of the lunch, planning my upcoming engagement party with my fake fiancé, whom I'm now sleeping with.

How could this possibly get any worse?

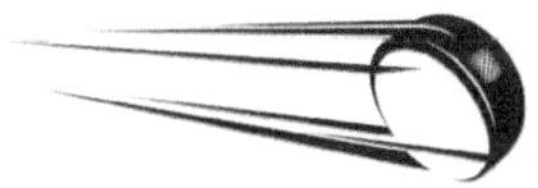

"That was…something."

I glare at Fox, though I'm not sure why.

Scratch that. I know *exactly* why.

"*I think the spring is nice.* Really, Fox? That's what you say to her?"

He winces. "I was just trying to be nice."

"Stop being so nice!"

It comes out louder than intended. I think.

Honestly, I don't know at this point. Maybe I mean it. Maybe I want him to stop being so nice, calm, accommodating, and helpful. I want him to tell me this is too much because it *is* too much.

But he won't. I know he won't.

"Is that what you really want?" he asks quietly, navigating toward my apartment because *of course* he offered to drive me home after my mother, who insisted I ride there with her, decided she had better things to do than take me back home.

"No," I say, just as quietly. "I love that you're nice, Fox. It's my favorite thing about you. I just… Isn't this going too far? First a proposal and now a party?"

"I don't know. Maybe? But what else are we supposed to do? Tell her no? I have a feeling she wouldn't take that so well and would call us on our bullshit. You want this to work, right?"

I *do* want this to work. It's been nice not having my mother call and berate me for a change. Sure, now she's going to be calling about party planning, but that I can deal with. I love planning. It's everything else that I don't love. Lying to people I care about, like Auden, who I've barely spoken to out of fear of blurting out how all of this is fake.

"Yes, I want this to work."

"Then we'll do it. Party and then we'll break up. You can dump me after the engagement party. No harm, no foul, except to your parents' pocketbook."

He's all smiles, but my stomach turns at the

thought. Not of my parents—I couldn't care less about that—but of breaking up with him. That was the plan all along, but having a timeline now makes it feel so much more real.

"What about your family? What are you going to tell them about all this?" For the first time since we started this whole thing, he looks panicked by my question. "Will you let them believe we're actually engaged, or will you lie to them too?"

He runs a hand through his hair. "I hadn't really thought about them in this whole thing."

No, I'm sure he didn't. We didn't think any of this through.

"We need to call it off."

He looks over at me, brows raised. "Are you serious?"

Shit. *Am* I serious? Do I want to stop this and go back to my parents trying to set me up? Go back to having them look at me completely disappointed instead of just mildly so? I hate that my answers are no and no. I hate that while I *should* call it off, there's a good chance I won't because I'm being that selfish right now.

I groan. "This wasn't supposed to be this stressful."

Fox reaches over, his hand landing on my thigh, and I like the weight of it far too much.

He squeezes me reassuringly. "Hey, it's okay. We'll

figure it all out. If it makes you feel any better, my parents would one hundred percent laugh about this whole thing."

"Really?"

"Oh, yeah, definitely. They have three raucous kids. Nothing would surprise them at this point."

"Even a fake engagement?"

"Regan pretended to be dating a boy for *three years* before coming out as a lesbian. I think a fake engagement wouldn't faze them one bit."

"Three years?"

"Yeah. They moved in together and everything."

"That's…"

"Fucking crazy? I know, but she was scared. What's funny is that it was completely unnecessary because when she finally confessed and came out, my parents didn't care one bit. We joke about it all the time now." He squeezes my thigh again. "This'll just be another story we bring up at holiday gatherings for the next, oh, ten to twenty years."

That makes me feel marginally better, but I still don't feel right lying to *everyone* we know and love.

"I think we should tell Auden."

Fox peeks over at me, brows raised. "Are you sure?"

"I'm sure. I feel horrible lying to her. She should know."

"All right. Then we'll tell her."

"Hutch will know, too, then. They tell each other everything."

He grimaces at that but nods. "Okay."

There's a small part of me that's irritated he's being so accommodating yet again, but it's squashed the second he tightens his hand on my thigh, his grip having slid two inches higher without me noticing. My dress is bunched up dangerously high. If I were to move at all, I'd practically be flashing him.

Fox must notice, too, because I swear the air in the car shifts. We're both very aware of our close quarters and what happened the last time we were alone together. I don't know about him, but I damn sure felt relaxed afterward. I could use more of that right now, and I'm betting he could too.

"Are you ready for your game today? Are you feeling…relaxed?"

He swallows hard. "I could be…more relaxed."

The double entendre of our words is loud and clear, so it's no surprise that when Fox parks his car in front of my apartment building, he follows me inside without a word. The second my door is closed, he grabs me around the waist, tugging me against him and pressing his lips to mine in a hard kiss. It reminds me of the one in the restaurant, only this time, there's no one here to witness it. This kiss is all ours. It's not for show.

It's *real.*

Pressing my back against the door, he kisses me until I'm a breathless, panting mess. Even then, he doesn't stop. He just drags his lips lower, trailing them over my chin and my neck and right down to the top of the dress that just kisses my collarbones.

"This dress covers too much of you," he complains. "I want more."

"Then take it off."

With quick fingers, he unsnaps the buttons that come all the way up to my throat, his mouth following along with each flick of his wrist. He drags his tongue over my stomach, and the cool air that chases after the warmth sends shivers down my spine.

When he reaches the end of the buttons, he drops to his knees, bunching the skirt of the dress around my waist. His head disappears under it, and he picks up right where he left off. He doesn't stop, not even when he reaches my simple white cotton thong. No, he simply fits his mouth over me—through my underwear and everything—and licks.

"Holy…"

It's all I'm able to get out because I can only concentrate on him feathering his tongue against me, the material between us creating a deliciously playful barrier that makes this all that much hotter.

"Fuck," he says, his lips brushing against me. "I missed the taste of you."

I nod even though it's not a question because I missed this too, which is ridiculous if you think about it. We've had no business missing this at all, yet here we are, pawing at one another like we're unable to control ourselves.

Fox grabs my hand, bringing it to his head. "Show me how you like it, Lilah. Show me what you need right now."

I know what he's doing. He's giving me permission to take control again. And fuck if that doesn't make me like him even more.

I grip his hair tightly and tip his head back so I can look him in the eyes. "What I need is for you to stop talking and eat me like the good boy I know you can be."

His coffee-colored gaze sparks, and it's the last thing I see before I force his mouth back to me and get completely lost in ecstasy. Fox drives his tongue against me, sliding it over me again and again, and it's fucking magnificent. I don't have to tell or show him what I like. He knows. Still, I keep my hand in his hair, holding him to me tightly, not wanting to lose this feeling that's racing through me.

His touch is just the right amount of pressure and

just the right speed, and he's not just tasting me. He's worshipping me, stealing all the breath from my lungs. I don't know when he moves my underwear out of the way, but suddenly he's sucking my bare clit between his lips, and my orgasm barrels through me in a flash. My hips buck off the door, but Fox doesn't dare relent, and I ride his face through each and every wave that passes through me. He takes it all, enjoying it quite a bit if the pleasured growl that rolls through him means anything.

When the last of my shudders subside, Fox finally gives me some reprieve, pressing soft kisses to the inside of my thigh as he works to catch his breath.

"That was…" But he doesn't finish. He doesn't have to. I know exactly what he means.

I nod anyway and say, "Yeah. That was."

I'm not sure how much time passes before Fox finally pushes to his feet and slips his lips against mine. I don't even care that he tastes like me. Our kiss is slower and softer than before, but it doesn't make me want him any less. I drop my fingers to where his pretty shirt is tucked into his slacks and tug it free, needing to touch him in any way I can. He hisses when my hands slip underneath and I drag my nails over his soft skin.

"You're teasing again, sugar," he says, that drawl of his that only comes out every now and then thick.

"*I'm* teasing? You just ate my pussy like it was your last meal."

"Yeah, but that's all I had time for. My game."

Shit. Right. I completely forgot he has a game tonight. He probably has a million things to do before it, and I've already taken up enough of his time today.

"But you didn't…" I slide my hand lower, palming his cock that's lying hard against his thigh.

He grabs my wrist, stopping me with a shake of his head. "It's okay. I'm okay. That was enough."

"Fox—"

But he silences my protest with his lips, kissing me hard. So hard I can feel it in my chest.

Ba-boom.

Ba-boom.

Ba-boom.

Wait. That's not my heart.

It's my door.

"Lilah Jane Maddison! Open this door right this instant!"

Auden.

Fox's eyes widen, mirroring the surprise on my face.

"What the hell is she doing here?" I whisper.

He shrugs. "How am I supposed to know?"

"You're engaged?!" she yells through the door, which she promptly bangs on again. "To my boyfriend's goalie?! You'd better open this door or I'm using my key! Five!"

"Oh, fuck." I shove on Fox's chest, my fingers flying over the buttons of my dress, trying to make myself as presentable as I can after the orgasm I just had. "She means it."

Fox gulps loudly and shoves his shirt back into his slacks hastily.

I wipe at his mouth, still glistening from my orgasm. "Go wash your face."

He nods, thundering his way through my apartment.

"Left, left!" I whisper-yell when he goes right toward my spare bedroom instead of left to the bathroom.

He throws up a hand, then tucks himself inside. I blow out a breath, running my hands through my hair, hoping like hell that's enough. I'm sure my cheeks are stained red and my lips are swollen, but there's not much I can do about that.

"Come on, Lilah. I know you're in there. You think I can't hear you?" Auden says much quieter this time, almost pleadingly.

I can hear the betrayal in her voice, and it nearly kills me. I've been keeping something huge from her. I have to fix this. With one last fortifying breath, I pull open the door and come face to face with my very hurt-looking best friend.

"Auden, look, I can—"

"Explain? Oh, you bet your ass you're going to explain." She marches past me, barely missing running into me—though I don't think that was her intent—and whirls around, shoving her phone in my face. "What the hell, Lilah?"

It takes a second for my eyes to focus, and when they do, I can't believe what I see.

Lilah Maddison, Heiress to Maddison Holdings Empire, Engaged to Seattle Serpents Goaltender Arthur Fox

There's a photo of us from two hours ago, Fox on his knee before me as he places the ring on my finger. I have no idea who took the photo. I didn't see anyone with a camera. But then again, I was so focused on Fox and his beautiful words that there's every chance in the world I could have missed it.

What I want to know is *how* this information got out so quickly. Who could have possibly cared that much? Who could have been so quick to sell this photo? Who could have—

"My mother."

Auden's brows pinch together. "What?"

"My mother!" I say again, gnashing my teeth. Of course she did this. *That's* why she was so insistent on having lunch at that restaurant. She had someone planted and ready to take the shot so she could profit off this in some way. "This was all orchestrated by her."

"You're telling me you're engaged to Fox because of her?"

"Yes!" I toss my hands in the air. Technically, that is true, just maybe not in the way I'm letting on right now.

"I…" Auden shakes her head. "I'm confused. How does your mother even know Fox?"

"It's… I…" I huff. "Can we sit down?"

She doesn't respond, just turns on her heel and makes her way to my living room, plopping down on the couch. She crosses her arms and legs simultaneously, and it may look like she's waiting patiently, but I know that's far from true. I follow behind her, sitting on the other end, a few inches more than striking distance away, just in case she flies off the handle at what I'm about to tell her.

"I am engaged to Fox."

She gasps. "What the hell?! I—"

"But it's not what you think," I interrupt before she explodes more than she already has.

"Really?" She lifts her brows pointedly. "Because this photo looks like he's proposing to you, and you're wearing that tacky ring you've always hated on your finger. I thought you weren't into Fox. I thought you *didn't* have a crush on him. Have you been lying about that, too?"

I wince, fiddling with the ring that's felt like it

weighs a hundred pounds since Fox slipped it on. "Yeah, I guess that does look pretty bad. But there's more to the story."

"Then you better get to telling it because I'm really losing patience here. I know I've kept things from you before," she says, referring to when she snuck around with Hutch before they officially got together, "but this is *marriage*, Lilah. I didn't think you'd hide something that huge from me."

"I'm not hiding it. Not intentionally. It just sort of…got away from us, and I didn't know how to tell you."

She tips her head. "Well, I'm listening now."

"Remember how I told my mother I had a boyfriend because she was on my ass about having a date for my father's birthday party?"

"Of course I remember. You told me you found someone. You did not, however, mention that *someone* was Fox." She cuts me a nasty look that I completely deserve.

"Surprise?" She huffs, and I continue. "We…didn't mean for it to be this big."

"*How* did it get this big? How did this even start?"

"New Year's Eve. I was on the phone with my mother"—I hold my hand up when she tries to interject, likely about to lecture me about answering my mother's call—"and Fox heard her grilling me and being her usual snotty self, telling me she didn't believe I had a boyfriend."

"Told you so," Auden mutters, and she's right. She did tell me so. Perhaps if I had listened to her then, I wouldn't be in this situation now. "Let me guess, then: he stepped in to help you and agreed to be your date for the night?"

"Yes."

"I mean, I get that. It's Fox. He's the sweetest man alive. I'm not surprised he wanted to help you. I bet he'd stop every lane on I-5 during rush hour traffic if it meant helping a turtle cross the street."

I smile. She has no idea.

"I don't get how it went from one date to an engagement."

"*Fake* engagement. We're not really getting married." I finger the gaudy ring. "It's all to keep my parents off my back. I...I didn't want to lie to you, Auden. I swear it. But I'm too afraid to tell my mother the truth because I don't want to turn into the bitter old woman she is."

That last part tumbles out of me before I can stop the confession. I didn't mean to say it, but it feels good now that it's out there. Especially because that's exactly why I keep letting myself play this game with Fox.

I *don't* want to end up alone and bitter. I'm still not over the moon at the idea of marriage, but the idea of a relationship… Well, it doesn't sound so wild anymore. This pretending thing has made me realize there are definitely perks to it. It's nice to have someone who cares and remembers all the little things about you and doesn't find your quirks to be strange, but rather cute.

Someone like Fox.

I shake that thought away, my eyes drifting to the door of the bathroom he's currently hiding in. Auden came in with such a blaze that I nearly forgot he was here. Can he hear all this? What does he think of my admission?

"That is…" Auden sighs. "That is the dumbest thing I have ever heard."

I whip my head back, surprised. "What?"

"First of all, you're not going to end up bitter and alone like that old…that old…bitch!"

A laugh bubbles out of me. "You just called my mother a bitch."

"Well, am I wrong?"

I shake my head, still laughing. "No. No, you're not wrong at all. She's a total bitch."

"Secondly, I can't believe you two are dumb enough to cook up this plan. I mean, seriously? You're practically feeding Fox to the sharks. You know if you give your parents an inch, they'll take a mile. How did you not see this coming?"

"I don't know. I thought it would just get them off my back for a bit. I figured they hate me, so they wouldn't be invested like they are when it comes to Sadie."

"Please. Your mother seizes any chance she gets to take control."

Something about that sends a shudder down my spine. Am I like her more than I thought? Because I want to have control in the bedroom? And possibly even in the boardroom?

"So, are you actually getting married?"

"No!" The single word bursts out of me quickly. "No," I say, softer this time.

She nods, pleased by that answer. "Do you think your mother knows this is fake?"

"If you had asked me that before today, I might have said yes. But considering she's currently planning our engagement party as we speak, no."

"A party? You're going to fake this in front of everyone?"

I shrug. "What choice do we have? Tell everyone it's just a big hoax? Just come out and say, 'Oopsie. Our bad'? No. We're going to have the party, then break up. That's the plan."

"At least you have a plan. I certainly didn't with Hutch. One day, we were having a little fun, sleeping together, and—" Her eyes widen. "*No.*"

"What?"

"Tell me you're not sleeping with him."

"Wh-What?" I force a laugh. "Of course not. I... We're..." I groan. "Oh, who am I kidding? Yes, we've slept together. But it was only one time!"

And a half. But I don't tell her that.

I squeeze my thighs together, a reminder of what just happened against my front door. It's safe to say my high from the orgasm is long gone, and I could definitely go for another to chase away the tension that's already crept back into my shoulders.

"Lilah..." She titters, relaxing back into the couch for the first time since we sat down. "You're playing a dangerous game, you know that?"

I don't say anything because I don't know what to say. Of course I know we're playing a dangerous game. I'm well aware of that. But I can't seem to stop it.

I wonder if that's because I don't *want* to stop it.

"Look," she says, folding her hands in her lap. "You're an adult. You both are, so whatever you two are doing is entirely your decision. I just...I think you should be careful, Lilah. I know you don't believe in love or relationships or any of that stuff, but Fox does. He pretends he's like the other guys in the Serpents Singles Club, but I don't buy that. He's too sweet for that. He has a big heart, and I don't want to see him get hurt."

She doesn't have to clarify that she doesn't want to see *me* hurt him, but Fox and I know this is fake, and we're not pretending it's anything but. We won't get hurt because there are no feelings involved.

"Thank you. I promise to take your words to heart."

She nods. "All right. That's all I want. Have you told Sadie?"

I shake my head. "Not yet, but I guess that's another phone call I need to make. I'm sure my mother has already spread the word across the pond."

"That woman. I swear," Auden mutters.

Then we're quiet. We stay that way for a long time, not really saying anything, and I am acutely aware Fox is still in my apartment, potentially listening to all of this.

"Well, I'd better get going," Auden says after a while. She stands, pulling her purse over her shoulder. "I have some errands to run—and apparently a new dress to buy for your engagement party."

I try to hold back my groan as I follow her, walking her to the door, where she throws her arms around me. I hug her tightly, needing it more than I realize. I hate that Auden found out about this from anyone other than me, but I'm glad the secret is out now. It's been killing me to keep it from her. Plus, having someone other than Fox to talk to about it will be nice.

"Are you going to tell Hutch about this?" I ask, worrying my bottom lip between my teeth.

"Yes. He's my partner. I don't hide things from him."

I nod, understanding. "That's fair."

"But I won't tell anyone else. Not even Rory."

I exhale heavily, relieved. "Thank you. You're the *best* best friend in the whole world."

"I know," she says coolly.

We hug again, and Auden leaves, her warning ringing loudly in my ears.

Be careful, Lilah. I don't want to see him get hurt.

I am being careful. I won't hurt him. We know what this is. We know it's fake. We're fine. *This* is fine, right?

I press my back against the door, squeezing my eyes shut tight. I can't help but laugh at how different this moment is from when I was in this same position just a half hour ago, Fox between my legs.

Sweet Fox. Kind Fox. Fox, who *does* believe in love.

It's fine. We're fine, I tell myself, but I can't help the little bit of worry that creeps in at the edge of my thoughts. What if we aren't fine? What if we're blurring the lines too much?

And what if…what if I do the stupidest thing of all and fall for my fake fiancé?

Chapter 14

FOX

I am going straight to hell.

I heard every word between Lilah and Auden and never once did I do anything to tune them out.

I'm too afraid to tell my mother the truth because I don't want to turn into the bitter old woman she is.

Is that what Lilah thinks will happen? Does she not see how incredible she is? With parents like hers who believe she's not good enough no matter what she does, I'm betting not.

They must have really done a number on her over the years if she believes she's like her mother, though. She's not. I know I haven't spent much time with the woman, but I know Lilah is nothing like her. Sure, she likes control, and her mother clearly does too, but it's different. Lilah doesn't want to control *other* people. She just wants to be in control of *her,* and who doesn't want that? Who doesn't want a say in their own lives?

I push off the tub's ledge, looking in the mirror for the first time. Fuck, I look a wreck. Thanks to Lilah's hands, my hair is sticking up everywhere, and I look tired, probably because this is when I'm usually taking my pre-game nap, not hiding in a bathroom. This whole thing has gotten much more out of hand than I ever thought it might. It was just supposed to be one party, one evening of faking it. Now, we're hosting an engagement party.

I could have said no, though. At any point, I could have told Selene to fuck off, and I could have told Lilah I was out. Yet, I couldn't. I took one look at the woman sitting next to me and saw that defeat in her eyes as her mother made snide remarks about her, and I couldn't do it. I couldn't leave her to battle them alone.

So, I got down on one knee, spoke from my heart, and asked Lilah to marry me. Sure, it was fake, but fuck, I'd be a fool if I didn't admit there was a tiny part of me that got lost in the moment. It almost felt real for just a fraction of a second.

We're going to have the party, then break up. That's the plan.

That's been our plan all along, and I've been fine with that, but now? Now, I don't know what I want. I rub at my chest, not liking the idea of breaking up with Lilah one bit, which is silly.

I shake away the thought and do my business, cleaning off my face and washing my hands. After spending far too much time in the bathroom even after Auden is gone, I do my best to gather my wits and gently pull the door open. I peek my head around the frame and find Lilah standing with her back fitted against the front door, just where I had her earlier.

She looks shaken, completely out of sorts. The urge to put her back together hits me strong, and I march over to her, intending to do just that.

"You okay?" I ask her softly.

Her eyelids flutter open at my intrusion. She nods. "I'm all right. Are you?"

"Why wouldn't I be?"

She points her thumb toward the door. "Because my mother is definitely the one responsible for the 'leak' about our engagement. It's splashed all over the internet now, and it won't just be Hutch who knows. It'll be all of them. There's no hiding this thing now."

She's right. We can't hide this anymore. But that was going to happen anyway with the engagement party, right? It's not like we could have kept hiding this for much longer.

"Do I love how this all came out? No, but we were going to tell Auden and Hutch anyway, right?"

"True. But—"

"Then it's okay." I close the remaining distance

between us. Not just because I want to reassure her but because I can't seem to help myself. I need to touch her. I tip her chin up toward me, her beautiful blue eyes a little duller than when I left her earlier. "It's okay. We're in this together, remember?"

She gives me a half smile. "Stop being so nice."

"No. You like that I'm nice."

She puffs out a breath. "Yeah. Yeah, I do. I just… Aren't you worried at all?"

"No."

"No? Do you think Auden knew you were here?"

"I don't know, and I don't care. The only thing I'm worried about right now is getting this dress off you."

Her brows pull together, but there's no mistaking the spark that comes back into her gaze. "But what about your game? Aren't you usually napping right now?"

I am usually napping at this time, but this whole day has already been screwed up as it is. Why not throw that out the window too? "Nap with me."

"With you?"

"Yeah. I have my suit in my truck already, and that's really all I need. I'm good. I can stay here as long as you want."

Her eyes brighten, as if she's surprised I knew what she needs right now is to not be alone. But she shouldn't be surprised. Lilah isn't that hard to read if you look for the right things.

"Are you sure?" she asks.

"Sugar, if you're asking me if I'm sure I want to go to bed with you, then yes, I am very, very sure of that."

She smirks. "I think we both know if we go back to my room, there won't be any sleeping happening."

"Oh, no. How sad."

She laughs at my monotone voice, and I haul her to me, kissing the laughter away. It's not long before it turns into something more, and I'm lifting her, her legs hooking together around my waist. My cock brushes right against her clit, which I know is covered by nothing more than a scrap of material.

"Arthur…" She moans my name, writhing against me. "I need…"

"I know what you need," I say, turning and carrying her through her apartment to her bedroom, her lips on my neck the whole time.

I drop her softly onto her bed, undoing the buttons she hastily redid to greet Auden, and I can't help my chuckle when I see just how many she got wrong.

"What's so funny?" she asks, eyes half open, already lost in the pleasure.

"Your buttons. They're cattywampus."

"Cattywampus?" She giggles.

"What? That's what we say in the South."

She shakes her head, rolling her eyes. "You're ridiculous."

"Yeah," I say, working the last of her buttons free and pressing my lips right above her belly button. "You like it though."

She sighs. "For the life of me, I can't figure out why, but I do."

"I'm telling you…" I trail my lips higher, kissing between her breasts. "It's the goalie stretches."

"Those damn"—a long sigh as I close my mouth around her nipple—"goalie stretches."

I tease her through her bra, loving the feel of the lace against my tongue. I don't know if she always wears lacy bras like this, but fuck, I hope so.

"God, that feels good," she murmurs as I pull her other nipple into my mouth.

It does. It feels so damn good. *She* feels good.

I tease her for I don't even know how long, but I know for certain I'm not getting a nap before the game tonight. It's worth it, though, especially hearing her little sighs and moans as I slip my hand beneath her dress, circling her clit with my thumb.

"Shit," I mutter. "You're so fucking wet for me, sugar."

"All for you," she agrees, panting and arching her hips to meet my touch, needing more.

She pulls at me like she's trying to drag me even closer than I already am.

I kiss up her neck until my lips are ghosting against hers. "What do you need, Lilah?"

"Your cock."

I smirk against her, loving her bluntness. Why does she have no problem speaking her mind to anyone but her parents?

"Yes, ma'am," I say, and she hums happily.

"I kind of like that."

I thought she might, but I don't say that. Instead, I do as she requests, working myself free from my pants, not bothering to undress fully before I press against her. She widens her legs, giving me space.

"Fucking hell," I mutter, kissing the corner of her mouth. "How do you feel this good with something between us?"

"How do *you*?" she asks, sliding her soaked pussy against me.

I rock against her again, even though I know I shouldn't. I need a condom, but the last thing I want to do is move. I just want to feel her. *All* of her.

"Please," she begs. "Fuck me already, Fox."

"Condom," I tell her, and she shakes her head. "No?"

"IUD. Haven't been with anyone in six months."

"Me too." Longer, actually, but I don't tell her that. "My last test was good."

"Then what are you waiting for? I need—"

Lilah doesn't finish that sentence. She can't. She's too busy not breathing as I pull her panties aside and slam into her without warning.

"Holy fucking shit."

I bury my head into her neck with a groan, unable to move. I'm scared if I do, I'm going to come instantly. She's so warm and tight and absolutely perfect. Nothing can ever get better than this.

"Move," she pleads into my ear. "I need you to move."

"I don't know if I can."

"Why?"

"Because, Lilah, your cunt is wrapped around me like a vise, and if I move, I'm going to come." Her breath stutters in my ear, and I pull back, looking down at her. "Is that what you want? You want me to fill you up, sugar?"

"God, yes," she says as I rock into her lightly. "Fill me, Arthur. Fuck me hard and fill me with your cum."

So, I do. I pull out until just the tip of my cock sits inside her, then I slam in again. Over and over, fucking her hard and fast with no remorse until her nails are digging into my back and she's arching into me, screaming my name in my ear.

"Come," she demands. "Come with me."

I thrust into her again and again, and then I'm doing just as I promised—I fill her up until I can feel myself leaking out of her. I don't know what drives me to do it. Maybe it's the heat of the moment or something else animalistic inside of me, but I pull out of her and replace my cock with my fingers, pushing all that cum back inside her, wanting to know that while I'm in net tonight, she's sitting at home with a bit of me inside her.

I pull my cum-soaked fingers from her, taking them right to her mouth. She opens willingly, tasting the two of us together, moaning around my digits with appreciation. She giggles when she feels my cock twitch against her leg.

"Ready again so soon?" she asks, her tongue teasing me still.

I slide my eyes to hers. "I just watched you eat my cum off my fingers. Yes, I am definitely ready again."

Another laugh as she pulls me down for a kiss, and I let her because I need to kiss her again. We stay like that for a long while, our mouths moving together until the last minute when I absolutely have to move or else I'm going to be late to the game.

"So much for a nap," she says as I pull away, somehow knowing what's coming next.

"Maybe it's for the best. I wasn't playing the greatest before. This could be a new tradition."

"I've always wanted to be someone's good luck charm."

"You can be mine, Lilah."

I kiss her again, then push off her, tucking my cock back into my pants. I pull her up, then make my way to her adjoining bathroom, where I wash up the best I can.

"Hey, Fox?" she calls, and I peek my head back into the room.

She's sitting on the edge of the bed, her dress still undone, her tits visible through the lace of her bra. Her hair is a complete mess, and if I look close enough, I can see the spots where I nipped at her neck as I fucked her. Is it wrong for me to want those marks to stay?

"Yes?" I say.

"How did you know?"

"Know what?"

"How did you know I like…" She exhales heavily. "That I like being in control?"

I don't know how I knew. Maybe it was just intuition. Maybe it was something else along the way. Or maybe it was even *me* wanting to give up that control. Either way, I had a gut feeling it was something we both needed.

I use the towel hanging near the door to dry my hands, then pad back out to her, stopping at her feet. I tip her head back until she's peering up at me.

"I don't know. But you like it, right?"

It takes her a moment, but she nods. "I do. Do you?"

"I do." Her shoulders relax at my affirmation. "And that's all that matters, isn't it?"

She nods again, pushing her shoulders back, that confidence of hers that I admire so much coming back full force. "Yes, that's all that matters."

I kiss her again, this time keeping it brief, and she walks me to her door with a promise of watching my game. Not until I'm tucked inside the elevator do I realize just how well and truly fucked I am.

Because this thing with Lilah? It's starting to feel less and less fake, and damn if that doesn't scare me.

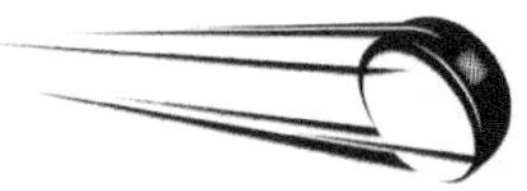

"Well fucking well."

I groan inwardly as I step into the locker room about twenty minutes behind my usual arrival time, something I'd gladly do again if it meant feeling Lilah come apart beneath me like she did. As I expected,

Lawson, Hayes, Keller, Hutch, and Locke are all standing in a circle near my stall.

And all of them are looking right at me.

"I take it you've heard."

How could they not? It was plastered all over the internet in record time. I've already had a phone call from my brother and sister, both of which I've ignored.

"Oh, we've heard all right," Lawson says, apparently speaking for everyone. "We heard you're a snake who doesn't tell us a damn thing. I *knew* something was going on with all that bumping and grinding you were doing on the dance floor at the party."

Keller smacks him on the back of his head. "Stop saying that. It's lame."

"You're lame," Lawson tosses back, rubbing at the spot Keller just hit. He turns back to me. "Got anything you want to say to us?"

"Uh, your mom says hello?"

Hayes snickers, holding his fist out for me to bump. "Nice."

Lawson ignores us both, barreling ahead. "I can't believe you didn't tell us you're getting married. To *Lilah*. We, like, know her and shit."

I shrug. "It's not like I was planning it. It just sort of…happened."

A snort draws my attention, and I look directly at Hutch for the first time. The smirk on his lips tells me he's already had a discussion with his girlfriend and is well aware of the predicament Lilah and I are in. I snap my gaze away from him, afraid I might break down and confess everything if I don't.

"What do you mean you weren't planning on it? Did you just propose randomly? That's not very romantic."

"What the hell do you know about romance, Lawsy?"

"Guarantee it's more than you, Mr. Never Been Kissed."

Keller opens his mouth to respond but closes it just as quickly, shaking his head like arguing with Lawson isn't worth his time.

"Wait. Holy shit!" Lawson's eyes are wide. "Is that your thing? Are you a virgin?"

"No, and your mom can confirm it."

Lawson steps toward him, and Keller grins, only further proving my theory that he enjoys fighting just a bit too much.

Locke grabs them both, pulling them apart. "All right, all right. That's enough. We don't need a fight before the game. And besides, we're not asking the important questions." He looks at me. "When did you and Lilah start dating?"

"A while ago," I say, keeping it vague like Lilah had before.

"Is *that* why you were bumping and grin—*oof.*" Lawson doubles over from the punch Keller lands on his stomach. He rubs at it, grimacing and throwing daggers our grumpy teammate's way. "Is that why you were dancing together on New Year's?"

"Yeah, that's why."

"Then why didn't you tell us?" Lawson actually sounds hurt, and I hate the guilt that moves through me.

I also hate all the lying.

You're doing this for Lilah, I remind myself. *Just play the part.*

"It was new," I explain. "We've been quietly seeing one another for a while, and on New Year's Eve, I just had a moment, you know? Like one of those 'fuck it' ones. I looked over at her and knew she was the one."

It's not entirely untrue. I did look over at Lilah and say "fuck it" when I stepped in to help her. The rest is a lie, though.

Hutch snorts again, but I ignore him, worried if I look his way, the truth will be written all over my face, but Locke doesn't disregard him. No, he looks over at our captain, and I watch a silent conversation move between them. What they're saying is as clear as day.

You know something, Locke's gaze says.

You bet your ass I do, Hutch responds.

He's lying? Locke asks.

Oh, he's big-time lying, Hutch confirms.

I gulp, glad Keller, Lawson, and Hayes are locked in an argument about whether my impromptu proposal was romantic or stupid. If you ask me, I don't think any of them would know romance if it bit them in the ass, especially Lawson. Maybe that's why Rory is so into him. She's not touchy-feely, and Lawson is as unromantic as they come.

Lawson finally throws his hands up, fed up with it all, and steps forward, wrapping his arms around me and hugging me until I'm forced to hug him back.

"Completely idiotic or not, we're happy for you, buddy. And I, for one, can't wait to be your best man."

"Thanks," I tell him. "You're not my best man, though."

He pulls away, his face crumpled in hurt. "But… but…best friends."

"For fuck's sake." Keller rolls his eyes with a groan. "Go get ready for the game."

Lawson walks away, grumbling something about friendship hierarchy, and I'm certain I've not heard the last of his feelings on it.

Keller steps up, clapping me once on the shoulder. "Congrats, man. I think you're dumb as fuck for getting married because it ruins your life, but congrats."

"Thank you. I think."

He shrugs, then pushes past me. He heads for his stall to get ready, his brows drawn tighter together than I've seen in a while, like something has him upset. I make a mental note to check in on him later.

"Happy for you," Hayes says, giving me an awkward pat on the head. "Quinn likes Lilah, so that's good enough for me."

I nod at him as he moves away. Then it's just me, Hutch, and Locke, both looking too smug.

"What?" I ask.

They exchange a glance. I don't like it one bit.

Locke breaks first, grinning. "Nothing, man. Very happy for you with this sudden turn of events."

But he doesn't *sound* happy. He sounds like he knows something, and it's got me feeling all kinds of nervous.

"I think you and Lilah are perfect together."

"You do?"

"Sure." Again, he doesn't sound sure, but I don't have the chance to say anything else before he walks away, leaving me to face Hutch alone.

When I finally get the courage to look my captain in the eyes, I know I'm in for a major ass-chewing.

I sigh. "Just get on with it."

"Get on with what? I wasn't going to say anything."

I grind my molars together. "Yes, you were, so just say it."

He lifts a shoulder. "I really don't have anything to say, Fox, and if I did, I'm sure it wouldn't be anything you didn't hear earlier from Auden."

Fuck. I guess that confirms that Auden knew I was in Lilah's apartment.

"Look," I say, stepping closer and lowering my voice so the other guys don't hear, "I know it sounds crazy, but it's totally fake, okay? We know what we're doing here."

Another grin, and for the first time ever, I want to take a page out of Keller's book and throw a punch to make it disappear. I'm not usually a violent man, but I hate this feeling, as if Hutch has one up on me or something. I don't think he'd ever do anything to betray Lilah and me and tell anyone, but still. It makes me feel so…bad.

I hate feeling bad. I want to be good.

Good boy.

Lilah's words ring through my head, and I try to push them away. I don't need to be having thoughts like that right now. The only thing I need to be focusing on is this game. That's it.

"As long as you don't let whatever this is get in

the way of your game, I don't give a shit what you do in your free time, Fox. Even if I do think you're playing the biggest game of chicken I've ever seen and think it's going to completely bite you in the ass. That's your game and your ass. I'm staying out of this one."

Even though his words aren't entirely encouraging, mainly because he thinks what we're doing is monumentally stupid, they still comfort me.

"Thanks," I mumble.

"But I will say this." Hutch takes a step toward me, so close now that I can smell the fancy Armani cologne I know he spent entirely too much money on. "If you hurt Lilah in any way at all, I will break every bone in each of your legs and laugh while I do it. I will hurt you so fucking bad you'll never play a game of hockey again. Understood?"

His words piss me off, and probably not in the way he expects.

"I would never do anything to hurt her. *Ever.* I'm doing her a favor, okay? I *want* to do this for her. So you don't have to worry about me hurting her. Lilah is…" I shake my head. "I would never hurt her, Hutch. Ever. I swear it on everything that I am."

His thick brows slowly inch upward, surprise coating his features, and I don't like it one bit.

"What?" I bark at him.

Yet another fucking grin as he shakes his head. "Nothing, Fox. Nothing at all."

Then he plops down in his stall next to mine and begins his all-too-familiar routine to prep for the game, leaving me gaping after him. I don't know how long I stand there, but it's so long that Coach comes into the room and asks me what the hell I'm doing.

"Sorry, Coach," I say, finally taking a seat and beginning my pregame process.

"You good?" he asks.

I nod as I start taking off the fancy dress shoes I changed into in my truck, the same place I put my suit on. I should have probably just taken it back up to Lilah's place to change, but I was too scared if I went up there, I wouldn't be able to leave again. "Yeah, I'm good."

He gives me one last look before continuing through the room, and I try my best to focus on the task at hand. It's hard, though. My thoughts are jumping all over the place, from Lilah to Hutch to Locke to Coach and back to Lilah again. Round and round they go.

And that's where they stay, even as we dress and hit the ice for warmups, all throughout the national anthem and even through the first period. It's not until we hit the locker room after the final buzzer and the guys going wild to celebrate my forty-one-save shutout that I realize I haven't once panicked about the game. It was the first time in a long time I wasn't completely stuck in my head and didn't force the team to play on their heels the entire time.

When I climb into my truck, my mind still reeling, I don't steer toward home. I go to Lilah's…and I think it's exactly where I'm meant to be.

Chapter 15

"Sadie is going to be so sad she missed this."

"I thought she was mad at you because she had to hear about your engagement from your mother."

"Well, yeah, but you know how it goes with sisters. We're mad, but if there's a common enemy, then…"

Auden nods, understanding perfectly. "Did you *tell her* tell her? You know, about the *fakeness*?" She mouths the last word, not that it was needed. I knew exactly what she was getting at.

"I did. She thinks it's brilliantly stupid, whatever that means."

Auden makes a noise I can't quite decipher, but I don't indulge her on it. I'm too busy watching my mother plan my whole life before my eyes. I sigh, and Auden follows my gaze.

"Remind me again why we're doing this?" she asks.

"Because it's fun?"

Auden's eyes slide right to where my mother is about thirty feet away, browsing through invitation options for my engagement party. "There are a lot of things I would say are fun, and going wedding shopping with your mother is not one of them. Especially for a fake wedding."

"Shh!" I admonish, glancing at my mother, who is paying us absolutely zero attention. That's pretty much been what the entire afternoon has been like, and I'm starting to wonder why I'm even here.

"She doesn't even know we're here. We could probably walk out of this store, and you wouldn't hear from her for an hour or more."

"And what? Miss picking out the perfect engagement party stationery that's going to inevitably end up in the trash?" I run my finger over the board that's full of paper examples. "This doesn't seem very green. Can't I just send everyone an e-invite?"

Auden snorts loudly, *finally* earning my mother's attention, but all she does is glare at us. Auden, being Auden, waves at my mother. Her glare deepens, and I have to turn my head, covering my lips with my hand so she doesn't see my smile. My mother turns back to the many paper options, back to ignoring us.

"Seriously, why are we here? It's not like this relationship is going to last past this party," Auden complains for at least the fourth time. "Let's go get burritos."

My stomach rumbles as if on cue. "Ugh, that sounds so good. I'm starving."

"Then let's sneak away. She'll never know."

"Are you kidding me? Selene knows all."

"She doesn't know you're faking it with the goalie."

"Auden!" I hiss at her, and all she does is grin.

Teasing me has become her favorite pastime since she learned about Fox and me. Even when the Serpents were on their bye week and I spent the whole time rolling around the sheets with my *very* flexible fake fiancé, she was still texting me daily with jokes, GIFs, and memes. Now, with the team on a six-day road trip, I've become her focus with Hutch gone. She's made me recount everything going on with Fox at least ten times. When we aren't talking about it, I've been talking about it with my mother, who is suddenly *very* invested and wants to be part of every moment, especially planning our engagement party. Personally, I think she just likes the idea of being able to control yet another aspect of my life. If she can't pick who I'm marrying, you bet your ass she's going to have a say in everything else.

It somehow makes Fox's absence even harder because now I don't even have anyone to relieve all this stress with, and I could really relieve some stress right now. And maybe some of his cheesy jokes. His Southern drawl. A few well-placed *sugars*. Really, anything to distract me from the fact that we're planning a party that doesn't mean a thing other than to signal the end of the weirdest contract negotiation of my life.

"You're thinking of him, aren't you?"

I peek over at Auden. "What?"

"Fox. You're thinking about him."

I huff out a laugh. "Uh, no. I am not."

"Yes, you are. Naughty thoughts, too." She pokes my cheek. "You're blushing."

I swat her hand away. "Stop it. No, I'm not."

"You are. You are, and you like him. You really like him." She sings this, not a care in the world who hears her. "You wanna fu—"

"Ms. Sinclair!"

Auden's back snaps straight, and her eyes widen. Slowly, she turns to look at my mother, who is standing right behind her, a pinched expression on her face. "Hi, Selene."

My mother narrows her eyes at her. "We're finished here. Let's go grab lunch."

"Wait," I say. "We're done?"

"Yes," my mother calls over her shoulder, already moving past us to the door. "You're doing cream with pearlescent for the engagement party. There's a classic silver ribbon for the engagement invites. I would have loved to have knocked out the wedding invitations today too, but since you're dragging your feet about setting a date, this will have to do."

Auden snickers, and I shoot her a glare.

"Shouldn't we wait for Fo—Arthur to make the final decision?" I ask my mother.

She huffs. "It's like decorating a house. Men don't want to be part of this kind of thing. Trust me."

"Actually, Reed was heavily involved in the decision-making for building our house, especially when it came to decorating," Auden says.

"When are you getting married again, dear?"

She's baiting Auden, and my best friend is doing her best not to bite.

"We're not engaged."

"Ah, right." My mother smiles victoriously over her shoulder, effectively ending the discussion.

Auden and I look at one another, rolling our eyes simultaneously as we trudge up a hill after the Wicked Witch. I have no idea where we're going, but I'm guessing this was all planned as part of her outing today. When she called this morning and asked if I had looked at invitations yet, I asked her if she was completely insane because it was six AM, but I wasn't at all expecting that to lead to us spending the day together. Yet here we are.

She's wrong, though. I think if this were real, Fox *would* care what kind of invitations we have. Well, maybe not exactly that, but he'd want to be involved. He doesn't seem like the kind of guy who just sits back. He'd want to have a say in his own wedding.

Guilt climbs up my throat, and it's not the first time that's happened today. Doing anything wedding related feels so…wrong. Not just because this is fake but because I know how Fox really feels. I know that, unlike me, he wants a relationship someday, a wedding —a *real* one, not whatever this has turned into.

Party, then break up, I remind myself. I'm not stealing anything from him. It's just a party.

As we pass by a store, something sitting on the glass shelf in the window stops me in my tracks. It takes Auden a moment to realize I've stopped and my mother even longer.

"What are you doing, Lilah Jane? We have a reservation we need to make."

"I just need a moment. I need to…"

I pull open the door to the shop, heading right to the display I saw from the street. I gently pick up the turtle figurine that looks like it's made of glass, rock, wood, and I don't even know what else. It's so unique and so Fox that I have to have it. I carry it to the register at the back of the shop, Auden behind me the whole time while my mother stands in the doorway of the kitschy little shop looking like she'd rather be anywhere else in the world.

"What is that?" Auden asks, standing behind me as I hand it to the person behind the checkout counter.

"It's a turtle made from materials found on Alki Beach. Beautiful, isn't it?"

"Very," I tell them, tapping my card to pay.

"Would you like it wrapped?"

"That'd be wonderful."

"Since when are you into turtles?" Auden asks as they wrap the adorable figurine I know Fox is going to love.

"It's not for me."

Her brows pinch together. "Then who is it—" Her face lights up. "Oh."

"What?" I say, not at all liking the look she's giving me. It's one of those obnoxiously knowing looks. I just wish I knew what she knew.

"Nothing," she says with a shrug.

"Here you go," the worker says, handing me the wrapped gift.

"Thank you," I tell them before turning back to Auden. "What were you going to say?"

"I wasn't going to say anything."

I hold back my irritated groan. "Yes, you were. About the turtle."

"It's a lovely turtle. That's all."

I glare at her, but she doesn't budge, refusing to tell me whatever it was she was going to say. No, she just smiles, and it's the most annoying smile in the world.

"Whatever," I mumble, exiting the shop with another thank-you to the worker and another dirty look from my mother.

She speeds ahead of Auden and me—seriously, how does she walk so fast in those heels with these hills?—as we continue on our way to the restaurant. We don't talk, we just keep walking, my mother complaining about how late we are because I just *had* to stop for a little trinket.

I ignore her, my mind thousands of miles away, all the way in Toronto. I wish I could say this is the first turtle I've bought since Fox has been gone, but it's not. It's just the first one Auden's seen me buy. I can't seem to stop myself, though. Every time I come across a turtle now, all I can think of is the sweet Southern boy who has made it his mission to save each and every one.

"It's for Fox," I tell Auden quietly as we stand inside the restaurant, my mother talking to the maître d', explaining to them that we're late because of her daughter. I'd be bothered by her throwing me under the bus if not for Auden, who is *still* sporting that damn grin.

"I kind of figured."

"He collects them."

"That's cute." Still grinning.

"It's not a big deal."

"Okay," she says, but she doesn't sound like she believes me at all. If anything, it sounds like she thinks it *is* a big deal. A very big deal.

And worse? I think she might be right.

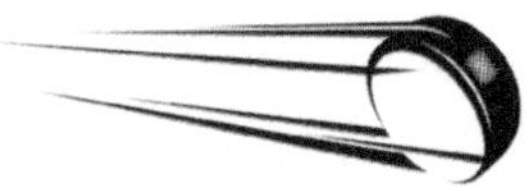

"Go, go, go!" I scream at the TV, knowing full well Lawson can't hear me as he flies down the ice, the puck on his stick as he skates farther and farther away from the opposition.

He drags the puck back, and it goes right over the goalie's shoulder and into the net.

"Yes!" I jump off my couch, stomping my feet in excitement as the camera pans over to Fox, who skates to the bench where the other players are going wild.

The Serpents are up three goals, the only one from Minnesota coming from a deflected shot that Fox had no chance to stop. Or at least that's what the commentators said, and I trust their judgment more than mine considering I still don't really know much about hockey, just that I've come to love watching it. I've found myself glued to my TV since Fox has been on the road, not wanting to miss a single minute of his games. I've tried not to read too much into that.

The players on the ice skate along the bench, high-fiving their joyful-looking teammates, and each one gives Fox a tap. Even with his nerdy *The Lord of the Rings* mask featuring a drawing of Gandalf surrounded by "You Shall Not Pass" in elvish-styled font, you can see him smiling.

He's having fun. He's having *so* much fun. It's so different from the Fox I watched a few weeks ago. He looks relaxed, totally at ease. Even when the teams start battling in front of him, shoving their sticks anywhere they can get them, he still looks calm and collected, like nothing in the world can touch him.

I don't know for certain if it has anything to do with our "relaxation" sessions, but I certainly don't think they've been hurting things. We have video-chatted every night since he left. It all started when I sent him a picture of his sock, which he couldn't seem to find the last time he was here. It was stuck behind my dresser, and I still have no clue how it got there since we didn't even get close to it. Still, I sent him the photo one night after his game, and he called me immediately. One thing led to another, and I ended up with my clothes off, both of us panting into the phone.

They've won every game since.

The puck is dropped at center ice, and this time,

Minnesota wins it back. They dump the puck into the Serpents' zone, then chase after it, winning it in the end. It all happens so fast—Fox is calm, making save after save as they throw pucks on net repeatedly, then the next, he's on his ass, and the goal horn sounds throughout the arena.

The crowd goes wild, and the Serpents stand there stunned. So do I.

"That was interference! That was goaltender interference right there!" the commentator for the Serpents says emphatically. "No way that goal isn't coming back."

The woman on the other mic agrees with him, and they begin talking rules and blue paint and even bring in some analyst who used to be a referee while the officials on the ice huddle by the penalty and watch the play over and over on a tablet. They show the clip on TV, the commentators breaking down exactly why the goal is going to be turned over, and I couldn't agree more. There's no way it's going to stand.

"Oh, oh. We've got a decision. We have a decision," the female commentator announces as the official skates to the middle of the ice.

"After reviewing the play, it was determined there was *not* goaltender interference. We have a good goal."

The arena erupts, and the camera pans to the

Serpents' bench. They're pissed. Hell, *I'm* pissed, and I'm not even playing the game.

"That was bullshit!" I yell at my TV, again not caring that they can't hear me.

But all of our arguing is pointless. The game continues, and even after conceding that goal, the Serpents manage to score on an empty net and pad their lead. They walk away all smiles because they've won their fifth in a row.

Not that I'd ever admit it to anyone—not even Auden—but I spend the next two and a half hours pacing my apartment, my phone in hand as I wait on his call. I've all but given up, tucked cozy in my bed and nearly asleep when my phone rattles against my bedside table. I flick my light on, grinning when I see the name on the screen.

"That was one hundred percent interference."

Fox laughs at my greeting and sits back against the headboard in his hotel room. "Yeah? You a rules expert now?"

"Of course I am. I also have eyes. His own teammate pushed him into you. They should have called it back."

He scratches at the stubble on his cheek, and I try to act like I don't miss the feel of it between my legs. "Yeah, probably. But we still won."

I smile. "You still won." I settle into my own bed. "Where are you?"

"The Sinclair St. Louis. We just got in. It was a quick flight." He lets out a yawn. "How was your day?"

My heart thumps in my chest. It's such a simple question, but I like it all the same. I've never really had someone who cared about how my day was before.

It's all fake, Lilah. Don't get used to it.

"It was good," I tell him, ignoring the thoughts trying to push through my mind. "Auden and I got pedicures."

"That sounds nice. Been a while since I've had one."

My brows rise. "*You* get pedicures?"

"Yeah. Why does that surprise you?"

"I don't know. I don't think I've ever dated a man who admitted to that," I say as he shifts around in the bed, trying to get comfortable.

There's a slight pause, and it takes me a moment to realize what's caused it.

I don't think I've ever dated a man who admitted to that.

Shit. It makes it sound like what we're doing is real. I don't know why I phrased it that way. Perhaps just a slip of the tongue or maybe something more. Either way, Fox continues, acting as if nothing happened, and I'm surprised at the relief that floods me.

"Not manly enough of me?"

"No, no." I shake my head. "If anything, I like that you admit it. Most guys wouldn't. They'd just sneak in and out of the shop, then scoff when other men bring it up."

"I used to go with my mom."

"You used to get pedicures with your mom?"

"Stop looking at me like that." I'm rewarded with another one of those rare scowls of his, and just like before, I enjoy it far too much.

"Like what?"

"Like that's the sweetest thing you've ever heard."

"Well, that *is* the sweetest thing I've ever heard."

"Even sweeter than me trying to save the turtles?"

I look at my nightstand where three figurines sit, the ones I've collected for him in his absence. I can't believe how excited I am to give them to him.

"Eh, I don't know about that," I say, looking back into the camera.

His signature grin comes back. He flicks his chin toward me. "Did I wake you?"

I look down at my flannel pajamas dotted with white circles on a pink background. "No. I wasn't asleep yet." It's not technically a lie. "Too wound up over that bad call to sleep."

He laughs. "Careful, you're starting to sound like an actual hockey fan."

I think I *am* an actual hockey fan now, and it has

everything to do with the brown eyes grinning at me all the way from Missouri.

"Since you played tonight, you won't be playing tomorrow, right?"

"Nah. It's Dash's net tomorrow night. But that's good. He has a better record against St. Louis than I do."

"Do you keep track of all that stuff?"

"Eh, sometimes. Usually, I try to ignore all the stats and shit like that, but sometimes it comes in handy. Some teams just have a goalie figured out, you know? Don't want to hop in the net if that's the case and give up those two points."

"You guys are number two now, you know."

"Heard some rumblings."

It's clear from the smile teasing his lips he's well aware of this and damn proud of it. He should be, too. I've seen how hard he's been working. I know their play earlier in the year weighed on him, especially his own, but it seems he's finally finding his groove.

He sits forward, then tugs his shirt over his head, falling back against the headboard, his hair now a wreck. Though I've seen him shirtless countless times, I still find my mouth drying at the sight of him, the dim hotel light casting the most delicious of shadows. He looks tired, but a good tired. Like he's spending his time doing what he loves and wouldn't trade it for anything in the world. I like him like this.

"Lilah?"

"Hmm?" I ask, pulling my attention back to him.

He chuckles lightly. "I asked what color you got for your pedicure."

It's so silly, but I like that he asks, that he cares enough to ask.

Fake, Lilah, I remind myself, something I've had to do much too frequently lately.

"Blush. We figured since Valentine's Day is coming up, we'd get something girlie."

He frowns. "We're on the road then."

"When?"

"Valentine's Day."

Disappointment tumbles through me, and I try to push it away as quickly as it comes. Why the hell I'm disappointed by that, especially when I've never cared about Valentine's Day before, I don't know.

I lift a shoulder, trying to appear unbothered. "That's okay."

"I'll make it up to you."

"Fox, I don't expect you to take me out for Valentine's Day."

"What if I want to?" he challenges, tilting his chin up.

If it were anyone else, I'd fight them on this, but for some reason, I *want* Fox to take me out.

"Fine," I relent, rolling my eyes to make it seem like I'm doing *him* a favor. "We can do something."

"Good." He grins, and I have to shuffle around because I swear the simple action goes right between my legs. "I'll plan something."

"I like diamonds. Big ones," I tease.

"Noted," he says, and it's a little *serious*.

"I'm kidding. Don't you dare get me diamonds, Arthur Whatever Your Middle Name Is Fox."

"Francis."

I can't help it—I laugh, and it warrants *another* scowl from Fox.

"I'm sorry, I'm sorry," I say once I finally settle down. "Arthur Francis? Are you sure your parents love you?"

"Very much. I might even be the favorite child."

"You're the oldest, which means you're automatically *not* the favorite. Trust me, I know from experience." I have never been my parents' favorite, not even in all that time before Sadie came along, and *especially* not after. "The youngest always wears the favorite crown. Though I'm not exactly sure how that works if your younger siblings are twins."

"That'd be Russ, then. He's the baby by five minutes." He yawns, reaching up to scratch at his chest. "And that's not always how it works. Your parents just suck."

I snort. "You can say that again."

He opens his mouth to do just that, and I cut him a glare. He laughs, but it's cut short with another yawn.

"Sorry," he says, scrubbing a hand over his face. "These long road trips start to catch up to me near the end."

"Do you like them?"

"I used to love them."

"What changed?"

He doesn't say anything, but he doesn't have to. The red stealing up his cheeks says it all for him.

Me. I'm what changed that for him. The craziest part of all? I *want* to be the reason he misses home. My breath quickens, and for the first time since our nightly phone calls began, it has nothing to do with anything sexy.

No, it's the realization that this thing with Fox hasn't just gotten out of hand with my mother planning us an engagement party. It's gotten out of hand because I like spending time with Fox far, far too much. Because he's the first person I think to call when I find something funny. Because I've been buying turtles for him.

"I'm tired," I announce suddenly.

For a moment, Fox looks hurt. Then he nods.

"I should probably get to bed myself. Never know if they'll need me in net tomorrow or not."

"I'll watch," I promise, telling myself I'm not watching for him but because I'm a hockey fan now.

It's just because you love the Serpents. That's all it is, Lilah. It has nothing to do with wanting to catch even the tiniest of glimpses of Fox waiting in the wings. Nope. Not at all.

"Thanks." He gives me a soft smile. "Good night, sugar."

"Good night, Arthur…Francis."

He groans, and it's the last thing I hear before I end the call. When I tuck myself into bed, I do everything I can to not think of Fox and the fact that he misses me. Even more, I try not to think about how much I miss him and what that might mean.

As I drift off to sleep with a smile, I know I've failed on both counts and am oddly at ease with it.

Chapter 16

Lawson: I have something that's been weighing on me, and I need to get it off my chest.

Keller: I don't care.

Lawson: Shut up, Kells.

Keller: Good one, Lawsy.

Locke: What's going on?

Hayes: Everything okay, man?

Keller: Christ, have you gone soft too, Hayesy?

Hayes: I'm not soft. Just being a good friend, you dick.

Keller: And proud of it.

Lawson: Anyone else completely hurt that Fox never told us he's been seeing Lilah?

Lawson: Like, I thought we were besties, Fox. How could you not trust us with this?!?!

Keller: You are a grown-ass man, Lawson. Why are you calling other grown-ass men your bestie???

Hayes: To be fair, this is Lawson you're talking to. Is he really that grown?

Keller: Excellent point, Hayesy. I like you again.

Hayes: Whatever.

Locke: For once, I'm on Lawson's side. How could you not tell us, Fox?

Fox: It's a little thing called privacy.

Lawson: There is no privacy amongst teammates.

Fox: There was when Hutch was sleeping with Auden and breaking the rules.

Fox: And when you were seeing Rory in secret.

Fox: And when Hayes was banging his nanny.

Hayes: Hey now…

Fox: I'm just saying. We have plenty of secrets among us.

Fox: I'm sure Locke and Keller are hiding something too.

Locke: I'm an open book. Ask me anything.

Lawson: Keller?

Keller: I'm not telling anyone shit.

Lawson: You're totally hiding something. I can feel it.

Keller: Or hear me out: I just don't like you and don't want to tell you a damn thing.

Hutch: You're going to have to stop saying you don't like him. People are going to start believing you.

Keller: Good. It's true.

Locke: If it were true, you wouldn't be in this group chat with him. Or the club.

Hutch: We are NOT a club.

Lawson: Shut up, Hutch. Yes we are.

Lawson: And you do too like me, Kells. Just say it.

Keller: Never.

Hayes: He doesn't need to say it. We all know it's true, even if he never admits it.

Lawson: Speak for yourself, Hayesy. I want to hear him say it.

Keller: Again, never.

Lawson: Booo!

Fox: Yeah, booo!

Lawson: Hey, you're still here. Good. Why didn't you tell us about Lilah?

Fox: Busy, busy, busy.

Lawson: You aren't busy! Come back here and explain yourself!

Fox: There's nothing to explain. We were seeing each other, it got serious, and now we're getting married. What else is there to say?

Lawson: Why didn't you tell us you were dating?

Fox: P-R-I-V-A-C-Y

Lawson: N-O

Fox: I'm done with this conversation.

Lawson: Aw, don't leave too.

Hutch: Shouldn't you be napping? We have a game in a few hours. Go sleep.

Lawson: Are you saying that as my captain or as your regular old grumpy self?

Hutch: Whoa. I am NOT old. That's Locke.

Locke: Gee, thanks, Hutchy.

Hutch: Sorry not sorry, bud.

Locke: For the record, I'm not that old.

Lawson: LOLOLOLOL

Lawson: Yes you are.

Lawson: You were born in the '80s.

Lawson: That's old.

Locke: I'm starting to understand why Keller hates you.

Keller: FINALLY!

Lawson: All right fine. You're not old. You're just…seasoned.

Locke: That makes me feel like I'm a steak or something.

Fox: Mmm. Steak sounds good.

Lawson: That's what you should serve at your wedding.

Fox: That sounds expensive. I thought you were cheap.

Lawson: I am. With my money. That's your money. I'm not paying for it.

Fox: Just reaping the benefits?

Lawson: Now you're getting it.

Keller: I'm not going to the wedding unless there's steak. Everyone gets obnoxiously mushy during them.

Locke: Huh. I wonder why. It's almost like it's a ceremony celebrating love.

Hayes: He's just jealous.

Lawson: SO jealous.

Lawson: Oooh. Maybe we should try to find Keller a date for the wedding.

Lawson: We can all band together and find someone who will tolerate his grumpy ass.

Keller: Don't even fucking think about it.

Hayes: Why not? Getting laid regularly will help your attitude problem.

Keller: Bold coming from you. It didn't help yours.

Hutch: Or mine before someone tries to throw me under the bus.

Locke: Like you did to me by calling me old?

Hutch: Again, not sorry about that, bud.

Hutch: Sure is fun to try though, isn't it, Hayesy?

Hayes: Very much so.

Lawson: Yes, I also love trying.

Hayes: Shut up, Lawson.

Hutch: Shut up, Lawson.

Locke: Shut up, Lawson.

Lawson: What? Nothing from you, Kells?

Keller: Nah. They got it covered.

Lawson: Fox?

Fox: Who said ANY of you assholes are invited to my wedding?

Lawson: Of course we're invited. I'm the best man, remember?

Fox: But you're not, remember?

Fox: My brother would be my best man.

Lawson: We are brothers, brother.

Fox: My ACTUAL brother.

Lawson: Ouch. Not gonna lie, that hurt.

Hutch: Are you saying Greer wouldn't be YOUR best man?

Lawson: Of course Greer would be my best man, just like I was his.

Lawson: God, I wish you all could have seen the look on Grady Miller's face. He was devastated. It was hilarious.

Locke: Still can't believe that guy is married. Thought he'd never settle down.

Keller: Settling down is for the weak. No offense, Fox.

Fox: Thanks?

Lawson: Stop being such a sourpuss, Kells.

Keller: Why? I've perfected the scowl. No reason not to keep using it.

Lawson: You're never going to get a woman like that. They don't like scowling.

Keller: Not what your mom said.

Hayes: Walked right into that one, Lawsy.

Hutch: Speak for yourself on the scowling thing. Women like it just fine, Keller. Trust me.

Lawson: Ah, yes, Mr. Grump Butt. How could I forget Auden's little nickname for you?

Hutch: If you know what's best for you, you'll forget it.

Lawson: I'm not afraid of you.

Hutch: You should be.

Fox: Guys…

Lawson: Yeah, Hutchy, settle down.

Fox: I was talking to you, too, Lawson.

Lawson: Hey, be nice or I won't be your best man.

Fox: For the last time, you are NOT my best man.

Lawson: We'll see about that.

Chapter 17

FOX

"Arthur Francis Fox!"

I pull the phone away from my ear, though it doesn't do much considering how loudly my mother screeches at me. It's a damn good thing I didn't answer this back in the locker room. Everyone would have heard her.

I suppose she has every right. I have been engaged for weeks now and have yet to tell her about it. I knew the moment I saw I had four missed calls from her, she'd found out about it. I've been psyching myself up to call her back ever since.

I should have called her when it first happened. I know that. But I've been avoiding it, and I'm not entirely sure why. Maybe because I didn't want to hear her get her hopes up just to let her down. Or maybe because I wasn't ready to admit just what a mess I'd gotten myself into. I don't know. All I know is it's time to face the music and hope my mother doesn't completely hate me afterward.

"Hi, Mama," I say, climbing into my Denali in the parking lot of the practice barn.

"Boy!" she hollers, her voice filling every inch of the cab of my truck. "Don't you 'mama' me. Explain yourself."

"I'm not sure what I'm in trouble for." I play stupid, but it's pointless. We both know what this call is about.

"Bullshit." My mother doesn't curse often, so when she does, I know she means it. "You know exactly what I'm talking about. You told me you weren't dating anyone, and now I see *this*. On the internets, no less!"

"Inter*net*, Mama. Not internets."

"I don't care what it's called! I want an explanation."

"Mama, I—"

"I swear, if another excuse comes out of your mouth, I will fly to Seattle this instant, and we can settle this in person."

Shit. I believe her, too.

I exhale heavily, then tell her everything going on with Lilah as I pull out of the parking lot and find a spot in bumper-to-bumper traffic on the freeway. She's quiet for a full minute after I get her up to speed on our situation. Then suddenly, she's laughing. And laughing some more.

In fact, she laughs for another full minute before I'm finally able to get a word in, my fingers flexing on my steering wheel as traffic moves just twenty-five feet or so.

"Are you good?" I ask her.

"I'm sorry." She coughs lightly, another chuckle. "I'm sorry. It's just between you and Regan, I don't know what to believe about my children's love lives anymore."

"I'm sorry I didn't tell you. I didn't think it would go this far."

"Obviously not."

"Are you mad?"

"I'm not exactly happy. I mean, I thought when you got engaged, it would be because you're in love and not just doing your friend a favor, but I guess I can't fault you for that, can I? Especially after hearing how awful her parents are. That poor girl." She sighs. "What have you gotten yourself into, Artie?"

I don't even have it in me to be annoyed by my childhood nickname. I'm too busy asking myself the same thing she is. It's what I've *been* asking myself for weeks now. My teammates—mostly Lawson—have been on my ass about why I didn't tell them about this before, Locke and Hutch are still looking at me like they know something I don't, and I'm somehow suddenly playing some of the best hockey of my life. All of this while getting myself more and more involved in Lilah's life every day.

So, no, I have no idea what I've gotten myself into. But I do know I don't hate it. In fact, I like it. Possibly even too much.

"You have a good heart, and I know that's why you're doing this. I guess I just can't understand why you're lying to yourself."

Her words shock me. Lying to myself? What the hell am I lying to myself about? "What do you mean?"

"I mean, you keep emphasizing how fake this arrangement is, but I can hear in your voice that you have some very real feelings for this girl."

I could deny it. I could tell her she's making stuff up or seeing more than what's really there, but that'd be a lie too, and…fuck, I'm tired of lying.

I do have feelings for Lilah. I had an inkling I might before we left for the road trip, and that feeling has just grown since we've been gone. It's not just because nearly every night I've talked to her has ended in some incredible phone sex. It's more than that. It's the phone calls and the way she makes me laugh and how she watches my games. It's me ordering nachos at every restaurant we've been to just because they remind me of her. It's so many little things and even all the big ones.

"Is this why you haven't called me lately? Because you like this girl?"

"I've called you."

"Three two-minute phone calls in the last few weeks isn't calling me. Not properly."

Shit. She's right. I guess I have been sort of avoiding talking to her. Not because I thought she would judge me for what's going on with Lilah—who I wasn't lying to about the likelihood of my mother's reaction—but I guess I just didn't want to talk for fear of this exact thing right now. My mother knows me better than anyone. She would know if I were hiding something even if I had been hiding it from myself.

I sigh, conjuring my favorite image of Lilah: sitting at my kitchen table with a bit of nacho cheese sauce on her lip, completely oblivious to it. It's ridiculous I love it so much, but I do. It's so real. So *her*.

Of course, *other* images also come to mind, but I won't think of them now while on the phone with my mother.

"You really do like her, huh?"

"Yeah." I clear my throat that's suddenly heavy. "Yeah, I do. I don't know exactly when it happened, but yeah."

"Does she know?"

"Nah. She's not interested in a relationship. I have to respect that."

"That doesn't seem very fair to you."

I swallow. It's not fair to me, but it's what I signed up for. I knew going into this how Lilah felt, and it's nobody's fault but my own that I'm in this predicament now. And that's okay. I'll play the part of doting fiancé for Lilah. I'll do what she asks, and I'll keep my feelings out of it all the while. Sure, it might hurt when we end things after the party, but I'm a big boy. I can take it.

"Promise me you won't let yourself get hurt."

I can't guarantee that, but still, I find myself saying, "I promise, Mama."

"Good. I love you, you know."

"I love you too."

"Then don't hide things from me anymore. Deal? No matter how insane it is, I want to know these things. And don't worry—I'll keep your secret, even at your party."

"Thanks, Mama. I appreciate it."

We end our conversation just as I pull up to the parking garage for my building, and I press my card to the monitor. I make my way up to my apartment, my mother's words ringing in my ears.

Promise me you won't let yourself get hurt.

I promised, and I lied.

I lied because, after ten minutes in my quiet

apartment and an outfit change, I'm racing right back down to my truck and steering it toward Lilah's. Twenty minutes later, I'm riding the elevator to her floor, then my knuckles are rapping against her door.

Nothing. No answer.

I knock again, and the result is the same.

Shit. I didn't even think about the possibility of her not being home. I just had to see her, which is a little ridiculous because I just saw her last night, crawling beneath her sheets shortly after our plane landed. When I snuck out this morning for practice, I had every intention of staying away.

Look how well that turned out.

I head back to the elevator, telling myself it's for the best because I'm getting too attached to her. Still, I can't help but be disappointed while waiting for the car to arrive. It dings, and I look up just as the doors slide open.

Cerulean. It's all I see.

Lilah.

Her jaw drops as I take her in: white towel hanging over her shoulder, black leggings that leave nothing to the imagination, and a matching jacket hanging open to reveal a lavender top. There's a strip of skin showing off her soft stomach that I want to drop to my knees and press my lips to. Her hair is up in a high ponytail.

It's clear she's just come from the gym, yet she still looks absolutely fucking gorgeous.

"Fox? What are you"—she pushes the button to open the doors on the elevator as they begin to close again—"doing here?"

"I wanted to see you."

She quirks a brow. "You just saw me this morning."

I shrug. "I wanted to see you again."

"Is that so?"

"That's so."

She finally steps out, coming to a stop so close the tips of our shoes are touching. "Hi."

"Hey there, sugar."

I swear she shivers as I slip my hand up her neck, my fingertips dipping into her hair that's slightly wet at the roots. I bend, brushing my lips over hers in the softest of kisses, and I love the little whine that leaves her as I pull away.

"I'm glad you wanted to see me," she says.

"Yeah?"

She nods, swallowing hard. "Yeah."

I kiss her again. "What do you say we go on another date?"

She smiles up at me. "Yeah, I think I'd like that."

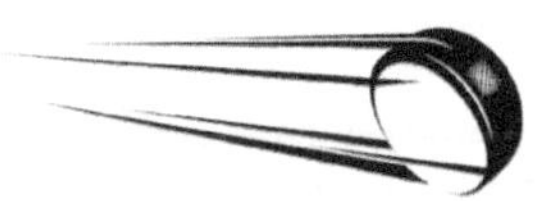

"When you said another date, I thought you meant like grabbing dinner or something."

"We are getting dinner."

Lilah rolls her eyes at me. "And that requires a ferry ride?"

"Do you want the best pizza of your life, or do you want adequate pizza?"

She huffs, tugging her jacket tighter around her. "The best pizza of my life sounds nice, but I wish I had known so I could have grabbed a warmer jacket. I'm in a skirt, for goodness' sake."

"A very *sexy* skirt, if I do say so." I slide my hand over her ass that's covered by a tight silky black skirt, her deep blue long-sleeved shirt tucked into it. I sling my arm around her, pulling her to me as she shivers. "Better?"

"Much." She snuggles in closer, and I press a kiss to her head. "I know this is so silly because I grew up here and taking the ferry is just part of everyday transportation for many people, but I *love* ferry rides." It's cute the way her eyes light up as she says it.

"Yeah? How come?"

She lifts her shoulders. "Maybe it's because my parents always used a car service to take us wherever we wanted, and they forbade us from using public transportation. Or maybe it's just how beautiful the scenery is. I don't know. I just love it."

"It is really nice out here."

"Have you ever been out here when they've stopped for the whales? It's so cool."

"Can't say that I have. Now I feel robbed."

"You should. It's a lot cheaper than an actual whale scouting tour, that's for sure." I laugh, and she pokes at my stomach. "What? Why are you laughing at me?"

"Nothing. I just find it funny that you're…well, *you*, and you're complaining about the price of a boat tour."

"That's how the rich stay rich, baby. Save money where they can."

"You sound like Lawson."

"Ew. Don't compare me to him."

"He's not that bad." She gives me an offended look, and I laugh again. "All right. Fine. He *can* be that bad."

"Poor Rory."

"Now you sound like my mom."

"Does she know Lawson? Or any of your teammates?"

"No, but I talk to her enough that it feels like she knows them." I exhale heavily, thinking of my conversation with her just this morning. "Speaking of my mother…"

Lilah peers up at me, her teeth sinking into her bottom lip. "Why don't I like the sound of that?"

"It's not bad. I, uh, I actually told her about us."

"You did? What did she say?"

"Well, as expected, she laughed."

Lilah sighs, relieved. "Good. I think. She thinks we're nuts, doesn't she?"

"Very much so."

"That seems to be the consensus, doesn't it?"

I shrug. "Yeah, but who cares? Are you happy with what we're doing?"

She hesitates. It's only for a moment, but it happens.

Finally, she says, "I'm having the best orgasms of my life. How could I not be?"

She smiles, but there's a wobble to it like she's hiding something. I want to call her on it, but that'd make me a hypocrite. I'm hiding something, too. Like the fact that I'm not only happy with what we're doing but want to do it for real. Maybe not the whole engagement part—that's way too fast—but the relationship part. That's what I want.

I don't tell her any of that. I keep it buried deep, not wanting to scare her away. I have a feeling if Lilah were to get even an inkling of indication that what we're doing is becoming real, she'd run. I don't want her to run. I want her to stay right here with me.

"Good," I tell her as she snuggles into me again. "Good."

We don't talk much as we reach the end of our ferry ride, the big boat pulling into the terminal nestled against the coast of the small town of Kingston.

"This is so cute," she says as she looks up the street lined with shops. "How did you find this place?"

"I try to explore as much as I can when we're not playing. Sometimes, I just drive and see where the road takes me. In this case, I hopped on a ferry and found it."

"You're so much braver than me. I don't even explore that much, and I've lived here forever."

"To be fair, you've spent the last ten years working your ass off creating something magical with your best friend. You didn't exactly have time to explore."

I hate how surprised she looks at my words, like praise isn't something she's used to getting.

"Stop looking at me like that."

"Like what?" she asks, still doing it.

I stop, tugging her to me, and she lets out a soft gasp. I place my hand on her cheek, tipping her head back until I'm peering down into the blue eyes I can't get enough of. I need her to know I mean it, know I see her.

"Like you don't think you deserve my words. You did something incredible with Auden. Sure, it might have been her company, but you were as much a part of that as she was, Lilah. Don't let anyone try to steal that from you. Especially not your parents, okay? Don't let them diminish everything you did, everything you worked for. Auden wouldn't have been able to sell her company for half of what she did if it weren't for you, and if you think your bestie doesn't know that, too, then you're wrong. You're a damn incredible woman. I hope you know that."

She swallows once, twice. "I do now."

Then she presses up on her tiptoes and lays her lips softly against mine. It's a quick kiss, a chaste one, yet somehow, it feels like so much more.

"What was that for?" I ask as she pulls away.

She shrugs. "Because I wanted to."

She tugs on my hand and leads us across the street like she's the one who knows where we're going.

Her eyes widen when she spots the crêperie to the right. "Please tell me we can go there after dinner."

I grin at her excitement. "That was the plan."

"God, I love you."

I stumble. I lose my footing on flat ground, nearly taking us both tumbling to the sidewalk as I run right into Lilah. We both know *how* she meant it, but it feels far too real considering our situation.

I don't know which one of us recovers first, but we continue walking as if nothing happened. She pretends she didn't just say those three words, I pretend they didn't make my heart hammer in my chest, and we both pretend we're not in way over our heads.

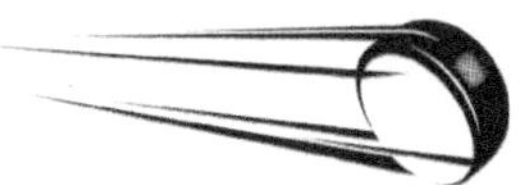

"You were right. That was the best pizza I've ever had," Lilah says, sitting on the ferry with her hand on her stomach. She unzipped her skirt the second we sat down. "And that crepe? The ice cream? I think that might have been my favorite date ever."

"Better than the nachos?"

"Sorry." Though she doesn't sound sorry at all, but I'm okay with that. "Can we please talk about that pesto and garlic chicken pizza again?"

"To be fair, it's all you've talked about since your first bite."

"Can you blame me? It was incredible. Well worth the garlic breath I have right now."

"I like your garlic breath."

"It's great garlic breath," she agrees. "And that sourdough crust? Ugh. It was perfection."

"It's one of my favorite parts of living here. Seattle loves its sourdough, and it's my favorite kind of bread. My mother used to make it all the time growing up."

"I love the way you talk about your family."

"They're my favorite people in the world. I wouldn't be where I am without them."

"How'd you even get into hockey living in the South? It's not huge there, right?"

"There have been a few renditions of professional hockey in Atlanta over the years, but as a whole, no, it's not huge there. My dad was a fan after going to college with a guy from Canada. He got him into it, and after that, he was hooked. Never missed a game on TV. I used to sit in the living room and watch along with him, and my obsession grew from there. I asked for my first pair of skates when I was six. The rest is history."

"That's actually really sweet, Fox. I bet he's proud of you."

I think of the text he sent me before the last game, a quick *Good luck, kid*. He sends the same one before every one of my appearances in net.

"Immensely," I tell her. "Doesn't let me ever forget it, either."

She squeezes my thigh. "I'm glad you have that."

"I'm sorry you don't."

"That sounds—" She yawns, the rest of her words stolen.

I chuckle. "I'm sorry. Did I bore you?"

"No." She shakes her head, turning sideways as the ferry disembarks. She stretches her legs out over mine, and I run my hand over her idly. "Sorry. I'm just wiped. So, why goalie? Don't they always say you have to be a little crazy to be a goalie?"

"Maybe, but I like to think it's that you're a little brave. I mean, facing down those shots? That's not crazy. That's courageous."

"I like that you"—she yawns again, her eyelids growing heavy—"think of it that way."

I laugh again. "Rest, Lilah."

"Huh?"

"Rest."

"No. What if I fall asleep?" she asks, her eyes barely open now, and I have no doubt she *will* fall asleep.

"Then I'll carry you to the car."

She huffs out a half-hearted laugh. "You're ridiculous."

"Only when it comes to you."

She smiles, mumbling something I can't quite make out, her breaths already evening out as she falls fast asleep, and that's how she stays through the rest of the ride. Not even the announcement that the ferry is approaching the destination rouses her from her sleep. So, I do as I promised—I haul her into my arms and carry her off the ferry and all the way to the car. She doesn't stir until I'm buckling her into the seat. Only then does she blink open her eyes.

"Did you carry me?"

"Of course I did, sugar."

She smiles, her eyes fluttering back closed. She sleeps the whole car ride back to her apartment and I carry her right to her door, where I barely get her on her feet to unlock it.

"I'm sorry. I don't know why I'm so tired."

"It was all the food."

"Mmm," she agrees, swaying on her feet a bit as she pushes the door open. She moves inside her apartment, leaving the door ajar like she expects me to follow.

I tell myself I do it just to make sure she's okay, but the truth is, I don't *want* to go home to my apartment. I don't want to be alone tonight. I want to be with her. I trail behind her as she makes her way to her bedroom, kicking her shoes off along the way. Next comes her shirt, and then her skirt hits the floor.

She looks back over her shoulder at me, a tired smile playing on her lips. "You coming?"

I should say no. I should leave. I should do a lot of things, but I don't. Instead, I keep going, pulling my clothes off right along with her. When we finally make it to her bedroom and slip beneath her sheets, I pull her as close as she can possibly get.

"Have you been buying turtles?"

"Hmm?" she asks, already half asleep.

"Have you been buying turtles?"

"Oh. That." She shrugs. "I might have found a few. They're for you."

"For me?"

"Of course. What do I need turtles for?"

I want to point out that I don't need turtles either given the robust collection I already have, but I don't.

Lilah bought me turtles.

I grin.

"Stop," she grumbles. "I can *feel* you smiling."

"No, you can't."

"Yes, I can." She pinches me, then kisses the same spot. "Stop being weird about it."

"I'm not being weird. I think it's sweet."

"They're just turtles."

"Just turtles," I agree, but they feel like so much more than that. I know it, and Lilah knows it too.

She snuggles even closer to me, her breaths beginning to even out.

"Good night, Lilah Jane Maddison."

"Good night, Arthur Francis Fox."

She's asleep moments later, but I lie awake for hours thinking about how Lilah, the girl who doesn't believe in relationships or love, thought about me while I was gone.

And how I thought about her too.

Chapter 18

LILAH

"Nothing gets me hotter than watching hockey in person."

I laugh at Rory, who hasn't taken her eyes off the ice since we sat down. She's barely even touched the nachos in her hand, and the urge to reach out and eat one has been bugging me all game, even though they're likely soggy as hell by now.

"What? It's true. Lawson is like a whole other person after a game," she says, still not looking away as the Serpents race up the ice with possession.

But I'm not watching the puck. My focus is solely on the man in net bent over trying to catch his breath as he watches his teammates attempt to score so they can increase their lead.

I don't know what's gotten into the team lately, but

they're on a hot streak, having won their last five games. It's been fun to watch at home, but it's even better to be sitting here at the arena. This atmosphere is electric, and the fans are on their feet for every incredible save Fox makes. It's been that way the whole game, and now at the start of the third period with the Serpents up three goals to one, they're really buzzing.

Fans groan when Lawson misses his shot up over the net, and the Florida team takes it back down the ice. Fox gets into position, his glove up while he tracks the puck as they get closer…closer…and the puck goes right into the webbing of his glove. The crowd roars again, and I join right in with them, standing to cheer him on. Rory is right—it *is* hotter to watch hockey in person.

I cup my hands around my mouth, yelling loudly along with the crowd. "Foxy, Foxy, Foxy!"

Knowing Fox, he's likely blushing right now with all the attention, but he doesn't let it distract him. Florida takes another puck down his way, and he stops it with his blocker. They gather the rebound and try again, but Fox is quick, pushing over and flipping his leg out and sealing it against the net. Save after save and the arena is so loud it's deafening.

All I can think is *That's him. That's my guy.* And I don't even panic about it, too entranced by the stellar performance in front of me. After another fifteen minutes of the same, the Serpents earn their sixth win in a row, only allowing one goal. The team gathers around Fox, tapping him on the head before saluting the crowd and skating off.

"That was incredible! Did you see Lawson?!" Rory shouts, clapping wildly and grinning bigger than I've ever seen her. It's strange at first, considering the woman hardly ever smiles, but it's so cute how much she clearly loves him.

Auden's no different, her face lit up with excitement, especially as they flash Hutch's picture up on the screen.

"Tonight's third star of the game, with two assists, is your captain, Reed Huuuuuutchinson!"

The crowd extends his name along with the announcer, the hordes of spectators stomping rhythmically. Hutch waves to the crowd, tossing a stuffed snake into the sea of people across from us.

"Tonight's second star of the game, scoring twice and earning his 500th NHL point, is Lucas Laaaaaawson!"

Once again, the crowd roars to life, Rory maybe even being the loudest of all as her boyfriend takes a lap, tossing a stuffie into the crowd and blowing them a kiss because *of course* he does. He's Lawson.

"Stopping forty-six of forty-seven goals—"

The arena gets so loud I can't even hear them announce Fox's name. It's drowned out as the "Foxy" chants start once more. It's amazing to hear everyone scream his name like this, and all I can think is, *I get to scream his name later.*

Fox waves to the crowd, throwing his hands up, trying to pump the fans up even more, and they go even more wild as he skates to where we're seated. He stops, and those espresso-colored eyes of his lock with mine.

I swear time stops…or at least that's the only explanation I have because even though it's only moments he stands there staring at me, it feels like hours. He chucks the stuffed snake into the crowd, everyone clamoring for it, but I don't budge. I can't. I'm too busy locked in a staring contest with him as a smile curves his lips. Fox winks, and heat stains my cheeks.

Auden elbows me as he skates away, everyone still cheering around us. "I saw that."

"Saw what?"

She rolls her eyes. "You like him, Lilah. You're happy with him."

I *am* happy with him. Not even my mother's obnoxiousness about our upcoming engagement party is enough to get me down. I'm sure it helps that any time I start to get stressed about it, Fox helps me "relax" by distracting me with sex or getting me out of the house. Like for our makeup Valentine's Day date, when he took me to Pike Place and the aquarium and we spent the day playing tourists. Or last week when he took me to an arcade, and he spent over four hundred dollars just to win the giant stuffed turtle they had that he could have bought for a fraction of the price. Or last night, when, after a particularly stressful day of linen shopping with my mother, he showed up at my door with a pint of butter pecan ice cream. We didn't even fool around. He just kissed me and held me on the couch while I read to him from a fantasy novel about dragons and courage.

So Auden is right. I *am* happy with him, more than I thought I could be if I'm being honest. It's so strange. I've been a serial dater all my life, never staying with someone for more than a month and never seriously. This thing with Fox has been going on for longer than that, plus it's definitely feeling serious, and I don't just mean because of the engagement. It's more than that, and I can't quite place my finger on what that *more* is.

"So?"

"*So...*" She stretches out the word. "Remember what I told you, yeah?"

"I know, I know."

Be careful, Lilah. I don't want to see him get hurt. But I don't think Auden realizes it's not just Fox she needs to be worried about. It's me too.

And I don't know what to do about it.

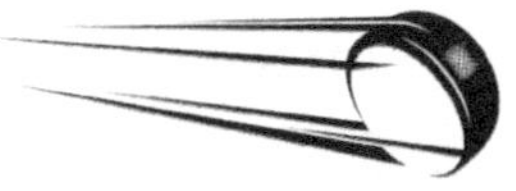

"That was quite the game, Artie."

He lifts his head, his whole face lighting up as he sees me standing against his car. He slows his pace, stuffing his hands into his pockets.

"Looks like I need to have a chat with security. They're just letting anyone in these days, huh?"

"Not just anyone," I say, pushing off his car and rocking back on my heels. "Only wives and girlfriends and *fiancées*."

His grin grows at that as he stops in front of me. "That so?"

"Yep. I just flashed this bad boy, and they let me right in." I hold up my hand, showing off the ugly-as-hell ring I've been wearing more and more lately. At first, I took it off every chance I got, only wearing it when I had to meet up with my mother, who has been far too invested in planning our engagement party. Then, one day, I forgot to take it off, and it's been there ever since. I try not to think too much about that, about how natural it feels on my finger.

"That's worrisome. Anyone can find an ugly ring and flash it."

"Hey! It's not ugly." I manage to hold my laughter in for all of two seconds before it bubbles right out. "Sorry, I couldn't even pretend."

Fox shakes his head, hooking a finger through a belt loop on my jeans. He hasn't even touched me yet, but my body lights up at his proximity anyway. "It's the most hideous thing I've ever seen, but it's kind of growing on me."

"It is not."

"Is too." He jerks me forward, and I fall against him. He catches me easily, his hands dropping to my waist as I curl my own around his biceps. I squeeze them, loving the way the defined muscle feels under my palms, especially when he's thrusting into me and whispering dirty things into my ear.

He leans down, his nose brushing against mine, his lips so close I can feel his breath ghosting over me. I don't think I've ever wanted to kiss him so badly before, but I chalk it all up to the leftover buzz of the game.

Yeah, that's all it is. Nothing else.

"Is not," I argue again.

"You make it pretty, Lilah."

And then he's kissing me, his warm lips pressing

against mine in a soft yet commanding way, and I'm wrong. I am so fucking wrong.

It's not the buzz from the game. It's Fox. All him and nothing else at all.

I should have known it was him. It's that same buzz I've had since the birthday party back in January, the same one that's been simmering just beneath the surface since. Fox's fingers dig into my hips as he draws me even closer, our bodies pressed together so tightly I don't know where he ends and I begin and vice versa. I don't care to know either. All I want is this—Fox's hands and mouth on me and that hum of pleasure rolling through me.

His touch inches higher, slipping beneath the Serpents jersey I'm wearing, the one with his name plastered across the back, and I shiver when he hits bare skin.

"Cold?" he asks, kissing the corner of my lips.

I shake my head, leaning it back to give him access to that spot on my neck he loves to taste. "Opposite."

He sinks his teeth lightly into me, then chases the sting with his tongue before trailing his lips back to mine, sealing our mouths together once more. I groan against him, pulling him closer if that's even possible.

"As hot as this is to watch, do you think I could get by?"

My eyes fly open, and I wrench my lips from Fox's

to find Keller standing nearby, his hip pressed against a familiar-looking truck.

"Uh, hi, Keller."

He grins as much as Keller can. "Hey, Lilah. You mind if I get into my truck?" He nods toward the vehicle we're standing just inches from.

I look at Fox, whose lips are rolled tightly together.

"I, uh, should probably mention this isn't my truck."

"What?" I look back at it. "Are you sure?"

"I'm sure." He points at the car Keller is leaning against. "That one is mine."

It looks identical. How did I not notice there are two of them?

"You have matching trucks?"

Keller points at his teammate. "He copied me."

Fox shrugs. "I copied him."

"Oh my god," I mutter, pressing my face to Fox's chest as he shakes with laughter. "Why didn't you tell me?"

"I was kind of distracted." He presses a kiss to the top of my head and tugs on me. "Come on. Let's let Keller have his truck back."

"Yeah, that'd be great," says the perpetual grump, shoving off Fox's car.

As the two men pass, they exchange a knowing

glance, and I hate it and love it all at once, especially when just a hint of jealousy passes over Keller's face.

"Always lovely seeing you, Lilah," Keller calls over his shoulder just before disappearing into his car.

The truck rumbles to life, and he races out of the garage at a high speed.

Fox rolls his eyes at his teammate and holds the passenger door of *his* vehicle open for me. "After you."

I glower at him as I climb inside. "You're paying for that."

"Promises, promises," he says with a grin.

Fox keeps his hand on my thigh the entire drive to my apartment, and it does nothing to quell the desire coursing through me. The sight of him driving one-handed makes me hotter than I ever imagined it could, and from the looks he keeps sending me every few minutes, he knows it, too.

He pulls into a parking spot. We hustle into the building, and I lose all sense of control the second we step into the elevator. Fox laughs when I shove him against the wall, but all the humor is gone when I press my lips to his in a rushed kiss. He groans against me, his tongue tracing the seam of my lips, then snaking inside.

We don't stop until the car arrives on my floor. Only then do we break apart, but only long enough to stumble out of the elevator and to my door. Fox presses against me as I push the key into the lock, his lips on the back of my neck, making it hard to concentrate on the simple task of unlocking the door.

"You taste so sweet," he mutters against my skin. "So fucking good. I can't wait to taste you more."

I groan with the promise, arching back against him, my ass sliding against the obvious erection he's sporting.

He hisses at the contact, teeth nipping at me. "Open the door already, Lilah."

"I'm trying!" Doesn't he see my hands are shaking? Doesn't he notice I'm barely hanging on by a thread right now?

I finally get the door open and spin, tugging Fox inside along with me. He follows after, hands on my hips the whole way until he's backed me against a wall. I don't even really know where we are even though it's my apartment. I'm too lost in Fox's touch to pay attention.

Our lips connect again, his tongue pushing into my mouth, and I moan. He shrugs his suit jacket off as my fingers find where his dress shirt meets his slacks, and I tug it up, needing to touch him properly. He groans when my bare hands meet his skin, and it spurs him on, his fingers flying through the buttons on his shirt until it's hanging open all the way. I slide my hands over him, tracing the ridges of his abs that

I know he works hard on, admiring every inch of him.

"Your hands feel so good on me."

"You feel good under my hands."

His palms slide over my ass. "I can't decide how I want you first."

"I love how you think you get to make that decision." I spin us suddenly until it's his back pressed against the wall.

He grins down at me. "Is that so?"

"That's so," I say, pressing my lips to his before dragging them down his torso, kissing every visible inch until I'm on my knees in front of him.

"Fuuuuuck." He drags the word out, biting his bottom lip as he watches me tug his belt free. "I won't last long, Lilah."

"You say that like I care."

I unsnap his pants and pull his zipper down, the sound sending another shudder of excitement through me. I grab his pants and boxer briefs, working them both down until his cock springs free.

"Like I don't enjoy the feel of you spilling down my throat."

I lean forward, running my tongue along his slit, loving the saltiness of his precum.

"As if I don't love the taste of you."

"Fuck. Shit. Fuck." He punctuates each word with

a knock of his head against the wall, and I laugh at how unhinged he's becoming with just a little teasing. "You're killing me already, and you've barely touched me."

"You like being teased."

He nods, his eyes hooded as he peers down at me. "Only by you."

I lick him again and am rewarded with another soft groan. I love him like this, compliant yet flirting with the urge to rebel. I like that he doesn't, that he gives me what *I* need, even if it means holding back his own pleasure.

He huffs out a breath. "Is it bad if I say I could come like this?"

"No." Another lick. "But don't."

"Is that a command?"

I nod, tasting him again, and he sucks air in between his teeth. "Yes. That's a command."

I tease him more, running my tongue over him again and again until he's literally shaking, but he does good. He doesn't come, though I can tell he's close, his balls tightening with each pass. I give them attention with fluttering touches while Fox lets out another string of curses.

"Lilah…" He groans, his eyes screwed shut tightly, the veins in his neck on full display as he holds himself back.

I know I'm pushing him, testing my luck.

"You're doing so good," I praise. "Being such a good boy."

His eyes spring open, and he looks down at me, his gaze hazy, almost drunk-like. I knew he liked it when I said that, but I didn't realize just how much. Seeing him like this now, knowing he's completely at my mercy…it's intoxicating.

He nods. "Yours," he says, voice thick with desire.

The single word unlocks something in me, and suddenly, I'm the one who can barely hold back, and I don't want to anymore. I suck him into my mouth, and Fox bucks against me as I finally give him what he wants. He's panting in a matter of minutes, his hands tightening to fists at his sides as he holds himself back from grabbing my head and driving into me like he wants to. His restraint spurs me on even more.

"Can I—*fuck*."

He groans as I pull him to the back of my throat, entirely cutting off his ability to speak. He's nothing but harsh breaths and incoherent noises as I work him over.

"Lilah…" Another groan. "I need to come."

I pull off him. "Come for me, Arthur. Come on me."

And he does. He grabs his cock, pumping once, then twice before he's spilling his heavy load right on my tongue and then some. It spurts all over my cheek, running down my chin, but I don't care. I love seeing him undone like this. I drag my fingers through the mess he's made, then suck them one by one into my mouth, not wanting to miss a drop of it. Fox gulps in air, watching me the whole time with eyes that promise I'll get mine too.

I kiss my way back up to his lips, and the second I touch them, he comes alive again, gripping my head so hard it nearly hurts, but I don't care. I want the hurt. I want the wild side of him. Fox lifts me into his arms with ease, his tongue working against mine as he leads us through the apartment, setting me down on the arm of my pink sofa. He pulls away long enough to shrug his shirt off the rest of the way. He rids himself of the rest of his clothes until he's standing before me naked, and I'm still fully dressed.

He strokes his cock, looking so hot with his hair a mess and his lips swollen from our kisses. I almost want to drop to my knees and suck him again.

"Turn around, Lilah. Hands on the couch," he instructs.

A part of me wants to be defiant, but when he pumps his cock again, I lose all the rebelliousness nipping at my heels and do as he says, wanting to feel him inside me more than I want anything else. With zero finesse, he yanks my leggings and underwear down just enough to expose me to him. He palms my bare ass, spreading me open, and he sucks in a breath.

"God, you're beautiful, you know that?" He slips a finger between my cheeks, running the pad of it over my back hole. "You ever been fucked here?"

I shake my head. "Not yet."

He chuckles. "Does that mean you'll let me?"

I shrug, trying to play it cool even though I'm barely holding myself up as he presses his finger harder against my rim. "Depends on how much of a good boy you are."

He growls—growls—and fills me in one hard thrust, knocking my breath from my lungs as I wasn't expecting it. I moan as he pulls out and slams back into me. His finger is still resting against my hole, the movement adding just the perfect amount of pressure.

I hear it before I feel it and tremble with lust as his spit lands against the top of my ass and slides down between my cheeks, right to where his finger is pressed against me, allowing just the tip to slip inside with ease.

"Oh god," I mutter, pushing back against him, loving the feeling of fullness that's overtaking me. He's barely even inside my ass, but I already know I'm going to want more.

He slows his pace, but only enough for his finger to slip inside me further until he can't go anymore. He adds more spit, then fucks me slowly, a vast difference to how he was just rutting into my pussy.

"Fuck, you have no idea how good you look right now." He pulls his finger out, then pushes it back in slowly. "My name across your back…my finger in your ass… I want to taste it, bury my tongue into your hole. Want to taste all of you, Lilah."

I nod. I'll agree to just about anything right now if it means feeling like this.

"But later. Right now, I want to make you come just like this, all over my cock while your tight little ass squeezes my finger."

I try to nod again, but it's no use. Not when he's back to fucking me with a relentless force, pounding into me over and over until my arms feel like they're about to give out, and my legs shake as I hold back my orgasm.

"So fucking pretty." Another hard thrust. "Wish you could see yourself taking my cock."

I don't know what it is—his punishing movements, me holding back, or how full I feel with his finger stretching my ass—but suddenly my eyes are stinging with tears. I want to come. I want to come so badly I can't stand it, but I can't.

He folds himself over me, his lips finding my ear. "Let go. It's okay to let go. I got you, sugar."

I do. I let go of everything, and I can't seem to help

the tears that fall from my eyes as I come, his cock still drilling into me, his finger still in my hole. I have no idea why I'm crying, but I have a sinking suspicion that what Fox said has a lot to do with it.

Yours.

He is mine. I don't know when it happened, don't know how it happened, but Fox isn't just my fake fiancé anymore. He's *mine*, and I'm *his*.

The scariest part of all? The realization doesn't terrify me nearly as much as I thought it would.

It doesn't terrify me at all, and that scares me more than anything else.

Chapter 19

"That's it. You're officially no longer allowed to plan our dates."

I chuckle, hands on my hips as I stare down at the girl doubled over, her own hands on her knees as she tries to catch her breath. We've been hiking for the last hour and a half and have stopped no less than ten times. Every time, Lilah has told me I'm no longer allowed to plan our dates. Every time, I laugh because even though she's complaining, she loves our dates.

I've lost track of the number of times she's had so much fun she's fallen asleep in my arms at this point. As much as I love having sex with her—and I *really* fucking love it—I love these dates and the nights she falls asleep on me even more, even if she is currently glaring at me like she's plotting my murder.

"I thought you did Pilates."

"I *do* do Pilates. *This* isn't Pilates, Fox. This is torture."

"It's just a small hill. This is no different than walking around Seattle."

"I *don't* walk around Seattle, though. I drive or Uber for this very reason. Walking up and down hills is pure agony."

"I think you're being a little dramatic."

"You're dramatic," she counters, rising back to her full height, her breaths still coming in fast. "Fine. Let's get this over with. I'm starving and want a giant, greasy burger. No, wait—cheese fries. No—chicken strips."

I lift a brow. "Are you going to order the whole menu?"

"I just might," she says, brushing past me.

I shake my head at her, catching up easily as we continue to climb. We don't talk much as we go, but I don't mind. I like being out here in the woods all the same. And fine, it *might* have something to do with the view in front of me, Lilah's leggings clinging to her sculpted ass.

"Stop staring at my butt!" she hollers over her shoulder when I've fallen behind for the tenth time when I could effortlessly be lapping her.

"Stop having such a nice butt!" I yell back.

If anyone else were out here, I'm sure they'd think we're crazy, and I'm okay with that.

I catch up to her when she stops for *another* break, only this time, I don't tease her as I have before. Instead, I pull the water from the backpack I've been carrying and hand it over, gulping embarrassingly loudly when she closes her lips around the same spot I've had mine. It's ridiculous, given everything we've done with each other, yet I still find it insanely hot.

She runs the back of her hand over her mouth, then hands the water back to me, the bottle nearly empty.

"You drank it all."

She tips her chin up. "Did not. There's still plenty left."

"Plenty for who? A mouse?"

She rolls her eyes. "You packed more. We both know you did."

She's right. I did pack more. We argued for five minutes over whether we'd need it. She insisted we'd be fine with the one bottle she was *not* carrying, but I remained steadfast that one wouldn't even last us the trip up, never mind back down.

I was right.

She pushes off the tree she is resting against and resumes our hike, her pace slow and steady. This time, I don't let her get ahead. I stay beside her, wanting to savor this last little bit of the hike. We're nearly to our destination, and I want to see her reaction when she sees it.

"Are you ready for our party next week?" she asks.

"Are *you* ready for our party next week?"

"As I'll ever be." She tucks a stray hair behind her ear. "I'm honestly more nervous to meet your parents than anything else."

"Don't be. They're going to love you. I'm sure of it."

"I hope so," she says, not sharing my enthusiasm.

In a surprising move, Selene actually considered my family when planning, and we were able to settle on a date that worked for everyone. Sure, it's a Friday evening instead of the Saturday extravaganza she had originally wanted, but at least my parents will be there. The twins can't make it, but they swear they'll be there for the wedding. I didn't have the heart to tell them there won't be a wedding.

As promised, my mother has kept her word and hasn't told anyone about Lilah's and my... arrangement, not even my father, who was shocked by the news but excited to have a new daughter-in-law. It was torture talking to him about it because he was so genuine. I don't think I've seen him that happy since Russ came home and told us all he was going to be a dad.

I'd be a fucking liar if I said I was looking forward to the party. I'm not, but not because I have to endure another evening with Lilah's horrid family or wear a suit and fake an engagement. It's because it's been slowly tearing me up to continue to lie to everyone I love. My father, my siblings, my teammates who are like siblings —everyone. It's one thing to do it for a few minutes at a party here or a conversation there, but to deceive them all on such a large scale? It makes my stomach churn.

"Are you okay?"

"Hmm?" I ask, turning to find Lilah staring at me with pinched brows. "What?"

"You look like you're about to vomit. Do we need to slow down?"

She asks that last question a little too eagerly.

I shake my head. "Nah, I'm good. Just hungry."

But it's a lie, and that makes me feel bad too. She's the one person I don't want to lie to, but I feel like I have to. She can't know the truth, or I'll lose everything, and I'm not ready for that just yet.

"Holy shit!"

"*Ooof!*" Lilah's arm smacks me right in the stomach, and I double over at the sudden pain.

Then I realize *why* she's freaking out. We've reached the end of the trail, and the view is—

"It's breathtaking," she whispers, her eyes wide as she takes in the waterfall across from us.

I step up next to her. "Worth it, right?"

She sniffs and shrugs, trying to play it cool. "Yeah, I guess."

But I can see in her eyes she's just as amazed as I am. We stand there quietly in the early March morning. The sun is covered by clouds, fog swirling around the trees, and water rushes down the cliffside across from us. It's beautiful, one of the prettiest sights I've ever taken in. Yet somehow, none of it compares to the woman standing beside me.

I rake my gaze over her, taking in every inch, from her dark hair that's sticking out chaotically from under her hat to her azure eyes that are brimming with tears, over her pert nose and those damn pink lips of hers that say the damnedest things.

I love you.

The three words filter through my mind in the same way they have been for the last few weeks. I don't know exactly when it happened, but it was probably on one of those evenings when we were snuggled together on her couch as she tucked her feet beneath my leg and read to me from the other end until we both drifted off to sleep.

I've done the dumbest thing I could think of doing. I've fallen for my fake fiancée.

With any luck, she'll fall for me too.

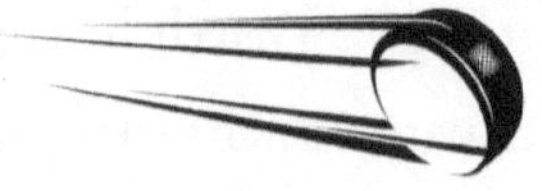

"I'm going to order the biggest, juiciest chicken sandwich ever."

"I thought you were getting a burger, cheese fries, and chicken strips."

"Oooh, you're right. A burger does sound good." She taps her chin. "Maybe I should get both. Or wait! You get one, I get the other. Then we can split it. Yeah, let's do that."

I laugh. "Do I get a say in this?"

"Nope." She bumps her shoulder against mine, then twines our fingers together.

I fully believe her, and the craziest part is I'd do whatever she asks.

Our trek back down to the truck is much easier, Lilah only stopping three times instead of ten. She seems much happier than on our hike up, and I'm unsure if that's because of the gorgeous waterfall or if she's just that excited for food. Either way, I love every moment of it.

When we finally get to the truck, Lilah runs ahead, the bouncing pom on her beanie just too damn cute for words.

"Come on! Feed me!" she calls, waving me over.

I chuckle the whole way there. "You act like you

didn't eat a stack of pancakes and hash browns *and* steal half of my bacon for breakfast."

"Hey, this is your fault. You're the one who kept me up late last night, burning extra calories."

"I didn't see you complaining while my head was between your legs."

She bites at her bottom lip. "No, I most certainly was not complaining about that."

I toss the backpack into the truck bed, then pull open the door for her. She stands there, looking at the truck like it's the most offensive thing in the world.

"Would you like a lift?" I ask with a chuckle.

She nods. "My legs are noodles, and my feet are killing me."

I lift her effortlessly, placing her on the passenger seat before dragging my hands down her legs and untying her boots, which look brand new. I wonder if she bought them just for this.

"Ahhh," she says as I pull the first one off. She tugs off her adorable hat, shaking out her hair. It's a total mess from the friction, but she still looks perfect. "That feels *much* better."

"You should have told me you weren't a hiker. I could have planned something else."

She shrugs. "You were so excited about it."

"Yeah, but I want you to enjoy our dates too, you know."

"I do. I like doing *anything* with you. Even if it is hiking."

I don't know why her words make my chest feel heavy, but they do. Maybe it's because I know she doesn't mean them in the way I hope she does. Or maybe it's because I'm kind of mad at myself for getting into this situation to begin with. I knew going in that I was lonely, that I was open to something more, but I swore I wouldn't let this turn into something bigger than what it was.

Yet here I am, completely in love with her, our engagement party days away, my heart threatening to beat out of my chest every time she looks at me. All the while, to Lilah, this is still completely fake.

"Hey," she says softly, tipping my chin up to her. "Are you okay?"

I nod. "Yeah. Sorry. Just got distracted trying to get these laces loose. Who tied these?"

"I did." She looks so proud that I can't help but smile. "What?"

"You're cute, you know that?"

She looks surprised, then grins back, flipping her hair over her shoulder. "I know."

Her confidence is so hot that I can't help but kiss her. She's so shocked by the sudden move that it takes her a moment to react, but then she kisses me back eagerly, her hands sliding into my hair as she pulls me closer. Before I know it, we're hanging out the side of my truck, her legs wrapped around my waist, my cock pressing against my jeans, Lilah rocking her hips into me.

She pulls away, gulping in air. "Back seat," she instructs through her pants.

"I thought you wanted food," I say—stupidly, because it *is* stupid to try to stop this right now.

Apparently, she agrees, kissing my jaw. "I found something else I want more."

Her words have me moving quickly. I tuck my arm under her ass and hold her up as I wrench open the back door, tucking us both inside. She sits in my lap, hands back in my hair as her lips find mine again.

"Why didn't you say hiking makes you horny?"

I chuckle. "Because I'm pretty sure you're the first person in the existence of the world to think that."

"Whatever," she mutters, kissing her way from my lips to my ear, nipping at my lobe, then moving back again. "Now take your pants off."

My truck is big, but it's not exactly two-people-in-the-back-seat-fucking big. Even so, I'm a determined man and somehow manage to wrestle my jeans down just enough, Lilah now sitting in my naked lap.

"Now yours," I tell her, hands already pulling at her puffy jacket, shoving it off her shoulders as she pushes up, working her leggings off.

There's nothing skilled or sexy about it, but it somehow makes it even hotter. We groan as she sinks down onto my cock, my hands on her hips as she settles there, adjusting to me.

"I don't think I'll ever tire of that," she says, moving her hips ever so slightly.

Don't, I beg silently. *Don't tire of it. Don't tire of me.*

Instead, I say, "Me either, sugar."

I lean forward, dragging my tongue over her neck as she gasps at the new angle.

"Arthur." She moans my name into my ear. "You feel so good."

"I could say the same thing about you."

"Then do it."

I laugh, but it turns into a groan as she squeezes me. "You feel so fucking good, Lilah. Love the way you take me."

She nods, her eyes screwed shut, hands on the ceiling of the truck as I fuck up into her. Sweat slides down my back under the layers of clothes I'm still wearing, and the windows fog from our hot breaths. If someone else were to pull into this parking lot right now, they'd know exactly what we were doing, yet somehow, I don't care. I don't care because this beautiful woman is bouncing on my cock, and it feels so fucking good that I don't think I could stop even if I wanted to, and I *definitely* don't want to.

"I'm so close," she murmurs. "Help me, Fox. Get me there."

"Anything," I tell her, meaning it wholeheartedly, and I'm not just referring to getting her off. I mean *anything*. I'd do it all for her. All she has to do is ask.

But in the meantime, I reach between us, pressing my thumb to her clit as she gets herself off on me. Apparently, it's exactly what she needs.

"Yes! God, yes!" she cries out, her hands going from the truck ceiling to my shoulders as she quickens her pace.

Seconds later, she's coming, her body shaking over mine, her breath in my ear. I grip her hips, driving into her, wringing out the last of her orgasm and chasing my own high, and she shudders all over again when I finally spill into her. Spent, I pull my hand from between our bodies and suck my thumb into my mouth, savoring the taste of her. She grins against my neck.

"What?" I ask.

"I like that you like how I taste."

"I don't *like* how you taste, Lilah. I fucking love it. Could spend a lifetime tasting you."

She snuggles against me closer, her face buried in my neck. And even though we really should be cleaning ourselves up right now, I allow it because, truthfully, there's nowhere else I'd rather be, including the rink.

"I lied earlier," she says after several minutes of me simply holding her, running my fingertips over her back in featherlight touches.

"About what?"

"My legs. *Now* they're like noodles." She kisses my neck softly. "Thank you for another great date, Fox."

I swallow the sudden lump clogging my throat. I don't know where it came from or why. Maybe it's because I just realized these dates of ours will be coming to an end after Thursday, when there's no longer any reason for us to have them. It's the last thing I want, but it's what I promised, and I'm nothing if not a man of my word.

So, I hug her closer, savoring every moment I can get for now.

"Any time, Lilah." I kiss the side of her head. "Any time."

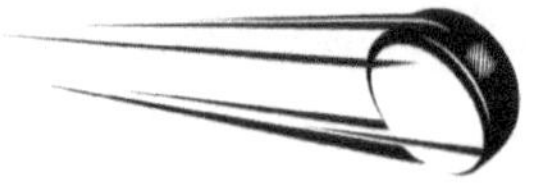

"My baby!" My mother throws her arms around my neck and pulls me into a hug like she hasn't seen me for two years instead of a few months. Her graying hair is pulled back in a half updo and she's wearing a sweater that says *Mama Bear* on it. "I missed you."

"Missed you too, Mama." I kiss her cheek. "I'm sorry I couldn't come to pick you up at the airport."

"Oh, nonsense. I know you have a busy schedule. Besides, we got to do some sightseeing, and your father convinced me to go up in that giant needle thing."

"The Space Needle is kind of neat, huh?"

"No, it was a waste of eighty bucks."

I grin, having expected nothing less from her. "How was the flight?"

"Amazing! But you have to stop spoiling us with first-class tickets. A gal like me could get used to that real fast."

"And that's the last thing my wallet needs," my dad says with a hearty laugh. He steps up to us, putting his hand on my mother's shoulder. "Let the kid go, sweetheart."

My mother huffs, but she does as my father requests. He takes her place and hugs me just as tightly as she did, the smell of fresh cut wood from his workshop reminding me of home.

"Good to see you, son. Did you see how much parking is at the airport? Thought I was going to have to cut off an arm *and* a leg for it."

"You guys didn't even drive to the airport."

"Still highway robbery, if you ask me."

"Oh, who cares about the parking, Roy. Is your *fiancée* here?"

It's funny because, like Selene, my mother emphasizes *fiancée*. However, unlike Selene, the word is filled with pure love and adoration, and she hasn't even met Lilah yet.

"She is. Did you want to come in or meet her at the door?"

"In, in!" She stomps her feet like a giddy child, and I can't help but laugh. I love that even though she knows the truth, she's not treating Lilah any differently than she would one of my siblings' partners.

I move aside, helping my father pull their bags inside. When I look up, my mother is gone. My dad notices, too.

He grins over at me. "That's your mother."

"Don't remind me," I mumble, taking off toward the kitchen where I have no doubt she currently is.

As I expected, she's standing in the middle of the room, her arms wrapped tightly around Lilah. What I didn't expect was to love seeing them together so much. My fiancée hugs my mother back, her head resting on the older woman's shoulder, eyes closed like every childhood trauma is being healed in this moment. And for Lilah, that might actually be true.

I love you.

The words rattle against my chest again, wanting

to be set free, but I lock them back where they belong, in the recesses of my mind for nobody else but me.

"Hey, now. I want my turn," my dad says, interrupting them.

My dad replaces my mother, hugging Lilah like she's part of the family and not someone he's literally just met.

"Great to meet you, sweetheart," my dad says, his accent thick on the last word. "I'm looking forward to getting to know the woman who finally got my kid to settle down so his mother can stop driving me nuts with worry that he's going to end up alone."

Lilah pulls away with a smile. "It's so great to meet you. Arthur has told me so much about you."

My mother looks at me, surprised. She knows how I feel about my first name. Hell, I complained to her about it enough when I was a kid. So she knows Lilah's casual use of it means something big.

We'll talk about this later, her gaze says, matching my own.

I nod at her in response, promising her just that.

"What would you like to drink with dinner?" Lilah asks them, turning to the cabinet where I keep my cups like it's second nature to her. We've spent an equal amount of time at my place as we have hers, so I guess it might be at this point. "We're just about done if you'd like to drop your bags and get comfortable."

"A beer, if you have it," my dad requests.

"And iced tea for you, Mama?"

She pats my shoulder as I pass by her. "You know me so well, son."

We shoo my parents from the kitchen, sending them away to get comfortable in my bedroom while Lilah and I finish making dinner—a simple meal of grilled chicken with a balsamic vinaigrette glaze, roasted rosemary red potatoes, and freshly chopped carrots. It was all Lilah's idea to make it. She wanted to impress them. I tried telling her it wasn't necessary, but she insisted.

"You're doing this big thing for me, Fox. Let me do this for you."

It was my shot to tell her the truth again, but I couldn't do it. So, I just nodded, helped her grocery shop, and now here we are, playing house with my parents in the other room.

"They're just like I imagined," Lilah says as she flips the chicken breast in the cast-iron skillet. I push the carrots around in the pan next to her. "You look just like your mom."

"I've heard that a lot. I've never really been sure if I should take it as a compliment. You know, since she's a woman and all."

"Oooh. You should grow your hair out more. It'll be sexy."

I slide behind her, and I love how her breath stutters the second I do. "Are you saying I'm not already sexy?"

She rests back against me. "I think we both already know I think you're sexy, Fox."

"I don't. Tell me."

She abandons the chicken, turning around to place her arms around my neck as my hands settle on her waist.

"You're sexy, Fox. I like your eyes and how they remind me of my favorite chocolate bar." She presses up on her tiptoes, kissing right beside my eye.

"The one with the crispies in it?"

"That's the one." She grins, then kisses the tip of my nose. "I like your nose, especially the scar on the bridge."

"Got that from Russ. He hit me with one of Regan's Barbies because I ate his last Pop-Tart."

"What flavor?"

"Brown sugar."

"Totally valid, then." She kisses the corner of my mouth. "I like your lips too, especially all the dirty things they say."

"Like when I say"—I brush her hair behind her ear, then lean in close—"if we were alone right now, I'd spread you out on this counter and eat your pretty pink pussy until you made a mess all over my face, then

I'd lick that little hole of yours I haven't yet gotten to taste until you were begging for my cock?"

She gulps. "Yes, like that."

I laugh darkly. "Anything else?"

"Definitely that Southern drawl. It doesn't come out often, but when it does, it's good."

"I'll try to remember that, sugar."

She groans, dropping her head against my shoulder when I use the exact accent she's talking about. "Stop it. It's not fair. You know that does things to me and we're not alone."

"Sorry, not sorry, sugar."

She pinches me for that one, then pulls away, her eyes finding mine. "You."

I cock my head to the side. "Me?"

She nods. "Your personality. Your kindness. Your good heart." She lays her palm over my chest. "Such a good heart. The best one ever, maybe."

It's yours, I want to say. *It's yours if you want it, Lilah.*

"Fox, I—"

"Oh my goodness!"

My parents come barreling into the kitchen and we spring apart like we've been caught doing something we shouldn't. What was Lilah about to say? Was she thinking the same thing I was? Could she want this to be real too?

"You have turtle hand towels in your bathroom!"

"That would be my doing, Mrs. Fox," Lilah says, pouring her a glass of iced tea, the special gallon of sweet I got just for her. She'd kill me if I tried to serve her anything without sugar.

"Mrs. Fox." My mother laughs with a shake of her head. "There's no need for formalities, sweetheart. You can call me Bonnie or Mama. Your choice."

A look I haven't seen before crosses Lilah's features: longing. I know instantly what it is she's yearning for, and it's the familial love my mother is offering her with open arms.

"Anyway," my mother says. "Did you know our boy here made it his life's mission to save the turtles when he was younger? Cutest thing ever."

"Bold endeavor, too," my father says as Lilah hands him a beer from the fridge. "He probably brought home at least twenty of those suckers through the years before we finally put a stop to it. Now he's got a hundred figurines instead."

"And now even more." Lilah tosses me a wink. She's given me no less than six since she first learned of my collection. I'd never tell my parents or siblings, but the ones from her are my favorite.

We settle at the kitchen table, our plates full of good food.

"I hope you like everything," Lilah says, lifting her mug of lemonade to her lips.

"I'm sure we will. It looks great," my mother says, my father already digging into the meal, his mouth full as he nods along with her. She points with her fork to the mug in Lilah's hand. "Did we take the last of your cups?" She looks to me. "Do you only have two proper glasses, Artie?"

"Oh." Lilah's shoulders tighten, and I can see the worry that settles into her eyes. "Um, no. I just prefer to drink out of a mug."

My mother laughs. "I *love* that. I always eat my ice cream out of a mug. There's just something about it that makes it taste better. Don't ask me why. I'm pretty sure it's science."

That same longing look from earlier creeps back in as Lilah's shoulders settle. She and my mother discuss different flavors of ice cream while my father sits by quietly, shoveling his meal into his mouth. I sit back, and I fall even more in love with Lilah than I already have.

After dinner, my father does the dishes, insisting on it since we cooked, and we relax in the living room with my mother, who is still gabbing with Lilah like they're old friends. Lilah's hand sits on my leg the entire time, my own curled around the back of her neck. It's easy. Comfortable. *Right.*

Eventually, my mother yawns, and my father stands.

"That's my cue," he says, helping my mother from her spot on the couch. "Come on, BonBon. Let's get you to bed."

"That's a lovely idea." She holds her arms out.

I look to Lilah. "That's *our* cue."

She laughs as we stand, my mother wrapping Lilah into her arms first.

"I can't wait to hang out with you again tomorrow," my mother tells her sincerely.

"You'll have to tell me more about Arthur's treehouse adventures."

"You bet, sweetheart." My mother pats her cheek before moving to me, that familiar perfume of hers that I swear she's been wearing all my life tickling my nose. "Thank you for bringing us here."

"Any time, Mama."

"I like her, Arthur," she says quietly so only I can hear. "She's a keeper."

She is a keeper, and that's exactly what I want to do. I want to keep her, want to make her mine for real. And with our engagement party so close, I'm losing the chance to make it happen.

My parents retire to my room, and Lilah and I take turns getting ready in the hall bathroom before slipping beneath the sheets of the temporary bed I've set up in my spare bedroom. Lilah rests her head on my chest like she's done so many nights before, and I hold her close, hoping she can't hear my heart beating wildly, which always seems to be the case these days.

"Your parents are wonderful, Fox," she says into the dark room, and there's no denying the emotion packed behind each of those words.

"They are, aren't they?"

She nods, then sighs. "I'm…I'm sorry this can't be real for them."

I'm sorry, too.

But I don't say that. I can't bring myself to do it.

So, I press my lips to her forehead. "Good night, sugar."

"Night, Arthur."

Lilah falls asleep first, while I stay awake late into the night, unable to stop thinking of how I'm going to tell her the truth about how I feel.

Chapter 20

"Does your mother even know you? I mean, she could have at least had this at The Sinclair."

I laugh at Auden, who stands beside me. We take in the party before us, which is stuffed to the gills with her friends and very few people I actually know and like. It has Selene Maddison written all over it, not an ounce of Lilah Maddison to be seen. The flowers are all wrong, the dress code she insisted on is so not me, and I hate everything on the buffet table.

Everything about this party is the exact opposite of anything I could have possibly wanted.

"Not at all."

My eyes land on Fox standing with his parents across the room. He's sipping on what I know is a glass of sparkling apple juice, his dad has a beer from the open bar, and his mother is clutching her sweet tea like a lifeline. They're all three laughing about something. I don't know what, yet it still makes me smile.

Roy and Bonnie are everything I expected and then some. They're kind and loving, and they clearly support their son no matter what he does, not that I know what that feels like. They've accepted me so easily it's almost too much to handle sometimes because, after this party, I'm going to have to give it all up. I run my hand over the base of my throat, massaging the lump that's settled there.

"How are you holding up?" Auden asks.

"I'm okay."

"You sure? Because with the way you're smiling right now, I'm worried you might crack." She pokes at the grin on my face, and I glower at her, poking her back.

"Behave, Lilah," my mother snaps from behind me, and I instantly bristle. "I mean, my god. Acting that way at your own engagement party and causing a scene. It's absurd. And fix your hair."

"My hair is fine, Mother," I mutter, teeth gritted.

"Tell that to a mirror, dear."

I square my shoulders back, ready to go toe-to-toe with her. I don't care if she finds out this is all fake. I have officially had enough of this. I'm done being her puppet. I'm done playing her game. I am just *done*.

"Mother, I—"

"Selene, there you are," Fox says smoothly, cutting in at just the right time. My mother gives him that same smile she's been giving him since day one. The one that says, *I don't like you, but I'm smiling so it* looks *like I like you, and once you turn your back, I'm going to talk shit about you and break you and my daughter up, then laugh all the way to the bank.*

The fact that she *still* thinks Fox isn't good enough for our family makes no sense to me. I'm the one who isn't worthy of him.

Auden squeezes my arm and sends me a tightlipped smile before slipping away, Fox taking her place beside me.

"I've been wanting to introduce you to my parents. Is Deacon around?"

"Oh, he's just right here." She turns. "My love!" she calls out, but he's too engrossed in a conversation—business, I assume—with one of his friends to pay her any attention. My mother sighs, then snaps her fingers. "Deacon!" she bellows.

That gets his attention—and nearly everyone else's, too. Talk about causing a scene and being absurd.

My dad excuses himself and makes his way over to us.

"Sorry, my love. Got swept up talking numbers." He looks down his nose at Bonnie and Roy. "And who is this, Lilah?"

Fox slips his hand into mine, squeezing it three times.

I'm right here.

I squeeze his back twice.

Thank you.

I clear my throat. "Mom, Dad, this is Roy and Bonnie Fox." I turn to Fox's parents. "This is my mother, Selene, and my father, Deacon."

My mother's smile doesn't reach her eyes as she extends her hand as if she's royalty and expects Fox's parents to kiss it.

"Oh, now, now. We're about to be family." Bonnie throws her arms around my mother before she can protest, hugging her tightly like she's an old friend and not standing stiffly in her arms. "It's so wonderful to meet you," the sweet Southern woman says.

"Hmm. Yes, wonderful indeed." My mother's words are cold, whereas Bonnie's are warm, and she pats her back awkwardly.

Bonnie does the same to my father, and I have to smother my laugh at the surprise on his face. I'll admit, I was shocked by Bonnie's penchant for hugging as well, but the moment the woman put her arms around me, I felt nothing but calm. I can count on one hand the number of times my parents have genuinely hugged me, and never did I feel even close to what Fox's mother's hug invoked—safe, warm, and, above all else, loved. I don't know if I've ever been held like that before. Except for maybe by…

I look up at Fox, who is having a hard time hiding his pleasure at my parents' discomfort, too.

"Nice to meet you, Deacon," Roy says, slinging his arm around me. "You've got a great gal here. Can make a mean biscuits-and-gravy breakfast." He pats his stomach. "And she's whip-smart, too. Did the crossword in the *Times* in under ten minutes. It usually takes me a full workday."

My father raises his brows. "Well, that is impressive, Lilah. It's too bad you've not put that to more use over the years."

I feel Roy's spine stiffen at my father's words, and I get the feeling that while this big Southern man is as sweet as they come, he's not afraid to protect the ones he cares about. In this case, that's me.

"Thanks, Roy," I tell him, laying a hand on his chest to hopefully help calm him down. "My father here collects antique furniture. You two might have something to chat about, given your line of work."

"Are you a dealer?" my father asks, suddenly interested.

"I guess you could say that. I make furniture."

My father's bushy brows rise. "You *make* furniture? As in you design it?"

"And build it with my own two hands."

Their conversation takes off from there, and feeling like I've done my duty, I take the opportunity to slink away, checking in on Fox, who is standing between our mothers as Bonnie explains her shifts at the hospital—twelve hours, three days a week, even on holidays. It's something my mother can't even fathom. I tip my chin at Fox, and he grins at me, then excuses himself, leaving them to chat.

"My mother looks bored as hell," I say to him as we walk a few feet away.

"Don't worry. My mama can charm anyone, even the coldest of cold."

"Selene Maddison is another level of cold."

Fox huffs. "Don't have to tell me twice."

Even though Fox and I have shown her we are nothing but a loving couple, my mother is still convinced he's beneath her and finds a way to insult him whenever I talk to her. Of course, he takes it like a champ, but I hate it all the same.

"Dude! You're getting married!" Lawson slings his arm around Fox's shoulder, ruffling his hair. "And I'm your best man!"

"He's your best man?" I ask Fox, though I don't know why.

There is no best man. He knows it, and I know it too. We haven't talked about how this party means the end. We haven't even talked about *how* we're going to break up or when. We just know this is it. That was the deal, right?

But now that it's here… Well, I don't know how I feel about it.

"Sure am." Lawson smiles proudly, dragging me back to the present. "And look, I know Auden's like your bestie and all, but if you could do me a solid and pick Rory as your maid of honor, I'd really appreciate it. I'm pretty sure Hutch would saw my nuts off if I had to slow dance with his gal."

"With a rusty spoon," says the man in question, strolling up with a glass of whiskey in hand, two ice cubes floating jauntily, and Auden on his arm.

She hands me a glass of champagne with a wink. "Looks like you need it."

She's right. With this party, I might have to rethink my recent no-booze stance.

"How do you even saw with a spoon, Hutchy?" Lawson's still grinning as Rory fits herself against his side like it's her rightful place.

They all look so…well, in love. Like couples. And I don't want to gag at the sight of it. I don't even want to call them fools.

What the hell is happening to me?

"You okay?" Fox asks, his own arm curling around my waist. I instantly settle back against him, and all my anxiety disappears with his simple touch.

I nod. "Yeah, I'm good."

And I *am* good. Sure, I'm at my engagement party with my fake fiancé holding me in his arms and I'm having a mild internal freakout because this whole thing with Fox has turned me into some weirdo who doesn't recoil at the idea of love, but still. I'm good.

At least I hope I am.

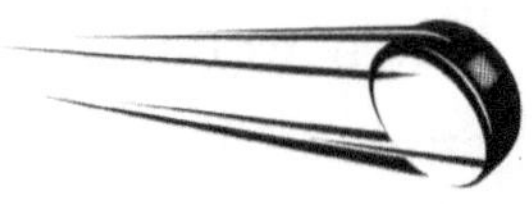

"For crying out loud, push your shoulders back, Lilah Jane. Stop slouching."

I haven't slouched once this evening, yet it doesn't stop my mother from picking me apart. I'm not sure why I expected the night of my engagement party to be any different, but I hoped she'd lay off for once in my life.

Still, I find myself pushing my shoulders back even more as a photographer—one I didn't even know she hired—snaps photos of Fox and me toasting the gathered crowd, our parents on either side of us. The flash from the camera is blinding, and I swear the only thing getting me through it is Fox's hand on my waist, holding me steady. Everyone around us cheers, and we're finally freed from our hostage situation.

"You smile like a crazed woman," my mother says through a grin.

That's rich coming from her.

She turns on her heel and marches away, her nose upturned the whole way.

"Well, isn't she just a ray of fucking sunshine." Fox glares after her, his jaw pulsing.

Bonnie smacks her son's arm. "Arthur Francis Fox, be nice! I raised you better than that." But even I can tell by her tone that she agrees with her son.

Aside from my mother being the frigid woman she is, this party has actually been…well, nice. Sure, I've had to remind myself several times that it's all for show, and soon, this fake relationship with Fox will be a thing of the past. I'll go back to either being harassed by my mother or well on my way to becoming the bitter old woman she swears I'll become, but it's nice all the same.

Someone tugs on the back of my long, cream-colored dress, and I turn to find Flora, Hayes's adorable niece, standing behind me. I bend to match her height.

"Well, hi. How are you, Miss Flora?"

"I like your dress, Ms. Lilah."

"Thank you. Your dress is gorgeous, too," I tell her, trying not to laugh at the pickle pattern dotting the fabric. "Did you pick it out?"

She nods, smiling softly. "Uncle Adam and Just Quinn took me shopping and said I could get whatever I wanted." She points to Quinn and Hayes where they're standing next to Lawson and Rory.

I don't even think they realize they're doing it, but her uncle and former nanny take turns casting glances over here to check on her. It's cute. I know the little girl has had a rough life, but damn, is she loved now.

Quinn shoots me a wave, and I smile at her.

"There you are, you little turkey," Lawson says, coming up behind her and tugging on one of her braids. "You were supposed to be stealing me a cookie, remember?"

"Stealing's bad, Uncle Lawson!" she says through giggles.

"Yeah, but you're all cute and shit. They don't care if kids do it."

"Go get your own cookies, Lawson," Fox says, "and stop encouraging a life of crime."

"What the hell else are kids for?" he grumbles, taking Flora's hand. "Come on. Let's go steal 'em together."

The kid giggles again, and they scurry off to cause havoc. I push to my full height, only slightly worried about what's in store for the dessert table. I'm sure Flora will keep him in check.

"Well, that was precious," Bonnie says, her hand over her heart as her eyes shine with unshed tears.

"Mama…" Fox warns. "Don't be getting ideas. You know this."

"I know, I know. I'm sorry." She nods, then sighs. "It's just… Well, you two look so good together. And a mother has dreams for her kids, you know? She wants them to find love and happiness, and I swear I see that you…" She shakes her head. "Never mind. Just ignore me."

Bonnie gives me a long look, then pats her son on the cheek before disappearing into the crowd of people I hardly know.

"Hey," Fox says, his hand on my elbow. "I'm sorry about that. She knows our…" He peeks around to make sure nobody is listening in. "Our arrangement. I don't know why she said anything like that."

I shake my head. "It's okay."

But…it doesn't *feel* okay exactly. In fact, this whole party is starting to not feel okay. Like too much. Like the whole room is closing in on me. Like I can't breathe. Like I might pass out at any moment.

"Whoa," Fox says, grabbing my other elbow as I sway. "Lilah. Hey, hey." He sets me straight. "You okay?"

I nod, but it's not very convincing when it takes every ounce of energy I have to do so. Fox notices.

"Come on, sugar." He wraps his arm around me and leads me away from the party, somehow knowing what it is I need without me saying a word.

Of course he does. He's Fox. He always knows what I need without me telling him.

He tugs me into a small room that looks like a supply closet, pulling on a light hanging overhead, the bulb swaying back and forth, and the only thing I can focus on is how I haven't seen a light like that in ages. My mother rented a big, fancy room at the top of a five-star hotel, yet the closets don't even have proper lighting.

Fox sets his sparkling apple juice aside, then takes my untouched champagne from my hand and puts it next to his. Then he gathers me in his arms, pulling me close, my face buried against his chest until all I can smell and think of is him, him, him.

He rubs my back as I focus on my breathing, trying to calm myself. I think I'm having a panic attack, and I've never had a panic attack before. Why am I freaking out right now? Why am I having such a hard time?

"I got you, sugar," he says softly, and it takes me back to the last time he said those words, when he was pounding into me, and I remember how good it felt to just let go. I want to let go like that again.

Suddenly my fingers are desperately moving

against the buttons on his crisp white shirt. I need to touch him, need to feel him against me. I simply need him. I lean forward, pressing my lips to his chest, kissing the skin I'm exposing button by button. He groans as I kiss him, his fingers flexing tightly against my waist where they've fallen. I tug his shirt from his pants, then drop my busy hands to his belt, undoing it with ease.

He stops me when I reach for his zipper. "Hey, hey, hey. Hang on. I want to make sure you're okay."

"Fine," I say, pressing another kiss to the base of his throat as I unsnap his dress pants. "Just want you."

I drag his zipper down, and he hisses when I slide my hand into his boxer briefs and grip his cock, stroking it just the way I know he likes. He's hard and hot and heavy in my palm and I want to taste him just as badly as I want to feel him inside me.

"Fuck," he mutters. "God, that feels good."

I stroke him again, moving my lips up his throat and over his chin until my mouth is on his, and then it's like something takes over him and he can't keep his hands off me either. He slips his tongue between my lips, his hands crashing into my hair as he takes control of our kiss, my hand still between us as I jack him. He drags his hands down my sides and over my waist, pulling my dress up inch by agonizing inch until I feel the cold air hit my bare skin. It takes him palming my ass for him to realize my surprise.

He yanks his mouth from mine. "You're not wearing any underwear?"

I shake my head with a grin. "I'm not wearing any underwear."

"Fuck." A kiss. "Fuck, fuck, fuck," he chants against my lips, which I have no doubt are already swollen.

Then he hauls me into his arms, and my back is pressed against I don't even know what, and I don't care, not even when it digs into my back. I welcome the pain. I *need* it. His own hand replaces mine as he grips himself and lines it up with my already slick pussy. We groan together as he presses the head of his cock inside me.

"Fuck," he says again, and I want to make a joke, ask him if he knows any other words, but I don't. I can't, especially when he slips inside me further, stretching me so wide and so perfectly that I need more.

"I can't believe how good you always feel," he says, his lips on my throat. "Never going to tire of it."

"Me either," I tell him as he sinks even deeper, my nails digging into his scalp as I hold him close, not wanting an ounce of space between us.

He groans when he finally pushes in fully, then he

backs out slowly. He doesn't move. He just holds himself there, his breath quick in my ear.

"I'm sorry," he says quietly, and I note how hoarse his voice has grown.

"Sorry?" What does he have to be sorry for? Because it certainly can't be this. Not when he feels so fucking good even when he's not moving.

But he doesn't explain. He fucks into me again, just as unhurriedly. It's painfully slow, and I want more, yet I can't seem to make myself ask for it when I usually have no problem being vocal and telling Fox what I want.

We maintain the excruciatingly slow pace. Over and over again, dragging us both closer to the edge as the party goes on around us. I can hear people talking, and the music, which is so not my taste, plays softly in the background. Lawson's loud laugh echoes. I hear someone else say something loudly. A pair of feet pass right outside the door.

Yet, even though I know we should be out there right now, none of it matters. Not as Fox continues to rock into me, as I hold on to him like he's going to vanish before my eyes.

"Gonna come," Fox says. "Fuck, I'm gonna come."

"Do it," I tell him. "I want to feel you inside me."

"You first." He wedges his hand between us, rubbing my clit in hurried circles.

It's everything I didn't realize I needed, and I'm coming in just a few touches, my pussy clenching around him and urging him on. Fox loses all restraint, slamming into me until there is no doubt I'm going to have a bruise on my back that matches whatever it is I'm pressed against.

"Lilah, Lilah, Lilah," he says, punctuating each word with a hard thrust. "Fuck. I love you."

Fuck. I love you.

I love you.

Love.

His once rhythmic movements stutter, and it's the only sign that he really just said what I thought he did. He recovers the fumble quickly, and his thrusts return to the same delightful pace as before. When his hand digs hard into my ass cheek, I know he's close, and just a moment later, he stills. I feel him empty himself inside me, and he drops his head into the crook of my neck, our uneven breaths filling the silence between us.

His lips ghost over my collarbone in sets of three.

Kiss.

I.

Kiss.

Love.

Kiss.

You.

He does it again and again, and it does nothing to

help settle my heart rate that seems to be at an all-time high. That same feeling I had out in the ballroom slams into me all at once. The room feels so small. Fox now feels too close, and I'm working far too hard for each breath I take.

Kiss.

I.

Kiss.

Love.

Kiss.

You.

I need to move. I need to go, need to be anywhere else than here right now. I shove at Fox, and he jerks away instantly, his oak gaze finding mine.

"Lilah?" he asks, likely seeing the wild look in my eyes. "What's wrong?"

"I have to… I need to… I can't…"

He slips out of me, and I groan at the loss of him. He sets me back on my feet, tucking himself back into his pants as I drag my dress back down, trying to ignore the fact that I can feel his cum leaking down my leg, a reminder of what just happened between us.

I love you.

"Hey, what's—" I hold my hand up when he takes a step toward me, and it kills me to see his brows crush together.

But not as much as it kills me to hear those three words still crashing through my mind.

I love you.

"Why did you say that?"

He swallows, dragging his hand over his clean-shaven jawline. "Shit," he mutters, exhaling heavily before finding my stare again. "Because I—"

"Don't."

His brows furrow. "Don't what?"

"Don't say it," I beg. "Please don't say it again."

He clenches his jaw. "Why not?"

"Because you can't."

"I can too."

I shake my head. "We said it was fake. We said this wasn't real. We had a deal."

He nods. "You're right. We did have a deal, Lilah. We said this was just for fun, said we'd break it off after the party. But, fuck, I don't want to, okay? Something changed along the way for me. I fell for you. I fell for your laugh and your smile and the fact that you love to eat and drink everything out of a mug. You think butter pecan is the superior flavor when we all know it's for old people. You're smart and strong and so fucking capable of doing anything, and all I can do is stare in awe. You take control and you're not afraid of what you want. You make me feel good. When I told you I collect turtle figurines, you didn't laugh at me. When I told you I struggle to read, you didn't even bat an eye, instead you picked up a book and you read for me. You make me feel like I'm on top of the world no matter what." He rolls his tongue along his bottom lip and exhales. "I don't want to break it off. I don't want to go back to being acquaintances. I don't want to go back to barely knowing you. I want this. I want what we've built these last few months. I want *you*. For real this time."

My head moves back and forth as Fox takes a step toward me. I take one back but run right into something big, and I peek behind me.

Huh. It's a filing cabinet. So that's the cause of the bruise I feel forming along my back.

But that's not what matters right now. Not when Fox reaches out, tucks his fingers beneath my chin, and pulls my eyes to his.

"I'm sorry I broke the rules. I really am. But I'll be damned if I say I'm sorry for loving you because I'm not. I am in love with you, Lilah Jane, and I refuse to apologize for it."

I am in love with you, Lilah Jane, and I refuse to apologize for it.

My head swims, my vision going fuzzy at the edges until all I can see are the brown eyes I've spent so much time staring into as of late. The same eyes that lock on to me at a game after he makes an incredible save. The same ones that bore into me as he makes love to me. The same ones I can feel on me as we sit on my couch and watch horrible television even though I know he hates it. And the same ones I've spent so much time trying to tell myself I don't love.

I am in love with you, Lilah Jane, and I refuse to apologize for it.

I look right into them, and I say the only thing that comes to my mind.

"Oh."

Chapter 21

FOX

"I am in love with you, Lilah Jane, and I refuse to apologize for it."

She stares up at me, eyes wide.

Then, finally, she blinks. Once. Twice.

"Oh."

Of all the things I thought Lilah might say, that was not one of them.

Oh? That's it?

She stands there, saying nothing else, and now I don't know what to say either.

Oh.

That single word rings in my head over and over.

I run my tongue over my lips, tipping my head to the side. "Oh?"

She nods.

"Is that all?"

She nods again, this time slower. "We, uh, we should probably get back to the party."

I just poured my heart out to her, and she thinks we should get back to the party. Our *engagement* party. The one happening just outside the door. The one I completely forgot about, so damn focused on the woman before me.

The woman who doesn't care that I just told her I love her.

What the fuck am I supposed to do with that? What am I supposed to say? Do I tell her again? Do I say it until I get a response other than *oh*?

But I don't. I just nod, my fingers falling to my shirt that's still unbuttoned. We remain silent as I slip each button back into its rightful place, and it's damn near deafening, even despite the fun being had outside without us. Lilah runs her hands through her hair, pushing the messy locks back into place, and then rubs at her nearly gone lipstick.

None of it matters. She still looks like she's been thoroughly fucked, and I'm sure I do too. Just maybe not in the same way.

Oh.

That damn word echoes around my head again.

Once I'm righted, I clear my throat. "Do you want to go first?"

She nods. "Sure."

She brushes past me, and I can't stop myself from reaching out, the fingers that were just pressing against her and driving her wild circling around her wrist. She looks down at where I hold on to her, almost like she's refusing to meet my eyes.

What does "oh" mean? Do you feel the same? Why can't you talk to me? Where the fuck do we go from here?

I have so much I want to say, but I'm unsure where to start. So, I say nothing. I release her, and she stands there a moment, hope filling my chest.

Say something, Lilah. Anything. Just please say something.

But she doesn't, and all that hope I was feeling goes out the door right along with her. I have no idea how long I stand there beneath the muted yellow light, but it's not long enough to stop the questions that are still swirling.

Why did I have to say anything? Why did I have to go and ruin it? I wish I could say blurting it out was just the heat of the moment, but it wasn't. Those three words have been sitting on the tip of my tongue for quite some time now. It's a miracle they didn't tumble out earlier.

But why tonight? When we're surrounded by our friends and family and whoever else Selene invited? Now, I have to go out there and pretend the woman

I'm head over heels for didn't just completely crush me with one little word.

Oh.

I shake my head, forcing the word out of my mind, then pull open the door—and come to a halt. Hutch stands with his back against the opposite wall, arms crossed over his chest as he eyes me knowingly.

"What?" I ask, jaw tight as I run my hand through my hair.

"Want to tell me why Lilah came back out to her *engagement* party with tears in her eyes?"

Fuck. She was crying? I move to chase after her, but I'm stopped by my captain. It doesn't matter that I have two inches on the guy; he's still holding me back, not allowing me to pass.

"Hutch," I snarl at him. "Let me go."

He shakes his head. "Not until you tell me why. Because I told you what I'd do to you if you hurt her, and I meant every fucking word of it, Fox."

"I didn't hurt her," I say through clenched teeth.

"She was crying." He shoves at my chest again. "I fucking saw it. I just want an explanation for it. I want—"

"I told her I love her!"

His eyes widen, and he releases me. "You did what?"

"I told her I love her," I repeat, quieter this time. My shoulders slump forward, my throat closing in tight. "And she didn't say it back. She didn't say it back, Hutch."

I knew how Lilah felt about love and relationships going into this—she was fully against both—and I knew how I felt about them. I knew it was risky. I knew I was playing a dangerous game. Yet, I played. I played it, and now I've fucking lost. This is nobody's fault but my own.

Hutch sighs. "Fuck, Fox. Shit. I… I'm so sorry."

I nod because I don't know what else to do or what else to say. It's not like any of it will suddenly make Lilah run back here and tell me she loves me too.

"Give her time," Hutch says. "Sometimes, it just takes time."

I don't respond because I know he's wrong. Lilah's already made up her mind. She knows what she wants, and I'm not on that list.

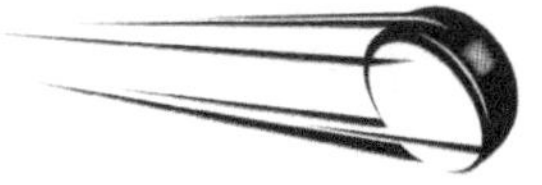

My parents didn't fight often growing up, so the times they did stick out like sore thumbs in my mind. I remember one particularly cold January night when we were on our way back from dinner—a treat in those days—and my parents didn't speak the whole way home. My father came home late, and my parents whisper-yelled at one another behind closed doors before all of us kids climbed into the car, and we went out as scheduled. I heard words like *gambling* and *extra shifts* and *the bar*. I had no idea what any of it meant and I still don't, but it made for the most awkward car ride of my life.

Until tonight. Lilah sits stiffly beside me in the passenger seat, her eyes focused on the road ahead of us, even though she might as well be looking a million miles away. My parents sit in the back just as quietly, and I imagine they feel just as I did way back when, like they have no idea what to do to break the tension.

So, they don't. After a night that's supposed to be full of joy and excitement, we ride home in utter silence. We don't speak even as I pull into my parking garage or when we all slide into the elevator, my parents and me on one side, Lilah standing alone on the other. Nor is a peep uttered when I push open my apartment door, a chill racking through me since I forgot to leave the heater on.

Or maybe that's just the iciness from Lilah. I can't tell which.

"I hope you don't mind if I turn in," Lilah says, her voice so sudden in the otherwise quiet apartment that it makes me jump. "I'm exhausted and can feel a migraine coming on."

Being the kind of woman she is, my mother smiles sweetly, meaning it to her core, and says, "Of course not, sweetheart. Go rest. We'll be fine on our own."

She wraps Lilah in a hug, and it's so fucking hard to watch the way she clings to my mother, like she'll never see her again. I have to look away.

When she turns to me, she hesitates, but it's only for a moment. She pushes up on her tiptoes and presses her lips to my cheek. I turn my head, inhaling the familiar floral scent I've come to associate with her.

"Peonies."

She pulls back, brows turned inward. "What?"

"I've been trying to figure out your perfume for months now, and I finally got it. It's peonies, isn't it?"

Her mouth floats open, her blue eyes bright with surprise.

Then she snaps it closed and mumbles a soft "Good night, Arthur" before hurrying out of the room.

I stare after her for a long time. So long that my father pats me on the back as he passes by, heading for bed himself, and it's just me and Mama left. She stands beside me, resting her head against my shoulder as I stare down the hall at the spare bedroom door. One and three-quarters inch. That's all that separates us, yet it feels like a thousand miles or more.

"Was this my fault?" she asks quietly, lifting her head from my shoulder.

I look down at her. "What? Why would you think that?"

"For what I said about wanting to see you happy. You two disappeared after that, and I was afraid I upset you."

"No, Mama. It wasn't you. This was… This was my fault, I think. I…messed up."

"Do you want to talk about it?"

I shake my head once. "No."

"I figured." She sighs. "Guess I'll do the talking, then."

"Mama, I—"

She gives me a sharp look that has me shutting my trap instantly. I nod, encouraging her to speak.

"I don't know what happened with you two tonight, son. I'm sure you'll tell me whenever you're ready, and that's fine. But I do know one thing that's certain, and that is that tonight, I watched the two of you closely, and at least not until you disappeared did it ever seem like you were pretending. Not a single glance or simple touch or secret smile…none of it, Arthur. That was real. That was *love*. And trust me, after thirty-five years of marriage, I know love when I see it. It's not always grand gestures and big presents or life-altering moments. It's the small things that add up. It's coffee dates. It's holding hands. It's showing up when the other person has had a bad day." She smiles softly, and I assume she's thinking of my father and the simple life they've always led. "You and Lilah… That's what you have. You have something real, and for most people, that only comes along once in a lifetime. When it does, you hold on to it. You don't let it go. You don't let it pass you by. You might have to wait on it a bit, but you never, ever give up. Like that play in hockey you guys do when you're down a goal. Where you go sit on the bench while your teammates keep playing."

"Empty net," I provide.

"Yeah, that. Why do you do it?"

"Because we want to score. We want to win. We want to keep playing until the final buzzer. Because we…"

"Never give up. That's what you need here." She pats my cheek. "Don't give up hope, Arthur. Play until the final buzzer. And even if you have to, play some more. The real thing is worth it."

I want to believe her, I really do, but it's hard when you pour your heart out to the woman you love and she barely acknowledges you've said anything.

She sighs heavily, then gives me a tightlipped smile.

"Get some sleep, son, and think about what I said, all right?"

I nod, not trusting myself to say anything right now. She tells me good night, and I watch as she makes her way to my bedroom, then I pull my eyes right back to that door. I stare and stare and stare some more until my eyes and legs grow as heavy as my heart feels. Only then do I force myself from the spot, moving down the hall and past the door.

I do my business in the bathroom, taking my time because, fuck, I'm not even sure if Lilah wants me in that room next to her. It has to be well after midnight by the time I finally find myself standing outside the door, my hand hovering above the knob. And at least another ten minutes before I convince myself to actually use it.

I push the door open as quietly as I can, careful not to wake Lilah, then slip beneath the blanket she's already hogging. The second I lie down, exhaustion from the evening sets in, and my eyes fall shut of their own accord. I'm just about asleep when Lilah shuffles next to me, and I hold my breath, knowing she's awake and waiting for her to say something.

But, just like earlier, she doesn't. Instead, she rolls over and puts her head on my chest just like she has so many times before, and just as I have, I wrap my arm around her and hold her close.

Play until the final buzzer. And even if you have to, play some more. The real thing is worth it.

Mama is right. The real thing is worth it, and I believe what we have is real, so I'm going to keep playing. I'm going to wait. I'm going to give Lilah all the time in the world. Whatever she needs.

I'm playing until the final buzzer.

Chapter 22

LILAH

"I'll have a large butter pecan latte, extra hot, please."

"Of course," the barista says. "Anything else?"

"A blueberry scone. Oh, and an old-fashioned donut."

"Make that two donuts, avocado toast, and a small decaf honey oat milk latte."

"You got it." The barista punches our order into the tablet. "That'll be thirty seventy-eight."

Auden hip-checks me out of the way, placing her black card against the reader.

"Auden! You aren't buying my breakfast for me."

She ignores me, and I shake my head at her as I follow her toward the back of The Coffee Spot, a local shop we've taken to meeting up at over the last year. She sets her oversized tote on the floor—never mind it costs as much as some people's rent—then pulls out her laptop, setting it between us.

"What's this?" I ask.

"It's nothing. Something I want to talk about later. First, I want to know how *you're* doing."

Auden watches me carefully, gauging my reaction. I don't give her one, careful to keep my face neutral. While I have an idea I know *why* she's asking after me, I am not giving anything away, hoping maybe if I don't, she'll move on.

The last thing I want to do is sit here and discuss Fox. In fact, for the first time in months, I don't want to think about Fox at all. His parents are still here, so I'm staying at his place, and it's slowly killing me because he's walking around like nothing has changed. Hell, just this morning before he left for practice, he kissed the hell out of me until I thought I was going to fall over right there in his entryway.

We still haven't talked about what happened in that supply closet. He's just continued on like we've spent every other day together—full of laughs and fun and really, really, *really* great sex. He's not outright said *I love you* since, but he's said it in so many other ways. My coffee made just right every morning. A mug of ice cream brought to me late at night after he hears my stomach rumble. Every kiss, every simple touch. The way he looks at me like he's never seen a more beautiful person.

And I have no damn clue what to make of any of it.

I am in love with you, Lilah Jane, and I refuse to apologize for it.

"What do you mean?" I ask Auden, pushing Fox's voice out of my head.

She arches a brow. "I mean, you and Fox disappeared at your engagement party, and Hutch said he saw you crying afterward. And even though you look well fucked right now, you still look frazzled. So, something is clearly up. I'm just curious what it is."

The barista stumbles, nearly dropping our beloved pastries to the floor before setting them on the table with a clatter.

"I, uh, sorry. I'll be right back with your avocado toast and drinks."

Auden flashes them a smile like she didn't just openly discuss my sex life in front of a virtual stranger.

"What is wrong with you?" I practically hiss.

"What?" She tears off a piece of her donut, popping it into her mouth. "It's totally what happened, isn't it?"

"Yes, but did you have to broadcast it all over the coffee shop?"

"Uh, in case you haven't noticed, we're the only ones in here."

I roll my eyes, but she's right. Aside from the baristas, it's just us, and I assume they've heard way worse. People will talk about anything in a coffee shop, even things they shouldn't.

I grab my donut and shove it into my mouth. "Mmfinve," I say around the fluffy dough.

Auden gives me a pointed look. "Want to try that again?"

I chew and swallow. "I said I'm fine."

"Oh, that part I understood. I speak mouth-full-of-food fluently. I meant, want to try that without lying to me?"

All the strength I've been using to hold myself up these last few days evaporates. My shoulders fall forward, and the tears that have been stinging my eyes finally fall.

"Oh, Lilah." Auden rounds the table, gathering me into her arms.

She holds me, letting me cry it all out, something I never do. I try to remain stoic, try to keep my emotions in check just as I was taught growing up, but screw that. I need to let this out. I need to cry. Because Arthur Fox is in love with me, and I think I love him too.

I think I've known for some time that it's true,

which makes my reaction the other night that much worse. But when he dropped that bomb on me, I froze. I completely shut down as worry after worry filtered through my head. I tried to shut them out. I've *been* trying to shut them out. But I can't seem to stop the bad thoughts from spinning.

At some point during my breakdown, the barista must bring over our drinks, because when I finally pull away from Auden, my face hot and wet and covered in snot, our coffees are sitting in front of us with two glasses of water as well.

Thank goodness, too, because suddenly, I'm thirsty as hell. I chug nearly all the water as Auden settles back down across from me, her lips downturned as she lets me recover from my cryfest. I clean up my face as best as I can and even take a sip of my coffee before finally blowing out a heavy breath.

"So, maybe I'm *not* okay."

Auden barks out a laugh. "Yeah, I'd say. Want to tell me what happened? Did you two break up?"

I shake my head. "No. We haven't. His parents are still here, and we have a thing with my parents tomorrow. It's the opposite."

"The opposite?" Her brows pull together. "Well, that would be marriage." She gasps. "Did you two sneak away and get married?"

"What? No!"

"Well…" She shrugs. "I'm just saying it's possible. Pretty sure there are websites that can make it happen in under twenty-four hours, and with the way you two have been lately, it wouldn't have surprised me."

"The way we've been lately? What do you mean?"

"You know, acting like you're all in love and stuff. Like you've gone and turned this real and like—oh my god. Something happened, didn't it? You caught feelings for Fox."

"Fox caught them."

She gasps, her hand covering her mouth, eyes filling with tears. Looks like we're both emotional today.

"That is just… Oh, Lilah. I'm so happy for you. I'm… Why do you not seem happy about this? You do like him, right?"

My chin wobbles, and I sniff, holding back the tears trying to spill. Yes, I like him. I more than like him. But it's not that simple.

"He told me he loves me, and I said *Oh. Oh*, Auden. That was my response."

She pulls her lips to the side. "I don't understand. Why did you not tell him how you feel?"

"Because I… Because I *can't* have feelings for him."

"Why not?"

"I don't know *how*."

"I'm not following." She looks just as confused as I feel, popping another piece of her donut in her mouth.

I look down at the mug the barista put my coffee in, grinning at the turtle on the side. Why wouldn't it be a turtle?

"I've never been in love before. I've barely even witnessed love. You and Hutch and Lawson and Rory…that's it. We didn't have love in my house growing up. My parents don't even love me now. I don't know how to do this. I don't know how to love someone. I don't know how to be in a relationship. What if I hurt him? What if he hurts me? What if we wake up one day and look at each other and realize this isn't what we want and we've just wasted so much time? What if we just don't work? If this was all a fluke?" I look up for the first time, my throat scratchy and my eyes burning yet again. "What if he doesn't really love me, Auden?"

She sets her donut down and reaches across the table, taking my hand in hers. "I think you know better than anyone I can relate to the whole parents-not-really-knowing-love thing. I mean, look at my relationship with my mother. It's about as convoluted as yours. So, I get it. I understand your hesitation. I wish more than anything I could sit here and say you're never going to hurt Fox or he's never going to hurt you, but I can't guarantee that. Nobody can. Is opening yourself up to another person scary? Every damn day. But what's life without taking a little risk?" She smiles, and I have no doubt she's thinking of the big risk she took with Hutch. "What does being with Fox make you feel like?"

"I don't know. Good."

"Good? That's it?"

"Well, what do you want me to say?" I toss my hands into the air. "Do you want me to tell you he makes me laugh over the most ridiculous things? He's the first person I want to tell a funny story to? The person who makes me feel calm after a chaotic day? Should I say I think about him when he's not around and I want him around all the time? My heart literally aches thinking of life without him, and even though the thought of marriage still scares me, it doesn't sound as scary if it's with him? How 'bout I tell you how every time I look at him, I swear I lose my breath a little? If I lose him, I'm going to feel like I'm losing a piece of myself? I am so impossibly and irrevocably in love with him that I can't think straight? Is that what you want to hear?"

I take a breath for the first time in what feels like minutes, and Auden stares at me, her lips twitching at the edge, a piece of donut stuck there, but I don't think she cares.

I care, though. It's annoying how she's just watching me.

"What?" I snap when she doesn't say anything.

It just makes her smile wider.

"Stop it."

"I can't."

"Can too."

"Fine. Then I don't want to." Her lips pull back over her teeth even more. "And yes."

"Yes?"

"Yes, that's what I wanted to hear. But more than that, I think it's what you *needed* to say."

My immediate reaction is to refute her words, but I think...I think she's right. I did need to say it. I *do* need to.

"I love him, Auden."

"I know you do."

"I love him so much and I'm so scared and I don't know what to do with my hands and I—"

She grabs my hand once again, pulling me back from the ledge I'm so ready to jump over. "Breathe, Lilah. Just breathe. This is the exact same reaction I had when I found out I was preg—"

She pauses, and my eyes flash to hers.

"Shit," she murmurs, squeezing her eyes shut on a wince.

"You're pregnant?"

She peels her eyes open one by one and nods slowly. "I'm pregnant."

"What?! How? Well, not how, I know how and I really don't need the details considering Hutch is basically like a brother to me, but… When? When did you find out? How did you find out? I—oh my god, you're pregnant!"

I'm out of my chair, flying around the table to her. I haul her into my arms and hug her tightly. When we part, we're both a crying mess *again*.

She laughs, wiping at the tears under her eyes. "We found out around Valentine's Day. I've been dying to tell you, but I know you've had so much going on with your mother and the engagement party and all this stuff with Fox, so I didn't want to add this on top of all that. Plus, they say you should wait to tell people, and I didn't want to jinx it."

"Auden…I would have been there for you no matter what else was going on. You know that."

"I know. I do. I don't know. Maybe I was just trying to get used to it myself."

"And have you? How are you doing? I know you always told your dad he was never going to be a grandfather."

"I meant it too. I didn't want kids. I truly didn't. Then we found out, and well…" She shrugs. "It happened, so we're doing it."

"Are you freaking out?" I ask as I slide back into my chair, handing her a napkin.

"Yes!" She laughs, then blows her nose. "Yeah, definitely. Hutch is too, though he won't admit it. You should have seen his face after I took the test and it was positive. I thought he was going to pass out, which was really rude, because *I* felt like I was going to pass out. Who would have caught me?"

"Ugh. Men."

She chuckles. "Right? I'm feeling better about it now. Only having mini panic attacks instead of big ones. Progress, right?"

"Majorly."

She blows out a long breath, fanning her face. "Gosh, look at us. Two big life changes. I just…I never thought we'd be here."

"You and me both," I agree.

I'm in love and so is Auden. She's pregnant, and I'm engaged.

Wait…am I still engaged? Am I marrying Fox now?

"What's wrong? You look like you're freaking out again."

"No, no," I say. "Well, maybe. I just don't know what to tell Fox. I don't know if this means we're really engaged now or what. I… Shit. I guess I need to talk to him."

"I think that's a great idea. This is an…interesting situation you two are in, to say the least, but I'm sure you'll figure it out. You know, since you're in *love* and all," she teases, singing *love*.

"Shut up." I throw my spare napkin at her.

"Hey, hey! Be nice. I'm with child."

"You only get to use that excuse for so long, you know."

"Which is why I have no problem milking it to the fullest extent." She grabs her donut again, taking a huge bite before sipping on her decaf coffee.

Huh. I guess that should have been my first clue. I've never known her to forgo caffeine. I was too stuck in my own head though, too busy worrying about Fox.

Fox.

I smile just thinking of him, already buzzing with the desire to talk to him. I want to call him now, but I think this is a better conversation to have in person.

"Now that we have our personal lives all figured out, do you think we can discuss our business lives?" Auden asks, rearranging the numerous plates on the table until she's able to open her laptop.

"What business lives? I thought you left that behind for roots."

"I did," she says, click-clacking away on her keyboard, eyes darting all over the screen. "And I have roots now. It's time to water them."

"Okay…" I stretch the word out, unsure where she's going with that.

She spins her laptop my way. "I give you water, AKA our next project."

I look at the screen filled with inspiration photos she's pulled from various websites. There are lots of upscale homes and architecture mixed with warm and cozy interiors. If I'm not mistaken, the photo on the right is one of her East Coast hotels.

"It all looks gorgeous, but I'm not following, Auden."

She sighs, pulling the laptop back to her and clicking a button on the keyboard. A new slide pops up that reads *Maddison Sinclair Designs – Your Home, Your Way*. I peek at Auden over the top of the screen.

"What is this?"

"I told you, it's our next project…if you'll have me, that is."

"Have you for what?"

"Oh. Duh." She clicks the next slide, and I can't believe what I'm seeing on the screen: a business proposal.

Auden clears her throat, then sits up high, and I instantly recognize this version of her—the badass CEO who *will* get what she wants.

"Good morning, Sharks," she says, and I laugh,

remembering all the time we spent in our dorm room watching *Shark Tank* together, Auden promising she'd have a killer business idea like one of them one day. She did, but she never needed the show to make her dream happen.

Just like she doesn't need me now. No, she *wants* me now. And I'm not sure why.

"I'm here today to submit a proposal that you, Lilah Maddison, buy into Maddison Sinclair Designs, a company that specializes in not only building your dream home but decorating it too. You would get fifty-one percent ownership of the company in exchange for a quarter million dollars for startup."

Next to Auden telling me she's pregnant, this is the absolute last thing I expected to happen today. Yet…it's exactly what I want.

I've been trying to figure out what I want for over a year now, and now that it's sitting in front of me, I can't believe I didn't see it before—I want to work with my best friend again. It was my favorite part of working for Sinclair Properties. She's smart, has great business sense, and isn't afraid to take risks. Watching her over the years was magical. Running a business with her is a no-brainer, especially when it perfectly combines her love of building things and my passion for planning and decorating. It's genius.

Wait. Did she say…

"Fifty-one percent?" I ask. "But that would mean…I'd be majority owner?"

"Yep. Not to brag or anything, but I kind of already had my fun running an empire."

She did, and damn did she do it well. But I don't know what to say to this. Literally no words come to mind. It's all mush.

Auden closes her laptop, folding her hands together and leaning forward. "Look, I know it's a lot, but I've been thinking about this for a while, since Hutch and I built our house last summer. It was *so* fun, and you spent so much time over there helping me do it."

"Do you remember those terrible cabinets the contractors tried to put in?"

She laughs. "You threw a fit, and you have no idea how happy I am that you did. It's what you used to do at Sinclair Properties too. You were always there to help steer me in the right direction when it came to decorating, and we both know you held that company together with your organization. This would be that, but in a different way, and we could do it on our own terms, at our own pace. *We* decide the clients we take on. *We* decide the pace. No shareholders. No boardroom meetings. Just us taking on the world. Besides, don't you think it's time for the world to see just how badass Lilah Jane Maddison truly is?"

She has no idea what her words mean to me. All

the times my parents have put me down. All the times they told me I was wasting my potential. Every damn time they told me I wasn't good enough.

They were wrong.

I am.

And Auden—the smartest, most business-savvy woman I know—betting on me proves that. I want to bet on me too.

"Okay."

"Come on, Lilah, I—wait, did you say okay?"

I nod. "Okay. Let's do this."

"Really?"

"Really."

"Ahhh!" she screams, as if we haven't already been enough of a disturbance in this coffee shop. She claps giddily. "Oh my god, oh my god! We're starting a business together! And I'm pregnant and you're in love and oh my god!"

Her excitement is palpable, and I bounce a little in my own chair. That weight I've been carrying for over a year now as I've tried to figure out what I want to do with my life fades away like it was never there, and I know without a doubt I've just made the right decision. I reach for my phone, eager to tell Fox, but I stop at the last minute.

"Call him."

I look up at Auden, who is watching me with a grin that slips as she continues to stare at me.

"I can't."

"Why?"

"Because if I call him, I'm going to tell him I love him, and I really think I should do that in person, don't you?"

Just like that, her grin is back. "You're, like, *so* in love."

"Shut up," I protest.

"You loooooove him!" she sings. *Loudly.*

"Auden Sinclair! Stop it!"

"You want to kiss him."

"Duh."

"You want to marry him."

"Ew."

"You want to have his bab—"

I cut her a look. "Finish that sentence, and I swear, I will walk away from our deal like that." I snap my fingers to assert my point.

Auden mimes locking her lips and throwing away the key, but she's still bouncing in her chair. As much as I hate to admit it, I'm practically doing the same, because I am in love.

So, so fucking in love. And I can't wait to tell Fox.

Chapter 23

"Well?"

I look around the room at my fellow Serpents Singles members, and they all stare back at me, displaying a mixture of emotions. Hutch and Locke are grinning. Lawson's jaw is dropped, and Hayes has his brows raised. Keller looks unbothered, per usual. The rest of the gym has already cleared out, everyone going home to catch a nap before tonight's game I assume. We're the only ones left.

"Is anyone going to say anything?"

"What do you want us to say?" Keller asks, sounding bored. "You fell in love with Lilah. Big fucking whoop."

I rub a towel over my head. "Uh, okay. I just figured you guys would be pissed because I've been lying to you and we're not really engaged."

"We knew."

This comes from Lawson, which surprises the hell out of me.

"You knew?"

He nods. "Yeah. Why do you think I've been screwing with you about being your best man so much?"

"I don't know. Because you're obnoxious?"

He grabs his chest. "I am highly offended, Arthur Fox."

I roll my eyes at him. I don't think Lawson has been offended a day in his life. "How did you know?"

I slide my eyes to Hutch and Locke. One of them has known for certain nearly this whole time, and I suspect the other sussed it out a long time ago. They both hold their hands up in innocence.

"I kept my lips sealed," Hutch says.

I look at Locke, who shakes his head. "Wasn't me."

"Then how did you guys know?"

Hayes raises his hand. "Makes you feel any better, I had no clue until just now."

"Dude, how?" Lawson asks him.

"I don't know. Maybe because I've been busy raising a kid and juggling a new nanny and Quinn's school schedule."

"Whatever, but it was pretty obvious."

"How was it obvious?"

Lawson shrugs. "I don't know, man. Kinda weird how he was allegedly secretly seeing Lilah before New Year's and then suddenly they were engaged when they spent Thanksgiving *and* Christmas apart. You don't exactly do that with someone you're so in love with that you're getting engaged that quickly. Just didn't add up."

"Shit," Hayes mutters. "I guess that does make sense."

I look at Keller.

He lifts a shoulder. "Just knew you were full of shit. Good at reading people and you're a terrible liar."

"I am not. We fooled plenty of people."

"Maybe old, senile people. Locke excluded, obviously."

"I'm not fucking old," Locke growls at Keller, though I don't know why he bothers anymore.

I look at each of them. "So none of you care?"

They all shake their heads, and that relief I've been dying for hits, but it doesn't completely chase away the ache that's been in the middle of my chest for days.

"You don't look entirely good with that. Should we be upset?" Lawson asks.

"No. I mean, yeah. Sort of. I lied, so that's pretty shitty of me."

"Fuck's sake. Here comes the 'good boy' complex."

Keller drops his head back on a groan, but all I can focus on is two words.

Good boy.

They send a shiver right down my back, and unfortunately for me, they notice.

"Okay, one, that was gross." Lawson points at me. "I know that reaction there, *good boy.*"

I narrow my eyes at him for using it again.

"Two, you don't *always* have to be so…so…well, honorable. You're allowed to just be a regular shitbag like the rest of us."

"Speak for yourself on the shitbag front," Keller says.

Lawson flips him off, eyes still on me. "It's not like you lied to be malicious. You did it for a good reason."

"Ever the *good boy.*"

Now it's *me* who flips Keller off. He snickers.

"So, we're good," Lawson says. "Stop worrying that handsome head of yours, okay? Need you focused in net tonight. We have a playoff spot to keep."

Everyone gets pumped at that. We've managed to not only recover from our slip to fourth place but jump all the way to second. We're crushing it right now, and the only thing I want more than to continue that is for things to go back to normal with Lilah.

"Shit, guys." I pull the towel from around my neck

and toss it into the laundry bin. "Thanks, I guess. For being so cool about it, I mean."

"Oh, we're not really 'being cool.' We're going to mock you endlessly for this one," Hayes says. "Give it time."

I can't even fault them for that. I have it coming, and we all know so. Apparently "time" means minutes, since the second we get back to the changing room, Lawson pretends to propose to Hayes, and he's all dramatic screams as he accepts. It's fucking ridiculous and over the top and just enough to distract me for a few minutes. It's officially the quietest my mind has been in days, but it doesn't last long, as I reach into my bag and my fingers collide with something foreign.

I pull it out and am surprised to find the tiniest turtle I've seen yet, no bigger than a thimble and cute as hell.

Lilah.

"That from her?"

I turn to find Hutch still hanging around, his bag slung over his shoulder.

I nod, swallowing thickly. "Yeah, it's from her."

"What is it?"

"A turtle."

He frowns, not understanding, but he doesn't question it. "Have you talked to her at all?"

I shake my head. "No, not yet. I'm…I'm giving it time, you know?"

He nods. "Sometimes that's all you can do. And if it doesn't work, then… Well, fuck, I don't know what, but you'll be okay. It's going to suck, but you'll come out the other side."

"Like you did after being left at the altar?"

He looks surprised I've brought it up. It's something he's mentioned in passing before but hasn't gone into great detail about.

"No, not like that."

I pull my brows together. "Are you saying you're not over that, then?"

"No. I mean, yes, I'm over that." He scratches at his short beard. "The whole being-left-at-the-altar thing… I know I don't talk about it a lot, but it's complicated. I was fucking crushed for a long time and had a huge chip on my shoulder because of it. But the more time I had away from it, the more I realized it was the best thing to ever happen to me. I thought I knew what love was back then, and I was wrong. I had no fucking clue. I was just going through the motions with proposing. Thought it was what I was supposed to do, you know? But it wasn't right. We weren't in real love, and I didn't realize that until Auden came along." He smiles softly. "Then I knew. It was real. It *is* real with her."

"And if something happened with you and Auden? Would you survive that? Would you come out the other side?"

He floats his mouth open, then snaps it shut, like he's never even considered the option of them not working out. I wish I were that confident in Lilah.

"No. I don't think I would. But I also don't think about it, and it's not something you need to be thinking about either. You're talking like you've already given up, like Lilah's already made up her mind."

I roll the tiny turtle between my fingers. "What if she has? What if she doesn't feel the same?"

"She does."

"How can you be so sure?"

"Because I am. Because I know her. Because I know you. Because it's impossible *not* to love you."

I look up at him, unable to keep from smiling at the sour look on his face.

He crosses his arms over his chest. "Shut up."

"You getting soft, Hutchy?"

"That's it." He backs away, holding his palms up. "I'm out. You're starting to sound like Lawson, and I can't handle two of him."

I chuckle as he disappears around the corner, and I sit there, still playing with the turtle. When did she even slip this into my bag? How long has it been in there? Was it recent? Is it a sign?

"Hey, Fox?"

I lift my head. "Hmm?"

"It's real."

"What?"

"With Lilah. It's real. Just remember that."

With that, he taps the doorframe twice, then takes off down the hall for good this time. I sit there for a long while, trying to convince myself he's right.

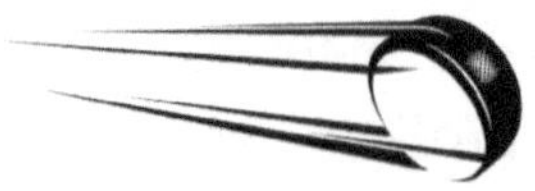

With everything going on, the last thing I want to do is have breakfast with Lilah's parents. However, it's *my* parents' last morning in Seattle, and there is no way I'm missing that, especially not with their flight a few hours away. If we're lucky, this breakfast will finish on time so they can get to the airport. And if I'm lucky, I'll get at least one glance from Lilah, who still hasn't looked at me all morning.

When I came home from my game last night, she was passed out on the couch, a blanket half hanging off her and a notepad sprawled across her chest. As badly as I wanted to talk to her, I couldn't bring myself to wake her. So, I scooped her into my arms and carried her to our makeshift bed, where she curled against me like she does every night.

We haven't said much since then, and now, we sit beside one another, our legs pressing together as her parents ignore everyone's existence like *they'd* rather be anywhere else. This was their idea, and I'm starting to think it was just to show off their betrothed daughter to all their stuck-up friends. We're at the same restaurant we got engaged at, and my parents stick out like sore thumbs in here. My father's cowboy hat sits on the edge of the table, and my mother's dress—while completely gorgeous—is so far out of current trends it's not even funny.

I should have never brought them here. Not because I'm embarrassed by them—that's not the case at all—but because I can *feel* these people staring. I fucking hate it. I'd rather be in net taking shot after shot with no goalie stick while my team is down a man. Literally anything else than this.

"So, Lilah," Mama says, breaking the silence. "I couldn't help but notice your sketchpad on the kitchen counter this morning. Those designs you were working on were gorgeous."

Selene snaps her head toward her daughter. "Designs? What designs?"

"Oh, uh." Lilah tucks her long dark hair behind her ear, setting her fork on her plate. "Well, Bonnie, I...I'm starting a business. With Auden."

I whip my head to her. "You are?"

"You are?!" her mother squawks over me. "This is the first I've heard of this. Deacon, are you hearing this?"

"I'm hearing this, my love." He scoffs. "Can't believe I am, but I hear it."

Lilah ignores them, her eyes trained on me for the first time today.

"You're starting a business with Auden?"

She nods. "Yeah. I'm sorry. I wanted to tell you last night, but I fell asleep. We talked about it yesterday at the coffee shop and just dove right into planning. It's been a whirlwind." She nibbles on her bottom lip. "Are you mad?"

"Mad? No. Why would I be mad? I think it's incredible. You're going to be great at it."

Red tints her cheeks, and she grins. "You don't even know what it is."

"I don't have to, Lilah. I always think you're great."

"Well, *I* think it's a terrible idea." Selene titters. "Can you imagine the power imbalance with Auden's net worth? And what happens when she decides she's bored and wants to sell the company?"

"Actually, I'll be the majority owner."

"You're kidding." Selene laughs haughtily, and the sound grates on me so badly I have to grit my teeth to keep from saying anything.

"Majority owner?!" Her father laughs. Literally

fucking laughs. "As if you have the competence or the skill. You've spent the last ten years being a secretary, Lilah. Running a business takes far more than that. There is no way you're going to make it. You won't even last a year. You—"

"Enough!" My chair screeches against the floor as I stand, slamming my hand down on the table so hard every dish rattles from the force.

Everyone in the restaurant freezes, and now all eyes are *definitely* on us, but I don't care. I can't bite my tongue any longer. I glower over at a startled Selene and Deacon.

"Do you have any fucking idea how incredible your daughter is? Any clue how smart she is? How talented she is? Hell, do you know anything at all about her? Huh? Do you?"

They don't answer, not that I expected them to. They're too damn busy staring at me like *I'm* the problem here. If they want a problem, I'll give them one.

"I didn't fucking think so. You should be ashamed. You call yourselves parents, riding on that high horse of yours, thinking you're better than everyone else, including your own daughter." I shake my head in disgust. "Her favorite color is a dusty rose. She drinks water and lemonade and just about every other damn thing there is out of a mug because she thinks it makes it taste better. She texts her sister every day, even if it's just a thumbs-up emoji, to let her know she's thinking of her. Even though she hates that hideous ring on her finger, she wears it anyway because it's what you want out of her. And when she worked *alongside* Auden—not for, just to be clear—she was the one who schmoozed and impressed the contractors and investors and businesses that were brought in on each and every single Sinclair hotel. Lilah. Nobody else. She ran that company just as much as the woman whose name was on the building, and now she has an incredible opportunity to put *her* name on something, and you're what? Shitting on her because it's not what *you* want her to do? Well, fuck that. She deserves this. She deserves to finally be recognized for her hard work. She deserves to not live in your shadow or anyone else's. She deserves to fucking shine like the bright star she is. What she doesn't deserve is your bullshit. So why don't you do us all a damn favor and shut the hell up for a change."

I'm out of breath by the time I finish, my chest heaving with a mixture of exhaustion and pure fucking rage. I've had to endure far too much of this, listening to Lilah's parents trash her, and I'm done with it. I don't care if it pisses Lilah off that I've said something. I can't listen to it for another second.

I turn to my mother, who has been quiet through

the whole thing. "Mama, I'm sorry. I know you raised me better than to raise my voice at people, but, dammit, some of them just deserve it."

Her lips twitch, and she rolls them together, doing her best to look fierce and upset with me as she nods, patting my hand.

"Dad, I—"

He shakes his head, cutting me off. "Don't need to say a damn thing to me, son. Never been prouder of you in my life." Then he trains angry eyes on Deacon and Selene. "For the record, I agree with every damn thing my boy just said. And if you got a problem with that, take it up with me."

Fuck, I don't think I've ever loved him more. I take a steadying breath, then finally look to Lilah, who is sitting there with her mouth ajar, baby-blue eyes wide.

"I'm sorry, sugar," I say to her softly. "I know they're your parents and you love them, but I couldn't sit by and listen to them degrade you again. I just couldn't do it. Not when you're you, always taking their licks on the chin like a champ, pretending what they say doesn't have any effect on you when it does. They hurt you, cut you right down to the bone. As much as I admire the hell out of you for holding your head high despite that, I can't be a willing participant any longer. You deserve better than that, and I hope one day you'll realize that."

I stare hard at Selene and Deacon, who have pushed their noses into the air like the snooty bastards they've been since the day I met them. Still, after all that, they don't say a word.

I throw my napkin down on the table.

"This is ridiculous," I say. "I'm not sitting here a minute longer with them."

My parents don't waste a second, both pushing their chairs back and gathering their coats. I look at the woman I got down on one knee for in this very restaurant just earlier this year, but she doesn't move. Lilah just blinks up at us, never once making a move to follow.

No. Instead, she drops her head to her chest, effectively turning away from me, and it's crushing.

It's "Oh" level of devastating.

Hutch was wrong. This isn't real. And Lilah just proved that.

With one last long look at her, I turn, leaving my heart behind. Mama wraps her arm around me, her motherly instincts sensing I need comforting, and my father follows closely behind as we make our way to the front of the restaurant.

"I'm so sorry, son."

"Thank you," I say, but I feel anything but thankful right now. In fact, I don't feel anything at all.

"I'm proud of you, though. While you're right—I

didn't raise you to talk to people like that—I'm damn sure glad you did. Those people are awful."

I flex my fist, fighting the urge to turn back and lay into them more. They'd certainly deserve it.

But I don't turn back. I keep walking, and it takes every bit of effort I have to do so, to walk away from the woman I love, the one who clearly doesn't feel the same way.

I push open the door.

"Wait!"

I stop.

"Wait!" Lilah calls again.

When I turn, she's standing, hands on the table as she stares after me with fear in her eyes. She looks down at her parents, whose faces are turning redder and redder by the second.

"What are you doing?" her mother chides. "Sit down, Lilah Jane."

"No."

Selene tosses her head back like she's just been slapped. "Excuse me?"

"I said, *no.*" Lilah scoffs. "You know, I have no damn clue why I have no problem telling anyone else off, no issues speaking my mind or taking what I want, but when it comes to you two? I'm a fucking doormat. And why? All because I'm starved for your love and affection. Because I hoped one day you'd wake up and realize I'm your daughter, not your puppet. Fox was right—this *is* ridiculous, and I do deserve better. I deserve better parents, people who love me for me. Who don't try to shove me into a box and make me something I'm not. Who don't want me around just to show me off to all their friends." She waves her hand toward the other patrons, who are all completely entranced by what's unfolding before them. "I deserve more. I deserve…" Her blue eyes find mine. "I deserve to be loved."

I swallow, so fucking proud of what I'm watching.

Finally! I want to shout, but I don't. I let Lilah have her moment, because fuck, she deserves that too.

"Mother, Father," she says, "I'm not engaged."

"What?" her mother hisses. How is it *that* got her attention out of everything that's been said today? "Of course you are. You're engaged to this…this…*hockey player*."

My mother makes a move toward Selene, but my father grabs her, holding the small woman back. I'd laugh at it if this were happening at any other time.

"No, I'm not." Lilah pulls off the tacky ring she's been wearing, tossing it onto the table with a loud *thunk*. "I never have been, and Fox isn't my boyfriend. This whole thing was fake. Completely staged."

"What?!" Her mother begins to cry. "I don't understand this, Lilah."

"What part? That this is fake? That I lied and said I had a boyfriend, and this incredible man over here stepped in to play the part because he's *good*? Because he is. He's kind and loving and everything you're not."

"Why?" her mother manages between her fake sobs.

"Why? Because I was too damn scared to stand up to you and tell you to butt out of my life! Because I was so damn worried I was going to become the thing I feared the most—you. Bitter and old and alone. Because, while you might be married and appear happy and in love in front of everyone else, I know the truth: you're just as miserable as you like making everyone else."

"That's it!" her father shouts, tossing his napkin on the table and shoving to his feet.

I've never moved faster in my life, crossing the restaurant and putting myself right between Lilah and her father. He scowls up at me, Lilah's heat at my back, but I don't budge. This guy thinks I'm afraid of him? No. Fuck this guy.

"Deacon, I'd like you to back up now."

"That is *my* daughter, son."

"Yeah? And she's the woman I love. So I'm going to say it again—back up. Before I make you back up, *sir*."

His nostrils flare, but he must realize I am not joking, and he wisely takes a step back.

I turn to Lilah, my hands going to her cheeks. "Are you okay?"

She nods. "I'm all right."

"Good." I turn back to her parents. "We're leaving, and you will not follow us nor contact her. You won't bother Lilah at all until *she's* ready to speak to you, *if* that even happens. Are we understood?"

Deacon opens his mouth, ready to argue, but thinks better of it. He snaps it closed, then nods once. I don't even give a shit what Selene thinks. I simply place my hand on Lilah's lower back and usher her from the scene. Not until we're all outside do I finally take a breath.

"Holy shit," I say, running my hands through my hair. "Holy shit."

Lilah nods, gulping in breaths of air herself. "I agree. That was…"

"Yeah."

I don't know who moves for the other first, but suddenly, Lilah's in my arms and our mouths are moving against one another. We're kissing like I'm some soldier who's just come home from war, which is fitting because it certainly feels like I just went through a battle.

Somewhere in the back of my mind, I know my

parents are standing nearby, but I can't seem to find it in me to care. I can't stop kissing her, mostly because I'm scared if I do, she'll leave, and I really, really don't want her to leave.

Lilah's the first to break the kiss, her once frantic movements slowing to a more normal pace until our lips are barely ghosting against each other.

"Lilah, I—"

"I love you."

I jerk back, looking down at her.

Did she just…

"What did you say?"

"I said, I love you. But what I really meant was: I am in love with you, Arthur Fox, and I refuse to apologize for it."

It's my words. It's what I said to her in the supply closet.

She loves me. Lilah Maddison fucking loves me, and if that's not the sweetest damn thing I've ever heard, I don't know what is.

"Well?" she prompts. "Are you going to say anything?"

I say the first thing that comes to mind.

"Oh."

"Oh? *Oh?* Are you serious? I just told you I love you, and you—dammit, Fox!" She pinches me. "Seriously?"

I laugh, pressing a quick kiss to her pinched lips. "Fair is fair."

"That was mean."

"No, what was mean was making me wait days to hear you say that."

"I know." She sighs, dropping her forehead to my chin. "I know, and I'm sorry. I knew it then. When you told me, I knew how I felt about you. I just couldn't… I don't know. I couldn't get the words out. I locked up. Got scared."

"Scared? You? Nah, I don't believe it."

She pulls back, her blue eyes brighter than I've ever seen them before, and I don't know if it's because she's finally released herself of all her parents' bullshit or our conversation right now, but whatever it is, I love it. I love seeing her like this.

I just fucking love her.

"I know I act brave. I know I act like I know what I want, like I have…control. But I don't. I get scared just like everyone else. And yeah, loving you scares me, Fox. Scares the hell right out of me because I've never been in love before. Because I don't know how to do this. I don't know if I'm going to drive you crazy or if you'll drive me there first. I don't know if we'll wake up tomorrow and regret it all or if we'll stay together until we're old and wrinkled. I don't know any of it aside from the fact that I love you, Arthur. I love you so damn much. I didn't plan to. I didn't plan for this to become real, but it did. It did and I can't be sorry for it. I don't want to be. I just want you. I want us. I want *real*."

I'm nodding before she's even done talking because I want all that too.

"Yes," I say, slipping my hands over her cheeks, kissing the side of her lips. "Yes. I want it too."

"You do?"

"So badly, sugar. I want it all with you. All the messy." I kiss her cheek. "The good, the bad." Then the other one. "Everything in between." I trail my lips right to her ear and whisper, "*Especially* the old-and-wrinkled part."

Her eyes flutter closed as I kiss her mouth, showing her I mean it, every fucking word of it. When we finally come up for air, she's blushing, and it's a look I know I won't tire of anytime soon.

"You know your parents are standing like fifty feet away, right?"

"I know they're around here somewhere."

"So, we should probably, I don't know, stop making out, right?"

"We should."

But we don't. I kiss her again and again and again, just for good measure. When I finally pull away, it's long past appropriate, but judging by my mother's smile when I find them hiding out around the side of the building, they don't seem to mind one bit.

"Thought you two might want a minute alone."

"Probably a good call." I tug Lilah to my side, silently vowing to never let her go.

"I take it you worked things out?"

I look down at Lilah, who nods.

"Yeah," she says. "I'd say we worked it out, Bonnie."

"Oh!" Mama claps excitedly. "I'm so glad. So happy for you two. See, Artie? I told you it'd all work out if you played until the final buzzer."

"You did."

We stand around and talk for a few more minutes until my parents need to leave for the airport.

"Son," my dad says, "I think we might need to have a chat whenever your mother and I get back home."

I nod. "Yeah, I kind of figured."

"But for now, it looks like you have some more important things to deal with." My dad pulls me into a hug. "I love you, Artie."

"Love you too," I tell him, releasing him and watching as he wraps Lilah into a hug.

He whispers something to her, and whatever it is has her shoulders shaking with silent cries as she buries her face against him.

Mama takes his place, kissing my cheek. "Can I tell him everything?"

I nod. "Please. And I really am sorry."

"Don't apologize, Arthur. You're the exact man I hoped you'd turn into. That's all I can ask for. And you," she says, moving toward Lilah. "You beautiful soul, you. I'm proud of you, kid. I know I'm not your soon-to-be mother-in-law and I have no idea what the future holds for you and my son, but know this—I am only ever a phone call away. I'm in your corner. Forever, Lilah."

My girl, who is barely holding it together, nods, tears streaming down her cheeks as my mother hugs her tightly. I kiss her cheek and give her one last hug before they climb into their rental car, waving at us through the window as they pull out of the lot.

Lilah looks back at the restaurant, which her parents are presumably still inside.

"Do you want to go back and talk to them?"

She shakes her head. "No. I really, really don't."

"Probably for the best." I scratch at my chin. "Uh, I'm sorry for kind of exploding in there. I just…"

"Don't," she says. "I'm not even remotely mad. I promise. If anything, it just made me love you more."

"Say that again." I swing her around to face me. "That part where you say you love me."

She giggles. "I love you, Fox."

"God, that sounds good." I nuzzle my nose against her neck.

"Now you say it."

"I love you, Fox."

"Arthur…" she warns.

I chuckle against her. "I love you, Lilah."

It's all I can manage before our mouths are fused together again, and I'm so not complaining. I have no idea how long we stand there unable to keep our hands off each other, but we eventually make our way through the parking lot back to my truck.

"Hey, Fox?" she asks as I pull open the door for her.

"Yeah?"

"What'd your mom mean by the 'final buzzer'?"

I laugh, shaking my head as I help her into my truck. "I'll explain on the way home, okay?"

"Mmm," she hums contentedly. "Home. I like the sound of that."

"Yeah? Me too, sugar. Me too."

I make sure she's tucked inside, then I close the door, rounding the truck with a smile I don't think I'm ever going to lose.

And it's all because of her.

Chapter 24

LILAH

"That's it, baby. Yes, yes. Harder. Faster. Yes!"

Auden and I stare over at Rory, who definitely does *not* sound like she's watching a hockey game. She's sitting on the edge of the couch, her chin in her hands as she watches the puck zip around the rink.

"How horny are you right now?" I ask.

"What?" she asks, finally looking back at us, blinking like she's just realized we're in the room too. "As horny as I usually am when I'm watching hockey. Why?"

Auden and I laugh.

"Uh, because you look like you're about to lick Lilah's TV screen, that's why." Auden sets her hand against her stomach that's just now starting to show her pregnancy. "And here I thought *I* was supposed to be the horny one being pregnant and all."

Rory curls her lips up at her twin. "I really thought we pinky-promised on the whole baby thing. They're so…gross."

"Animals are gross too."

"Extremely gross," Rory agrees. "Which is why I chose only one. Animals or babies, animals or babies. I choose animals."

Auden rolls her eyes, plucking a spare pillow off my pink couch and chucking it at her sister's head. Rory doesn't care. She's back to watching the game, and it's just in time to see Fox make an incredible save. I wish I were there, but between Auden's sudden morning sickness issues and our late-night business strategy sessions, I'm perfectly comfy on my couch between my two best friends.

"Damn! Your man is on fire!" Rory claps loudly, cupping her hands around her mouth and cheering as if Fox can hear her from the rink downtown. With how loud she's being, he just might.

Your man.

She's right. Fox is my man, and just thinking it makes me smile.

It's been three weeks since our breakfast with our parents, and I can't remember the last time I was so happy. Things were good when we were faking it, but the real thing? I don't know. It just makes everything feel so much…*more*. Auden says that's what happens when you're in love, and I choose to believe her. How could I not with how he makes me feel? It's like I'm walking on air yet more grounded than I've ever felt. I don't understand, and I kind of never want to, either. I just want to accept it and revel in it.

The other good thing to come from that morning is I haven't heard from my parents. It's been crickets, and I'm perfectly okay with that. I meant every word I said to them, and I know Fox did too. He's already told me he'll respect me if I want to have a relationship with them and will try to be on his best behavior, but he couldn't make any promises. It made me smile far too much.

"Seriously, Lilah?"

"What?" I turn to Auden, who is watching me closely.

"You're thinking of Fox again, aren't you?"

"Ugh. Again?" Rory throws herself back against the couch. "You're so obsessed with him."

I don't contradict her. There's no point. I am obsessed.

"When are you two getting married again?"

I kick Rory for even asking that question. She counters with the pillow her sister threw at her.

Fox and I have decided to keep the option open for a wedding, but one far, far, *far* off in the future. We're not officially engaged, but we're not *not* engaged either.

It's complicated, which I suppose is fitting for how this whole relationship began, but it worked for us, getting us here, so we're rolling with it.

"Hey, hey, pregnant woman here!" Auden shields herself before stealing the pillow that's just hit me right in the face and settling it over her protruding belly. We manage to finish the game with minimal pillow fights, and before I know it, the final buzzer is going off.

The Serpents won. *Again.* The camera zooms in on the team as they line up to tap helmets with Fox, Lawson giving him an extra kiss to his dome before they salute the crowd and skate off. It's cute and makes Rory swoon, not that she'd ever admit it.

Shortly after, Auden and Rory call it a night, rushing to get home to meet their boyfriends, leaving me alone waiting for Fox. About an hour later, I hear his key in the door, and I grin from my spot on the couch as he pushes it open like this is his home too.

He lights up the second he sees me. "Lilah."

"Fox," I return.

Then I launch off the couch and right into his arms, his hands going under my ass as my legs wrap around his waist, our lips meeting in a rushed kiss like it's been days since I've seen him instead of hours. Naturally, it's not enough, and I don't think it ever will be.

"Fuck, I missed you," he murmurs against my skin, his lips on my neck.

"You just saw me."

"So?"

I laugh. "Good point."

I drag his mouth back to mine, our tongues rolling together until we're both out of breath. Eventually he sets me back on my feet, his hair a mess from my hands and my lips feeling swollen.

"Going to go take this off," he says, pointing to his suit. "Couch cuddles?"

I nod enthusiastically. "Please."

I grab the book we've been reading—a new one about a vampire brotherhood—and settle back into my spot. He emerges from my room a few minutes later in nothing but a pair of low-slung gray sweatpants. That's it. No shirt, no socks. Just him in all his glory. It makes it hard to focus as he settles between my legs, his head resting against my stomach, legs stretched out over the edge of the other side of the pink furniture that's far too small for him.

"Where'd we leave off?" I ask, opening the book and flipping through the pages.

"I bookmarked it with the Costco receipt."

"Good boy," I tell him, running my fingers through his hair. "Ah, I remember this one. She's just gone to the compound and met the other brothers."

"I think V is my favorite so far."

"Really? I like Z. He's mysterious."

"He's *hot*. You have a thing for his scar and you know it. Remind me to never introduce you to Adrian Rhodes."

"I don't know…hockey player *and* has a scar? Sounds kind of hot. Any chance he's a mega-flexible goalie?"

He tilts his head back to glare at me, and I hide my smile behind the book.

I read for a long time, or at least that's what it feels like. Fox interjects his feelings about the long-haired vampire every now and then and we debate the plot and whose book is next, but that's all we do. We lie there together, me reading to Fox, him snuggled against me. It's not the sexiest night in the world, not the most adventurous, but it's ours.

I wouldn't trade it for anything.

Epilogue

FOX

"Three, two, one!"

Lilah slams her thumb down on her computer, and with that, Maddison Sinclair Designs is officially launched. She throws her arms around her very pregnant best friend, who seems like she's due any day now, and they hold on to each other tightly as we burst into cheers around her.

Hayes and Quinn blow into noisemakers, Flora doing the same at their side. Locke and Keller clap loudly, the latter nearly smiling even. I look at Hutch over them, and he grins at me like *we're* the ones in on a secret, and this time, I know exactly what it is—we're lucky as hell to have them.

He's right. We are lucky. We needed them bad when we lost game seven of the conference final. It was rough. I don't think the group chat was active for a good two weeks afterward, everyone licking their wounds, but I was glad when the team that beat us at least went on to win the Cup. They deserved it, but next year… Next year is ours. I can feel it.

Lilah moves toward Hutch and Auden toward me.

"Congrats," I tell her, hugging her as best I can with her round stomach between us.

"Couldn't do it without our girl." She smiles, referring to Lilah.

I really don't think Auden would have gotten this off the ground *and* planned her wedding without Lilah's help. Why she decided to take on two life-changing endeavors *while* being extremely pregnant is beyond me. But she did, and she has Lilah to thank for the success of it all.

When my girl finally steps up to me, I can't wipe the smile off my face.

"Hey there, sugar," I say, the tips of my shoes pressed against hers.

"Hi."

"How do you feel?"

"Honestly? Still stressed, but also relieved. It's weird and hard to explain."

"You don't have to. Not with me. Never with me."

She tips her head to the side, squinting at me. "Why are you so good to me, Arthur Fox?"

"Because you deserve it, Lilah Maddison."

With that, she hurls herself into my arms, and I catch her just like I will every time. Our lips connect like old friends, and I slip my hand up her neck as I hold her to me, not wanting to let her go. Not because I'm afraid I'm going to lose her—I don't fear that anymore—but because I can't get enough of her.

When we've kissed long past what's appropriate, we finally pull apart.

"I'm proud of you," I tell her.

That earns me a blush. "Thank you. I couldn't have done it without you."

"Yes, you could have. You can do anything, and you don't need me for any of it."

"Well, I didn't want to, and I *don't* want to. I always want you by my side."

I sigh, dropping my forehead against hers. "I like the sound of that, being by your side."

"It does sound nice." She huffs out a laugh. "God, can you believe we did it?"

"Yes."

"It's been a busy summer. The playoff run, the proposal, the wedding planning, the baby that's due any day now, *and* launching the company."

"And yet, you did it all."

"In heels, too."

I laugh, thinking about the nights those heels were digging into me as I helped her relax through it all. "I told you, you're an incredible woman, Lilah Jane."

"You believe in me too much, Fox."

"And you don't believe in you enough." I kiss the tip of her nose.

She sighs. "Keep saying things like that and I'll…"

"What, sugar, what will you do?"

"I don't know. Marry you or something."

I pull away, looking down to see if she's serious, and fuck me, but she is.

"You'd let me put a ring on your finger? *My* ring this time?"

She nods slowly. "Yeah. Yeah, I think I would."

Her words nearly knock me down. The thought of seeing Lilah walking down the aisle toward me rattles something deep inside me, something I've been holding on to for a while now, and the urge to drop down on one knee like I did all those months ago hits me. But I don't. I keep the desire tucked down, buried away for another day.

This day is about her company, her accomplishments. I can wait. I can ask Lilah to marry me another day. Besides, I have a feeling she'll say yes.

"Okay, break it up, break it up." Lawson pulls me away from Lilah. "This is a party, not your sex den. Let's celebrate!" He picks up a red cup and holds it in the air. "To Lilah!"

"Hey!" we all say, holding our cups up as well.

"To Auden!"

"Hey!" we cheer again.

"And to Hutch's inability to pull out, which means we're getting a second generation! Long live the Serpents Singles Group Chat!"

"What's pull out mean?" Flora asks, sending everyone who is not Hayes and Quinn into a fit of laughter.

Hutch smacks him on the back of the head, and even Rory shakes her head, annoyed, though I see her smile as she takes a sip of her drink.

The doorbell chimes through the house.

"I got it!" Lawson calls, racing toward the door.

"Anyone else think he's getting extra exhausting lately?" Hayes asks.

"He's *always* extra exhausting. It's like you people never listen to me," Keller grouses.

"That's because you hate everyone and everything. You don't count," Locke says.

Keller shrugs, indifferent as usual.

"Uh, Hutchy?" Lawson calls, walking back into the room.

"Yeah?" our captain answers.

"Someone's at the door for you."

"Who the hell is it?" Hutch growls, irritated by Lawson's vagueness.

"Was hoping you'd tell us."

Our star forward steps aside, revealing a tiny blonde woman standing behind him. Auden gasps, then looks up to her fiancé, but he's too busy staring at the woman clutching a bag to her side.

"Uh, who is that?" Lawson asks in a hushed voice, which for him isn't so quiet. Everyone hears it.

Hayes speaks up. "I think that's his sister."

"*Step*sister," Hutch corrects, brows tilted inward. "What are you doing here, Vanessa?"

"Sorry, I…I didn't mean to intrude," she says, pushing her hair behind her ear. "It looks like you're having a party. I just…"

Her eyes slide around the space, looking each of us over like she's looking at a room full of strangers, and shit, I guess she is—that is until she lands on the man standing at the back. The one with the salt-and-pepper hair at his temples, the wrinkles at the corners of his eyes. The veteran.

Locke stares back, looking like he's seen a ghost from his past.

And I think maybe he has.

**

THANK YOU FOR READING!

I hope you loved Lilah & Fox as much as I do! These two were so fun to write. Such opposites, but still so in love. If you enjoyed this book, I encourage you to leave a review on your favorite platform.

Want more?
Keep reading for a bonus scene!

Bonus Scene

LILAH

"Are you serious?"

"I am."

"No, Fox!"

"Why not?"

"Because I… I… No!"

He rolls his lips together to keep from laughing, and I get it. I do. I'm sure I look nuts right now, waving around a hairdryer and wearing nothing but pantyhose and heels, a full face of makeup, and all my jewelry.

We were moments away from walking out the door when I stopped for what I thought was going to be a quick drink and *of freaking course* my lid wasn't on my bottle tight enough. Water went all over my dress.

So, here we are, me drying my dress with the hairdryer while Fox sits on the bed and waits for me to be ready to go again.

"I'm just saying, I wouldn't complain."

I narrow my eyes at him and his relaxed form. He's leaning back on his arms, his long legs spread wide, his bowtie loosened around his neck once again.

I want to be annoyed by that since we really do have to leave as soon as I dry my dress, but I can't seem to be. He looks too damn good right now for annoyance.

He lifts his hand, running it over the scruff lining his face, and fuck if that's not hot, too.

I set the hairdryer on the counter and walk toward him, not stopping until I stand between his legs. I don't know what I'm doing. We have to leave. We're already going to bc latc for Coach Smith's birthday party, but I can't stop myself.

Fox doesn't seem to mind as I slip my hand into his hair. He leans into the touch, his eyes growing heavy. I bend, pressing my lips to the corner of his mouth, and he groans softly.

"What are you doing?" he asks, his hands finding my waist, his fingertips digging into me as he holds me tightly, like he's trying to hold himself back. "We're going to be late, Lilah."

"As if you care." I kiss the other side.

He chuckles. "I really don't."

"Then shut up and let me kiss you, Arthur."

"I'm yours for the taking, sugar."

And take I do.

I press my lips to his, not caring in the least that it means I'm going to have to redo my lipstick, and he opens for me instantly. Our tongues meld together, reuniting like old friends as he drags me closer. My dress doesn't require a bra, so I'm not wearing one, and I'm reminded of the fact as my nipples brush against his suit jacket. The touch is soft, yet I feel it everywhere.

Fox must feel it too, as another soft groan leaves him. The sound vibrates through me, spurring me on. I shove on his chest, and he falls back with the pressure. I climb on top of him, our bodies lining up perfectly, mouths still fused.

His fingertips dig into me even more, no doubt leaving behind little indentions on my waist, and I can't help it when I roll my hips against his hard cock that sits right between my legs.

Another groan, and I laugh against him, then do it again.

And again. And again. Until he's a panting mess under me, moments away from coming in his fancy attire. I want him to. I want him to make a complete mess while he's fully clothed and I rub myself against him. While he's at my mercy.

He wrenches his mouth from mine.

"You're mean," he complains, trailing soft kisses over my jaw. "So damn mean."

"No, I'm not. You love this."

"I do." He nods against me, his lips teasing at my neck. "I really fucking do." He drags his tongue against me. "Fuck, you taste so good."

"I bet my pussy tastes even better."

He stops moving. Stops breathing. Then he's choking on a strangled laugh. It sounds pained as his fingers dig into me so hard, I'm sure I will bruise later. He's physically holding himself back from hauling me up and burying his face between my legs to see if I'm right.

"Don't tempt me," he warns, dragging his tongue against my neck again. "I'm liable to give in."

"Then give in," I tell him, grinding my already swollen clit against him again. "Taste me, Fox. Taste all of me."

My permission is all he needs before I'm dragged up, up, up until my thighs are bracketing his head.

I'm still wearing my pantyhose, but it doesn't deter him. No, he rips the sheer material with ease, then spears me with his tongue in one swift motion.

"*Oh, god*," I cry out.

He laughs against me, then laps at me again, his hands now on my thighs holding me steady. I wish we had moved farther up the bed so I had something to hold on to, but I guess his hair will have to suffice.

I grab his dark brown locks, holding on for dear life

as he sucks my clit into his mouth with just the right amount of pressure. I'm not surprised. Fox knows my body better than anyone else at this point. He's explored it enough times in the last year and a half not to.

He eats me, tasting every inch and not once relenting in his torment. I don't want him to either. Somewhere in the back of my mind, I know we should stop. That we have somewhere to be. But I can't bring myself to care. Not when having his hands and mouth on me feels so damn good. So damn right.

"Fox," I whine, tugging on his hair. "I'm close. So close."

He quickens his pace, the flicks of his tongue driving me closer and closer to the edge that I'm already close to tipping over.

"Come on, sugar," he says between long licks. "Give me what I want. Make a mess all over my face."

I tug on his hair again. "I would if you'd stop talking and start licking."

Another deep chuckle, and the vibrations from it are just what I was missing.

My orgasm races through me, my legs shaking on either side of Fox's head as I hold on to him and ride the wave.

But he never relents. No, he keeps tasting me again

and again until I'm shaking for a second time, making the mess he asked for.

When he finally gives me a reprieve, I slump forward, barely catching myself from face planting onto the bed and ruining my carefully done makeup.

As I struggle to catch my breath, all I can hear is my heartbeat in my ears and the clinking of metal as Fox undoes his belt.

Then I feel him and his hard cock pressing at my entrance. His hand grips my waist as he pushes inside me slowly. Torturously slow. So damn slow that by the time he's fully seated, I'm ready to come again.

"Fuck, sugar, you should see yourself. Your pretty pussy stretched so perfectly around me, ass in the air. I wish we didn't have anywhere to go. Wish I could stay inside you like this all night."

I nod. "I wish it too."

"But I can't," he says, slowly dragging himself back out until just the tip of him is sitting inside of me. "I can't. Which means I'm going to fuck you hard and fast, Lilah, and I refuse to apologize for it."

Then he slams back into me with a force that has me scooting up the bed. It doesn't matter. He chases after me, thrusting into me over and over.

It's hard and fast, just like he promised, and I wouldn't have it any other way, especially not with my third orgasm racing through me.

"Fuck, fuck, fuck," I chant as he continues to rut into me relentlessly.

"Fuck is right," he says, voice gravelly. "You feel so damn good squeezing my cock, Lilah. So perfect. So mine."

I am his. I've been his since the moment he told my mother he was my boyfriend when he most certainly was not. I just didn't know it yet.

But now… Now I know it, and I'll tell anyone who listens.

"Always yours," I tell him.

"Damn right," he grits out, pumping into me harder and faster than before. "Gonna come in this sweet pussy of yours, sugar."

"Do it, Fox. Fill me up."

And he does. He slams into me again, then comes with a force, filling me up as promised. It's so much that I feel it leaking out, and I hate that a little. I want to feel him in me for the rest of the night, throughout the party and even after.

When he's finished, he slides out, using two fingers to push the cum that's leaked out back inside of me.

Guess he wants me to feel him too.

Fox leans over me, kissing the back of my neck. "We really should go."

"Ugh. You're right. We're going to be late."

He laughs. "We're already late."

"But soon we'll be so late that everyone will know what we've been up to."

"Please. We all have bets on whether Coach will even show up to his own party on time because of what he's certainly up to with his wife."

"Do you blame him? She's hot."

"She is, but you're prettier," he tells me, kissing me again, and I know he's not just saying it because he thinks it's what I want to hear. He's saying it because he genuinely believes it, and that's what I love most about him—the way he loves me.

Fox drags me until I'm in a sitting position, then grabs my chin and brings my lips to his in a scaring kiss that could easily lead to more sex if we're not careful.

But we are. We know our limits. Or at least Fox does, since he's the first to pull away.

I whine, and he chuckles. "I know. Make it up to you later?"

I nod. "You better."

He helps me off the bed, buckling his pants as I head to our dresser.

We bought a small house together earlier this year after he signed another four-year deal with the Serpents. I've never lived with a guy before, but I have to say I don't hate it. Not at all.

I pull open the top left drawer, but in my post-orgasm haze, I quickly realize it's the wrong one, so I close it.

But it's too late—I saw it.

A black box.

It is not just *any* black box. Not one that would house a watch, a necklace, or even a bracelet.

No. It's the kind of box that would contain a ring. *The* ring.

We've talked about marriage a few times, but they've all been brief conversations. Nothing lengthy. Nothing serious.

A ring is definitely serious.

A kind of serious that I want.

I might have been engaged to Fox before but none of that was real. I want real. I want him. I want to be his wife. I want to be with him forever.

But there's clearly a reason the ring still sits in the drawer, not on my finger. He's not ready to ask, and I'm not about to push him to.

So instead, I pull open *my* drawer, grab a fresh pair of pantyhose—thankfully, I always buy multiple pairs —and pretend like I saw nothing as I remove my now ripped clothes.

"Lilah?"

I don't turn around. He's going to see it all over my face if I do. "Yeah?" I say, pulling on my new pair of stockings.

"You saw it, didn't you?"

I trip, and Fox catches me before I hit the ground.

"Jesus, are you okay?" he asks once I'm righted.

I blow my hair out of my face, ignoring how my knees shake. "Yeah, yeah." I clear my throat. "I'm good. Totally fine."

One side of his lips kicks up. "Hmm. I'm sure you are."

"I am."

"And?"

"And what?"

Now he's full-on smiling. "You know what. You saw the box, didn't you?"

I nod, swallowing thickly. "I saw…something. I don't know what it is or what it means. I just saw—"

"An engagement ring. And it means I want to marry you."

He pulls open the drawer and snatches up the box.

He exhales heavily before slowly falling to one knee in front of me.

I gasp, even though I know exactly what's happening. Still, I can't believe it.

Fox is on one knee before me. He's holding a black box. He's looking at me like I'm his everything.

"Lilah Jane Maddison" My name falls off his lips like a love song. "I did this once before. I got down before you and I asked you to marry me. It was for show, and I told myself it meant nothing." He laughs quietly. "Man, I was wrong. It definitely meant something. Hell, I think it meant everything. And I meant those words more than I ever realized I did. So, I'm going to repeat them, this time knowing their full weight."

He clears his throat.

"I fell in love with you on our first date. You were radiant, eating nachos and drinking sparkling jalapeño lime lemonade at my kitchen counter. I knew then that our love was the kind you hear about in fairy tales."

A smile breaks across my face, thinking of our first date.

"I wasn't looking for forever, but that's exactly what I found in you. You brought something into my life I didn't know I was missing."

Just like the first time he said it, his voice softens, his words growing heavier, more serious. The rest of the world fades away. It's just me and him. His hair a mess from my hands and my pantyhose not even pulled all the way up my legs.

We look so ridiculous, and I don't care. I wouldn't have it any other way. Not with Fox.

"You're brilliant and kind and beautiful," he continues. "And your wit might be my favorite thing about you. You make me laugh and smile. And you make me really, really damn happy. It would be an absolute honor to be your husband."

He grins and mine widens, because I know what's coming next. And I know exactly what I'm going to say.

"So, what do you say, Lilah? Will you marry me?"

The words are barely out before I nod and say, "Yes, yes, yes!"

He jumps to his feet, his arms going around me as he kisses me hard, and I let him. Sure, I'm going to have to redo all my makeup now, but I don't care. This moment is worth it.

I have no idea how long we kiss. I'd say too long, but I don't think that exists with Fox.

Either way, when we finally pull apart, I have to wipe away the tears spilling from my eyes. Fox does the same.

"Shit. I told myself I wouldn't cry. Guess Lawson won that bet."

"You made a bet you wouldn't cry? With Lawson? Wait, does everyone know?"

He nods. "Yeah. I mean, not the when or the how, but they've known for a while that I wanted to propose. I was waiting for the perfect moment."

I look down at my half-dressed state. "And it was now?"

"Well, you saw the ring, didn't you?"

"I saw a *box*. I haven't seen the ring yet."

"Oh, right." He holds the black box before him, and it pops open with a distinctive sound.

A gorgeous teardrop-shaped ring with two smaller diamonds sits in the middle of a silver band. It's simple yet elegant.

"Fox, this is…" I shake my head, those damn tears stinging my eyes again. "This is gorgeous."

"Yeah? I'm glad you like it. I was nervous. Wasn't sure how you'd feel." He takes it out of the box, tossing it aside. "May I?"

I hold my hand out to him, watching as he slowly slides it into place.

"A perfect fit," I say, marveling at the ring on my finger. "A perfect ring too."

He grins. "See those smaller diamonds? Those are from your grandmother's ring."

About six months after the scene we caused at the restaurant with Fox's parents and my own, my grandmother's ring arrived in the mail with a note that said, "*This is still yours.*"

That was it.

I knew instantly that it was from my mother. It's the only contact I've had with her since, and likely the only contact I'll have for a long time to come. I'm still too angry at my parents to speak to them.

But knowing that Fox took the ring I always

loathed to wear and turned it into something I now *want…* Well, it just proves the kind of man he is—a good one.

"It's gorgeous. It's perfect. It's…" I look up at him. "Thank you, Arthur. Thank you so much."

"Thank me? I should be thanking you. You're the one who said yes."

"And I'd say it again a thousand times over."

"Yeah?" He smiles, wrapping his arms around my waist, pulling me until I'm tucked against him. The perfect fit. "A thousand times?"

"Ten thousand."

"I like the sound of that."

"Yeah? Me too." I push to my toes, pressing a soft kiss to his lips. "I love you, Arthur."

"I love you more, sugar."

I want to argue with him because it's impossible, but I don't. Instead, I let him kiss me again. Softly. Slowly. Sweetly.

This time when he pulls away, I don't whine. I don't complain. Because I know that I get to do this for the rest of my life, and I can't imagine anything better.

"Now," he says, grinning down at me, "let's get to that party, *fiancée.*"

Other Titles by Teagan Hunter

SEATTLE SERPENTS SERIES

Body Check

Face Off

Delayed Penalty

Empty Net

Top Shelf

CAROLINA COMETS SERIES

Puck Shy

Blind Pass

One-Timer

Sin Bin

Scoring Chance

Glove Save

Neutral Zone

ROOMMATE ROMPS SERIES

Loathe Thy Neighbor

Love Thy Neighbor

Crave Thy Neighbor

Tempt Thy Neighbor

SLICE SERIES

A Pizza My Heart

I Knead You Tonight

Doughn't Let Me Go

A Slice of Love

Cheesy on the Eyes

TEXTING SERIES

Let's Get Textual

I Wanna Text You Up

Can't Text This

Text Me Baby One More Time

INTERCONNECTED STANDALONES

We Are the Stars

If You Say So

STANDALONES

The DM Diaries

Best Friends for Never

Stay on top of my new releases, cover reveals, sales, and more by visiting:

www.teaganhunterwrites.com

Thank You

My husband, Henry. Forever my number one. Thank you for providing me with meals, space, and time to write this one. I love you.

Laurie. Ten years. That's how long I've been publishing, and I've been so grateful to have you by my side every step of the way. Thank you for believing in me.

My editing team. Caitlin, Julia, Judy… The real heroes! I couldn't do this without you and all your hard work. Thank you for sticking with me all these years.

Kim, Nina, Meagan, and the VPR team. Your support is incredible. I wouldn't be able to write these books if I didn't feel so confident in the team standing behind me. Thank you for everything.

Tidbits. Thanks for being my safe space.

sMother. I love you.

You. Thank you for taking this journey with me. This book was a true labor of love, and I hope you felt that in every word.

With love and unwavering gratitude,

Teagan

TEAGAN HUNTER writes steamy romantic comedies with lots of sarcasm and a side of heart. She loves pizza, hockey, and romance novels, though not in that order. When not writing, you can find her watching entirely too many hours of *Supernatural*, *One Tree Hill*, or *New Girl*. She's mildly obsessed with Halloween and prefers cooler weather. She married her high school sweetheart, and they currently live in the PNW.

www.teaganhunterwrites.com

www.ingramcontent.com/pod-product-compliance
Lightning Source LLC
Chambersburg PA
CBHW061037310726
48969CB00004B/994